The Invasion Begins . . .

As soon as he got to the complink, Doug used his ID to set up a conference with the other six members of the commission. It took less than five minutes to get all of them on the net. The sonic booms had apparently awakened everyone.

But no one knew what had caused the noises. With all seven commissioners trying to talk at once, any communication was difficult. One or another of the members occasionally broke away from the conference to make or take another call.

An outbreak of small arms fire came almost simultaneously with news. "Federation troops have landed at the starport. They're advancing toward both towns." Sam and Max were little more than three miles apart, with the starport farther from the river, completing a roughly equilateral triangle with the towns.

Thirty seconds later, Franz Bennelin was suddenly cut out of the conference hookup. The others caught a flash of military battledress before Bennelin's complink went dead.

"They're coming for us."

The Buchanan Campaign
by Rick Shelley

D1014041

Ace Books by Rick Shelley

UNTIL RELIEVED
SIDE SHOW
JUMP PAY
THE BUCHANAN CAMPAIGN
THE FIRES OF COVENTRY
RETURN TO CAMEREIN
OFFICER-CADET
LIEUTENANT
MAJOR

THE BUCHANAN CAMPAIGN

RICK SHELLEY

ACE BOOKS, NEW YORK

If you purchased this book without a cover, you should be aware that this book is stolen property. It was reported as "unsold and destroyed" to the publisher, and neither the author nor the publisher has received any payment for this "stripped book."

This is a work of fiction. Names, characters, places, and incidents are either the product of the author's imagination or are used fictitiously, and any resemblance to actual persons, living or dead, business establishments, events, or locales is entirely coincidental.

This book is an Ace original edition,
and has never been previously published.

THE BUCHANAN CAMPAIGN

An Ace Book / published by arrangement with
the author

PRINTING HISTORY
Ace edition / December 1995

All rights reserved.
Copyright © 1995 by Rick Shelley.
Cover art by Chris Moore.
This book may not be reproduced in whole or in part,
by mimeograph or any other means, without permission.
For information address: The Berkley Publishing Group,
a division of Penguin Putnam Inc.,
375 Hudson Street, New York, New York 10014.

The Penguin Putnam Inc. World Wide Web site address is
http://www.penguinputnam.com

ISBN: 0-441-00292-7

ACE®
Ace Books are published by The Berkley Publishing Group,
a division of Penguin Putnam Inc.,
375 Hudson Street, New York, New York 10014.
ACE and the "A" design are trademarks
belonging to Penguin Putnam Inc.

PRINTED IN THE UNITED STATES OF AMERICA

10 9 8 7 6 5 4 3

THE BUCHANAN CAMPAIGN

Prologue

As a member of the Buchanan Planetary Commission, Doug Weintraub was, in theory at least, one of the seven most important people on Buchanan. Since the total population of Buchanan was only thirty-seven thousand, theory didn't count for much. Someday, the commission might be as grand as its name, but at present it was little more than a glorified town council. Like the other members of the commission, Doug put most of his working hours into the operation of his farm. A third of the farm's output actually involved the cultivation of crops in soil. Apart from a few head of livestock, the rest came from nanotech food replicators.

But Doug wasn't working at three in the morning. He was hunting, something he did at least once a week, looking for the world's tastiest native treat. The hippobary was also the largest native herbivore. Like the hippopotamus that gave it half its name, the hippobary was mostly aquatic, but came ashore at night to graze along the river that flanked Buchanan's two towns, Sam and Max—the original colonists had been rather quixotic in many respects. Hunting hippobary wasn't the safest pastime. An adult male might reach a thousand pounds. A female could top twelve hundred. Although they preferred the comfort of water to support their bulk, hippobary could move rapidly on land, and their short, curved tusks could kill a human. It had happened more than once in the 150 years that Buchanan had been settled.

Doug had hunted hippobary since he was fourteen years old. He was good, careful. Part of his care was that he never went out until well after the middle of the night. By two or three in the morning, the hippobary would have eaten their fill. A full belly made them sluggish.

Now in his mid-forties, Doug was tall, thin, and very fit. Working a farm by hand insured that. His face was weathered and deeply tanned. His hands were rough and calloused, with long, gaunt fingers. His sandy-brown hair was beginning to go gray. His rifle was an antique, from the original stock brought to Buchanan with the first settlers, and patterned after a design that had originated on Earth a thousand years before. But the weapon was fully serviceable, and powerful enough for hippobary, and night-vision goggles let him see where to shoot.

A path led from Doug's backyard to the river. Wide and shallow over a soft bed, the river had never had any name other than the Muddy. Even at the flood, the Muddy rarely got deeper than eight feet. The marshy flood plains gave the water too much room to spread, away from Sam and Max.

Two hundred feet from the river, Doug turned right and followed the edge of the marsh grasses. Every few steps, he stopped and scanned the area between him and the water. His goggles depended on available light, rather than infrared, but they were better than nothing and had the added attraction of local manufacture. Better equipment would have to be imported, and imports were prohibitively expensive.

I want a big one tonight, Doug told himself. He liked large portions of hippobary. The native meat was only partially digestible, partially nutritious for humans. "Half an hour and you're hungry again" was the local complaint, which was usually coupled with "But that means you can eat more hippobary that much sooner."

A flash of light in the sky to Doug's right distracted him. "Can't be a meteor," he mumbled, shaking his head. "Can't be a transport shuttle either. There's nothing due." He would have heard of the arrival of an unscheduled ship within minutes of its arrival. "I'll ask Hans in the morning," he decided, turning his attention back to his hunt.

Then a sonic boom disrupted the night. Doug looked up again, as two more streaks of light raced across the sky. After a few seconds, there were two more sonic booms.

All thought of continuing the hunt ended. Doug started back toward home. He wanted to get on the complink and find out what was going on, which might not be easy in the middle of the night. Buchanan didn't have a full-fledged starport. The landing field was manned only when a ship was expected, or when an unexpected ship radioed its arrival.

Doug's wife Elena was standing in the kitchen, looking out the back door, when he got home. "What's going on?" she asked as soon as Doug reached the porch.

"I don't know. Anything on the net?"

"I didn't look. I wanted to see if you were around."

Doug hurried through the kitchen to his den, Elena following right behind. As soon as he got to the complink, Doug used his ID to set up a conference with the other six members of the commission. It took less than five minutes to get all of them on the net. The sonic booms had apparently awakened everyone.

But no one knew what had caused the noises. With all seven commissioners trying to talk at once, any communication was difficult. One or another of the members occasionally broke away from the conference to make or take another call.

An outbreak of small arms fire came almost simultaneously with news. "Federation troops have landed at the starport. They're advancing toward both towns." Sam and Max were little more than three miles apart, with the starport farther from the river, completing a roughly equilateral triangle with the towns.

Thirty seconds later, Franz Bennelin was suddenly cut out of the conference hookup. The others caught a flash of military battledress before Bennelin's complink went dead.

"They're coming for us," one of the other commissioners said, and hands reached to disconnect the net conference.

Doug swallowed hard as he broke his connection to the others. His hand was shaking.

"What's it all about?" Elena asked. She had seen and heard everything that he had.

"Invasion." Doug stood and gripped her arms hard. "Get Jamie. Both of you go down into the storm cellar and *stay* there until someone comes."

"Where are you going?" Elena asked.

"No questions. There isn't time. Just get Jamie and lock yourselves in the cellar. *Now.*"

Elena wanted to argue, but the look on Doug's face stopped her. "Be careful, dear," she said. Then she went to get Jamie, the only one of their three children who still lived at home.

Careful? There's no time left for careful, Doug thought. War was one evil he never would have dreamed could come to Buchanan. An invasion by Federation troops? It was unthinkable, even as it happened.

He looked around his den, then pulled open a drawer, took two boxes of cartridges for his rifle, and stuffed them into the oversized pockets of his hunting overalls. Going through the kitchen, he grabbed an empty canteen. He could fill it at the river. Elena and Jamie went through the kitchen and down into the storm cellar. Elena looked terrified. Ten-year-old Jamie seemed to be more asleep than awake.

Doug slipped his night-vision goggles back in place, picked up his rifle, and went out the back door. He trotted across the yard to the barn. His plans were taking shape on

the fly, his thoughts not fully coherent. *The Federation at-*
tacked us. We need help. Only the Commonwealth can help
us, if we can get word to them, if they choose to help.

One thought led to the next. Communications were a
problem. A radio appeal would take years to reach the nearest settled world. Buchanan had no ships capable of Q-
space transits. There was only one possibility, and that was
why Doug ran to his barn. There were three message rockets on Buchanan—small, high-acceleration rockets that
could transit Q-space. One of those might avoid interception. And one of those rockets was in Doug's barn.

If there's time, he thought. *If I can get it off before sol-*
diers come for me. If it can elude whatever ships are in
orbit. Too many "ifs."

The rocket had always been a nuisance. Twenty-six feet
long and fifteen inches thick, it took up too much room; it
was, or always had been, useless. Custody of it was the
major penalty of Doug's membership in the commission.
The rocket was at the back of his barn, near the second set
of large double doors. He pulled the tarp off of the rocket
and found the small programming module. There was no
time for uncertainty. Doug had read through the instructions
for the MRs when he was given responsibility for his. That
alone wouldn't have been enough if the programming module hadn't provided constant help. He keyed in his commission ID as authorization, then had to key in the message.
For security reasons, it couldn't be done orally. Finally, he
had to enter transit instructions. Those took time, as Doug
had to navigate the computer's system of menus one window at a time. He had never programmed one of these
rockets before. No one on Buchanan had. They were an
emergency device, something to use to signal extreme need
when no other means was available. Like now.

The message was simple: "Federation forces have invaded Buchanan and appear to be taking planetary com-

mission members prisoner.'' Doug programmed the rocket for Buckingham, the capital world of the Commonwealth. Flight instructions . . .

Doug hesitated. He looked away from the rocket and listened for any hint of soldiers. There were only the familiar noises of the night. *These rockets are supposed to get well away from any planet before they distort their way into Q-space,* Doug reminded himself. It would take days for the MR to reach a normal transit point, with no guarantee, and little hope, that it would escape the attention of the invaders.

''What happens if I program it to shift into Q-space right away?'' Doug whispered. He couldn't remember reading about that. What would transit in the neighborhood of a large mass do to the rocket? What would it do to the large mass? How dangerous would the distortions be?

''I'm going to find out,'' he mumbled, desperation overriding judgement. He programmed the rocket to transit five seconds after ignition. Then he rolled the rocket's launch cradle over to the double doors, opened them, and pointed the rocket across the river. He gave himself a ninety-second delay before ignition, and ran toward the path that led upstream, carrying the rocket's programming module with him. Even if soldiers arrived before the rocket blasted off, they wouldn't be able to stop the countdown. Maybe they could destroy the rocket with their personal weapons. Maybe they couldn't.

Doug ran as he hadn't run in a decade. He felt the ache of lungs and heart pushed to unaccustomed effort. He wanted to be as far away from that rocket as possible when it tried to insert itself into Q-space. *I hope Elena and Jamie stay in the storm cellar,* he thought, but there was no time to go back to reinforce his warning.

The flash of ignition was greater than Doug had expected. A cloud of fire and hot exhaust gasses ignited the barn even before the rocket started to slide up out of its cradle. Then the rocket sought Q-space. Doug had no way to be certain that it succeeded, but there was a shock wave, a distortion of local gravity, as the rocket opened a bubble of Q-space around it, forcing the air away, outward. There was a greater blast of fire than before, white and blue flames that started at the outside of the bubble and collapsed inward as the bubble disappeared. The shock of the rocket's transit completed the destruction of the barn, blew out the fire that was consuming it, and sent out ripples that flattened the tall marsh grasses.

The shock wave sent Doug flying to the ground, face first.

After a minute or more, he picked himself up. He ached all over, but nothing seemed to be broken. He looked back toward his home. The house was still standing, though the roof had been damaged.

He wanted to go back, but couldn't. Even if Federation troops hadn't been on their way before, the rocket launch would certainly draw them. His wife and son would be safe—he wouldn't. Doug tossed down the programming module, turned away, and continued trotting along the path away from his home and the settlements. He wasn't certain where he would go. Some five or six miles away, there was a string of low hills, and several caves. They would give him at least momentary safe haven.

And time to think.

Part 1

1

A four-note call from a bosun's pipe sounded over speakers through His Majesty's Starship *Victoria*. The traditional announcement, "Insertion into Q-space in thirty seconds," followed, and every complink displayed a countdown. For a century, there had been no real need for the warning. In the early centuries of Q-space travel, it had been necessary to shut down a ship's artificial gravity before making the transit to or from Q-space because the early Nilssen generators had been unable to support the power demands of both of their functions simultaneously. Current engines had no such difficulty. In addition, the dimensional translation was no longer accompanied by the gut-wrenching sense of dislocation that the early generators had produced. But traditions died hard within the Royal Navy of the Second Commonwealth.

Two thousand feet aft of the ship's bridge, in one of the six dozen troop bays that occupied the bulk of the ship's volume, Sergeant David Spencer of the First Battalion, Second Regiment of Royal Marines looked up from his inspection of the Intelligence and Reconnaissance (I&R) platoon to the nearest speaker when the bosun's call sounded.

"Third time pays for all," David whispered after the announcement. After fifteen years in the Marines, David had lost count of his Q-space transits—well over a hundred.

But this was the third transit of this particular voyage, the final jump.

There were no noticeable feel to the ship's translation to Q-space. *Victoria*'s navigator locked onto a point-mass dimensional complex. The ship's Nilssen generators deformed the point and expanded the resulting sphere around HMS *Victoria*. David knew the rudiments of the theory, though the mathematics were beyond his imagination. During the jump, the ship existed in a virtually independent universe, a bubble whose diameter would be scarcely greater than the longest dimension of *Victoria*—slightly over five miles. Once inside Q-space, the ship would rotate until it was aimed at the proper exit point, and then transit back to normal-space. The amount of distortion forced on the sphere during the exit determined the normal-space distance covered during the jump. Properly plotted and executed, three Q-space transits could carry a ship to any point in the known reaches of the galaxy. Two snags kept Q-space transport from being effectively instantaneous between any two points. First, a ship had to climb away from the gravity well of a planet before making the first transit of a voyage. Second, ships had to make lengthy normal-space passages between Q-space transits, traveling away from their last jump points in normal-space until the last distortion ripples had damped out completely. That meant five days in normal-space before the first transit and three days after each jump. A captain in the Royal Navy didn't cut corners, not if he or she wanted to retain that commission.

Victoria's journey home to Buckingham from Devereaux had been something of a lark for most of the troops. Their posting to Devereaux had been long and boring. The first, second, and engineering battalions of the Second Regiment had spent nearly two years helping the new colonists stake out townships, build houses, clear forest, prune back the local predators—that sort of job. It hadn't been proper military work, but it was work, and Marines had to be kept busy, if only to keep them out of mischief. But there had also been time for military training. The Royal Marines never passed up the opportunity to train their people on new terrain. Now the Second Regiment was going home, looking forward to catching up on overdue holiday leave and a little civilized debauchery. A colony in its first years had little to offer visiting military men—no pubs or dance halls, no unattached and available young women.

Sergeant Spencer finished his inspection, then moved out into the cross aisle. "All right, lads. Do try to keep the area looking shipshape longer than thirty seconds. You've earned your free afternoon. Dismissed."

"Three more days," Jacky White said, immediately dropping onto his bunk. The men chosen to serve in the I&R platoons tended to be rather below average in height and weight. Stealth was an important weapon for them. But Jacky was slightly shorter than average, even for the I&R. Fully dressed, he looked slight, no particular threat to anyone. But there was a wiry, muscular body hidden beneath those clothes, and the bland face concealed the mind of a proficient infantryman. "Three days to home and then it's civie street for me. Bloody time too. My enlistment was up six weeks ago."

"You're not a civilian yet, White," Spencer said. "You know the drill, 'Enlistment continued for the Good of the Service.' "

"Aw, c'mon, Sergeant," Jacky said, laughing. "You mean, 'enlistment continued because the RM are too cheap to provide special transport home.' "

"As you will." Spencer held back his smile until he turned away from Jacky. His face was so weathered that his men sometimes said that his smile could start babies crying. "Mind, you've had your lark. I haven't had a decent day's work out of you in longer than six weeks.''

''What will you do with your leave when we get home, Sergeant?'' Lance Corporal Tory Kepner asked. Tory was still on his feet. Spencer turned to him, liking what he saw. Kepner looked as if he had stepped out of a recruiting poster, tall and obviously strong, clean-cut, the exception to the ''small men go to I&R'' rule. He would make full corporal soon, replacing Norwood Petty, who had transferred to the Second Battalion when he made sergeant.

''I know what *you*'ll do,'' David said, avoiding the question. ''You'll be off to see that new son of yours.''

''Not so new. He's eighteen months old, and I haven't seen him yet.'' Tory had bored his mates to tears through most of those eighteen months, and through the last five months of his wife's pregnancy, talking about his wife and child.

''Not to worry,'' Alfie Edwards called from across a half dozen bunks. He was the only man in the squad shorter than Jacky, but outweighed him by fifteen pounds. He had grown up in a rough, lower-class neighborhood and looked it. Even though his hair was worn short, there was no mistaking the ''almost red'' color or the fact that it was uncontrollable. Alfie had been dangerous in a fight before enlisting. Training camp had merely refined his skills. He had never been bothered by any yearning for a ''fair'' fight, wanting every possible advantage. ''You were there for the important bit.''

''He thinks,'' Jacky said, sotto voce.

''I didn't hear an announcement that we've left Q-space,'' Roger Zimmerman said. He leaned against the end of a tier of bunks. ''Hasn't it been long enough?'' He was less worried about the transit than he was about the discussion he was interrupting. Roger fancied himself the glue that kept the I&R platoon's first squad from disintegrating into a constant brawl. He claimed to be older and wiser than the others, but had stopped mentioning that when the others said it was a matter less of years and wisdom than of the fact that he was simply going bald.

"Maybe the navigator's got the shakes and can't line us up," Alfie said, and there were laughs from most of the others.

Then the transit announcement came. After another thirty-second countdown, *Victoria* was back in normal-space, and in its home system.

"I'll be in my room," Spencer said. "Lunch will be called soon. Leave a bit for the rest of the battalion, will you?" He used that as an exit line, heading for the hatch on the inboard side of the compartment while the squad groaned and called out retorts. Sergeants were quartered separately, normally four to a room—except for company lead sergeants and above, who were two to a room, and the regimental sergeant major, who had a cabin to himself. On this voyage, with only half the regiment aboard, David shared a stateroom with only one other sergeant, Malcolm Macdowell, HQ Company's quartermaster. And Macdowell used the room only to sleep in.

There was a message flashing on the complink screen when David got to the stateroom. "SERGEANTS' CALL AT 1215 HOURS IN THE SERGEANTS' MESS."

"Right after lunch," David mumbled. "I wonder what's cooking now." He smiled at his pun. Finally alone in his sanctuary, David let his body relax. After fifteen years, it was an automatic reflex, the putting on and taking off of proper military posture. Barely thirty-two years old, David had enlisted while he was still underage. He had planned from the start to make a career out of the Royal Marines, and he had worked with almost maniacal determination to make himself the best Marine he could possibly be. Almost textbook average in height and weight, David looked deceptively mild, with pale blue eyes and thin blond hair. The·

look was simply another advantage to make use of.

He glanced at his watch. Mess call wouldn't sound for twenty minutes. *Twenty minutes to kip out*, David decided. He lay on his bunk and stared at the overhead. It would be good to get home to Buckingham and civilization. Two years was an unusually long posting to a frontier world like Devereaux, and David was no different than his men—he was anxious to enjoy some of the pleasures of a civilized world again. The twenty minutes of daydreams were only a start.

David put on a fresh uniform before he went to the mess, undress blues with standing collar. Captain McAuliffe could sometimes get sticky about appearance. Heading back to garrison after a two-year absence, he was almost certain to start.

Lunch was served from 1100 to 1200 hours, ship's time. Most days, David made it a point to get to the mess late enough that he didn't have to stand in line. But today there would certainly be rumors about the meeting. There might even be hard information.

"It's all three battalions," H&S Company Lead Sergeant Landsford told David just inside the entrance to the mess. "Colonel Laplace himself will be conducting the meeting."

"What's on the cooker?" David asked.

Landsford shook his head. "Something about the war is all I've been able to find out. No idea what."

"The war's still on then?" David asked. "The war" had been something of a joke on Devereaux. The Confederation of Planets had formally declared war on the Second Commonwealth—rather, on the worlds that belonged to the Commonwealth, since the Federation didn't recognize the existence of the Commonwealth itself. The Federation had reasserted its claims to sovereignty over all of the worlds settled by humans. But they had *always* claimed that. No word of any actual fighting had ever come to the troops on Devereaux.

"Colonel had officers' call ten minutes after the last jump," Landsford said. "Must have been a priority signal waiting." There wouldn't have been time for *Victoria* to report its return to Buckingham and get a message back.

"You know what I think?" David said sadly. "I think we've wasted our time making plans for furlough."

"I dare say," Landsford said.

"You know, Peter, if this war has turned real, it won't be like any of the campaigns we've known before. This won't be a mop-up of a tiny colonial civil war."

"We'll earn our pay," Landsford agreed. "But it's no good speculating. The colonel will have his say and then we'll know, won't we?"

The speculation didn't stop, of course. David got his meal and took a seat. He ate slowly, listening to the talk— questions and speculations, no solid answers.

The regimental sergeant major and the three battalion sergeant majors came in together, just after 1130 hours. RSM Dockery brushed aside the first questions directed at the group, quite brusquely, and the questions ceased.

"They know what's up," David mumbled.

"But they'll not let the cat out of the bag," Sergeant Eric Dealy of Engineering Battalion said. "Dockery could keep mum about his pants being on fire if he was ordered to."

The laugh that earned was subdued, but prolonged.

"They'll sit there in their corner and pretend there's not a thing different about this meal," Macdowell said from the next table.

"You don't think they'll send us out again straightaway without even a stopover on Buckingham, do you?" Norwood Petty asked.

"We'll have to reprovision, if nothing else," Macdowell

said. "*Victoria*'s been out for two years, after all. The old girl needs her bit of maintenance, and she needs to fill her larders and storerooms."

"Doesn't mean they have to let us ground out," David said, just to puncture Macdowell's confidence. "They could load the rest of the regiment, do a rush job on the tune-up, and have us heading out-system in forty-eight hours."

"That'd sure have the lads feeling mean enough to fight," Macdowell said.

"It would have *me* feeling mean enough to fight," Dealy said. "And I'm a pacifist at heart." That earned a generous laugh. In his younger days, Dealy had been one of the most frequent barroom brawlers in the regiment. It had taken him extra years to earn his stripes because of that.

Precisely at noon, Sergeant Major Dockery got up and spoke with the chief mess steward. A moment later the stewards started setting pitchers of coffee and tea on the tables. Then they cleared away dishes and closed down the serving line. By 1212, the last of the mess stewards had left the room. Two minutes later, the colonel arrived. A sergeant by the door called attention and everyone sprang to their feet.

"As you were," Colonel Arkady Laplace said without breaking stride. He had his operations chief and all three battalion commanders in tow. The regiment's executive officer had remained on Buckingham with the other three battalions. The senior officers marched to the head of the room. Colonel Laplace took up a position looking out at his sergeants, who had already returned to their seats. The other officers sat with the sergeant majors.

"I know how quickly rumors spread aboard ship, so I want to get the facts out even more rapidly," Laplace started. "I've already briefed the officers. Now it's your turn. If it were practical, I'd address all the men myself, but I could only do that over the speakers, and that's little better than hearing it in a letter-chip from home."

That earned a few laughs. After forty years in the Royal Marines, Laplace had his timing perfected. He was at ease with his authority, and felt no need to artificially protect his "dignity." His men tended to award him their highest praise for an officer: "He's better than most."

"There was a dispatch waiting for us on the buoy when we bounced out of Q-space," the colonel said. "I expect a few of you have already guessed this, but we won't get to take all of the furlough we've accumulated over the past two years. We'll be lucky to manage seventy-two hours in port before we're off out again." He held up a hand to forestall questions.

"I know. We should have at least six months in-system, plenty of time for everyone to take furlough and get in a score of pub crawls besides, but the war appears to have taken a turn. Fighting has actually started."

That brought a low buzz of comment. Colonel Laplace waited for it to fade before he continued.

"The news isn't particularly good. The first engagements apparently occurred in the system of Camerein. The only losses we know of were Commonwealth, three frigates. More recently, there's word that Federation troops have invaded an independent world on the marches between our respective core regions. I don't have full details, just the barest outline. But the Federation has taken a world known as Buchanan, and we're to chase them back off.

"The reason we're going straight out again is that there isn't another full regiment to be spared on Buckingham just now. Two regiments are being retained as home defense, in case it should come to that. The other three regiments based on Buckingham have already been dispatched on other missions, and Buchanan apparently can't wait."

2

Flight Lieutenant Josef Langenkamp was dozing in the fourth squadron ready room aboard HMS *Sheffield* when the alert klaxon sounded. Before the horn went silent, Josef and his comrades were moving toward the hangar and their fighters. They helped each other don and seal their helmets before stepping through to the ramp leading out to the airlock and hangar. They had been in their flight suits since coming on shift. The fourth was the alert squadron, on two-minute response. All of the pilots were young. A few were still teenagers, but most, like Josef, were in their twenties. Even the squadron commander was only twenty-six. Flying a Spacehawk required young reflexes.

This alert was almost certainly only one more training exercise in a seemingly endless series. After all, *Sheffield* was still in orbit around Buckingham and there had been no warning of any enemy fleet entering the system. But until they had confirmation that this was only a drill, they would treat it as real.

Crew chiefs waited for their pilots on the hangar deck. The multipurpose Spacehawk Zed-3 fighters were in their slots in the launch/recovery cylinders. Josef's fighter was in the third slot in the rotating cylinder.

''Going for a gang launch, sir,'' his chief, Andrew Mynott, told him as they connected Josef's air and power hoses in the cockpit.

"Thanks, Andy," Josef said. "You heard anything about our mission?"

"No, sir, not this time." The crew chief was a large, hulking man, in his early forties, but he could still manage the most delicate touch when he was working on "his" machine. He had spent more than twenty years maintaining Spacehawks, all of the way back to the Zed-1, the first of the series. Mynott finished checking connections, then tapped Josef on the helmet. "Clear now, sir," he said as he stepped back.

Josef nodded and closed the canopy while he worked through his preflight checklist. At the same time, he had a voice from Combat Control Center to listen to.

"Ground support mission," the C^3 voice announced. "Gang launch. Your computers have been programmed with the launch sequence and initial vector." The numbers were repeated for the pilots. Josef compared the numbers recited over the complink with the numbers showing on his screen. They matched. That was always a relief.

The preflight routine was controlled pandemonium, too hectic to allow Josef to worry. Launching a full fighter squadron needed three launch/recovery cylinders. Each LRC would be extended from the hull of *Sheffield*. Six fighters were launched simultaneously from pods that were barely seven feet apart in each LRC. The cylinders were emptied one after the other, with no more than ten-second intervals. Fortunately, not all launches were made in that hair-raising fashion. The fighters could be launched one at a time, with each pod rotating around the LRC to reach the solo launch slot—"The biggest revolver in the Galaxy," a sign on the hanger deck read.

Combat pilots wore neural implants to make their jobs more nearly reasonable than they would be for unaugmented human minds. A needle-thin jack connected the computing power of their helmets and fighters to their own brains. It was a three-way system. Combat command was on one channel with mission parameters. The Spacehawk needed attention from its pilot—through the neural implant, the pilot was instantly on line to his bird's systems. And finally, the pilot needed to pay attention to his environment, both inside and outside his cockpit. At first, the confusion had seemed absolute, but training and drills reduced the incomprehensible to routine, honed skills and reflexes, brought confidence. After four years, it was just another day at the office for Josef.

As soon as the service crews were through the airlocks, the LRCs were extended from the hull of *Sheffield*. A final ten-second countdown was both audio and visual. *Sheffield* kicked the fighters out of the LRC. The ship was in assault orbit, 160 miles above Buckingham. The Spacehawks' rockets fired five seconds later. While the fighters slid down toward the atmosphere, the squadron commander, Lieutenant Commander Olive Bosworth, briefed her pilots.

"First run is missiles only. Our target is a cluster of six buildings in the desert, rigged with everything but people."

"What, no live targets?" one of the pilots asked.

"Clamp down on that, now," Bosworth said sharply.

As Josef's fighter punched through a few high wisps of cirrus clouds, he got visual identification of the target. The squadron was over ocean at present, but the coast was less than forty seconds away, with the target another eight seconds beyond.

Red lights started flashing inside Josef's cockpit. Status codes jumped straight from green to red. A warbling alarm siren sounded.

"This is Red Three," Josef said, struggling to remain calm. "I show full hydraulic failure."

"Eject, Red Three," Commander Bosworth said. "We'll have the rescue team on the way before your chutes open."

There was no choice unless Josef wanted to accompany

his Spacehawk into the ground at thirty-five hundred miles per hour. He pulled up the safety cover to his left, armed the ejector, then lifted the trigger housing on his right and punched the button.

His Spacehawk was crossing the coastline as the cockpit pod was blasted clear of the rest of the fighter. The ejector explosives cancelled much of the escape pod's forward momentum. A first series of drag chutes righted the cockpit capsule in the seconds they were deployed. Three small rockets provided additional braking as the first series of chutes broke free. When the rockets fell silent, the main chutes deployed. Josef clenched the armrests of his seat and flinched with each shock.

I hope Andy got all the straps tight, Josef thought just before the crash bags inflated around him and the capsule hit the ground. The impact was still enough to knock him out. *It's almost inevitable,* the briefing went. *We do everything we can to reduce the force of impact, and the cockpit of a Zed-3 has a thousand years of safety engineering behind it, but the human body still tends to get indignant when subjected to certain levels of abuse. And when it gets too indignant, it goes on strike.*

When Josef regained consciousness, he heard a voice in his ear, but he didn't pay attention at first. He ached all over but was—apparently—not critically injured. He moved his arms and legs, tentatively at first, then with more vigor—as much as the cramped confines of the cockpit would permit. *Nothing broken,* he thought, and he repeated that after two deep breaths convinced him that no ribs had been fractured either. He touched a stud on the side of his helmet and the visor displayed his vital signs: heart rate elevated; blood pressure slightly depressed; respiration normal.

"Red Three, do you copy?"

Josef finally became aware of Commander Bosworth's

voice. He keyed his microphone, uncertain that he would be able to transmit. The cockpit capsule was on its side, rocking. At least one of the braking parachutes had to be attached yet, pulling at the pod.

"I appear to be in one piece, Commander," Josef said. "I guess I took a little nap."

"Affirmative, Three. I showed you out for ninety-three seconds. Can you free yourself from the capsule?"

"I think so. My vitals are sound and nothing seems to be broken."

"Take it slow and easy, Josef. You're in a sandfield. Your chutes are dragging you but there's nothing ahead to make that dangerous."

"Uh, thanks, Commander. How long do I have before pickup?"

"Nine minutes. Medevac will be coming in from the northwest."

"Roger, Commander. See you later."

Josef took a deep breath and looked out at the sand. He spotted the edge of the parachute that was dragging him.

"I guess I should get out and cut that loose," he said softly. "No need to slide halfway across the flipping desert."

He had to crank the canopy open by hand, and the crank was underneath him, down by his legs. Slowly, he pulled himself out of the capsule, getting a mouthful of sand when the canopy opened. He took off his gloves and dropped them back inside, then took the knife from the sheath on his right leg. In the deep, loose sand, the capsule slid as rapidly as Josef could walk. He sawed at the parachute cables, holding on to them, letting them drag him along. Finally, the last cable parted and the parachutes blew away. Josef fell against the pod. Even through his pressure suit, he could feel the residual heat in the composite skin of what was left of his Spacehawk.

Josef checked his compass, then looked northwest. The medevac plane was already visible, a dark shadow low in the sky. It landed fifty yards from the pod. Josef fetched his helmet from inside the capsule, then walked toward the plane. A hatch opened and two crew members came down the short ramp.

"About time you got here," Josef shouted across the sand. "I could have got terminal sunburn."

"Didn't anyone tell you that those birds aren't disposables?" one of the medtechs asked. "They cost a trifle more than your undies, you know."

"Really?" Josef feigned surprise as he climbed the ramp. He had to duck his head to get through the open hatch. Josef had come within a quarter-inch of being turned down for fighters because of his height. He barely fit in the cockpit of a Spacehawk. "They chafe just the same."

"Have the flight surgeon prescribe a cream," the tech said. "Might help your disposition as well."

"Let's strip you out of that suit," her companion said as they entered the shuttle's triage chamber. "Make sure you don't have chafing serious enough to require a trauma tube."

Before the medevac flight landed at the naval port facilities in Westminster, Josef had been pronounced fit. He wound up sitting in the passenger cabin, sipping a glass of juice. He had tried a little innocent flirting with the female medtech, but she had proven unresponsive.

"You've got more important things to worry about, Lieutenant," she told him in a bantering tone.

"Such as?" he asked.

"Such as explaining how you managed to scrap a seventy-five-million-pound Spacehawk."

That did give Josef something to think about. *I can't help it that the hydraulics went south*, he thought, trying to reassure himself. But would command feel the same way?

"What's the routine here, love?" Josef asked the female tech as the plane taxied to a halt at its hangar.

"There'll be a car for you, I imagine. Since you don't need an ambulance, that is." She flashed teeth. "Yet," she added.

"Ouch." Josef laughed and grinned.

There was a car waiting, though, with a naval rating to drive it. "Flight Lieutenant Langenkamp?" the driver asked when Josef came off of the plane.

"Yes."

"I'm to conduct you to base operations, sir."

The driver proved to be totally uncommunicative throughout the five-minute drive. When he finally parked, the driver turned to Josef and pointed at the building.

"Through the door, sir. They'll guide you from there."

In less than two minutes, Josef found himself in the office of an assistant base operations officer, Commander Owen Neely.

"No injuries, Lieutenant?" Neely asked after returning Josef's salute.

"No, sir. Thank you."

"Relax, lad. Have a seat," Neely said finally. He gestured to a padded chair by the room's single window. "Even without injuries you must be feeling tatty. I understand you went in rather hot."

"Yes, sir. Not all the training in the galaxy prepares you for something like that, sir." Josef went to the chair. Neely perched on the corner of his desk.

"Actually, the Navy rather prefers to avoid the situation. We'd rather train pilots to not have to leave their fighters so abruptly." Josef tensed a little, but the commander waved a hand casually.

"Sorry, that wasn't meant as a criticism. It's not as if your bicycle had a puncture now, is it? You can't just pull over to the verge and wait for a maintenance lorry.''

"No, sir," Josef said, still too nervous to feel relieved.

"Our report said you reported complete hydraulic failure."

"That's what the telltales said, Commander. There wasn't time to do more than accept that."

"Of course not." Neely stood. "I think that's all I need from you. There'll be a board of inquiry, but that's nothing for you to worry about. A formality. The admiralty likes its measure of red tape." He smiled, briefly. "And just to impress you with our efficiency, I guess I could tell you that the replacement Spacehawk is already being ferried up to *Sheffield*."

"Oh?" Josef stood when the Commander did. "I was hoping to fly it up myself, sir."

"Ah, but you're a downed flyer. *King's Regs* require a pilot to stand down for seventy-two hours after, and I'm afraid we couldn't wait that long to replace your fighter."

"Sir?"

"Nothing, Lieutenant." Neely hesitated, then said, "That 'nothing' is quite official. Let's just say I spoke out of turn. You're not to carry that out of this office."

"Whatever you say, sir," Josef said, more puzzled yet.

"Under the *Official Secrets Act,* Langenkamp."

"Yes, sir."

3

Commander Ian Shrikes was a light sleeper. Even as a child, the slightest noise woke him. Each time he transferred to a new ship, there was a difficult period of adjustment. And each time he returned to Buckingham and his family, his system had to relearn the noises and movements common there. But he could always get by with the softest of alarms, and often woke before it went off. This morning, his hand was already reaching for the alarm when it started to buzz. Dawn in Westminster was two hours away, but duty called, even though Ian was in a staff position now, aide to Admiral Stasys Truscott. Today the admiral was moving his flag up to HMS *Sheffield.*.

"Already?" Antonia Shrikes asked sleepily as her husband got up.

"Already. Sorry, dear, I didn't mean to wake you."

"Silly. You know you can't get out of here without waking me." She yawned and stretched, then sat up.

"There's no reason for you to get up yet, Toni. It's just four-thirty."

"So I'll nap after the kids leave for school," she said. "I'll fix breakfast while you're showering."

Ian was wide awake. He was always fully alert as soon as he woke. He moved through his morning routine with economical efficiency, and fifteen minutes after getting out of bed, he was leaving the bedroom, ready for duty.

Duty was an important word to Ian. He had spent twenty-four years in the Combined Space Forces, doing his duty to King and Commonwealth. His appointment to the Royal Naval Academy had been won in open competition. Each slow promotion had been won the same way, through ability and dedication. Ian approached his current staff duties with all the diligence he had brought to every other posting. It was a necessary step forward in his career. At the conclusions of his tour with Admiral Truscott, Ian knew he could anticipate promotion to captain and command of his own starship.

Before he went downstairs, Ian looked in on the son and daughter he had seen too little of over the years. Ian Junior was thirteen. His room was decorated with models of starships, one of every vessel his father had served on. He was already working on a model of *Sheffield*. Ruby was nine, an old nine. Her dolls had already been relegated to one corner of her room and received only occasional attention. Ruby spent most of her free time on the complink, showing an aptitude that amazed her parents.

Looking in on the children almost disrupted Ian's schedule. It was the only thing that could. But, finally, he broke away and went downstairs. Antonia was just putting his breakfast on the table.

"Aren't you going to eat?" he asked when she sat across from him with only a cup of tea.

She shook her head. "Not if I'm going back to bed."

"Sometimes I wonder if you ever eat," Ian joked. "Are you afraid you couldn't fit back in the cockpit of a fighter?"

"They don't let old ladies into those cockpits. I got out while the getting was good. There were too many former fighter pilots and not enough upper division postings."

They put off any farewells until the car from fleet headquarters arrived. Then they held themselves to quick good-byes and a brief hug and kiss. Restraint, holding back on any overly demonstrative displays—it was a routine they had perfected over fifteen years of marriage. That this was the first time Ian might be leaving for a major military engagement made no visible difference.

But each of them felt it.

There was little traffic on the roads so early, even in the housing development that was home to so many Marine and Navy families. In the last few months, the reality of the war had started to make itself felt in the CSF community. Men and women had failed to come home from cruises, their fate not yet explained. You could feel the difference in the still morning air. The staff car moved at the speed limit through the suburbs to the naval base on the east side of the Westminster Spaceport.

At the gate to fleet headquarters, they stopped for an ID check. While he waited for the guard to verify his identity, Ian looked off toward the maintenance hangars, a mile away. There were lights banked on around the command shuttle that would take the admiral and his staff up to *Sheffield*. The guard came back out of the gatehouse, returned the ID chips, and saluted. Ian returned the salute with casual correctness, and his driver put the car back into gear.

"Fleet ops building, sir?" the driver asked.

"Yes, that's right." Ian had originally expected to go to the admiral's house and accompany his chief in, but Truscott had specifically indicated otherwise.

"I'm not certain just when I'll be heading in, Ian," Truscott had told him the evening before. "I'd rather have you at the office, making sure everything's ready for us."

There were armed guards at the entrance to the Fleet Operations building—Marines in full battledress, not the usual Shore Patrol in dress uniforms. They also checked Ian's ID before they saluted and allowed him to enter the building.

You'd think there was a war on, Ian thought without

humor. After nearly two years, fleet headquarters seemed to have finally decided that the Federation's declaration of war might be serious.

Ian took a lift tube to the sixth floor. Admiral Truscott's temporary offices there would be vacated sometime within the next several hours. None of the staff clerks were in yet. Only one communications technician was in the outer office.

"What do we have for the admiral this morning, Gabby?" Ian asked.

"A bit of the usual, sir," Louis Bierce said. "Nothing that looks particularly urgent. But that's just my guess, isn't it?"

"Do you even remember the last time you were wrong about something like that?" Ian laughed. Gabby always seemed to know how important a piece was likely to be.

"I've got it writ down in a diary somewhere," Gabby said.

"Too bad you're not going out with us, Gabby. I don't know how we'll do without you."

"I'm just as happy to be staying, and I don't mind saying so, sir. I've already put thirty-five years in uniform. The Navy's well off putting me out to pasture." In his younger days, Gabby had been a prizefighter, winning the fleet heavyweight championship three times. Even though trauma tubes had always removed the most obvious signs of damage, there were still the physical clues, the thickening of the ears, the way he carried his head just slightly forward, the way he moved on his feet.

"There's no such thing as mandatory retirement because of age or years in service," Ian reminded the chief petty officer.

"But the pension doesn't build past what they'll give me now, sir. Anything beyond thirty-five years is a gift from me." Gabby chuckled. "I never was that much for charity."

"You must know where some important skeletons are buried, Gabby, getting your retirement approved with this war on."

"War ain't become real enough yet, sir. That's another reason to get out while the getting's good."

"Okay, okay. Better give me the night signals, so I can have them ready for the admiral when he comes in."

Gabby's fingers danced on the keys of his compsole. "Downloaded to your desk, sir."

Ian went through to his office, the smallest of the six offices in the admiral's suite. He opened the curtains on his windows. The curtains had been ordered by the admiral. "We get enough of bare walls aboard ship," he had told Ian when they moved into the offices. "Let's make this place look a little more pleasant, what?"

Ian ran a hand over the fabric of the curtains now, smiling warmly at the memories that came back, not just of this office—they had only been here a few odd months—but of a long career. The trickle became a flood. Ian moved around the office in something of a fog. The tea cart—it offered much more than just tea, but naval tradition insisted on the ancient name—had been switched on before Ian arrived. He usually drank coffee, but this morning, he dialed up tea and sat at his desk to work through the night dispatches.

The memories kept building. Ian stared at his complink screen. Instead of reading the message printed there, he thought about the day he had reported aboard his first ship, the frigate HMS *Avenger*. The first officer's orientation talk played back. *Our frigates are the spiritual and lineal descendants of the frigates that sailed the seas of Earth as much as fourteen hundred years ago. There is a* Golden Hind *in the fleet. The original was Sir Francis Drake's ship when Queen Elizabeth I ruled England. Avenger* had seemed impossibly cramped to Ensign Shrikes, fresh out of the Academy. But when he took his first shore leave three months later, he had felt nervous with all the excess room of an atmosphere around him. He had spent most of his two weeks ashore inside one building or another, going outside only when he absolutely had to, and he had kept his eyes down then.

That memory brought a chuckle, and the laugh brought Ian's mind back to the present. He blinked several times, looked at the clock, then took a long drink of his tea. It was getting cool, so he got up to get a hot refill. Then he turned his attention to his work.

It was just after 0630 when Gabby stuck his head into Ian's office. "The admiral is in the building, sir, in the lift coming up."

"Thanks, Gabby." Ian stood. "I have absolutely no idea what the schedule is for today. The admiral said we'd have to wing it."

Stasys Truscott came sweeping into the office with a booming "Good morning, lads." He wasn't the sort of man who would appear overly impressive out of uniform. Only a little above the average height for Buckingham, and considerably below the average weight, Truscott might have appeared to be a mid-level civil servant in mufti. But his uniform transformed him. Nearly eighty years old, Truscott had worn the uniform of His Majesty's Royal Navy for sixty of those years, and he had frequently told Ian that he planned to stay in the RN however long it took him to make first lord of the Admiralty. "And Long John Raleigh didn't get *his* appointment until he was a hundred and seven," Truscott would always add. Sir John Raleigh was the current first lord.

"Ian, we're due at Long John's office at 0730. We'll have to leave here no later than 0710," Truscott said as soon as he had blustered through his morning greetings. Social pleasantries remained a foreign language to him, but he always made the attempt to get through them in something approaching proper fashion.

"Aye, sir, I'll call for a car straightaway," Ian said.

"No need. My car is waiting." Truscott started toward the door to his private office. "Gabby, would you come in with me?"

"Of course, sir."

"Oh, Ian, before I forget," Truscott said. "Ring up Captain Hardesty and tell him we'll be coming up immediately after the briefing. We'll go to the shuttle from the Admiralty."

"Aye, sir." Mort Hardesty was captain of *Sheffield*. "Any idea how long the briefing will last, sir?"

Truscott had already resumed his course toward his office. He just shook his head in answer.

Gabby was only in the admiral's office three minutes. Ian had just completed his conversation with *Sheffield* when Gabby came in, a dispirited look on his face.

"What's wrong, Gabby?"

"My retirement's off," Gabby said, his voice crustier than ever. "I'm going up to *Sheffield* with you."

"The admiral couldn't help?"

"No, sir. He said the new orders are quite precise."

"I'm sorry, Gabby. Anything I can do to help?"

"The admiral said I should ask you to get a staff car to take me home to pack. I'm to go straight to the shuttle from there."

"Sure, Gabby." Ian made the call immediately. "Be waiting for you in five minutes. You called your wife yet?"

"No, sir. I'm a bit scared of *that*." Gabby managed a wan smile. "I'd best do it now though, before I just show up home."

Ian brought up the matter during the ride to the Admiralty. "Gabby had his heart set on retiring, Admiral. Isn't there anything you can do?"

Truscott sighed and shook his head. "I tried, but no go. I went straight to the top, but this order originated at the Palace. All retirements and discharges are off, indefinitely. All I could do was give Gabby a choice. He could stay here or move up to *Sheffield* with us."

"He sounded terrified of telling his wife."

"In his place, I might be too. She'd have made a fine Marine leading sergeant." His laugh seemed to find some humor, about halfway through.

On normal visits to Sir John Raleigh, Ian waited in an outer office while Truscott went into the inner sanctum alone. This time, Ian was ushered in with the admiral.

"Good morning, Stasys," Long John said, getting up and coming around the desk. Raleigh did not appear to be past middle age. As a senior officer, he had long been eligible for the full course of treatments to keep the effects of age at bay. There was as little gray in his hair as there was in Truscott's. He stuck out a hand for Truscott, and after they shook, Raleigh turned to Ian. "Morning, Shrikes. I know you're caught a bit off the mark, but what I have to say to your boss will involve you."

Ian nodded.

"Let's move next door and get comfortable." Raleigh led the way to a door at the side of his office. Ian had never been through that door, but he knew what was there in a general way. Raleigh had a very comfortable den filled with overstuffed leather chairs, books, and book viewers, and various bits of memorabilia, few of which had any connection to the RN. A standard naval-issue tea cart was the only object in the room that had any air of the CSF to it.

"Drop the bomb, First Lord," Truscott said, a little stiffly, as he sat in one of the chairs. "You're being so damn polite you must be ready to chop my head off.''

Raleigh laughed heartily, but it rang false. Ian took his seat more slowly, his eyes darting back and forth between the others. Raleigh's body had started to show the effects of many years of a sedentary lifestyle. His cheeks had a plump softness, and weight that had once been hard muscle had turned to sagging fat on his torso. But there was nothing wrong with his mind. That was as hard and sharp as ever.

"Nothing so dramatic, Stasys," Raleigh said. "Tea, coffee, something else?" He moved to the tea cart.

"Coffee," Truscott said with a sigh, "straight."

"Ah, yes. And you, Shrikes?"

"The same, sir."

Raleigh served his visitors, then took tea for himself. "Nothing like a good brew," he said. He went to his chair and sat, then took a sip. He looked at Truscott over the rim of his cup.

"The bomb," Raleigh said finally. He shook his head. "It's really a simple matter, Stasys."

"How simple?" Truscott was more suspicious with each passing second.

"A temporary addition to your staff. His Majesty has requested that we accommodate an observer from the Privy Council."

"A *politician*?" Truscott let his dismay show clearly in his voice.

"Actually, no," Raleigh said. For a moment, he seemed preoccupied with inspecting the remaining contents of his teacup.

Ian figured out the answer before anyone spoke. *If it's a member of the Privy Council, but not a politician, then it has to be . . .*

"Prince William Albert Windsor, Duke of Haven," Raleigh announced. "His Majesty's youngest brother."

Truscott closed his eyes, took a deep breath, and let it out noisily before he opened his eyes again. "It could be worse. At least the duke knows the Royal Navy."

"He served for six years," Raleigh said. "I don't believe you ever served with him?"

Truscott shook his head. "No, but I have met His Highness on occasion."

"Now, Stasys, I want to be crystal clear about this. His Highness will be attached to your staff, but only as an observer. His commission hasn't been activated. He isn't going along to issue orders or interfere in your operations. That is the express order of His Majesty."

"And what if the duke decides that he wants to take a hand?" Truscott asked.

"If the lad gets out of line, you'll have to be firm, but diplomatic." Raleigh gestured to Ian. "That's why I wanted you in here for this, Shrikes. I imagine that a considerable portion of the 'keeping in line' will fall to you. I'll repeat it straight out. The Duke of Haven will be along strictly as a civilian observer without naval rank. Since that is His Majesty's order, the Duke of Haven is in no position to appropriate any other status. His only brief is to invite the rightful government of Buchanan to apply for membership in the Commonwealth."

"Yes, sir," Ian said. "I'll do my best. I met Prince William at the Commonwealth Day ball last year. Not that he has cause to remember me."

Raleigh nodded. "I'm certain you'll do fine. In any case, even if His Highness had his commission activated, you'd still outrank him. His reserve commission is lieutenant commander, and you know the protocol. When a member of the royal family is serving on active duty, family connections give him absolutely no privileges beyond what his naval rank entitles him."

"So I've been told, sir," Ian said.

"Believe it," Raleigh said. "The RN couldn't function any other way." He turned to Truscott. "The commander's been with you too long, Stasys. Your cynicism is rubbing off."

"I'd like to get moved up to *Sheffield* as soon as possible," Truscott said, rather than responding to Raleigh's jibe. "When can we expect His Highness?"

"Tomorrow afternoon." Raleigh stood. His visitors immediately rose as well. "One of the last supply shuttles, I imagine."

4

The air in the low entrance to the cave was nearly lethal with concentrations of carbon monoxide and carbon dioxide. But no smoke showed outside the cave, and that was the important consideration. Doug Weintraub had watched the mouth of the cave all night, dozing only intermittently, anxious that his fire not give away his location. Occasionally, he had scurried into the cave on hands and knees, breath held, to make sure that the low fire hadn't burned out or grown too strong, or to add wood to the fire.

Just before dawn, Doug made another trip into the cave. This time he laid two thick hippobary steaks on the coals. Half an hour later, his breakfast was cooked. It tasted extraordinarily good after two weeks of raw meat and whatever wild fruit and vegetables he could find.

Doug hadn't dared to go home since the night of the invasion. Twice, he had gone near the settlements, moving carefully in the night. His reconnaissances had provided little information. He had been too cautious, too nervous, to take chances. He assumed that the Federation soldiers would have the latest equipment, not just weapons but also *detecting* gear. Doug had only his night-vision goggles. If Federation soldiers were looking for him, they would find him.

The invasion was still a shock, and Doug had been unable to guess at the reason. Buchanan had no great reserves of people, no special natural resources. There had been no warning, no demands. Driven to distraction by his futile search for a motive, Doug had finally turned his mind to more practical considerations, and found almost as much confusion. *What the hell do I expect to accomplish out here? One man, one foolish man.* Against an army.

One man? What did it matter? There was no way that Buchanan could possibly stand against the Federation, not if it really wanted Buchanan. The Federation probably had more ships than Buchanan had people. Doug didn't count on receiving help from outside. The Commonwealth might not have received his message rocket. The rocket might have destroyed itself in the immediate Q-space transit. Even if the Commonwealth *had* received Doug's message, they might not respond. Again, Buchanan had nothing in particular to offer.

It boils down to, "How much are we worth to them?" That was where Doug always came up against a blank wall. How could one man make the cost of holding Buchanan too great for the Federation?

Doug finished his steaks, then stared at the entrance to the cave he had used for cooking. There had been more to the exercise than breakfast. He had killed a hippobary the night before last, then stretched its hide on a frame and set it in the cave to smoke-dry. He had cut sixty pounds of meat into narrow strips to smoke and dry as well. The meat would keep longer as jerky, and he could carry food more easily that way if he had to move his camp.

There was still work to do. Hippobary hide was thick, an excellent insulator. Doug planned to cut and sew the hide to provide himself with a thermal shield, something to help conceal him from the infrared detectors he assumed Federation soldiers would have. With that extra layer of protection, he would be able to move around near Sam and Max with less chance that he would be discovered. He needed information, and he needed recruits.

One man had no chance. A group of men *might*.

Another four hours of sleep would have been nice. Doug was tempted to take those hours, put off his foray until the next night. It had taken him until mid-afternoon to stitch together his hippobary heat shield with fibers from a rivergrape vine and a needle fashioned from a sliver of a hippobary leg bone. Now it was sunset, and sleep was more tempting than a long walk and the danger of being discovered by patrolling soldiers.

"I've wasted too many days now," Doug told himself firmly.

After he left the cave, he followed hippobary paths along the river. The spring floods had been gone for nearly three months, and the ground was firm enough that it wouldn't show footprints. The Federation soldiers were new to Buchanan. They would probably avoid hippobary. Right now, those animals were the only allies Doug could count on. They gave him food, his thermal shield, and some protection. *If only they had guns and a willingness to fight on our side,* Doug thought, smiling in the dark.

The barn had burned to its foundation, or been blown apart. Even the course of plascrete that had supported the walls was damaged. At the rear of the barn, where Doug had launched the message rocket, the plascrete had been fused into something unrecognizable. The back of the house was scorched, the wall warped, if not as badly as the barn's foundation. The roof shingles were blackened, and many were missing. There were no lights on in the house.

Doug lay motionless in the reeds for twenty minutes. *It doesn't mean anything,* he told himself. *They wouldn't stay here. They'd have gone to Marie's.* Marie was Elena's oldest sister. She lived in Max, near the Park, the greenbelt between the two settlements.

He crawled to the house, just in case it was being watched. He had to go inside, look for any message that Elena might have left, and unless the invaders had looted the place, he hoped to find supplies.

After pausing again below the porch, Doug went up the back stairs and through the kitchen door quickly. He dove into the house and rolled to the floor under the table. When he came to a stop, his rifle was up, ready for action. Doug gave himself a moment, until he was breathing normally again.

I must be alone, or I'd already be dead or a prisoner.

He scooted out from under the table, stood, and closed the outside door. He made a quick tour through the house to make certain that he was alone, and to see what his wife had left. Clothes were missing from his wife's dresser and closet, and from Jamie's. A piece of paper on the corner of the dresser carried one word: "Marie." Doug closed his eyes in relief, then turned the paper over and printed his initials on it. If Elena came home, she would understand.

Then Doug went to work. He found a knapsack and filled it—clothing, ammunition, supplies, and food. The first pack filled quickly. He filled a second as well. He could have filled a dozen, but this was all he could carry back to his hideaway. Doug needed only an instant to suppress the instinct to grab a portable complink. The advantages of communications were infinitely outweighed by the simple fact that even the most basic scanning equipment could pinpoint his location the instant he turned the complink on.

Got to get moving, Doug told himself. *I've been here too long already.* The night's work wasn't over yet.

Gil Howard came out on his back porch and stood there silhouetted against the light from inside his house. He jumped when Doug rose from the tall grass and walked toward him.

"We thought you were dead," Gil said when he recovered from the start. He hurried down off the porch and moved to meet Doug. "Where the hell have you been?"

"Hiding," Doug said. "What's going on? I've been completely out of touch since the night of the invasion."

"There hasn't been much," Gil said. "The Federation people say they've decided to 'assert their rightful sovereignty,' as the new governor told us over the net."

"How many troops did they land?"

"No more than a couple hundred, but their ship is still in orbit. No telling how many more men they have up there." Gil looked around, nervous. A little shorter than Doug, he was only a couple of years older, although he looked older than he was. Buchanan did not have the sophisticated nanotech equipment to hold down the appearance of age. But he was also a farmer, fit and healthy from a lifetime of physical work.

"And everyone's ready to sit still and let them steal our world?"

"There's not a hell of a lot we can do, now, is there?"

"Maybe, maybe not," Doug said.

"What do you *think* we can do?"

"We can try to make the price higher than they're willing to pay," Doug said. "We can make sure they know this is our world."

Gil lowered his head and turned away. Doug waited, almost holding his breath. Did *anyone* feel as strongly about this as he did? Finally, Gil turned back to him.

"What do you want me to do?"

Doug took a deep breath, then let it out. "Help me organize. Get some of the men. Have them put together field packs and weapons. I can't go house to house recruiting. The Federation people may be looking for me. I managed to fire off the message rocket before I went to ground. If it got through, we *may* get help from the Commonwealth—eventually. But we can't count on that, and we can't very well let strangers come in and do all the work.''

Gil spent a moment pacing before he answered. ''Okay, I'll do what I can. But when I've done that, I'll join you. I don't much like the idea of strangers barging in and taking over.''

Doug smiled. ''I was hoping you'd say that.''

Part 2

5

Admiral Truscott sat motionless through most of the ascent to *Sheffield*. Ian could almost hear his boss sigh with relief when the command shuttle moved out of the atmosphere into the freedom of space.

"It's been decades since I really felt comfortable ashore," the admiral said. "I would almost have passed up the chance to get my flag if I could have stayed in space full-time."

Ian sat across from the admiral and looked out a porthole, almost as avid for space as Truscott. *This is why I joined the Navy,* he thought. Man had been trespassing in space for a thousand years, and there were still all of the absolutes. Space was unforgiving of error. A moment's distraction could be deadly.

"You know, Ian," Truscott said as the shuttle pilot matched orbits with *Sheffield*, "this mission may take us into completely unknown territory."

"Sir?" Ian had allowed himself to become distracted by the outside view. *Sheffield*'s bulk had dominated the view for some time. The bundle of three tangent cylinders stretched for miles, comforting in its bulk.

"We've never had a real space war. Apart from a few minor skirmishes, we've simply used space for transportation. The wars have all been down in the dirt, just as they've been since one caveman first hit another over the head with a club. We haven't the foggiest notion whether any of the tactics we've dreamed up at the War College will work when it isn't just a drill. We don't know anything about the business of war in space.''

"We're as ready as we can be, sir," Ian said. "After all, the Federation has no more experience at this than we do.''

"On the contrary, Ian. We have to assume that they've already won at least three space engagements.''

"Camerein?''

Truscott nodded. "Camerein. We still don't know what happened there. All we know is that three ships haven't returned from that system. *Northumbria* was there when the Federation declared war. *Suffolk* and *Hebrides* never came back from their missions to Camerein.''

"Not to mention Prince George," Ian said.

"Not to mention." Truscott nodded again. "That may be why we're to be honored with the presence of his younger brother, to keep William out of His Majesty's way for a time. It is my understanding that the Duke of Haven has been pressing His Majesty for an all-out assault on Camerein to rescue their brother.''

"I'm a bit surprised that we haven't been ordered to do something like that, instead of this Buchanan go," Ian said.

"No, not yet," Truscott said, and then he held up a hand to forestall any further conversation. The shuttle was about to slide into its hangar bay on *Sheffield*.

Admiral Truscott was welcomed aboard with full honors, sideboys, flourishes, and whistles. Rear Admiral Paul Greene, commander of *Sheffield*'s battle group; Captain Mort Hardesty of *Sheffield*; and a half dozen other officers were there to greet the admiral. Truscott suffered the formalities with cheerful resignation. Under peacetime conditions, he had welcomed the ritual and pomp. The Navy wasn't fully conditioned to war yet, and rituals were hard to suppress.

It was twenty minutes before Truscott and the others reached the flag bridge. Ian went straight to the tea cart to provide refreshments for the senior officers.

"I want a full conference, as quickly as you can set it up, Paul," Truscott said while Ian passed around the cups. "Skippers and first officers of all five ships, Colonel Laplace of the Marine regiment, along with his top staff and battalion commanders, the commander of the air wing, and her squadron commanders." In addition to *Sheffield* and *Victoria,* the battle group would include the frigates *Repulse* and *Lancer,* and the supply and service vessel *Thames.*

"There's a chance some of those people are still dirtside, Stasys," Greene said. "Provisioning is still going full lick, and quite a few of the people from *Victoria* are getting in their bit of shore leave yet."

"Find out how many and who, and get those officers up here double-quick. I need to get this briefing out of the way today. We're going to war, not to a tea party."

A moment later, only Truscott and Shrikes were left on the flag bridge. "Get our people in here, Ian," Truscott said. "I might as well get them straightened away while we're waiting for the other lot."

"Yes, sir."

There had been considerable reorganization. As senior officer, Admiral Truscott got the prime flag territory on the battlecruiser. Admiral Greene and his staff had been bumped, and were in the process of transferring to *Victoria.*

The rest of Truscott's staff had gathered in the flag wardroom. Ian went in and exchanged greetings. Most of the team had been together for nearly two years.

"Pep talk time," Ian told the others. "On the flag bridge."

• • •

It was after 1700 hours before Paul Greene could report that all of the officers Truscott wanted present for the briefing had arrived. "They're waiting your pleasure in the main wardroom, Stasys."

"Thanks, Paul." Truscott clapped his friend on the shoulder. "You know, we may really earn our pensions on this voyage."

Paul Greene's answering smile was thin. "It all seems a bit foggy to me, Stasys. Unless you've been keeping secrets."

"Not intentionally, at least. I've routed everything to you since this flap came up." Truscott shrugged. "There may be the odd bit and piece missing. Hell, man, I'm not sure *I* know all of what's going on."

Ian opened the door for the admirals, then followed them along the corridors and down the lift tube. When he opened the door to the main wardroom, he heard the call to attention as someone inside spotted the admirals. A lectern had been set up at the head of the room. Truscott homed in on that and told everyone to be seated.

"Ladies, gentlemen." Truscott didn't waste time when he reached the lectern. A quick glance around showed faces that were attentive, curious, a bit apprehensive.

"We will depart Buckingham in less than twenty-four hours. Our destination is a world known as Buchanan. If you've never heard of it, don't feel bad. I hadn't heard of it myself two weeks ago." There were complink controls on the lectern. Truscott punched in a code and a chart of the Buchanan system appeared on the wall behind him. Next to the chart, a list of vital statistics for the system wrote itself on the wall screen.

"Nothing remarkable," Truscott said. "Seven planets, two of them gas giants with extensive satellite systems. Two well-defined asteroid belts. Only the one habitable world. Buchanan was settled about a hundred and fifty years ago. We have no population figures, no recent data of any sort. All we do know is that Buchanan has apparently been invaded by forces of the Federation.''

A hand rose in the audience. Truscott nodded at the officer and she stood.

"Lieutenant Commander Olive Bosworth, fourth squadron of the air wing.''

"Yes, Commander?''

"*Apparently,* sir?'' She put a lot of emphasis on the first word.

"Apparently, Commander,'' Truscott affirmed. "A message rocket was intercepted coming in-system. The cylinder itself was badly scorched. The early analysis was that the MR transited to Q-space deep in a planetary atmosphere. Yes, I know that the book says that can't be done. At least, there are strong recommendations against it. But the message in the rocket was that Federation troops had landed and were taking members of the governing planetary commission prisoner. The Admiralty takes the message seriously.''

Paul Greene cleared his throat and Truscott looked to him.

"Someone has to ask this, so it might as well be me,'' Greene said. "What's so important about Buchanan, other than the fact that Federation troops may have landed there?''

"Buchanan is on the fringe between the core regions of Commonwealth and Federation,'' Truscott said. "It has been independent, not a member of the Commonwealth, but not accepting the claimed sovereignty of the Federation either. It is apparently only lightly settled. Buchanan could give the Federation a toehold close to worlds that are vital to the Commonwealth. It could also give them a base close to an area that a lot of our ships use for making mid-course

Q-space insertions. If they set up shop there, they could be a real thorn in our sides, even perhaps threaten Buckingham. Other than location, the important thing is that they've requested our assistance in defending themselves. His Majesty's government have decided that we should grant that assistance.

"We'll have to gather our own intelligence going in. The scout ship *Khyber* has already been dispatched. We will rendezvous with *Khyber* before we make our final jump to Buchanan. Our preliminary analysis is that the Federation probably hasn't committed major assets. But the basis of that estimate is nothing more than the fact that, as far as we know, there's nothing to justify a major commitment. You can understand that, since Buchanan's location is strategically important, I don't place an excessive amount of faith in that assessment, which is one reason why *Khyber* is off doing a recce.

"Our mission is to engage Federation forces and liberate Buchanan. I will keep you apprised of developments as necessary. Once we have firm intelligence on the current status of enemy forces, we'll move toward tactical planning. In the meantime, I want every ship, every section, ready for combat. That's all for now."

After the briefing, Ian followed the two admirals back to the flag bridge.

"Just how strong do you think the Federation force on Buchanan is, Stasys?" Greene asked.

"There's really no way to know," Truscott grumbled, "but I'm hoping they've not assigned more than a single troop ship. Their Cutter class, if we're lucky."

"A single battalion?" Green asked, clearly skeptical.

"The colony on Buchanan can't number more than forty or fifty thousand people. They have no significant exports, almost no contact with other worlds. You know what it's like with a small colony. All they have is their location, their homes. Even if they plan to build it up afterward, there's no call for a major commitment of Federation troops at the start. Especially if they don't know that someone managed to get out a call for help. We have a chance to score a quick victory. We need something like that to drive home the point that this war is for real. A lot of civilians don't seem to recognize the peril yet.''

Ian felt a sudden chill at an uninvited thought: *A quick defeat might drive home the point even better.*

6

Turn and about—*hell of a way to run things,* David Spencer thought as he packed his bag at the Royal Albert Hotel in downtown Westminster. *Been gone twenty-four months and only get twenty-four hours ashore.*

It had been a spectacularly unsatisfactory shore leave, even though he had splurged on a room in the poshest hotel on Buckingham. Drinking alone had been no fun. Nothing tasted right. It was all flat, like the talk of the civilians around him. Finally, he had bought a bottle and gone back to his room. After scanning the day's headlines on the complink, David searched for news of the CSF and the war, linking back through all of the months he had been gone. He found the entries about the ships that were presumed lost: *Northumbria, Suffolk, Hebrides.* Each had carried a Marine detachment. David had done a tour aboard *Suffolk.* He knew men who were serving on *Hebrides,* perhaps also on *Northumbria.*

Turn and about. In some ways, David was almost glad to see this liberty end. There were no taxis handy when he left the hotel, so he started walking. It was a bright spring day in Westminster. The breeze was mild, coming from the ocean. Nothing that David saw showed any sign that there was a war on. He stopped on a corner and turned through a complete circle. People walked and rode past, caught up in their normal affairs, oblivious to anything else. Business as usual. David suddenly felt like screaming in frustration. *Don't you bloody sods know what's going on?*

For a moment, he trembled with something like rage. It wasn't until he was in the taxi heading out toward the CSF base in Cheapside that he managed to think his way through his reaction. *What do you* think *a war's supposed to be like at home? It's up to blokes like me to keep them feeling safe and normal.* Finally, his tension eased enough for a wry question. *And where's the fine text that says folks have to panic 'cause there's a war somewhere?*

David looked around, settled himself more comfortably in the backseat, and cleared his throat. "Driver, drop me at Northbridge and Woolsey, instead of going to the port." There was still time for a pint or two before he had to report back for the shuttle.

Buses ran along Northbridge every twenty minutes. David took a post near the front of the Tattooed Lady, put his bag on the floor between his feet, and set himself a time limit. This pub felt more comfortable than the fancy bar at the Royal Albert.

Almost like home, David thought. He drank down his first two pints of bitter quickly, then decided he had time for a third. When the third pint had gone the way of the first two, there were still four minutes left until the next bus was due, so David ordered a final half pint and tossed that off in one long swallow.

"There, lad, you've had your proper taste." He set the glass on the bar with exaggerated care. "No telling how long that has to hold you." He flipped a sloppy salute at the barman, picked up his bag, and headed for the door. His steps weren't nearly as crisp and military as when he came in. But he felt worlds better.

David whistled his way to the bus stop. He wasn't drunk—a slight buzz, nothing more. By the time he reported back aboard *Victoria,* he would be ready for duty. He probably wouldn't even need a killjoy patch to cleanse the alcohol from his system.

No one paid much attention to a slightly intoxicated Marine in Cheapside, not even in the afternoon. Drunken Marines were a daily, and nightly, sight there. The bus conductor, a former Marine himself, took note of where David sat in order to make sure the sergeant got off at the port. The conductor always did what he could for the Marines and sailors who came under his charge on their way back to base from a sortie into Cheapside. He knew what it was like.

David sat and stared out the window. He continued to whistle, but softly, absentmindedly. Behind him, the conductor smiled when he found himself whistling the same tune, just as softly. He nodded, thinking that very little had changed in the twenty years since he had mustered out.

The bus ride took less than ten minutes. David got up from his seat a half block before the familiar stop at the main gate and worked his way to the door at the rear of the bus.

"Good luck, Marine," the conductor said as David weaved by him.

David stopped and looked at him. "Thanks. And good luck to you." The conductor saluted with a grin and David returned both. He stepped down from the bus feeling better than he had in weeks.

A dozen people got off with David, all of them heading back to base. Others were converging on the gate, getting out of taxis or walking down the street. Down the block, David saw three of his people. Alfie and Roger were more than half carrying Jacky White. Jacky seemed scarcely conscious.

"No damn wonder," David mumbled.

"Hey, Sergeant!" Alfie shouted, still fifty yards away.

"We brought him back in one piece, sort of."

Jacky lifted his head and managed to open his eyes, but only briefly.

"Why didn't you slap a killjoy on him?" David asked when the men reached him. "We can't get him on the shuttle like that."

"Ain't right," Jacky mumbled. "They got no bloody right." Then he sagged toward the street, completely unconscious. Alfie and Roger were hard put to keep him from falling.

"We was afraid we couldn't get him back at all if he sobered up," Roger said. "Takin' a chance on company punishment seemed better'n him endin' up in the brig."

"Slap a patch on him now," David said. "Better make it two. I've never seen him so far in the bag."

Alfie supported Jacky's weight while Roger applied the medical patches to his neck. After a moment, Jacky groaned, but killjoy patches didn't work *that* quickly. He was still unconscious.

"We don't have time to wait for it out here," David said. "Keep a firm grip on him, lads, and let's get him inside. Maybe he'll wake up by the time we get to the shuttle."

David stayed close to his men as they went past the sentries at the gate. There was a detailed ID check before anyone was allowed through. The guards gave Jacky a close look, but after they had confirmed all of the group's identities, they waved David and his men through.

"Get him on a cart," David said after they were clear of the gate. "If he was awake, I'd make him walk all the way to the shuttle, all the way to *Victoria* if we could manage it."

There were open buses for transport on the base—flatbed trucks with simple benches, no doors or aisles. David and his men piled aboard one heading toward the shuttle terminal. Halfway there, Jacky groaned and started to sit up, one hand held up to his head. Even after he got upright, he held his head, putting the second hand up to help. His eyes were open, but his gaze seemed fixed on his toes.

"Where the hell are we?" Jacky asked.

"*You're* on the tightrope between the brig and company punishment," David said. It was enough to make Jacky look up.

"I'm a civilian, damn it," Jacky said. "My hitch was up seven weeks ago. They've got no bloody right to keep me in."

"They've got every right in the galaxy, lad," David told him. "There's a war on."

"I don't see any war," Jacky retorted. "I don't much care either. It's not my war. Let somebody else fight it. I've done my time."

"And you'll do a little more, White," David said. "The only question is where you'll do it, and that's entirely up to you. You can return to duty like a man, or you can spend your time in the brig." David wouldn't beg anyone to do his duty.

"He'll be all right, Sarge," Roger said. "We'll keep him straight."

"Anyone seen Tory?" David asked. It was time to start worrying about the last of his squad.

"He went straight home yesterday," Roger said. "Told us he'd see us back aboard ship."

"Then he'll be here. He knows his duty." David looked at Jacky. White was still leaning forward, holding his head. The killjoy patches would sober him in a hurry, but—especially with two patches on at once—they would give him a giant-killer of a headache.

Serve him right, David thought. He was upset at Jacky's condition and complaints, but not nearly as upset as he would have been if Jacky had missed ship. That would have been a certain court-martial offense, and in time of war, the sentence would be heavy. *We'll whip you back in shape, lad,* David promised silently. It was a rotten break for Jacky—and all the other marines, soldiers, and sailors whose enlistments had been extended indefinitely—but there was no help for it.

"They got *Suffolk,* Sarge," Roger said as the cart slowed for its halt at the shuttle terminal. "Three of the lads I went through training with were on *Suffolk.*"

"*Northumbria* and *Hebrides* as well," David said. "We've probably all lost mates. But we'll get our innings."

"Jacky'll see it clear soon enough," Roger said.

David nodded. "Let's get inside and check in for the shuttle."

Tory Kepner ran into the terminal at the last possible moment. He checked in just as the shuttle to *Victoria* was being announced. "That was close," he said when he joined the others from his squad.

"You made it. That's the important bit," David said. "How's the wife and son?"

"Fantastic. I hated to leave."

"We get this next job of work done, maybe they'll give us a proper breather." David herded his charges toward the gate.

"I've got hundreds of holos of Francie and Geoff," Tory warned. Francie was his wife, Geoff the eighteen-month-old son.

Alfie groaned. "An' I suppose we'll have to look at every bleedin' one of them."

"Half a dozen times." Tory grinned. "And that's before I parcel out the cake that Francie baked for you lot."

"Aw, c'mon, lad," Alfie said. "Can't let your missus's cake go stale waitin' for that. It'd be an insult to her."

"How would you know the difference between stale and

fresh?'' Tory challenged. ''You think the RM serve us gourmet meals.''

Everyone but Jacky laughed. Jacky was conscious now, but he hadn't said a word in quite some time.

ID chips were checked at the entrance to the shuttle. Besides the naval rating comparing the chips to a roster, there were two Marines in battledress, carrying loaded weapons. That was new. In all his years in the Royal Marines, David couldn't remember security ever being so tight.

''There's a war on, right enough,'' David whispered to himself as he took his seat in the shuttle.

7

Three days after his meeting with Gil Howard, Doug Weintraub left his cave just before sunset. He walked a mile west before turning north. The past days had left Doug feeling more nervous than he had been since the first hours of his flight. Sleep had become almost impossible. His nerves were stretched almost to the breaking point.

He reached a location that overlooked the rendezvous point an hour early. It was an area of tall grasses and scrub trees, with a fair amount of cover—for foe as well as friend. Doug settled himself in a prone position on the low rise and gnawed at a strip of hippobary jerky while he waited—more to ease his nerves than his hunger. He was delighted to see his recruits move into the area with some sense of precaution, spread out, rifles at the ready.

Almost military, Doug thought, though he had never seen a true soldier and suspected that professionals might not look so awkward. They certainly wouldn't be carrying such an assortment of hunting weapons.

Would I even see trained soldiers? Doug wondered. The doubt raised his level of nervousness. He made a wide, slow circuit of the rendezvous area before he moved in to meet the others.

"I was beginning to think you weren't going to show," Gil whispered when Doug arrived.

"I wanted to make sure you hadn't been followed," Doug replied.

He looked around the group. Everyone had night-vision goggles like his own. They were common on Buchanan; any hunter would have a pair. Doug recognized most of the men immediately, and the rest as soon as they talked. Gil and the Evander twins, Ronald and Robert, were wearing coveralls that looked as if they had been fashioned from thermal-seal tarps. They would give as much protection from infrared detection as Doug's hippobary hide, and wouldn't weigh a tenth as much. The others all wore ponchos that would give some protection—but not nearly enough. Albert Greer was probably the oldest of the group, near sixty. That would be nothing on a more civilized world, but Buchanan was too small and isolated to possess the latest medtech organisms and devices; Greer was grizzled in appearance and had taken to shaving only rarely. The Evander twins, not yet twenty, were the youngest. The others were George Hatchfield, Marc Bollinger, Timothy Connors, and Ash Benez. Despite the individual differences among them, all of the men showed some similarities. All were used to hard work out of doors. They all farmed, at least part-time. Even the twins had weathered and tanned faces. And they all were accustomed to firearms. On Buchanan, all of the men hunted.

"I had to be careful talking to folks," Gil said. "I probably could have got more men, but I figured it was best to be cautious."

Doug nodded. "By far. Let's get under cover before anything else. I feel naked as hell out here."

"Where we goin'?" Albert asked.

"The first caves south of the bend," Doug said. "I've been using the larger to sleep in, and the other for smoking hippobary." He thumped his hand softly on the hide he was wearing. "It doesn't look like much, and it may smell awful rank, but it'll help hide you from snoopers. Better than that poncho, Albert."

Greer nodded, a jerky gesture the way he did it. "I thought of hippobary, but I didn't have any hide to hand and wasn't sure there'd be time to cure one before tonight."

"I've got enough for three of you," Doug said. "Let's get moving. Stay loose, stay alert, and keep some distance between. If anybody brought a complink or anything else that puts out any sort of energy, leave it here. We can't use electronics without giving away our position."

He didn't wait for acknowledgements or questions, simply turned and started walking toward the caves. This time, he held a course as straight as he could manage without maps or compass.

I wish I knew more about soldiering, Doug thought after they had been moving for a quarter hour. *I wonder how many mistakes we've made already.*

By the time the group reached the caves, Doug felt as if he were three hours short on breathing. Several times during the march he had realized that he was holding his breath and had to remind himself to start again. It accentuated his already considerable exhaustion, making him ready to collapse by the time he crawled into the big cave.

Gil Howard switched on a small battery lantern. The sudden light made Doug jump, but before he could yell, he saw that Gil had shielded the lantern, and Albert was already draping a poncho across the low entrance to the chamber.

"Be more dangerous to have people shouting 'ouch' all the time," Gil said when he saw the way Doug was looking at him.

Doug pulled in a deep breath. "I guess you're right. I've just been going without anything so long that . . . well, you know."

Gil nodded.

"I appreciate that you all came," Doug said, looking around the group. "I hope you know what you're getting into." A couple of them nodded. They all looked serious.

"There's plenty of jerky hanging there." Doug pointed. "Help yourselves. I hope you all brought canteens or water bags. Be more efficient if a couple of you take them all over to the river to fill them."

The Evander twins started collecting containers immediately. Both of the twins had jet-black hair and eyes that seemed undecided whether to be brown or hazel.

"As much as possible, we need to get everything done outside before dawn," Doug said before the twins left. "Night and thermal shields are the only protection we've got outside."

Albert Greer started chuckling.

"What's so funny?" Doug asked.

"Just thought you might like to know," Albert said. "I brought thirty pounds of explosives. Thought we might find a use."

Doug smiled. "We can sure as hell try. You have detonators too?"

"Stuck 'em in Gil's pack when he weren't lookin'. I know better than to keep caps and plastic together."

Gil looked startled. He picked up the knapsack he had so cavalierly dropped and went through the outside pockets until he found the small box with eight detonators in it.

"There's another box," Albert warned him, and Gil pulled that one out as well.

"Only one target worth using that much boom-putty on," Ash Benez said. "The shuttles the Federation troops came down in. There's three of them sitting at the port."

"Something to think about," Doug said. "If we can figure a way to get at them. They must have guards posted."

"They do, at least part of the time," Benez said, "but I

haven't seen more than three pacing around at a time.'' In peaceful times, Ash was one of the locals who worked the spaceport, on those rare occasions when there was any work to do there. He had paid special attention to it since the invasion.

"Let's sleep on it," Doug said. "We can't do anything before tomorrow night in any case."

By late morning, when everyone was back up, no one had any better target to offer than the shuttles at the spaceport.

"It's so perfect, I wish I had thought of it," Albert said. "What better symbol?" He didn't get any argument.

While the rest of the force turned to making the caves into a better bivouac, Doug, Gil, and Albert tried to find a low-risk way to strike at the shuttles. Late in the afternoon, Doug briefed the rest of his "troops," and just after sunset, all nine men started toward the spaceport.

There were clouds far out to the west, low on the horizon. They wouldn't complicate this mission, but there might be rain before noon the next day. Doug turned his gaze from the sky to the four men with him. Gil and three others were taking a route several miles to the west, with half of the explosives and detonators. Doug and the rest were following the river. They would move through the greenbelt between Sam and Max out to the spaceport. If one team were destroyed or delayed, the other team could still attempt the strike.

Doug's team was spread out, ten yards between men as they hiked along the river, almost in the riverbed. The land at their left sloped up to the level of their shoulders. There were dozens of hippobary visible, and the men gave the animals the right of way, standing motionless whenever one of the beasts came close. So soon after sunset, the hippobary were intent on getting to their grazing grounds. As long as they perceived no immediate threat from the humans, they would concentrate on feeding.

Hippobary will be the least of our worries before the night's over, Doug thought. All of the day's planning had skirted several important issues, like casualties and Federation reaction to the raid. No one wanted to talk about friends being killed or wounded. No one had any idea how the soldiers might respond. "All we can do is take it all one step at a time," Albert had said. "None of us know enough about this business to do anything else."

Ash Benez was on point when Doug's group reached the greenbelt between Sam and Max. The narrow strip had been set aside when the colony was founded. It was simply "the Park" and remained undeveloped, a statement of optimism: "Someday we'll be so populous that we'll need to have special areas set aside to remind us what this world was like before we changed it."

"Let's take a breather," Doug whispered when his team moved into the Park. "If there's any enemy activity, maybe we'll get lucky and spot them before they spot us."

Like most of the residents of Buchanan, Doug was intimately familiar with the Park. Its many small, secluded clearings were popular with courting couples—not that there were likely to be any young lovers to interrupt now.

Doug crawled ten yards ahead of the others and settled himself on his stomach to watch. No matter how hard he tried, he couldn't completely shut out his fear. *I don't want to get the lot of us killed.* If this attack resulted in disaster, would anyone else ever take up the campaign?

That afternoon, Doug had spent two hours questioning his men about the activities of the Federation troops, gathering as much intelligence as he could. Soldiers patrolled the towns, but not with any great frequency or numbers. Patrols consisted of three or four men in battle kit, but they didn't bother the local residents for the most part. There was no catalog of atrocities or outrages. The soldiers carried a variety of weapons, including beamers, needle guns, and slug throwers. Doug was just as worried about the combat helmets the soldiers wore—certain to be replete with sophisticated electronics, targeting capabilities, communications links, augmented sight and hearing.

Twice during the passage between Sam and Max, Doug signalled for his men to take cover. The first time, he decided that he really hadn't seen anything. After a few minutes, he cautiously moved forward, then signalled for the others to follow.

The second time, there was excellent reason for taking cover. The Buchananers dropped to the ground and remained motionless while a Federation patrol passed no more than twenty yards in front of them—four men walking single file on the main path from Max toward Sam. Doug and his companions lay motionless, hardly daring to breathe. Doug felt as if his body had gone completely rigid. He worried that the sound of his heartbeat might be loud enough to give them away. He had *thought* that he had known what fear was before, especially after setting off the MR the night of the invasion, but this was a numbing terror beyond anything he could even have imagined before.

The Federation patrol moved slowly past, the men looking casually around. It would not take much to give away the fact that there were locals hiding—armed locals. After the soldiers passed, Doug waited ten minutes before he gave his people the signal to get up and move on. Even then, he had to force himself to move. He was trembling with poorly suppressed fright.

Three minutes later, Albert came up to Doug and whispered against his ear. "We should be clear, at least until we get close to the port. I don't think they run more'n one patrol at a time. They'll go through Sam, then head back to their camp out by the port."

Doug nodded. It might have been better if there were more patrols out, more men away from the main encampment at the port. That might have made the job of getting in and out easier. There were platoon-sized detachments camped near each of the settlements, but most of the troops were held out at the port. Where they could protect the shuttles.

The shuttles. Doug and his men lay in the grass near the edge of Buchanan's rudimentary spaceport. A single plascrete runway stretched north and south. A small terminal and one large, now empty, hangar were the only permanent buildings. A cupola above the terminal provided Buchanan's only air traffic control. Antennas on the dome connected the colony to communications satellites overhead and gave incoming ships a link to the colony.

A year that saw two ships arrive was one that would be remembered for decades. Like the Park, the port was more a statement of the colony's faith in its future than a necessity for the present.

The port buildings were on the near side of the field, between the runway and the two towns. The main camp of Federation troops was to the north, on the terminal side. The three shuttles were parked in front of the hangar, facing the runway. The hangar was open on both ends. There were no lights or soldiers visible in the building. But Doug could see the tail end of the center shuttle, and that was the target.

"Tail's probably the only place those birds are vulnerable," Albert had said that afternoon while they were planning the operation. "The skin's got to be reinforced past all belief. All the stretch-boom I brought probably wouldn't even char it. All we can do is cram all that shit up the tailpipe and set it off."

"Come on," Gil had protested. "The temperatures and stresses *those* must be built to take?"

Albert had chuckled nastily. "Think, boy," he said. "They're built to funnel all that energy one way, out the back. We put a blast headin' the other way, we ought to be able to raise hell with the valves, vanes, whatever the hell they use to direct the exhaust."

"I don't suppose they'd be so considerate as to leave the doors open so we could blow up the cockpits," Doug had said.

"Not likely," Albert said. "The only other way I can see that we might do some damage would be to blow away the nose gears, and it probably wouldn't take much for them to fix that. But if we can screw up the fire boxes, it might slow them down a mite longer."

Not too much longer, Doug had thought at the time. He had no grandiose delusions. Even if there was only one troop ship in orbit, it had to carry more than three shuttles. The only certain result of this raid would be the grounding of more troops, and probably an aggressive search for the raiders. But they had to try.

"We'll never blow an opening between the firing chamber and the fuel tanks," Doug had said. "That would be pretty. Set off a hydrogen tank and the whole thing would go. One blast, on the middle shuttle, might take all three of them, if they're parked close enough together."

"Probably aren't," Albert replied, "and unless you've got some brilliant way to get at the tanks, it's all a dream anyhow."

"If only we had some way to find out about the shuttles, plans, schematics, *something*."

"Wish for a dreadnought while you're at it" was Albert's reply to that.

After fifteen minutes, Doug hadn't seen any sign of guards posted around the buildings or shuttles. There were two men farther away, but they stayed by the tents. *There must be guards,* Doug thought, *unless their electronics are so effective that human sentries aren't needed.* That possibility didn't cheer him at all. Human sentries might be evaded, or silenced. Electronics would give their warning long before they could be silenced.

''Let's go,'' Doug whispered, afraid that if he waited much longer he would loose his nerve completely. ''Be on the watch for *anything.*''

The last two-hundred yards seemed to take forever. Doug and his men didn't crawl, but they stayed low, crouched over, moving only when the sentry on the near side of the army camp was walking away from them, going to ground before he reached the end of his post, waiting until he made the return trip and turned again before they rose to move on.

Doug aimed toward the southern corner of the hangar, planning to go along the outside of that building. With the huge doors open on both ends, going *through* the hanger was far too tempting to chance. It was almost as if those doors had been left open as an invitation . . . a trap.

Of course, the whole setup might be a trap, Doug thought during one of the intervals while he and his men were flat on their faces waiting for the distant sentry to turn away again. For the first time, Doug realized, *I might die here tonight, any minute, even without warning.* It was that, more than the physical exertion, that had him panting for breath.

When they reached the hangar, Doug leaned against the wall to slow his breathing. His fear was almost strong enough to touch—almost enough to strangle him. Still, he edged along the building, moving slowly, stopping before he got to the far corner. He wasn't about to stick his nose out on that side, not more than a few inches above the ground.

Once he was on his stomach, Doug slithered to the corner

and stuck his head out far enough to look around. The shuttles were smaller than he had expected. From nose to exhausts, they were barely 140 feet long, hulking shapes that seemed to hug the ground. No more than three feet of tire showed below each shuttle. The tops of the wheels were hidden by wells in the belly of the shuttles. The wings stretched out to the sides, low extensions of the flat belly.

After more minutes of silent watching, Doug slid back from his exposed position and got up. "This is impossible," he whispered. "You'd think they'd have more cover on their shuttles even if they were on one of their own worlds, in the middle of one of their own bases."

"A trap?" Albert asked.

"It smells like it," Doug conceded. "I can't believe that they have so little doubt of their security that they wouldn't set up defenses."

"Hey, we're just ignorant farmers," Ash Benez said. "Maybe they figure we wouldn't even *think* about attacking them."

"There's been nothing in any of the new governor's orders on the net," Albert said. "They haven't even told us to turn in weapons."

We can't turn back, Doug thought, though there was nothing he wanted more at that moment. The other team would be coming in from the far side of the port, and there was no way to communicate with them. After a hesitation that couldn't have been half as long as it seemed, Doug nodded.

"We'll change their minds tonight."

It was another ten minutes before Doug spotted movement on the far side of the runway. He pointed so his companions would see.

"Okay, Albert," Doug whispered. "Let's go visit that middle shuttle. You start preparing the tail while the rest of us look for anything else that might be vulnerable."

Doug led the way out onto the apron in front of the hangar, his rifle up, ready to return any fire. The others spread out in a loose wedge behind him. Albert took his half of the explosives directly to one of the two exhaust nozzles, stuck a small flashlight up into the tube, and started looking for control surfaces that might be vulnerable. Doug crouched behind one of the main landing gear, keeping watch, his attention focused in the direction of the tents. The others did a quick survey of the accessible portions of the fuselage, looking for panels that might give a better explosive path into the interior.

It was Tim Connors who hit the jackpot, where the upper surface of the left wing met the fuselage. He whistled softly, and gestured when Doug looked his way. Carefully, Connors twisted a latch and opened the access panel. Albert looked along the side of the shuttle, holding off on his work, while Doug went to see what Tim had found.

In the recess, Doug saw the shuttle's fuel intakes, two pressure couplings. One intake pipe was labelled for liquid hydrogen, the other for liquid oxygen. Doug quickly waved for Albert.

"Could give us a real pretty show," Albert whispered.

"We have enough explosives to take out all three?" Doug asked.

"Don't want to spread it too thin," Albert said, which was easier than admitting that he didn't know. "Why not be satisfied with two of 'em? Maybe the blasts will take out the third."

"Okay. Get started on this one. I'll have Gil pack the one farthest from the camp."

"Yeah, you do that," Albert said. "Then I'll check to make sure he did it right."

Gil Howard's group had just reached the end shuttle. Doug ran across and scooted under the fuselage. Gil started to work with the explosives as soon as Doug opened the access panel.

"We'll let Albert set both timers," Doug said. "We want to be certain they go off together."

Doug moved everyone else away from the shuttles, giving them a headstart on their escape. Six men took up prone positions in a line fifty yards from the nearest shuttle, ready to give Doug, Gil, and Albert covering fire if necessary. Doug could feel sweat pouring freely down his face. There seemed to be a lump in his stomach a foot in diameter.

"Give us as much lead time as you can with those timers," Doug told Albert, who was priming both detonators at the same time.

"Five minutes from right now," Albert said, positioning one timer in the middle shuttle. He closed the access panel and twisted the recessed latch. Then the two of them ran to the other shuttle and Albert attached the second timer and secured that panel.

"Let's get the hell out of here," Albert said.

They ran hard. The rest of the men got up as the last three approached, and they all took off in the same direction. Doug looked at his watch every few seconds. The group started to slow down after a couple of minutes of racing at full speed. Albert was the first to lag behind. Doug held his speed down to stay with him. Soon Gil and Ash had slowed as well.

"Keep moving as fast as you can," Doug urged the others, feeling the extra effort that talking required.

By the last minute of the five, everyone had slowed down to the pace of the older men. None of these men were accustomed to this level of physical exercise. They might work regularly, but they had not trained as athletes.

"Keep going," Doug said when they were all fairly close together again. "We've only got thirty seconds."

When the count got down to fifteen seconds, Doug

stopped everyone. "Down on the ground." He took up a position looking back toward the shuttles. "We don't know what kind of blast effects there'll be." *And I want to see this,* he told himself. *It might be the only victory we have.*

Ten seconds. Five.

The night lit up with an orange-and-red fireball. Just as the sound of the blast reached the watching Buchananers, two more explosions sent even brighter light flashing out through the first cloud of flames. The hangar was blown to shreds, hurtling large panels of siding into the dark. The third shuttle exploded next, and the terminal building started to burn. Beyond that, tents were burning and blowing, and the fire spread into the prairie grass around the edges of the port. Glowing debris arced through the night and fell on all sides, starting more secondary fires.

"Okay, let's get out of here before they get their act together," Doug said. He got to his feet and started jogging toward the southwest. This time, it wasn't a full-out run, but a more moderate pace. It still hurt. Doug's lungs felt as if they might burst.

But, for a few minutes at least, the Federation troops would be too busy to give chase.

Part 3

8

"White, stick around. The rest of you, hit the showers.'' David Spencer mopped at his face with a towel while the I&R platoon filed out of the gymnasium. Jacky White just stood where he was, not even looking at Spencer. Since leaving Buckingham, the Second Regiment had been training ten to twelve hours a day. Physical conditioning was the first item on the daily schedule for the platoon, even before breakfast.

''You're still carrying a chip,'' Spencer said when he and Jacky were alone.

''What d'you expect? I've been shanghaied. You think I should jump for joy?''

''I think you're a Marine and should act that way,'' his sergeant said. ''You go into combat sulking like this, you'll be worm meat in five minutes, and maybe your mates as well. Is that what you want?''

Jacky didn't say anything.

''They're the ones you're going to hurt,'' Spencer said. ''So you think you got a raw deal. You're not the only man in the regiment who thought he was going back to civie street and didn't. There are at least a hundred others who've had their hitches continued. You can bet the story's the same among the Navy crew, and in every other regiment in the RM. What makes you so damn much better than all of them?''

When Jacky didn't reply, David shouted, "Say something, damn you."

"What? That it's okay I'm being screwed because a lot of other sods are in the same boat? That doesn't make it right, not by a sight. Don't worry, I won't let my friends down, but don't expect a damn thing more from me."

Spencer advanced on Jacky until they were toe to toe. "Look at me," Spencer ordered. When Jacky finally raised his eyes, Spencer said, "You've got until we make our last Q-space transit. You get your act in order or you'll spend the rest of this cruise in the brig. I won't risk my platoon on the moods of a crybaby."

"Is that all, *Sergeant*?" Jacky asked.

"Get out of my sight." After Jacky left, David relaxed the tight control he had been holding himself under. His hands trembled with suppressed rage.

The standard table of organization for a Royal Marine line company was simple. The basic tactical unit was the squad, eight men. If each slot in the squad was filled at its highest rating (a rare event) there would be one sergeant, one corporal, two lance corporals, and four privates. A squad could operate as a single entity, or split into two four-man fire teams. Four squads made a platoon. The highest ranking squad leader doubled as platoon sergeant. There would be a lieutenant as platoon leader for each platoon—again, ideally; more often there was one lieutenant for two platoons. A company consisted of three line platoons, a special weapons platoon, and a headquarters and service platoon (H&S), the last a catch-all for all of the necessary ancillary personnel—clerks, cooks, communicators, and mechanics. A battalion had four line companies and an H&S company. The intelligence and reconnaissance platoon was part of Battalion H&S. The next rung in the organization chart was the regiment, four line battalions, weapons battalion, and engineering battalion . . . and the inevitable H&S detachment, theoretically an "augmented" company at regimental level, though it could approach battalion size in practice.

There were a lot of new men aboard *Victoria* for this voyage. Manning levels in the RM had been low as long as David Spencer had been a member. Now, the Second Regiment was almost at full strength. New men meant dropping to a more basic level for training drills. Although some of these men had been in the regiment almost since the start of the Devereaux mission—replacements had been husbanded on Buckingham since the start of the war, attached to the battalions that had stayed behind—most still seemed to be raw recruits.

There were three new men in the first squad. Sean Seidman was a small, quiet man, except when he lost his temper. That had already happened once in the week since he had joined the squad. Like the other recruits, he was hardly more than a boy just out of school. Seidman's complexion was dark—and so was his temper. Even in the best of moods, he seemed to be perpetually one match short of an explosion, but he was one very proficient Marine, the best marksman in his training class on every light infantry weapon. Carlo Montez was a large, fair-skinned man, his hair a light blond. He was slow-moving, but a whiz with electronics and savage in unarmed combat. The third man was Henry, more commonly "Henny," Prinz, from the German-speaking world of Hanau. His English was fluent, but heavily accented. When he got excited, he was incomprehensible in either language.

Spencer had assigned each of the new men to one of his veterans, and told the old-timers to shepherd them along. Only Jacky White had been spared that duty. While Jacky had quit bitching constantly, he remained surly and uncooperative. If he hadn't been with the squad for nearly five years, David would have given up on him days before. *I may have to brig him yet,* he reminded himself, and the possibility hurt.

Once a Marine was sealed into the helmet, his senses were amplified and extended, turning the brutal reality of combat's horrors into a virtual reality that was marginally less terrifying. A head-up display on the visor showed him things he could never see with his naked eyes, picking up infrared as well as visible light. It offered magnification when necessary, and plotted charts and data on targets or threats. Besides amplifying nearby sounds, the helmet's "ears" also provided abundant communications links. Medical sensors funnelled through the helmet's complinks kept commanders apprised on the physical condition of every trooper.

"We'll run full diagnostics on every helmet," David said when his men were settled at the benches in the electronics shop. "Replace anything that doesn't show one hundred percent. We don't want marginal equipment now." The diagnostics were mostly automatic, and repair rarely needed anything more than unplugging a wafer module and replacing it. In theory, any Marine ought to be able to maintain the helmets equally well. In practice, some men seemed to have a more delicate touch, better results. In David's squad, the men with the touch were Tory Kepner and Roger Zimmerman. One of them would be the last to go over every helmet.

David watched his men work for a quarter hour, then said, "Alfie, let go of that for a minute, will you?" Alfie nodded and got up from the bench. He followed David out of the shop.

"What is it, Sarge?" Alfie asked. David just gestured for him to follow him and headed to one of the break rooms.

"Get yourself a cup," David said, getting coffee for himself. Alfie did as he was told, then followed the sergeant to a table.

"It's about Jacky, isn't it?" Alfie asked.

David nodded, then took a long sip of his coffee.

"I knew it was going to be rough for him," Alfie said. "Didn't figure he'd hold the grudge this long."

"You know what my problem is, don't you?" David asked.

"I'm not sure I do," Alfie hedged.

"If he doesn't shape up, I don't dare take him into combat. He'd bugger the works for everyone. And if I don't dare take him down with us, there's only one thing I can do, and I don't want to do that."

"Unfit for duty in a combat zone?" Alfie spoke the words reluctantly. He had been in the Royal Marines long enough to know *King's Regs* backward and sideways. It was a court-martial offense, no chance of running it soft under company punishment.

"I need help from you and the rest of the lads," David said. "I told Jacky he had until we make our last Q-space jump to shape up or I'd have to brig him. I had to give him the deadline, but I don't want it to come to that."

"We've all had a go at him, Sarge. We'll keep at him, you know that, but I don't know as he cares what happens to him any more."

"In all my years in the RM, I've never had to court-martial one of my men, Alfie. I don't want to start now, not with Jacky."

"We'll do what we can. We don't want anything to happen to him either. He's a good mate."

"But if you can't get him back on course, he'll be too much a danger to himself and everyone else," David said. "Do what you can, but don't try to cover for him. You could be cutting everyone's throat."

"I know," Alfie said, very soberly. He drank down the

last of his coffee, his hand shaking. "I'd best get back to work, Sarge."

"When do we find out what the job is?" David asked Lead Sergeant Landsford. They were alone at a table in the sergeants' mess. The fleet had made its second Q-space transit a few minutes earlier. "Don't they know what they want us to do yet?'

Landsford shrugged. "I'm not sure we've even got a map of the bloody planet. No one seems to know a thing about this Buchanan. Bloody world of farmers that nobody goes to. That's why we're on our way to rendezvous with the ship that's been in to do a recce."

"Hell of a way to run a war," David said. "They'll probably give us five minutes to study an ops briefing—on our way down."

"We get that much, count yourself lucky," Landsford said. "It wouldn't surprise me a whit if they sent your lads down to take a look-see so the rest of us know where to go."

"Don't even think that," David said, groaning.

"Just in case, your lads ready for action?"

"We're ready," David said. "We'll do whatever we have to do."

"Likely to be a right balls-up, no matter what," Landsford said. "I've got a proper itch about this."

"Should have the medicos give you an ointment," David said, laughing. "They say they've got a cure for anything."

"Don't you start. Sergeant major's been riding me for days."

Rendezvous was still hours away, but there were already rumors floating through the regiment about what news the scout ship had. The rumors had started almost the instant that the ship had been sighted. David had dismissed the platoon. There was still an hour before supper, but he knew he wouldn't get much work out of them until they got some news. Besides, it gave him a chance to kick off his boots and grab a little rest before mess call. But he had scarcely closed his eyes before there was a knock at the door.

"Come in," David said, suppressing a sigh. He swung his legs off of the bunk and sat up. *I hope it's not an officer,* he thought, looking down at his stocking feet. *I'm out of uniform.*

"Sergeant?" Jacky White opened the door, but didn't enter.

"Come on in," David said, more softly. "Have a seat." He gestured to the bunk across from his. "What's on your mind?"

Jacky sat just on the edge of the bunk, and held himself stiffly, as if he were at attention.

"I wanted to let you know that you don't have to worry about me," Jacky said. "I'll do my bit. I still say I got a raw deal, but I won't let the lads down. I know my duty." There was tension in the voice, but not the open hostility of a few days before.

"I know you do, lad," David said. "I just had to make sure you'd remember. I owe that to you and the rest. The best thing we can do is get through this patch as fast as we can. Sooner it's over, the sooner we can go home." He paused, then added, "And the sooner you and everyone else in your position can get on with their lives."

Jacky stood. "I just wanted to make sure you knew."

David stood as well. "Thanks, Jacky. We're all counting on, you."

9

"**Captain of *Khyber*** on link, Admiral," Gabby Bierce said.

Khyber had been moving toward the fleet for three hours since appearing out of Q-space. Captain Dever Miles had reported in at once. Truscott had put him off, simply ordering him to collate all of the intelligence he had gathered, and to transmit the hard data as soon as possible. This follow-up was right on schedule.

"I'll take the call in my day cabin, Gabby," Truscott said, getting out of his chair. "Ian, you'd best come along. I may need you to tickle my memory later."

"Aye, sir," Ian replied.

The admiral's day cabin was actually two rooms and bath. The smaller room held a bunk, small table, and one chair. The larger room focused on a large tabletop complink monitor that could be used as a chart plot or to model battles. There were also projectors to let the admiral conduct full-scale holographic conferences in the room, with projections of as many as nine remote participants.

The admiral sat at the table in the chart room. "On the wall, Ian," he said. Ian turned on a wall monitor. Captain Miles's face appeared in close-up, larger than life on the fifty-inch screen.

"Afternoon, sir," Miles said.

"Dever." Truscott nodded. "You have everything I asked for?"

"Everything we could find, sir."

"I'm afraid I'm going to impose on you, Dever," Truscott said. "Feed everything through to this station on the blitz, if you haven't already. But I want you to shuttle over and give me a personal briefing in the flesh."

"Whatever you say, sir," Miles said. "There wasn't even a flicker of annoyance at the command to leave his ship for an unnecessary trip to *Sheffield*.

"I do apologize, Dever." The admiral put on a three-second grin. "But I'm getting old and I think better if I've got somebody to bounce things off of in person . . . and my aide is getting rather bruised."

"I'll be over straightaway, sir." Dever Miles matched the admiral's grin almost perfectly.

Truscott severed the connection and looked up at Ian. "Get on to Captain Hardesty. Let him know the shuttle is coming, and keep me posted. I'll ask you to go to the landing bay to escort Dever up here as well."

"Of course, sir," Ian said. "And I really don't mind having ideas bounced off me. I've gotten rather used to the bruises."

Truscott laughed freely, for the first time in weeks. "Get out of here before I do myself an injury, Ian. I'll stay here until Dever comes."

It was two hours before Captain Miles arrived. Ian was waiting when Miles stepped out of his command shuttle.

"I'm Ian Shrikes, Captain, Admiral Truscott's aide. He asked me to escort you to his day cabin."

"What's this chase about, Shrikes? What can I tell him face-to-face that I couldn't have told him hours ago on link?" Miles kept his voice level, showing only a trace of annoyance.

"Really, sir, I don't think there's any more to it than the admiral said. He prefers face-to-face whenever possible. And he's especially keen on meeting new senior officers under his command."

"Bloody waste of time," Miles said under his breath. The rest of the trip to flag country was made in silence.

"Good to meet you, Dever," Truscott said as Ian followed Captain Miles into the day cabin. "I know the commute is a nuisance. I apologize again. But we're going to be working together on what may be a tricky job of work, and I like to *know* my commanders. Can't do that over a flipping screen, not even on this holo cock-up."

Miles flashed a quick look at Ian, who had moved to the far side of the room. *No, we didn't rehearse our stories,* Ian thought, correctly interpreting the look. *I just know my boss. That's my job.*

"So far, sir, it doesn't look all that tricky," Miles said. "I trust you've had time to scan the data I sent over?"

"I've had my ops people going over it in detail, of course," Truscott said. "Here, have a seat. No need to be uncomfortable." He indicated one of the chairs at the flat-screen table. After the captain sat, Truscott took a seat across from him. Ian remained standing. "They've been flashing me highlights. It's going to take most of the night to process all of the telemetry and so forth."

"I can give you the main points very quickly, sir," Miles said, finally starting to loosen up.

"I hoped you'd be able to. How about something to make the talk go easier? Coffee? Tea?"

"Coffee would be good, Admiral. Thank you."

Ian did the fetching. The discussion stopped until both senior officers had coffee.

"The situation on Buchanan appears remarkably straightforward," Miles said after he sampled his drink. "The colony isn't much, a couple of concentrations of homesteads, rough spaceport, farms. No real industry. No doubt they have their share of nanotech facilities, but cottage scale. No sign of any settlement outside a semicircle seven miles along the base, four miles along the short axis. The base follows a river, of course.''

"And the Federation?'' Truscott asked softly.

"One ship in orbit, apparently Cutter class, though it differs in a few particulars from the specs I had available.''

"Anything of special interest?''

"Not on the ship, Admiral,'' Miles said. He raised his coffee cup to stretch the pause long enough to make the admiral bite.

"Then where?''

"The spaceport, sir. There appears to have been a fight. Our recce suggests that three troop shuttles were destroyed on the ground.''

"Means the locals have managed to do for themselves,'' Truscott said with pleasure.

"They've had a go at them, sir. That seems clear. Those shuttles were lined up in a pretty little row.''

"How many shuttles would a Cutter class carry, do you know?'' Truscott asked.

"According to our data, sir, seven troop shuttles and a command gig.''

"And the locals managed to put the chop on three of them?'' Truscott chuckled. "Magnificent. Any idea how recently the action occurred?''

Dever Miles closed his eyes briefly. "Before we arrived, and the ground had cooled too much to gauge from residual heat. Must be at least ten days since now, perhaps considerably more.''

"Then we have to strike fast, while it's still simple,'' Truscott said. "If there's opposition, they might bring in reinforcements.''

10

His Royal Highness, Prince William Alfred Windsor, Duke of Haven, entered the flag bridge wearing an undress khaki uniform without insignia or badges of rank. Despite the almost requisite participation in various sorts of athletics, and his stint in the Royal Navy, William's face at least exhibited much of the softness and pallor of the full-time courtier. Only his hands showed that his life had not been wholly wasted in such pursuits; his grip was firm and strong; there were muscles concealed by the tailored uniform blouse. Although height had ceased to be a sure indication of class long before his ancestors left Earth, William was taller than most people on Buchanan, nearly seven foot tall. But Admiral Truscott no longer flinched when the prince came into the room. In private, Truscott had admitted to Ian that Prince William wasn't being as much of a pain as he had expected.

"I've seen fleet transits of Q-space before, but never from this vantage," the prince told Ian. "I thought I might get more than a one-ship view, as it were." He spoke softly, timing his statements so he wouldn't interrupt any duty conversations. He and Ian were off to the side.

"I hate to disillusion you, but there's really no difference," Ian said. "You may hear some of the ship-to-ship traffic before and after, but the screens will show the same pictures you'd get on the forward bridge."

William chuckled. "Disillusion me? Hardly a novelty. One gets used to that quite young in my position. When I was a child, I thought I might one day be king. I was third in line to the throne when I was born. There was more than a decade between my brother George and me, and fifteen years between George and Henry. But now? Henry has eight children and seven grandchildren. Even George managed to sire two sons before he decided that marriage wasn't for him. That makes me nineteenth in line for the throne now." His face went serious. He ran a hand through his hair, brown with auburn highlights, worn longer than most of the officers around. "No better than eighteenth, even if George has come a cropper on Camerein."

"No way to know what's happened there," Ian said.

"Not to worry. George has a positively uncanny knack for coming through the stickiest patch without a smudge. I don't think being spaced would do for him."

The image was too much for Ian. A smile quickly broke into a soft laugh. "I wouldn't want to put that to the test," he said.

"Ah, no, it might make for poor relations," the prince said.

Ian realized that he had missed something on the flag bridge when Captain Hardesty came in and went up to Admiral Truscott.

"You said there was something about the transit coordinates, sir?" Hardesty asked.

"Yes, Mort," Truscott replied. Ian edged closer. Prince William stayed at his shoulder. "I'm throwing the book away."

"Sir?" Hardesty said, cocking his head to the side.

Truscott tapped his fingers on the armrests of his chair. "If we make this last transit by the book, the Federation forces will have three days to prepare for us. That simply isn't acceptable.''

"There are good reasons for having exit points well away from planetary masses, sir," Hardesty said.

"Are there?" Truscott asked. "I've given this a lot of thought, twisted all of the data through the computers six ways from Sunday. Actually, there's no evidence quite so compelling as that MR we received from Buchanan. It made its first Q-space transit within a few feet of the planet's surface. And Buchanan is quite clearly still there."

"*Sheffield* masses considerably more than an MR, sir."

"We'll exit at considerably more distance, Mort. I'm not about to order the fleet to pop out of Q-space skimming air. But I do intend to reduce the warning that Cutter class ship has of our coming."

"Cut down by how much, sir?" Hardesty asked.

"Let me put the plan on screen." Truscott fiddled with controls, and a distant view of Buchanan, taken by *Khyber* on its reconnaissance, appeared.

"We'll jump to two separate points," Truscott said. "*Repulse* and *Lancer* will go in closest, to engage the Cutter class vessel from behind as quickly as possible." He looked up to meet Hardesty's eyes. "Three hours out at top acceleration. No braking. They'll go straight past the Cutter class, firing all weapons they can bring to bear, then move into a tight turn to come back for a second pass, if needed. The rest of us will come in from the opposite direction. We'll come in four hours out, moving to block the Federation ship's escape route. As soon as we jump, I want a combat patrol out. If the Cutter class survives its contact with *Repulse* and *Lancer*, we'll send Spacehawks against it as soon as possible."

"A bold plan, sir," Hardesty said. "If we can deal with the turbulence."

"Frankly, Mort, I'm totally discounting turbulence. That

MR survived its first transit, whatever turbulence there might have been, made two more transits to Buckingham, and arrived within fifty yards of its programmed exit point. We should be able to damp any residual effects without putting a strain on our Nilssen generators.''

Hardesty nodded abruptly. ''Whatever, it'll give us new calibration points for future ops.''

Truscott laughed. ''That's the spirit, Mort. Before this war's over, we may be jumping a hell of a lot closer than this.''

''Nobody ever said war would be easy,'' Hardesty said.

''I wouldn't attempt this if I didn't have full confidence in our people and ships, Mort. We go at 1605 ship's time.''

''You throw the shilling out, sir. We'll dance on it.''

''Is this going to be as dicey as it looks?'' Prince William asked Ian. They had left the flag bridge together to get an early dinner before the Q-space transit. Throughout the fleet, men and women were eating early. Once the fleet made this jump, they might be at battle stations indefinitely.

''I think the admiral has it right,'' Ian said. ''It doesn't stop the butterflies from flitting around my stomach, but I saw that MR. Apart from a few scorch marks, there was no damage at all. One of the techs said that the rocket must have made its first jump before it cleared the launch rack.''

The prince whistled. ''Must have been a brave man to dare that.''

''Make that a desperate man and I think you'll have it right,'' Ian suggested.

William nodded. ''Homeworld suddenly invaded. No forces to meet them. Only one hope. Desperate *and* brave. For all he could know, he was committing suicide.''

''I hope he didn't,'' Ian said. ''Before this is over, I'd like the chance to salute him.''

''At least.'' William leaned back and stared at the ceiling. "People like that, I hope they opt for Commonwealth membership. It's that sort who are the backbone of the Commonwealth. But folks like that are notoriously independent."

"They did come to us for help," Ian observed. "Maybe we were their only hope, but they did come to us."

"It's only a first step," William said. "Even after we liberate them, it may take bags of diplomacy to get them to opt for membership."

Before 1600 hours, Ian and William were back on the flag bridge. Admiral Truscott had eaten there. Out of habit, Ian glanced at the tray. Whatever worries the admiral might have about the coming maneuver, and the battle that certainly lay beyond it, they hadn't affected his appetite. The tray had been cleared.

At 1604:30, Admiral Truscott said, "Send the execute order, Gabby," and Gabby hit two keys on the console in front of him. The order had been prepared an hour before.

Klaxons sounded, followed by the standard transit warning. At precisely 1605, the ship's external video pickup went to the featureless gray of Q-space. For the duration of the transit, *Sheffield* was effectively alone in a universe all its own.

"Hardesty to the flag bridge" came over the speakers, thirty-five seconds after Q-space insertion. "Navigation sensors show slight abnormalities in the Q-space bubble around us, a greater than normal eccentricity."

"How slight?" Truscott asked while his own navigation officer scurried to access the raw data.

"No more than point naught-naught-four," Hardesty said. "Quite manageable if it doesn't increase. Well within standard tolerances. It's just the proximity of the fleet, I'd say."

"No doubt," Truscott said. "We'll monitor it. I'm more

interested in fluctuations at the other end. No difficulties with mapping our exit?''

"No, sir. Ah''—there was a slight pause—''exit in seven minutes, twelve seconds.''

"Right, Mort. Truscott out.''

Ian glanced at a time strip.

"I want that Cutter class on the main screen no more than five seconds after we exit Q-space,'' Truscott said. "We'll have a few minutes of observation time before our light reaches them.'' Someone called out a precise time for the light lag. Truscott ignored it. It wasn't vital. The opposing ships would be too far away to engage each other that soon.

"Are all four squadrons of Spacehawks ready to go?''

Lieutenant Commander Cawley, the fighter wing's flag liaison officer, said, ''Armed and ready, sir. First squadron is ready to launch and maintain a constant six-bird defensive screen. Second squadron is on two-minute alert. Three and four are on twenty-minute call.''

Truscott nodded. ''I trust a proper rotation is set up? This may continue for quite some time.''

"Whatever it takes, Admiral,'' Cawley said. ''We don't get many opportunities for this sort of go.''

Truscott gave Cawley a brief glance of annoyance, then turned to Ian. ''Would you have the mess stewards bring in a tea cart as soon as we complete the transit? My throat's a bit dry.''

When Ian left, Prince William went with him.

"The admiral's quite a showman, isn't he?'' William asked as they walked along the corridor.

"He has his moments. Sometimes I'm not sure if he's serious or light.''

"Sticky position for an aide,'' the prince commented.

•   •   •

"There it is, Ian," Truscott said as soon as his aide and the prince returned to the flag bridge. "Buchanan." The planet was centered on the wall monitors, and a white circle ringed the Federation ship that was keeping station over the planet.

"We have reports from *Thames* and *Khyber,* sir," Gabby reported. "Shouldn't be long before we hear from *Repulse* and *Lancer.*"

"Very good." Truscott leaned back and stared at the wall screen for a moment. He turned to Ian as a mess steward entered with the tea cart. "Tea, with just a hint of lemon, I think," the admiral said.

"Here you go, sir," the steward said as he handed the cup to Truscott.

"Thanks, lad." Truscott took a sip. "Just right. Ladies and gentlemen?" he said, raising his voice. "I think we all have time for a taste."

Prince William turned away, unable to suppress his grin. He looked at Ian and shook his head, just a fraction, and Ian smiled back. The admiral was pulling out all the stops.

"Fighter screen being launched now, Admiral," Commander Cawley announced.

"Thank you. The show will be starting soon," Truscott said after all of his staff had drawn their drinks and returned to their stations. "All we have to do is sit back and watch until *Repulse* and *Lancer* make their pass."

11

The unexpected success of their first strike had been heady. But the air of celebration had faded within seventy-two hours. And after seventeen days cooped up in the caves, Doug Weintraub could scarcely bear to look at his companions. The one cave had been too small for the nine men, socially if not physically, so three men had moved to the smaller cave, the one Doug had used for smoking hippobary before. They didn't dare risk fires now, not with all the care in the world.

Doug lay on his back near the entrance of the larger cave. He pulled an uncured hippobary hide over his head and shoulders. Eye holes had been cut in the hide. With that shield in place, he edged along on his back until he could see the sky outside without offering a target that enemy sensors could detect.

He didn't see anything overhead, but he heard the shuttle as it moved away from the area. Again. For seventeen days, the enemy had maintained continuous air surveillance over the region. Doug had no idea how many shuttles the Federation had left around Buchanan, but there was always one in the air, day and night, flying a regular patrol pattern.

The regularity of that pattern was a deep relief to the hiding men. It meant that the enemy hadn't managed to narrow its search yet. Doug and his men were probably still safe, except from chance discovery. For a time.

Doug kept his head outside the cave for as long as he could. The sound of the shuttle's jets kept fading. It would be at least thirty minutes before it returned. The shuttle was a noisy timekeeper.

"No change," Doug reported when he slid back inside.

"How long are they going to keep up the search?" Marc Bollinger asked, his voice tight with tension.

"As long as they're up there looking for us, they're not back at the settlements harassing our people, or knocking on our door here," Albert said. "Start to worry when they quit the flights."

The same conversation had played itself out in many variations during the days of quarantine. The men dared only brief excursions from the caves, always at night, always timed as the current patrol shuttle was moving away. They went to the river for water. They went out to make a hippobary kill. Even though they didn't risk fires, they had to eat, and the jerky Doug had made while he was alone had been exhausted more than a week before. Even Doug was finally sick of the taste of hippobary.

"When they give us a chance," he said, "we'll have to move farther away for a time. Move off, regroup, find a way to vary our diet. Then, once the Federation people have had time to grow complacent, we come back and have another go at them."

"Only thing left would be to ambush a patrol," Gil Howard said. "That's going to be chancier than blowing up their shuttles. Those didn't shoot back."

"Hell, we didn't think we'd be able to shred their shuttles, but we did," Albert said. "We manage to pick up a few Federations weapons and it'll make everything else go a little easier."

"Unless we can mobilize the entire population, we're never going to be able to do more than make the odd raid," Gil cautioned them. "I'm not saying we shouldn't do it, but maybe we let our hopes get too high.''

Doug sighed. ''The entire idea was to make the cost of occupying Buchanan higher than the Federation is willing to pay. We've made a damn good start, wiping out three shuttles, putting them to the bother of a constant air patrol. And the troops on the ground have to be more nervous than before.''

''It would be nice if we could pick up a few more people before we move,'' Ash Benez said. ''And news out of the settlements.''

''Nice but not necessary,'' Doug said firmly. ''The Federation is probably keeping close watch on folks in Sam and Max now. They can't know that we're on the outside. As far as the enemy knows, that attack might have come from one of the settlements.'' Then it was time to stop the conversation before it went on to the next logical area of supposition: conditions in Sam and Max. The talk had gone that far a few times before, and the results had been discouraging.

''We need to get a hippobary tonight,'' Doug said. ''Dump what's left of the last one. It's getting a little too gamy.''

''Hard to tell what's ripe anymore, with us all in here together,'' Albert said, sniffing theatrically. It got a few restrained laughs.

Better than thinking about what the Federation troops might be doing to our families, Doug thought. *Maybe I shouldn't have started all this.* He looked around the cave at the anxious, drawn faces. *Have I done more harm than good?*

Something's changed! At first, that was all that penetrated Doug's mind. He had dozed off, sitting against the side of the cave, close to the entranceway. His morose thoughts had lulled him into a fitful half-sleep. Then . . .

"The shuttle," he said. He looked around quickly. Most of the others had already noticed. A couple of them were on their feet. The rest looked more alert, leaning forward, ready to get to their feet in a hurry if they had to.

The shuttle had been coming back in the direction of the caves, at its usual slow speed. Then it had suddenly gone to high power. An instant later, there was another change in the sound.

Doug crawled out to the mouth of the cave, pulled the hippobary hide over his head, and looked out through the eye holes. The shuttle had increased power and turned away.

"I can't see anything like this." Doug pulled the cover away and slid it back into the cave. He got up and completely out of the cave entrance, his body pressed against the hill as he looked into the sky.

Albert crawled out into the mouth of the cave. "Can you see anything?" he asked.

Doug pointed at the visible plume of flame and smoke in the sky. "It's burning for orbit."

"Nobody runs that fast for good news," Albert suggested.

For a moment, Doug's mind couldn't work out the implications of that. Albert repeated it. Doug nodded absently, his eyes still locked on the rocket trail, already getting faint and distant.

"You don't think . . . ," Doug started after a moment. "The Commonwealth? It can't be, not this soon."

"You're the one who sent off the message rocket," Albert said. "You got another explanation for that shuttle scatting that way?"

Ash Benez pushed through the entrance and stood out in the open. By the time he located the shuttle's trail, it was almost gone. "We've won?" he asked uncertainly.

That was enough to restart Doug's mind. "We don't

know that. We don't know anything. It could be Federation reinforcements coming in. It's been long enough for that. Come on, let's get back inside. It may even be a trick to make us expose ourselves."

But before he followed Albert and Ash inside, Doug took another long look into the sky, his eyes following the fading contrail. It made a difference. No matter what the reason for this, they would have to expose themselves soon. They had to know what was going on.

But not before tomorrow night, Doug decided. *We'll see what tomorrow brings.*

Part 4

12

The space in front of Admiral Truscott on the flag bridge of *Sheffield* contained a holographic projection of the battle developing in the lower orbit of the Federation troopship. The frigates raced toward the Federation ship. At the scale permitted by the flag bridge holo, the movement was painfully slow, and slowed even more as the computer constantly adjusted the scale to increase resolution. It was easy to tell the Federation ship from any Commonwealth vessel. Unlike the Commonwealth's traditional sheaf-of-tubes approach to starship construction, the Federation held to even older designs, independent modules—spheres and lozenges—linked by beams and connecting tubes.

Repulse was north of the Federation ship. *Lancer* was south. Both frigates were in a slightly higher orbit, so their weapons wouldn't endanger each other. Even though it was a stern chase, they closed quickly. The Federation ship had been keeping station over the settlements on Buchanan. Within minutes of sighting the Commonwealth frigates, the Federation ship went to maximum acceleration, reaching for additional altitude, trying to escape. The remaining Commonwealth ships stood in the way of that escape.

''It's almost as if they don't see us,'' Prince William whispered.

''They see us,'' Ian replied, unable to take his eyes from

the display. "But as long as we're farther off, we're the lesser evil."

"They're looking for time to reach transit speed," William said.

"If they can." Ian glanced at a data screen. "If they use anything like our standards—our *old* standards—they've got a long way to go, and *Lancer* and *Repulse* should be launching their first strike any second now."

Six new objects appeared in the display as each Commonwealth frigate launched three missiles. The missiles spread out as they crossed the gap.

"It's a seven-minute run for the missiles," a technician announced.

Beams of light reached out from the troopship toward the missiles as laser defenses locked on. Anti-missile missiles followed. *Repulse* and *Lancer* launched a second spread of missiles as the first reached the midpoint of their run. The troopship's lasers had no effect on the hardened shells of the Commonwealth weapons, but five of the six were destroyed by the interceptor rockets, and the sixth was knocked too far off course to correct.

When the Federation ship launched intercepts toward the second flight of missiles, *Repulse* and *Lancer* launched another six missiles, than six more right behind them. The frigates' particle beam cannons fired up to knock out interceptor missiles before they could do their job.

"The range is too extreme," Truscott muttered to himself. "None of the beamers will do any good till you get closer."

The frigates started launching attack missiles as quickly as they could fill the tubes, attempting to overload the enemy's defenses.

"Damn waste of munitions," Truscott muttered, louder than before. He reached for a complink, but it was only *Sheffield*'s captain he called.

"Mort, how long until our Spacehawks are in intercept range?"

"Won't do us any good to launch for another thirty minutes, sir," Hardesty replied. "Just a waste of fuel. And if that Cutter class transits to Q-space, the birds will be a lot safer aboard."

"One way or another, it looks like the Federation troops on Buchanan are going to have to fend for themselves," Ian whispered to the prince. "Either we destroy their ship or it jumps out of the system."

"I doubt the admiral views it so simply," William replied.

For the next half hour, they all watched the battle. Several times, Truscott recorded notes. The captains of *Lancer* and *Repulse* wouldn't enjoy the admiral's after-action critique. The longer the engagement continued, the hotter Truscott became. The two frigates had fired a total of thirty-three missiles at the lone Federation ship before they scored their first hit, and *that* wasn't nearly enough to disable it. The troopship was firing back at *Lancer* and *Repulse* by then. The confusion of offensive and defensive missiles, particle and light beams, became so thick that it was difficult to make sense of the battle simply by watching the holo display on *Sheffield*.

Then the Federation troopship made good its escape. There were no spectacular visual effects, the ship merely disappearing as it jumped to Q-space. *Lancer* and *Repulse* started maneuvering to give the site of the jump as wide a berth as possible, to minimize any effects of turbulence as normal space-time flooded back into the volume displaced by the transit.

"Lost 'em, damn it!" Truscott swore. "Let them get away." He switched off the holo display with an impatient swipe of his hand. He turned away to stare at a bulkhead until he could control his emotions.

"Signal *Lancer* and *Repulse* to boost for a standard covering orbit above the rest of the fleet," Truscott said a moment later. "*Khyber* to a polar orbit for reconnaissance above and below."

While the flag signals officer, Lieutenant Commander Estmann, relayed that order, Truscott keyed his link to Captain Hardesty. "Mort, take us down to where that troopship was, station-keeping directly over the colony." After Hardesty acknowledged, Truscott turned to Estmann again.

"Signal *Victoria* and *Thames* to take their positions from us, in line, east to west. Put *Thames* in the middle."

Truscott stood and looked around the compartment. His face remained flushed. "We might as well stand down for now." His voice was audibly cycling down from the tension of combat, and the frustration of seeing their quarry escape. "It'll be hours before anything else happens. Get a meal and some sleep. Duty watches only. Ian, I'll be in my cabin once I've had a word with Captain Hardesty."

Ian scarcely had time to acknowledge before the admiral was off to his bridge.

"And that's that," Ian said, mostly to himself.

"That is not a happy admiral," Prince William said, almost directly into Ian's ear.

"It's a good time to be out of his line of fire," Ian agreed. "If *Lancer* and *Repulse* hadn't wasted so many missiles, he'd probably have them running drills before supper."

"I think I'll kip out for a while," William said, cutting off a yawn with a hand against his mouth. "You'll give me a shout if anything interesting happens?"

"Anything *interesting* happens," Ian replied drily, "and you'll hear the horns the same time I do."

"Quite," William said, chuckling as he turned to leave.

•   •   •

Ian stripped to his underwear before stretching out on his bunk. A fresh uniform was hanging on the rack over the foot of his bed. He lay on his back and folded his arms under his head. Several deep breaths helped to relax him and clear his mind. As soon as he closed his eyes, he was asleep. That was unusual. And within minutes, his sleeping eyes were twitching. The inconclusive battle he had witnessed replayed itself in his dreams.

With differences.

The Cutter class troopship first destroyed *Lancer* and *Repulse,* needing only a single missile for each of the frigates. Then it accelerated directly toward *Sheffield,* unconcerned with the swarm of Spacehawks that danced around it and the subsequent fusillade of missiles and energy weapons from the battlecruiser.

When *Sheffield* exploded, Ian woke.

He felt his body shaking, felt sweat welling up all over. He sat up and swung his legs off of the bunk. For a moment, he sat there staring at nothing. Then he looked at the clock. Barely an hour had passed since he left the flag bridge. He turned and looked at his pillow. Sleep no longer seemed so urgent.

Ian got up and went into the bathroom for a shower, spending longer than usual under the pulsing water. The heat and force of the spray relaxed him more than the short, disturbed sleep. By the time he turned off the water and dried himself, the nightmare had started to fade, as nightmares do. But he wasn't ready to lie down and risk its return. Instead, he dressed and walked up to the flag wardroom.

More than half of the people who had been on the flag bridge during the battle were already in the wardroom, drinking coffee or tea, or just sitting there staring at whatever happened to be in front of them.

"Welcome to the club," Prince William said. He raised

a cup in toast, then took a sip. "I do hope this doesn't become a habit."

Admiral Truscott sat alone in the larger room of his day cabin, at the side of the flatscreen chart table. Stasys had made himself comfortable hours earlier, after he chased Ian and the rest of his staff off to get some sleep. He had kicked off his shoes and donned old, comfortable slippers, taken off his uniform shirt and pulled on a threadbare robe that he had worn for twenty years—a favorite that he had refused to retire. His orderlies always learned quickly to make sure that the robe was cleaned regularly, and with some care.

A tea cart was close at hand. Stasys had a fresh, steaming cup of tea within easy reach. He hadn't bothered to count how many cups he had drunk over the past eight or nine hours. The drinking was an almost autonomous reflex. His mind was elsewhere—two-hundred miles below, on the surface of Buchanan, mostly, but ranging at need all of the way out to the boundaries of the solar system.

It had been a busy, and productive, workday. The fleet had been repositioned. *Lancer* and *Repulse* had been given a chance to dock with *Thames* to replenish expended stocks of munitions, then set to cover the fleet from likely incursion routes. The appearance of a Federation fleet so soon was unlikely, but the possibility couldn't be ignored. The scout ship *Khyber* was also positioned as part of Truscott's early warning system. *Sheffield* and *Victoria* were in low attack orbit, maintaining position under power, close enough to launch fighter and shuttle sorties against the surface. *Thames* was still in line between the two larger ships.

Truscott knew, almost up to the second, where every functioning battle helmet on the surface of Buchanan was. Although there was no way to intercept and decode the communications transmissions, the orbiting ships could detect those transmissions, locate the sources, and trace any movement. Those locations were plotted on the flatscreen on the admiral's chart table. Each Federation helmet was a tiny blip of red light. When the helmet moved, the light blinked, the rate depending on the speed of movement. When the movement stopped, the light went back to steady.

The battle orders had been written. Stasys had worked with a light pen on a complink slate, scratching out his drafts and editing the printed versions the complink returned. The final orders were awaiting only the transmit sequence: orders for each of the ship captains, the fighter wing commander, and the commanding officer of the Second Regiment of Royal Marines.

Stasys leaned back and stretched. He was finally tired, but it was a pleasant exhaustion, coming from work he knew was as good as he could make it. He got up and paced around the table, making two complete circuits before he reached for the controls on the table, and pressed the XMIT and CONFIRM buttons at the top of the screen.

"Done." But only the beginning. Truscott went out to the flag bridge. There were only three people on watch: the duty officer, a communications technician, and an orderly.

"Orders for the day have been posted and transmitted, Lieutenant Halverdi," Truscott told the duty officer. "I'm going to bed. Leave word to have your replacement wake me at 0430. I'll be in my day cabin."

"Aye, sir, 0430 hours," the lieutenant replied. "Will there be anything else?"

Truscott smiled. "I don't think so, not tonight. The excitement doesn't start until morning."

13

Reveille was at 0300 hours in the troop holds of HMS *Victoria.*

David Spencer had lined up all of his gear the night before, gone over every item to make certain that it was serviceable. Waking, he slipped into his field skin and was putting clothing on over that before the field skin had settled itself against his own. A field skin was a living organism, designed in the nanotech labs. It provided insulation, helped to recirculate moisture, and added a small measure of help in case of injury. David put his mind completely into the task at hand. With three other sergeants in the room hurrying to get dressed at the same time, concentration was essential. There was little talking, except for local traffic control as everyone moved through to the head.

Mess call sounded. David was the first in his room ready, but the sergeants' mess was already crowded when he arrived. In addition to the other sergeants who were coming in, many of the regiment's officers were present. Sergeant Major Dockery was at the entrance, repeating the same line every time a new batch of noncoms arrived. "Get your food and take your seats. We get our briefing while we eat."

It wasn't until he heard that announcement that David realized that the mess call had been different: "All sergeants *will* report to their mess." *You must have been half-*

asleep yet, David told himself. *You shouldn't miss clues like that.*

The mess hall filled quickly. No more than four minutes after David's entrance, it appeared that everyone had arrived. Many of the sergeants were still in the serving line when Colonel Laplace stood and started talking.

"Those of us who are going down in the first assault waves will man the landing boats in fifty minutes," he started. "Second and Third Battalions will be the primary strike force, landing on the flatlands west of the settlements on Buchanan, striking in from northwest and southwest, linking just before you reach the spaceport. At the same time, First Battalion and C Company of Engineering Battalion will land east of the settlements, across the river, to cut off escape routes for the Federation soldiers. The engineers will be on hand in case a bridging operation becomes necessary. The river isn't particularly deep, but it's too much for a man in battle kit to walk across with his head above water, and the bottom is too soft for wading, so air tanks are also out. Fourth and Special Weapons Battalions will be held in reserve. Company commanders have their orders." Colonel Laplace hesitated a moment, looking around the room.

"This should be an easy drill, men," he said. "We have numbers, position, and no enemy air or heavy weapons to worry about. But don't let anyone go cock-of-the-walk. The Feddies down there aren't toy soldiers. Be careful. Let's keep casualties to an absolute minimum."

There were no concluding formalities. The colonel and his staff filed out of the room. The company commanders of the units that were making the landings headed for the sections of the mess hall where their sergeants were gathered. Only a few noncoms had to move. For the most part, they had clustered with others from their own companies.

"I&R platoon will be first down in the jungle," was

Captain McAuliffe's first statement when he got to the HQ Company sergeants.

Tell me something I couldn't guess, David thought.

"You'll have the engineers just behind you," McAuliffe continued. "H&S and Alpha Companies will hold the center of our line. Bravo and Charley will have the flanks. Delta will be our mobile reserve, back with the engineers."

"Sir, is there room for the shuttles to actually *land*?" Sergeant Macdowell asked.

"Apparently not," the captain replied. "The first units down will use ropes. The engineers will make a clearing to bring in their equipment, but that won't be until after we establish our perimeter."

"Sir, what's the count on the opposition?" David asked.

"Intelligence is tracking 675 active helmets," McAuliffe said. "A shorthanded battalion, if their TO is anything like ours."

"And if they haven't got more helmets to switch on when we're not expecting them," David said, and the captain nodded.

"Always that chance, Spencer. A good point to bring up. As far as we know, there was only the one Feddie ship here, and that would put an upper cap of roughly nine-hundred men they could have landed. But don't take even *that* figure as gospel. They've had time to position a reserve, even a whole company lying doggo to catch us by surprise."

"If they have, my notion is that they'd most likely be somewhere in that jungle we're jumping into," David continued.

McAuliffe smiled. "So tell your lads to mind their arses. Besides, you'll have the engineers behind you to worry about." That brought a laugh from everyone sitting at the table and from the two lieutenants who stood flanking the company commander. Ezra Franklyn handled communications and operations, strictly a staff type. Manuel Boronski was titular platoon leader for both HQ and I&R platoons of First Battalion's H&S Company. But since the company had only half its complement of officers and Boronski was also second in command, he was normally relegated to running the backup command post and communications node. Which left David Spencer to run I&R with little operational interference from Boronski, which suited them both.

"We'll have air cover, won't we, sir?" Lead Sergeant Landsford asked. He liked to get even the obvious questions answered.

"*Sheffield* will launch the lot from what I hear," McAuliffe said. "Fire suppression ahead of us, close cover while we land, and whatever help we need from the plugheads after. Now you'd best hurry up and get to your men. They're going to be getting right antsy."

David gave his platoon a quick summary of their part in the coming operation, then led them to the armory for weapons and ammunition. He ordered a quick helmet check, to make sure that every man had a fully functional helmet while they waited to be summoned to their shuttle.

"By squads now, lads. Squad leaders, make sure everybody's got everything." David walked the line of first squad, giving them a quick inspection—functional, not decorative. When he got to Jacky White, David gave him a grin and slapped his shoulder.

"Jacky, I don't know that we'll get the chance, but if any Federation blokes come our way, remember, *they're* the ones keeping you here."

Jacky managed a weak smile. "I've been trying to see it like that. Heaven help any of that lot who get in my way."

"That's the way, lad."

Second and Third Battalions were called to their shuttles.

Then First Battalion's I&R platoon. They would be the first unit down east of the settlements.

"What if they come after us straightaway, don't give the rest time to land?" Alfie asked. "The lads on the other side of the river won't do us a bit of good if all them Feddie blokes dash straight for us."

"Just hope nobody notices we're there in all the bother," David said.

14

The soft knock on his door woke Ian instantly. "Oh-four-hundred, sir," the orderly said. "The admiral left word to be called at 0430. Landing operations are about to begin."

"Thank you," Ian said. He had left his own "night orders" with the duty officer, to be wakened thirty minutes before Admiral Truscott. "Would you wake the Duke of Haven, and give him the same message?"

"Aye, aye, sir."

Ian took a couple of deep breaths and got out of bed, amazed that he had managed any sleep at all. He even felt curiously refreshed. *Excited,* he decided. *Despite everything, I'm actually looking forward to this operation.* At least there had been no further nightmares once he returned to bed.

He hurried through his normal morning routine, wanting to be ready for the day before the admiral was wakened. As soon as he was dressed, Ian went to the flag wardroom for coffee and buttered toast—just enough to postpone any hunger pangs, not enough to spoil his appetite in case the admiral wanted his company for a full breakfast. Prince William came into the wardroom just as Ian was beginning to eat.

"We get an early start, no?" the prince asked. He sat

across the table from Ian, and the mess steward came to take his order.

"Apparently," Ian replied. "I haven't seen any operations orders. The admiral must have done it all during the night."

"I assume he does sleep occasionally."

"Sometimes I wonder," Ian said. "When his mind is really going on a project, he can get by for days with only an occasional catnap."

"My brother Henry is much the same," William said. He normally avoided references to the king, and especially avoided using the title. "He gets a bug in his bonnet and he's a veritable dynamo. I think that's one reason I stay away from court as much as possible. You might find this hard to believe, but there have been many occasions when I seriously considered emigrating to some frontier world and making a place for myself."

"I seem to recall that it's been done a few times before by members of your family," Ian said.

"Ah, a historian as well." William chuckled softly. The mess steward brought his breakfast and left. "Yes, it's been done, perhaps more often than you realize. One might almost say that the founding of the Second Commonwealth itself resulted from that sort of wanderlust. Buckingham might well drown in royalty if some of us didn't move off-world now and again."

Ian smiled politely, then decided to risk another sally. "I recall a report that stated that sixty percent of the children born on Buckingham can already claim *some* relationship to the royal family."

The prince nearly choked on his tea, the laughter sprang out so quickly. He set the cup down and brought a napkin to his mouth, staring at Ian over the napkin for a moment.

"You do have your moments, don't you?" he asked when he took the napkin away from his mouth. There was a smile on his face. "You caught me properly with that one."

Ian's smile was tentative. "Part of the job description. You do know that the position of aide can be traced to medieval court jesters on Earth?"

William was ready for that one. "And you see yourself as a throwback to your primal roots?"

"Touché," Ian admitted with a laugh.

"Actually," William said, "if you stretch the genealogies back to the founding of Buckingham, the percentage related to the royal family would probably be much higher. Luckily for everyone, there are limits to how far relationship carries."

"Sometimes." Ian raised his cup as if in salute.

"Ah, well, we'd best get a move on or the admiral will think we're sleeping in."

Ian glanced at his watch and took one final gulp of coffee. "You're right. The orderly will be knocking at his door any second now."

"I'll see you on the flag bridge," William said as Ian got up from the table. "I'll be along soon."

Ian went directly to the flag bridge. If the admiral wanted him, the word would go there. If there were no earlier call, Ian would go to the admiral's cabin fifteen minutes after the wake-up call. That would give Truscott his usual time to start preparing for the day. While he waited, Ian scanned the orders that the admiral had issued for the day's operations. There wasn't time for a detailed reading, but Ian knew enough about the admiral's style to glean the essentials quickly.

"Cautious," Ian mumbled when he saw the extent of the operation. In these circumstances, that was a word of approval.

"*Victoria* has her first landing boats ready to go, sir,"

the duty officer told Ian. "We have Spacehawks on the match as well."

Ian nodded. "The boss had a busy night."

"Sure looks that way," the duty officer agreed. "Word is, he did it all himself, right down to writing the orders."

"If anyone in the fleet could do it, he could," Ian said. That wasn't merely loyalty; it was Ian's honest opinion.

The tech at the communications console looked up. "Commander Shrikes, the admiral wants you in his day cabin."

Truscott was already dressed when Ian got there. "Have you seen the orders?" the admiral asked.

"Just had time to skim them, sir."

"Put everything we could into this, Ian. The more we use going in, the less it should cost. Now, everything depends on how well we perform, how fiercely the Federation troops resist."

"Knowing they've been abandoned ought to hurt their morale," Ian said.

Truscott frowned. He had no quarrel with the decision made by the Federation captain. In similar circumstances, Truscott knew he would make the same decision. "Not as badly as if we'd managed to destroy that ship. This way, they can hope for reinforcements if they hold out long enough."

"You don't think they can hold out that long, do you, sir?"

"If we can't reduce a short battalion with a full regiment of Marines and *Sheffield*'s fighter wing before that Cutter class can fetch support, you may have to tie me to a chair to keep me from exploding."

"They're cut off, with a hostile population around them, and us moving in. I wouldn't want to be in that position," Ian said.

"Nor would I," Truscott agreed. "But the Federation is used to imposing itself on unwilling hosts."

"Would you like your breakfast on the bridge, or in here?" Ian asked.

"On the flag bridge, and no more than a cup of tea just now. I'll eat later, perhaps. It's just about that time."

15

The ride down was rough for David Spencer and his platoon. The men were packed shoulder to shoulder in the shuttle. Lap straps were scarcely necessary once the shuttle got low enough for gravity to hold the men in place. David kept his eyes on a panel at the front of the compartment. During the descent, a large red light burned. Once they reached three thousand feet, a yellow light came on below it.

"Release safety belts," David shouted. "Ready to stand to the ramp. Look and make sure you're wearing your gloves."

Four reels were recessed into the floor of the compartment, forward of the hatch that would drop to form a short ramp. As soon as the hatch opened, the ropes would be unreeled and the thirty-two men would rappel to the ground. With any real luck, their descent would only be thirty feet. That depended on how precise the pilots were in finding their assigned drop zone. There wouldn't be time to look for a better spot if the first was bad.

The shuttle's rockets went into full reverse thrust, then died as the craft switched to jets. The angle on the jets was changed to slide the ungainly craft into a hover. As a green light replaced the red and yellow, a siren sounded and the ramp was dropped.

"Stand to the ramp!" David shouted as winches uncoiled the ropes. "Go! Go! Go!"

The men started down. David moved near the head of the line on the closest rope and was third down it. Sergeant Hugo Kassner, third squad leader and the second-ranking noncom in the platoon, would be the last man out of the shuttle.

Getting the line coiled around his waist and legs was almost automatic. David checked his grip and dropped off the ramp. The greatest danger, other than the chance of hostile fire, was building up too much speed on the rappel. Over any major distance, friction could burn through the best gloves or leave a man with too much momentum for a safe landing.

Thirty feet? The pilots had struck gold. There were only twenty feet above a small clearing.

Even on the way down, David was broadcasting orders, linking with the first men down, directing them out from the drop zone to form an initial perimeter. He hit the ground, moved away from the ropes, and took cover. He scanned the vicinity to verify the information being relayed from the shuttle's detectors, that there were no enemy forces on this side of the river . . . that there were no active enemy *electronics* within a one-mile radius. He had to remind himself of the distinction.

As more men came down, David directed them to positions on the perimeter, and widened the diameter, stretching the circle toward the river and Buchanan's two settlements. The shuttle was a deafening shadow overhead, but—comfortingly—there was no enemy fire coming in.

The last men came down. "You're clear, we're off," the pilot reported to David. "Good luck. Kick some butt."

"If they leave us any," David replied. "Thanks for the ride."

The shuttle slid away horizontally, getting clear of the men on the ground before it climbed for altitude, then switched to rockets for the burn that would carry it back to *Victoria*. They might have to make as many as six more round trips to get everyone to the ground.

David clicked his complink over to the noncom frequency to confer with the squad leaders. "Get out your mapboards."

The mapboard was a specialized complink, a twelve-inch flatscreen that folded in thirds to fit in a pocket, less than a quarter-inch thick folded. The maps were centered on the location of the platoon, and carried all of the data available to the main computers on the ships above. The scale could be adjusted from a distant view that would encompass the entire planet, down to a detailed scale of one inch to fifty feet. The map was photographic, enhanced by a variety of overlays, with red lights to show the position of active enemy electronics—mostly helmets—and green lights to show the position of friendly forces.

"No surprises," Hugo said after he had time to scan his. "Looks like the main landing is on schedule."

"Right, so let's not get *our* schedule out of whack," David said. "Put a fire team out on each flank until the rest of our lads and Alpha get down. Use fourth squad for that. Take your squad to check out the rear. See if you can spot anything to help Delta and the engineers. I'll keep first and second squads here."

So this is Buchanan, David thought as the squads started to move on their assignments. He looked out at the terrain rather than at the display on his helmet visor. The clearing was covered with soft, ground-hugging shrubbery—long, tangled vines, thin and flexible. Around the clearing were several different types of trees. None looked particularly familiar, but David wouldn't have recognized an apple tree unless he saw apples hanging from it.

There was little undergrowth beneath the trees, only a scattering of grass. There was also no immediate sign of wildlife, but that didn't surprise him. The noise of the shuttle and the presence of so many intruders would likely silence most animals for quite some time. There *were* animals, even fairly large ones, in the area. The close scans had shown thousands of bloated piglike aquatic or semi-aquatic animals.

A call on the command frequency brought him back from his nature watch. The rest of H&S Company was coming in. And the first detachment of engineers was on final approach.

"How far east of us are they?" David asked. "I don't show them." He clicked through displays on his helmet. "Wait, there they are. They're three miles from where they're supposed to be."

"Last-minute change," Captain McAuliffe said from his shuttle. "They spotted an easier site to knock down a landing strip. You'll have to send a squad back to them. Delta won't be down for another hour."

"They'll be on the ground long before we can reach them," David said, "but we're leaving now."

"Link with them on this channel, Spencer."

"Should we move our whole perimeter back?"

"Negative. The engineers will have to find a way to move their equipment up to the river."

"You sound as if you doubt they can." David was already drawing in first squad and moving the other squads to cover the gap.

"I'll believe it when I see it," McAuliffe said.

David could see shuttles lining up to drop the rest of H&S Company as he explained to his men that they had to make a quick hike through the forest to find the new location that the engineers had decided on for their landing.

"Just going out of their way to foul things up," Alfie said. "Engineers figure they know everything."

"Captain sounded ticked about it too, Alfie," David said. "Makes us no difference. We've still got to go back and hold their hands until they bring in the rest of their people. Zimmerman, you've got the point. Thataway." He pointed. "Everyone, keep your eyes open. Just because we don't show any enemy helmets in the area doesn't mean it's clean. They may be smart enough to turn them off long enough to spring an ambush."

"Now, that wouldn't be very nice of 'em," Alfie said.

"Put the lid on that chatter. Let's not get careless."

The new men were scattered through the middle of the line. David kept special watch on them, and would, until he had seen them in action. New men made David nervous. He had no way to predict how they might react to anything.

Roger Zimmerman stayed to the animal trails he could find—after clearing that decision with his sergeant.

"Might as well," David told him. "Keep a close watch on your sensors, but I doubt that the enemy's laid booby traps out here. No damn reason to." It was a questionable decision, and David knew it, but if there *were* booby traps out in the middle of the forest, then the entire landing might be in real trouble.

Tory Kepner was behind Zimmerman, followed by Seidman, Alfie, Henny, Jacky, and Montez. David took the back end, where he could watch his men as well as the terrain behind them. It kept him busy. But the others were doing their jobs. Even the new men seemed aware of the basics: watch the sides, avoid unnecessary noise. The squad's spacing was too tight. Several times, David passed the word to spread out. "We don't want to be a row of ducks in somebody's shooting arcade," he said once.

Don't let an ambush take out an entire patrol. That was one of the first maxims of infantry training. *If you are ambushed, make sure at least some of your people survive to answer the incoming fire.*

David stopped the squad once for a short break, and to give himself time to check his mapboard and make contact with the lieutenant who was leading the engineer detachment. After the break, he rotated Jacky White up to the point.

"The engineers have a sentry out, here," David told Jacky. He pointed to the spot on his mapboard. "Still a mile off. Be watching for him."

Jacky nodded and moved off. David signalled for the rest of the squad to follow.

The engineers had already started their work by the time David and his squad arrived. A survey crew was laying out lines. Trees were being sawed off at ground level with cutting beams. Men with drag lines and portable winches were hauling timber and shrubbery out of the way. A small earthmover was levelling terrain with the blade on its snout and spraying the first layer of plascrete from a rig on its rump. But the engineers hadn't bothered to put out sentries, except for the one man who was watching for the I&R squad.

And one man was just standing by, watching the rest work. David didn't need to see insignia to know that was the lieutenant.

"Sergeant Spencer?" the officer asked when David reached him. David nodded. "I'm Lieutenant Guran."

"Lieutenant." David lifted his visor and looked over at the earthmover. "I hope that thing has a real high gear on it, sir."

"How's that?"

"You know you're going to have to build a four-mile road to get your bridging equipment to the river. The terrain's all like this, some worse."

"We needed a decent place to set down, Sergeant."

"Yes, sir, but what if the admiral decides he wants those bridges today?"

"Not my problem. We can only do the possible."

If you'd set down where you were told to, it would be possible, David thought, but he couldn't say that to an officer he didn't know.

"By now, sir, just about everyone's down this side of the river, except for the rest of your people and heavy equipment," David said. Delta Company of the first was landing just then. "The line has been established three miles west of here. There'll be patrols out on the flanks and such, but that's too much area to cover adequately. Your people will have to watch for infiltrators or ambushes."

Guran lifted his visor. "We were supposed to have infantry cover so we could do our work."

"Excuse me, sir," David said, in his most respectful tones, "but you were supposed to be two-and-a-half miles west of here, where you would be close enough for that cover, where our Delta Company is landing now." *You might as well have stayed aboard* Victoria *for all the good you'll do here,* he thought. *Or even back on Buckingham.*

Guran held up one hand to stop David. With the other hand, he pulled down his visor. Even though David couldn't hear anything, it was clear that Guran was referring the matter to his superior. David decided it was time to let Captain McAuliffe know what was going on as well.

"I've been monitoring you," McAuliffe told him. "I've already contacted the colonel on this. Watch your mouth, Spencer. You know what I'd do if you back-talked me like that?"

"But I've never know you to pull a boner like this, Captain. You're a pro, like me."

McAuliffe chuckled. "God help you if you ever pull a mouthful when you're in the wrong."

"I do my best, sir."

"For my sake, David, ease off. Let the facts stand. Don't

confuse the issue by letting Guran claim you're insubor-
dinate.''

"Yes, sir," David said meekly. He had made his point.
The higher-ups could haggle all they wanted to.

Guran's call took longer. When he lifted his visor again,
his face was red, and he had trouble keeping his voice in
check. David kept his own face as blank as possible, but
he couldn't help wishing that he had been able to overhear
the other conversation.

"Two companies of the reserve are being sent down to
provide cover," Guran said. "As soon as they arrive, you
can take your squad back to your company."

"Yes, sir," David, said, as respectful as a boot in his
first week of training. "I'll get my men posted."

The men would be spread painfully thin, but that
couldn't be helped. The engineers were cutting a landing
strip three thousand feet long. Loaded with heavy equipment, even an STOL shuttle needed room. David gave the
eastern side to Tory Kepner and his fire team. David kept
the rest on the western side, where any threat, however
unlikely, was most apt to appear.

"Full active sensors," David said. "Active links to the
eyes above. Keep your own eyes open though. The sensors
won't pick up anyone with thermal shielding and an inactive helmet.''

"We *know* all that, Sarge," Alfie said.

"Humor me, lad," David said. "I like to hear myself
remind you. That way, when you doss out and get yourself
fried, I won't have to feel guilty about it."

As the morning erased itself, David had his men improve
their defensive positions. "Dig in, it'll help pass the time,"
he told them. From time to time, David made contact with
Captain McAuliffe or Hugo Kassner, keeping track of the
rest of his platoon and the rest of the war. The main land-

ings on the far side of the river remained on schedule. Resistance was light, but Federation helmets had been turned off in considerable numbers as the enemy went to ground. The Second Regiment hadn't gone hunting for the occupying forces yet. The operation was still in its first stage, landing and establishing initial positions. The Spacehawks from *Sheffield* were the only Commonwealth units actively seeking out and engaging Federation forces.

Meanwhile, the combat engineers raced to complete their landing strip. Foot by foot, they cleared obstructing trees, levelled the course, and sprayed the surface of their strip with quick-drying plascrete, several coats. It was a noisy procedure, and occasionally some of David's men had to move quickly to stay out of the way of falling timber.

It was noon before the extra line troops arrived, rappelling in over the first completed sections of the landing strip. David answered a call on his command link and went to meet the first load of troops who came down.

"Sergeant Spencer, I'm Asa Ewing."

David lifted his visor. "Good to see you, Lieutenant. Your men ready to take over minding the engineers?"

Ewing grinned. "Baby-sitting is better than sitting it out completely."

"There's been no sign of threats here, sir, but I'd sure like to get back to my platoon."

"So I hear." Ewing was still grinning. "Give me a few minutes to get my squads into position and you can take off."

"Thank you, sir. We'll take lunch while your men settle in."

Just knowing that they were about to leave perked up David's squad. Alfie even found time, and the materials, to erect a "Foxhole to Let—CHEAP" sign. The return march took less time than the march out, even though David kept slowing his men down and nagging everyone to keep close watch. Even after they passed through the pickets Delta Company had posted behind the battalion's main position, David tried to keep his men fully alert.

"Get your men in position," McAuliffe told David. "You're several hours behind in digging in." When David started to flush, McAuliffe laughed and held up his hand. "Don't bother. I know, and so does the whole chain of command, all the way to Admiral Truscott."

"Is it my butt being fried?" David asked.

"Just don't let any of the engineers catch you alone on a dark street for a time," McAuliffe suggested.

"I'll watch it," David promised. There are always men in the regiment with long memories for grudges. "Anything interesting going on over on the other side?" David asked.

"Quiet, so far," McAuliffe said. "The last update I had was that the Feddies have turned off most of their helmets."

"I take it they're not dropping dead of fright?"

This time, McAuliffe's smile was thin. "No such luck. Somebody on the other side spent time preparing this. They're going to try to hold out. They must expect reinforcement."

"Well, sir, *we'd* expect it, wouldn't we? I mean, even if the ships had to bug out."

"The RM take care of their own," McAuliffe said. It was an article of faith.

"Feddies must feel the same way." When McAuliffe nodded, David took a moment to think, then said, "I'll get my lads busy, sir."

"Let them get what rest they can this afternoon. You'll have to put out patrols tonight."

"Aye, sir. I expected that."

16

When the pilots of fourth squadron were sent to their fighters, it was no panic scramble. They had been sitting in their ready room watching what little action there was below on their complinks.

"We'll be looking for targets of opportunity," Commander Bosworth told her pilots. "Keep your spacing, and stay alert. We'll stagger the three flights, high, low, and periphery, and move them around, just like a drill."

Just like a drill was the cliché of the day.

"Don't go getting any dirt on her nose," Andy Mynott told Josef while they were getting him strapped into the cockpit.

"Haven't you got any *new* advice?" Josef asked.

"Can't get you a new bird out here, sir. You don't bring this one back, we're all out of work until we get back to port. And I make a *terrible* spectator."

"I'm not overly fond of the sidelines either, Andy."

"Third squadron must be raising hell about getting back," Andy said just before he lowered the canopy over Josef. "You're going out in a gang launch. The rest have been single shot."

Josef held himself to a soft grunt as the canopy came down and sealed itself.

"Green lights across the board," he told Andy over the intercom. "Unless you want to ride along, you'd best get your butt back through the airlock.''

Andy pulled the jack on his headset, flipped Josef a casual salute, and hurried toward the airlock.

''Red three ready for launch,'' Josef reported over the squadron channel.

''Stand by,'' Commander Bosworth said. ''Ready for cylinder extension.''

Josef felt the movement as the LRC slid out from the fuselage of *Sheffield* and he lost the ship's artificial gravity. He scanned his screens and telltales again to make sure that no problems had surfaced on board, then toggled the switch that turned full control of his Spacehawk over to the launch master.

The countdown went without a hitch and the six Spacehawks of red flight were kicked out of their tubes. Around the fuselage of *Sheffield*, blue and white flights were also ejected from their LRCs.

During the first minutes, Josef focused his attention completely on the flight, ready to overrule the automatic pilot if necessary. With the neural jack active, he was as much a part of the Zed-3 as any of its other instruments or controls. Like most fighter pilots, Josef nursed the conceit that he could react more rapidly to an emergency than the automatic systems. In any case, he had to be prepared to react if those systems failed.

''Okay, red flight, follow me down,'' Commander Bosworth said once the Spacehawks cleared the immediate vicinity of *Sheffield*. ''We've got the first lowball detail.''

Suits me, Josef thought. He watched the commander nose her Spacehawk over until it was pointed directly at the spaceport. Both main rockets kicked him. Off to her right and just behind her, Bosworth's wingman, Ensign Seb Inowi, matched her maneuvers precisely. Ten seconds later, Josef put his bird into its stoop, and a quick glance at his monitors showed Kate Hicks stuck to her position off to his side.

Red flight corkscrewed around to approach the settlements from the north. They would brake below the sonic barrier well away from the settlements, sparing the colonists sonic damage. After each run, the Spacehawks would climb south to turn and make another run. Even at stalling speed, the birds had only seconds over the target area. Targets had to be acquired early, or transferred to the next Spacehawks coming through.

All of the fighters showed the first targets of this mission. "Lock on those blips," Bosworth told her wingman. "We'll each shoot two moles." Moles were thin missiles that would follow an electronic signal back to its source, even if it was several meters underground, below reinforced plascrete.

"I have a lock," Seb replied.

Josef automatically noted the targets on his screen, even though he wouldn't get a shot at them. If Bosworth and Inowi missed, maybe the last pair of Spacehawks in the flight would have time to lock on. Josef and Kate certainly wouldn't. They would be past the targets before the results were certain.

The sky was clear, but there was some thin haze low. Commander Bosworth went below five hundred feet as she lined up her targets and released her missiles. Almost simultaneously, Seb launched his moles, and the four missiles left thin vapor trails as they dove toward their targets.

Fully occupied with his own Spacehawk, Josef was only able to spare the lead pair of birds the slightest fraction of his attention. Eyeballing out the canopy had to be balanced against the demands of the monitors inside the cockpit. It was pure chance that he saw the plume of the fifth missile.

"Fire coming up!" he shouted over the command channel. Before the words were out of his mouth, the last missile had struck Seb Inowi's Spacehawk. Fighter and missile erupted in a golden ball of fire. Smoke and debris were hurled away from the fireball. Josef pulled back on the control yoke of his bird, fighting to get above the fragments.

"I've got a lock," Kate's voice said, and Josef saw the trail of two missiles launched from her Spacehawk, heading for the ground and the point of origin of the missile that had hit Seb's fighter.

"Seb didn't get out," Kate added, before her missiles hit.

The knot in Josef's stomach doubled in size, but there was no time to think about Seb now.

"Let's go back around for another pass," Commander Bosworth said, her voice under precarious control. "Watch your butts."

There was a numbed air of unreality about the rest of the patrol. The demands of flying and, rarely and briefly, fighting left little room for emotion or extraneous thought. But the memory of Seb Inowi's loss was there, reduced perhaps to an icon at the moment, ready to expand into full-screen awareness as soon as there was time. Seb was the squadron's first combat loss ever. It had been many years since a pilot had been lost even through accident. When Josef popped the canopy on his bird and Andy Mynott helped him out, there was none of the usual chat. The pilots headed to the ready room for the inescapable post-mission debriefing.

"A rescue and recovery team has been down," Commander Bosworth announced when she stepped up to the podium. "They didn't find anything."

That was all that Josef would ever remember of that debriefing.

17

Nightfall turned the world pale green for Marines in combat helmets. Their optics extended vision into the infrared, showing the results in ghostly overlays on normal vision. From time to time, David Spencer scanned the positions of his men. If a Marine's uniform, helmet, and field skin were all properly fitted and functional, the man was virtually invisible in infrared. Traces of movement were the most reliable guide to location then. Early this evening, thin, high clouds blocked much of the light of the stars and the one moon that was above the horizon, but there was still a little visible light, enough to detect gross movement on the ground. But the Commonwealth camouflage pattern was well suited to Buchanan. It did not stand out in light or dark.

Shortly after sunset, David sent his third and fourth squads out on separate patrols to cover the mile-wide strip of forest between the battalion's position and the river. After those patrols returned, the first and second squads would go out. Until then, David had little to do but wait.

That didn't mean that he wasn't busy. David kept track of the early patrols, listening in on the squad and noncoms' frequencies. Captain McAuliffe relayed the main points of the evening briefing from fleet command. Before sunset, the two settlements and spaceport had been ringed. Second and Third Battalions had linked up and had extended their lines to the river on either side of the two towns. No attempt had been made to advance into the towns yet. Opposition remained light. The Federation troops refused to engage. Three-quarters of the troops originally pinpointed by their helmet electronics had switched off and moved almost immediately. Now there wasn't a single Federation helmet being tracked. Very few of the missing enemy had been located so far. Commonwealth losses had been light on the ground; three killed, two wounded and evacuated to *Sheffield*. The one major loss was the single Spacehawk and pilot lost to a surface-to-air missile. The engineers were still working, trying to get their road built through the forest.

That last item brought a smile to David's face. And even though Captain McAuliffe had been speaking by radio, from somewhere farther along the line, he had apparently sensed, or guessed at, David's reaction. The captain switched from the noncoms' frequency to a private one and said, "Don't gloat, Spencer."

"I'll try not to," David promised. "But it's going to be hard."

"Just remember, could be our backsides in a sling next time."

Once his men had eaten, David put the first and second squads on half-and-half watch. In each pair, one man would be on watch. The other would get what rest he could. With half of the night devoted to patrolling, and the need to keep watch during the other half, no one would get much sleep. The longer there was opposition in the field, the farther behind the men would get on sleep.

And these Federation blokes won't make it easy, David thought. It was time for him to try for a little shut-eye of his own.

Jacky White lifted his head just enough to get a better view of the forest in front of his position. Some of the underbrush had been flashed out during the day, but there had been no way to clear a proper kill zone. Heavy forest was too close for comfort. The green blips that identified the men of I&R platoon who were out on patrol had moved out of range, third squad to the south, fourth squad to the north. There were no red blips visible, but Jacky didn't assume for a second that there were no Feddies out there, perhaps even within a hundred yards of his own position.

Switch my helmet off, and I could creep within twenty yards of an enemy without him seeing me, Jacky thought. He took a deep breath and let it out slowly, trying to pace his tension.

I should be back on civie street, he reminded himself. Jacky couldn't get that out of his mind for long, but it no longer brought blinding rage in tow. There was something else much more important now.

Lord, don't let me screw up. Don't let me get any of my mates killed.

Moving slowly, and as quietly as possible, Jacky rolled over on his left side to stretch his right leg and arm. Then he rolled back to repeat the moves on the other side, trying to keep limber. Action, if it came, would likely come without warning.

I wish they'd come out and let us get this over. At times, Jacky let himself hope that this one campaign would do the job, end the war between Commonwealth and Federation. He knew better. He knew that securing Buchanan wouldn't win the war for the Commonwealth, but—just maybe—it would be enough to calm the big shots back at the Admiralty and the Ministry of Defense on Buckingham. Perhaps they would start to let enlistments expire.

Fat chance. He focused his attention completely on his watch then. *One bleeding step at a time.*

•   •   •

"Coming back in, David."

Spencer sat up and quickly relayed the word to the rest of his platoon and to the platoons on either side.

"Bring 'em in, Hugo," Spencer replied over the non-coms' circuit. "We're watching for you."

The third and fourth squads came slowly into view, visible more for occulting the landscape behind them as they moved than because they stood out in the night. David counted bodies as they came through the line. *All present,* he assured himself.

"Get your men in position," David told the squad leaders, "then give me your reports so we can get out."

The reports took no time at all. Neither squad had come across any evidence of either Federation soldiers or local residents. "We went down to the river, and patrolled close to the shore," Hugo Kassner reported. "There's some nasty-looking beasties coming out of the water, but they're not human and they're not carrying weapons." On a mapboard, the squad leaders showed David the routes they had followed.

"Good enough," David said. "Give it to the captain. The rest of us will be going for our walkabout now. Hugo, that makes you senior until I get back. I haven't the foggiest idea where the lieutenant is."

"Thanks for nothing," Kassner replied.

David led his squad directly west, then south, turning not nearly as close to the river as third squad had. During the first stretch, David took the point position himself—hardly by-the-book. It was a way of using adrenaline, paradoxically calming himself by putting himself where he had to channel his tension into the work. Once the squad was moving parallel to the Commonwealth lines, David moved Alfie up to the point, with Sean Seidman behind him, and David took a more normal command position in the third spot.

Early on, David decided to push his men farther south than Hugo's squad had gone. Local dawn wasn't until 0530. And no rule-writ-in-stone said they had to traverse the entire front a second time to return to their lines where they had left. They could clear a passage anywhere, communicate directly with the platoon and squad leaders to make sure that they didn't come under friendly fire.

Their first break was one David hadn't planned on. Two large animals were blocking their path, obviously mating. Since the two beasts combined outweighed David's entire patrol, he decided to let them finish without interruption. But he squelched the first comments from the men with him. "Save it for the head when we get back to *Sheffield*," he told them over the squad frequency.

"Hope somebody saves the vid," Alfie said.

"Part of the record," Tory replied. "Just have to do a databank search."

"Stuff it," David said, more sharply. "Mind your flanks."

It took the animals, hippobary, another ten minutes to finish and move off the path, back toward the river. They took no notice of the spectators. David got his men moving again, with Jacky on point. Twice more, the squad paused to give hippobary time to get out of their way. These interruptions were shorter, each caused by a single animal.

"We're getting near the end of our lines," David told his men shortly after their third hippobary encounter. The last green blips showing on his mapboard east of the river were fifty feet south of where he was standing—and a half mile east. Beyond that corner, there would only be occasional patrols and checkpoints on the flanks.

"How much farther are we going?" Roger Zimmerman asked.

"At least another half mile. Depends on what we find." David stopped to let the entire squad move past him while he did a slow survey through 360 degrees. Even without enemy electronics to lock onto, his own sensors might provide early warning of an ambush. Highly directional microphones could pick up the slightest noise. Under perfect circumstances, they could identify a human's heartbeat or breathing at a hundred feet. Motion detectors could pick up gross movement, if nothing so small as a soldier's rifle tracking a target.

Nothing's perfect, David reminded himself. It still came down to the sharpness of a Marine's eyes, the speed of his reactions, and luck.

On the point, Alfie had stopped. The rest of the squad stopped behind him. Suddenly (the way such things normally happen in combat, particularly at night) the head-up displays on the visors of the Marines showed an arc of red blips, as enemy helmets were switched on—much too close. The shooting started at the same time. Reflexes swung the Marines into action. They dove for cover and returned fire, blindly at first, only slowly able to search out specific enemy blips to direct their aim at.

David called for help as soon as he was down and confident that he had found the best available cover. Captain McAuliffe responded within seconds. And scarcely behind that call, fighter control assured them both that Spacehawks were on the way down to add their support.

It couldn't be soon enough. In the first seconds of the engagement, David could tell that his men were getting the worst of it. The enemy was dug in, hidden, showing only weapons and enough of themselves to aim and fire. David's patrol had been caught in the open, with only the casual cover they could find from the terrain itself. Two men had been hit in the first volley. David had lost any vitals on Henny Prinz, which meant that either he was dead or his helmet had been knocked out of commission, and the data from Roger's helmet showed that he had been wounded and was most likely unconscious.

David loaded a chain of grenades and aimed short, dropping the grenades a hundred feet out. That was closer than allowed by the field manual, scarcely beyond the kill radius of the grenades. But his men were as protected as possible. Just maybe, the rounds would do more damage to the Federation troops.

It gave them no more than twenty seconds, but David and his men knew how to use seconds to best advantage. They squirmed to new positions, getting as close to ground as they could, putting what vertical cover they could find between them and the red blips of the enemy helmets.

Then new fire entered the fray. The *sounds* of the weapons were different, definitely not standard military issue. David checked his display. The fire was coming from farther south, from a point where there were no blips, red *or* green. When he finally spotted muzzle flashes, David saw that the fire was directed toward the Federation ambush. For a few seconds, David kept his head down while he tried to process the information.

"We've got allies, to the south," David said, with some excitement, over the squad frequency. "Be careful with your fire. We don't want to kill friends."

Two Spacehawks came in then, from the south. The pilots provided just an instant's warning for friendly heads to get down before they opened fire on the red blips. The rapid-fire cannons made a deafening roar that would have been unbearable if it had lasted more than a second. When it ended, all of the red blips were gone from David's visor display.

"Let's see what we've got out there," he told his squad. "Keep an eye open for our invisible helpers. They may not know who's who."

18

It was incredibly foolish, dangerous, but Doug couldn't deny himself. When he heard the first missile blasts, he slid out of the cave and climbed up the hill to look toward Sam and Max. The first hint of dawn was in the east. To the north, there was one burst of light after another as fighters launched missiles at ground positions. It appeared that most of the activity was away from the towns, closer to the spaceport. Doug hoped that the rockets were sparing Sam and Max.

"They must be able to see their targets, one way or another," he whispered.

"They must," Albert said below him.

Doug turned his head and looked down. "They came," he said.

Albert nodded. "They came." Several others came out of the cave.

"Let's keep close to the surface, at least," Doug said, moving back down the slope. "We don't want to end up as targets ourselves."

"For either side," Albert said.

"I guess this means that your message rocket got through," Gil Howard said. "I don't think I really believed it would."

Neither did I, Doug realized. Down the line, the Evander twins and George Hatchfield came out of the other cave and ran to join the main group.

"What do we do?" one of the twins asked.

"Stay out of the way for now," Doug said. "Avoid showing ourselves until the Commonwealth has men on the ground. Then we make contact with them. If they haven't finished off the Federation bastards, we can help."

"You think they'll leave us anything?" the other twin asked. His brother laughed, but no one else did.

"Don't forget, we got the first blows in," Albert said, frowning at both of the Evander lads. "Taking out three shuttles without losing a man is nothing to sneeze at."

"In the meantime, let's not forget basic security," Doug said. "By the time the sun's up, we'd best be back inside. We'll keep one man out as sentry, and rotate the job every half hour. All we can do now is wait. We don't want to bollix it up so close to the end."

Wait was easy to say, harder to bear. Doug kept telling himself that he should get some sleep, but that was impossible. He found it difficult to stay inside the cave, under cover, but he knew that if he didn't hold himself in, he could never hold the others. Finally, he forced himself to lie down, even though he had given up on sleep.

You can at least think, he told himself. It had been easy to say, "We'll make contact," but would it really be that simple? The morning passed at a tortuously slow pace as he tried to devise a safe way to communicate with the Commonwealth forces.

The others were as restless as Doug. George and the twins had moved back to the main cave. It felt more crowded than ever with everyone packed in—and too nervous to sit or lie quietly.

"Listen, I've been thinking," Doug said at last, and all of the others turned toward him, except Ash Benez, who was out on sentry duty. "We're going to have to make contact in daylight, so we don't get shot up by mistake. But I think we should move as close as we dare under cover of dark.''

''You mean wait till tomorrow?'' Gil asked.

''Better late than dead,'' Albert said before Doug could reply.

''That's what it amounts to,'' Doug said. He looked around. The choice wasn't popular, but no one was confident enough to insist on going in sooner.

Shortly after sunset, the men moved back out of the caves, even though they knew it would be hours before they started toward home. One way or another, they were going *home*. They could see an end to their subsistence exile, an end to the fear, an end to hiding in caves and daring to sneak out only at night.

One way or another.

There were whispered conversations, but none of them lasted long even though Doug gave up any attempt to maintain silence. It wasn't as if his companions were capering about and shouting. In any case, the whispers were unlikely to bring disaster down on them, not this night, so far from the towns. *Let them get it out of their systems now, before we move toward home,* Doug thought. *We'll need the silence then.*

He climbed to the top of the low ridge above the caves. He didn't show himself above the crest, but lay just behind it. It was the clearest view he could get toward Sam and Max—not that he could see anything except the rare glare of missiles or gunfire. After a little while, he rolled over on his back and stared at the stars and the few wispy clouds overhead. And, remarkably, he fell asleep.

But it didn't last. Albert woke him. ''Are we going, or aren't we?''

Doug blinked several times and yawned. "What time is it?"

"Close to midnight."

"We could almost crawl back by dawn."

"Gil and I were talking." Albert hesitated for a moment, waiting for a prompt from Doug.

"About what?"

"Federation soldiers all stayed this side of the river, far as we know, right?"

"Far as we know," Doug agreed.

"We saw some of these Commonwealth folks come down on the other side."

Doug didn't need to have a picture drawn for him. "Cross the river and go back that way? That might help keep body and soul together. Cut down on the odds, at any rate."

"That's what we thought," Albert said.

The idea was too sound for Doug to find any fault with it. "You have everybody ready to go?"

"Gil and I didn't say anything, but most of 'em have been ready to go for hours. Been fidgeting all over the place."

There was a good ford across the river not more than a half mile farther south. This far upstream, the riverbed was more gravel than mud, and over one stretch it was shallow enough to wade across without any difficulty, shallow enough that hippobary avoided it as much as possible.

"We take it slow and careful all the way," Doug said in a whispered conference before they crossed the river. "No way to tell how far out the Commonwealth troops will have patrols, and there's no way to be absolutely certain there aren't Federation forces on the other side. Either one will probably see us long before we can see them."

"Best put Ash up front then," Albert suggested. "He's

got the best eyes for night I ever came across.''

"Ash?" Doug asked.

"Fine with me," he said.

"I'll be right behind you," Doug assured him. "Don't take any unnecessary risks, Ash, not now. The least hint of anything, we go down and wait it out."

"Fine with me," he repeated.

It made for a slow trek.

They were no more than a hundred yards away when the firefight started. Doug and his companions dove for cover. When it became clear that none of the fire was aimed at them, Doug snaked his way forward a couple of yards to get better cover—and a better view. He stared, trying to figure out who was who, which of these unseen soldiers were friends and which were enemies.

It wasn't until the string of grenades went off that he saw the crest of the Federation on the side of one helmet. Quickly then, Doug pointed the enemy out to his companions.

"Let's get a piece of this," he said. "That'll tell the others we're on their side."

It felt wonderful to put a Federation soldier under his sights.

Part 5

"Hey, are you Commonwealth people?''

The accent was strange, but not so strange that David couldn't understand it. ''We're Commonwealth.'' He kept his head down. ''Second Regiment of Royal Marines. You the folks who called for assistance?'' David told Tory to take over the radio traffic with Captain McAuliffe and with the nearest section of First Battalion's line. ''Get medical help here fast. And have everyone keep their eyes and ears open until we know for sure what's going on here.'' Then David turned his attention back to the locals.

''That's us,'' the same voice said. ''Didn't expect to see you folks quite so soon. Not that we really *see* you yet.''

''You showed up at an opportune time,'' David said. ''Thanks.''

''You put the hurt on them. Any of them still in one piece?''

''Probably not,'' David said. ''Their electronics went out rather suddenly. But we'll wait for reinforcements before we go looking. I've got a couple of men down.''

''We're not going to, ah, startle your reinforcements, are we?''

''I've already passed the word that we had help. You'd best stay where you are for now, just in case there are any Feddies left around feeling hostile. We'll have company in about four minutes.'' A voice on his command channel had just told David that the reinforcements would arrive in less than half that time. Caution, not distrust.

Two platoons from Charley Company reached the site, and put out their own security teams. Medics went to Zimmerman and Prinz. Roger would be fine after time in a trauma tube. Prinz was dead. Most of his head was missing. No trauma tube could handle that. There were five dead Federation soldiers, and two wounded who probably wouldn't survive to reach a trauma tube.

The Buchananers came up to the Commonwealth soldiers in a group, their rifles and shotguns held high above their heads.

"Keep your weapons," David told them. "We may run into more of these jokers. We'll take you back to our command post. I'm sure Colonel Zacharia would love to have a chat with you."

"We've a few questions of our own." The same Buchananer had done all of the talking for them. "I'm Doug Weintraub, a member of the Buchanan Planetary Commission."

"He's also the crazy man who set off that message rocket," another man said. "I'm Albert Greer."

First Battalion's command post had been set up close behind H&S Company's position. It was a bunker hurriedly dug in the clearing where David and his men had landed the morning before. The only lights inside were infrared. David took Doug in and introduced him to Lt. Colonel Zacharia.

"Your people took out those three shuttles?"

"A lucky chance. It's the only blow we've managed to strike for our own freedom. After that, all we could do was hide until you folks showed up. They had a round-the-clock air search going until you folks chased them off."

"Not the only blow," Zacharia said. "If you hadn't

managed to get that MR off . . .''

Doug shrugged. ''That was desperation. I set it to jump to Q-space immediately after launch.''

''I'd give you all an escort home tonight, but we haven't moved into your towns yet,'' Zacharia said. ''There are still Federation troops out there, and most of them turned off their electronics before we could account for them.''

''I think we'd prefer to help free our world, if you have places for us,'' Doug said.

''Could be useful, sir,'' David said after clearing his throat. ''If we're going to have to hunt down all the Feddies, it might help considerably to have locals who know the terrain with us.''

Zacharia hesitated. ''How does that sound to you, Mr. Weintraub?''

Doug grinned. ''Quite satisfactory, Colonel.''

''We'll get you and your companions proper battle kit, of course. By the way, what *is* that you're wearing?''

''Hippobary hide.'' Doug laughed. ''I imagine it's a bit rank by now, but it kept us hid from their infrared detectors.''

The sun was rising before David and his squad got back to the line. Weintraub was with them, in full Marine kit now, right down to the field skin. *That* had bothered Doug, and the other Buchananers, at first. It was something they had never heard of.

''A bit more compact than those hides,'' David said when he instructed them on how to put the field skins on. ''And a lot handier.''

''Be nice if we had a chance to clean up a little first,'' one of the other locals had said. ''We've been living in a cave for ages.''

David nodded. ''We don't have much in the way of facilities. But field skins are the next best thing. It's all nourishment to them.''

"They're alive?" one of the younger men asked. David had heard the name but didn't recall it, one of a pair of twins.

"Nanobugs," David said.

"Ages past anything we've got in the way of nanotech," Doug said.

"They're fairly recent," David admitted. "The first ones came into use about the time I joined the RM. Military secret until five years ago. The latest models are still on the restricted list.''

Doug and two of his companions would stay with First Battalion, Doug with David's platoon, the others with line companies. The other six Buchananers would be divided among Second and Third Battalions.

"We'll get you back to your families as soon as possible," David told Doug as they settled in on the line.

"It'll be good to get home," Doug said. "Damn good."

Doug stretched out in the shallow foxhole. A keppu log covered part of the hole, giving some extra protection. Finally, he had time to think, time to sort through all that had happened in the last few hours.

Taking part in the firefight had been strangely exhilarating, even if Doug and his friends had been largely ineffectual. He knew that they had been no more than a casual distraction to the Federation troops. But the Commonwealth Marines had welcomed them warmly, as companions in arms, eagerly awaited allies, not as useless farmers who couldn't be trusted to keep out of the way while the "professionals" did their work.

Right friendly sorts, Doug allowed. He felt fifty pounds lighter wearing the Commonwealth field skin and combat fatigues, even with the heavy battle helmet. Doug had quickly accepted that he couldn't hope to master half the capabilities of his helmet in any reasonable length of time. Spencer had explained the basics but, clearly, efficient use of the helmet required extensive practice as well as more detailed tutorials.

The fight shouldn't last that long now, Doug told himself with a grim smile. The Federation troops on the ground were on their own now, abandoned by their ship, and vastly outnumbered.

We can win. We can really win. It was a heady thought.

The sun was up. There was limited movement among the Commonwealth Marines—but no *unnecessary* movement, Doug noted. Immediately around him, Marines were eating and trying to get a little rest when they could, but not everyone at once. Doug had eaten two complete meal packets, one in the command bunker, the other after he joined the intelligence and reconnaissance platoon on the line. The extent of his hunger surprised him. The weeks of little more than partially digestible hippobary had sapped him more than he had suspected. He was still hungry, but decided that he wouldn't make an issue of it, not among the soldiers in the field. *I'll eat when they do.*

Doug looked out under the keppu log toward Sam and Max. He couldn't *see* the towns. The river was a mile away, through forest that was thick in places, and the settlements were beyond that. But Elena and Jamie were there, and Doug worried about them, caught in the middle of this pending battle. He could hear the sounds of war from time to time, Commonwealth fighters making combat runs, more rarely bursts of small arms fire on the ground—always at a distance. There had been no sound of activity anywhere near.

Better people who know their business than amateurs, Doug decided. *Less chance of folks getting hurt. Or killed.*

20

The larger room in Admiral Truscott's day cabin looked crowded. Truscott sat at the center of one side of the chart table. Captain Hardesty sat directly across from him. Commander Georgia Bentley, the fighter wing commander, sat at one end of the table. Ian and Prince William stood along the wall, behind the admiral, more spectators than participants in the conference. But Admiral Greene and the captains of the other ships in the flotilla were present only by full-scale holographic projection, as was Colonel Laplace, the Marine commander.

"I'm open to suggestions," Truscott told the others. "We have more than six hundred Federation soldiers, perhaps considerably more, on the ground. We need to locate and neutralize them as quickly as possible. The first constraint is that we must do as little damage as possible to the interests of the legal inhabitants. The second constraint is that I want to be as economical of our own personnel and matériel as possible. If a general abhorrence of wasting lives isn't reason enough for you, just remember that this war is young. One battle won't end it, at least not to our advantage. But if this task force should go missing the way the ships sent to Camerein have, the effect on Buckingham might be overwhelming." He turned and glanced up at the prince. "Would you care to elaborate on that, Your Highness?"

"You said it very well, Admiral," William said. "There is tremendous concern in the government already. Since the Commonwealth depends on the voluntary cooperation of member governments, and its military forces depend on voluntary enlistments, a continuing series of military disasters might lead to a serious erosion of support. I'm certain we can count on continued full support from Buckingham and the core worlds of the Commonwealth, but support on outer worlds would become less certain with each setback. And our base is, in any case, much narrower than that of the Federation. They control many times the number of worlds than are members of the Second Commonwealth, and many of those worlds are older and more populous than ours."

"Precisely. We have problems the Federation doesn't," Truscott said. "They have at least five times the number of worlds and perhaps a dozen times the population to draw on. There is still conscription in the Federation, and with their highly centralized political control, they have less concern about defections, either of worlds or individuals. Most of their worlds have been too thoroughly subjugated to provide trouble for them."

"Ah, excuse me, Admiral," the prince said. "I wouldn't count too highly on that information. Conscripts are unlikely to be assigned to high-risk enterprises outside the Federation itself. They tend to be posted as garrison within the Federation, or spread out among professional units on larger expeditions."

This time, Truscott turned completely around to look at the prince. "I assume that your information is more up to date than mine." Ian doubted that anyone else in the conference could pick up on the subtle change in Truscott's tone. He was upset, and holding it back, but Prince William wasn't the focus of that chagrin.

"Any information I have is available to you, sir," William said. "I would have offered to compare notes before had I suspected." He had obviously noted the change as well.

The admiral cleared his throat, nodded to the prince, then turned back toward the table. "In any case, we need to mop up this operation as quickly as we can without being wasteful of our resources, particularly human resources. The Federation soldiers on Buchanan doused their electronics and went to ground. How can we find them, short of patrolling every square foot of the surface and flushing them out one man at a time?"

"If they prepared their fallbacks carefully in advance, we can't," Colonel Laplace said. "It's that simple, sir. But my guess is that any preparations were likely rushed and incomplete. We must have arrived long before they could have expected us, if they had any cause to suspect that we would intervene at all. Our best bet is probably detailed mapping, including ultrasonic as well as the standard EM frequencies. That can turn up quite a bit in the way of shallow bunkers and caves. We can turn to the local residents for help as well. Past those measures, it may still come down to my Marines walking grids to flush the enemy."

"My people are working with the Colonel's intelligence staff to take directional sound detection devices down to the surface," Paul Greene said. "If we can't pick up locations from the air, we'll have to go that route. But rather than walk Marines into every potential ambush, we can search each grid with microphones. There's a chance we'll be able to pinpoint enemy positions by their unavoidable sounds."

"Heartbeats and respiration?" Colonel Laplace asked. Greene nodded. "I don't think that microphones will work a damn bit better than the detectors built into every combat helmet, and they're not doing a bit of real good. There's far too much interference for that sort of thing to work.''

"The first step, surely,'' Captain Hardesty said, "is to move troops into the settlements, make contact with the locals, get what assistance we can from them in locating Federation positions. The more data we can get that simply, the less we have to worry about these other possibilities. You did suggest that time is of the essence, Admiral.''

Truscott nodded. "Colonel Laplace, how are your troops situated for moving into the towns?''

"Whenever you order it, sir. But we have no idea how much resistance we'll meet. As quickly as they disappeared, a considerable number of the Feddies must be in the towns. The faster we move in, the higher the likelihood of civilian casualties.''

"Have your intelligence people talked with those guerrilla fighters yet?'' Truscott asked.

"At length,'' Laplace said. He shrugged again. "They've been out of touch with events in the two towns for too long to have any useful information about where enemy troops might be. The last contact they had was when they blew up those shuttles at the starport, two weeks before we arrived.''

"What value, if any, do you place on the cooperation of these guerrillas?'' Captain Miles of *Khyber* asked.

"Considerable, if it comes down to searching out pockets of Federation resistance in the countryside,'' Laplace said quickly. "They know the terrain, the wildlife, the most likely sites for caves or bunkers.''

"Ah, excuse me,'' Prince William said, very deferentially. "I'm not part of the military chain of command, and it's certainly not yet time for me to begin my diplomatic function on the surface. But may I point out that one of these resistance fighters is a member of Buchanan's governing planetary commission, a person of considerable importance to his own people, and therefore to us. Anything we can do to make these fighters feel a freely accepted commitment to us can only help ease the subsequent political phase. We hope to win their free adherence to the Commonwealth, not just a temporary alliance which they might see as political necessity. The trouble we take with the people of one world now will pay off thousandfold later, on scores, perhaps hundreds, of other worlds.'' The prince looked around, smiled apologetically, and spread his hands. ''My apologies for being a long-winded politician. It's a hereditary defect, I'm afraid.''

Truscott quickly suppressed a grin. ''Not at all, Your Highness.'' He looked around at the others. ''It's an important part of the equation, something we may have needed reminding of.'' Behind Truscott, Ian raised an eyebrow. There seemed to be nuances in the relationship between admiral and prince that he hadn't been aware of.

''Colonel Laplace, I think it's time to start moving your men into, er, Sam and Max. If and when they run into active resistance, we'll take each incident independently, as cautiously as possible, to minimize casualties and damages. That means that we won't be able to use our Spacehawks as freely as we might otherwise.'' He glanced at Commander Bentley, who nodded. ''The birds only go in if we can be sure of striking Federation targets without endangering civilians.''

''That's the way we'd want it in any case,'' Bentley said.

''You want more manpower for this, Colonel Laplace?'' Truscott asked. ''I'll release one more company of the reserve if you think you need them.''

Laplace took a deep breath. ''I think we can do the job with the assets we have dirtside now, Admiral. I'll strip the units east of the river of a couple of companies, bring them across to establish a beachhead behind the towns.''

''Let's get busy. I think that's all for now. Ah, Captain

Miles, if you'd stay on the link for a few minutes?"

"Of course, sir," Dever said.

Except for Dever Miles, the holographic projections were gone from the room. Hardesty and Laplace had gone as well. Truscott asked Prince William to remain. "I think this is something you should be aware of," he said.

"As you wish, sir," William replied. Ian had made no move to leave. If the admiral didn't want him present, he would expressly ask him to go. That didn't happen very often.

"Both of you, sit down and be comfortable. There's no need to keep this stiff." William and Ian sat across the table from the admiral.

"You have something additional for me, sir?" Captain Miles said after it was clear who was going and who was staying.

"Yes," Truscott said, turning his attention back to the only remaining projection in the room. "I'm cutting *Khyber* loose for a few days, sending you back to Buckingham on a special mission."

"That will put us out of this operation completely, sir," Miles said, a trace of puzzlement in his voice.

"I don't think so," Truscott said. "We—or, more precisely, *you*—are going to demonstrate that inter-system voyages don't need to take nearly as long as they've taken in the past."

"Sir?" Miles said.

"A continuation of what we've already seen and done here, Dever," Truscott said. "We made our entrances considerably closer than doctrine allows, without the slightest hint that we were crowding any real safety limits, and we have the example of that MR that made the transit to Q-space within feet of the surface of Buchanan, without any deviation in course or damage, either to the MR or to Buchanan.''

''Exactly what sort of demonstration do you have in mind, Admiral?'' Miles asked, beginning to see where this was heading.

''I have a number of dispatches for you to take to the Admiralty,'' Truscott said. ''I'm also sending duplicates via two MRs. One MR will be programmed to make the voyage in the customary three jumps, but with virtually no interval between Q-space transits, no significant spatial separation. The second Mr will be programmed to make the voyage in two jumps, with minimal intervals.''

''And *Khyber,* sir?'' Miles asked.

''I want *Khyber* to make the voyage in three transits as well, spaced not quite as closely together as the MRs. Twelve hours out before the first jump, twelve hours between transits, and entering Buckingham's system no more than eighteen hours out from the surface. That's likely to set off all sorts of defensive alerts back there, *if* the MRs don't get through first. But I believe they will.''

''Most likely,'' Miles conceded. ''The evidence of the Buchanan MR is overwhelming, the more so because it must have been a nearly obsolete model.''

''Quite,'' Truscott said with a short laugh. ''It was several decades old. That adds considerably to my confidence that we can safely take these steps. I wouldn't risk *Khyber* if I thought there was one chance in a million that it wasn't safe.''

''When should I leave?'' Miles asked.

''You could take a moment to start *Khyber* toward your first transit point now, Dever. I'll transmit the dispatches to you shortly.''

''Very well, sir. I'll be back online in thirty seconds.''

•   •   •

"Obviously you don't think there's the slightest risk to *Khyber* or Buckingham in this," Prince William said after the conference ended. *Khyber* was already accelerating toward its first transit point. Admiral Truscott had given orders to Mort Hardesty to prepare for the launch of the message rockets as well. "Is this just a matter of cutting down the time needed for strategic movements, or is there more to it? If I may ask."

"I don't think that 'just' is quite the word for it, sir," Truscott said. "It's a point I've suspected for a great many years but never had the opportunity to test. The early generations of Nilssen generators were so cranky and unpredictable that we're still quivering with fear of some unspeakable catastrophe. We tread around our Nilssens as if they were some bloody piece of magic that we're too damn ignorant to understand. We don't want to risk 'offending' the genie, or some such rot. That MR the Buchanan people sent was a particular stroke of luck. I never could obtain Admiralty approval for an experiment of that nature, even with MRs, and I tried. And although I don't have specific authorization for this experiment, I made it clear to Long John that I intended to make use of the possibilities that MR offered, and he concurred." Truscott chuckled. It hadn't been *quite* that simple, but his authority as fleet commander was broad enough to make up the difference—as long as the experiments worked.

"Think of the time delay for travel between systems," Truscott continued. "It takes fourteen days to go from a planet in one solar system to a planet in another solar system. We make three Q-space transits, the first to take us to an uncluttered region of space with maximum separation from any stellar masses, the second to take us more-or-less laterally toward the region of our destination, and the final jump to take us to the specific system we want to reach. That's a fortnight lost even if we're only going from Buckingham to Lorenzo.'' Lorenzo was only six light years from Buckingham, the nearest habitable world to the Commonwealth capital.

The prince started to speak, but Truscott waved him off. ''I know, Lorenzo is a poor example. We do that jump in one transit now. But it was *civilian* traffic that provoked that, and there are only a handful of one-jump routes, and still a five-day lag before and three days after the transit. Eight days to make a trip that could be done in less than one.''

''Demonstrating that will change life considerably,'' William ventured, ''and not merely in military affairs.''

''At the moment, military affairs are uppermost in my mind,'' Truscott said, ''but you're correct. It should tie the worlds of the Commonwealth together much more closely.''

''Do we have any idea how long the Federation takes to make transits?'' Ian asked.

''Not the military,'' Truscott said. ''The evidence we have for civilian traffic is sketchy, but some skippers are reputed to cut several days off of every journey. It's something they tend to be reluctant to discuss.''

''You apparently don't think that we have several weeks to enjoy freedom of action here,'' William suggested.

''Frankly, I'd be surprised if we have two weeks,'' Truscott replied. ''That is at the heart of the dispatches I sent to the Admiralty and to His Majesty. Referring to the losses we've apparently suffered at Camerein, I stated my considered military opinion that we're likely to face a massive response from Federation forces and asked for immediate reinforcement.''

''Using new guidelines for Q-space transits,'' William said.

''Exactly.''

''If I might be so bold, Admiral,'' the prince said.

''Would it be possible for me to add a dispatch of my own to the collection? For what good it might do, I would like to add my endorsement.''

''Thank you, Your Highness.'' Truscott stood and gave the prince a formal court bow. ''I would appreciate that.''

''You've really got yourself around him,'' Ian told the prince when they finally left the admiral fifteen minutes later. William's dispatches had been added to the MRs and to those that *Khyber* was carrying. ''When we were first told that you would be accompanying us . . .'' Ian stopped and grinned. ''I suppose I really shouldn't talk about that. I'll just say that his reaction was rather less than enthusiastic.''

''People always expect me to be somehow different, just because of who my parents were, who my brother is.'' William sounded tired, or perhaps just discouraged by the topic. ''Royal competence always seems to come as a complete shock.'' He noticed Ian's raised eyebrow and grinned. ''Not a particularly diplomatic statement, was that?''

''Not particularly,'' Ian agreed. ''But then, I'm used to hearing statements like that. It's one of the burdens of my position.'' Both men laughed at that.

''That may be why we hit it off so well, Ian. In many ways, your position is very much like my own.''

21

David Spencer and Doug Weintraub made their way back to the I&R platoon from the battalion command bunker. It was close to noon, less than nine hours after the ambush.

"First the good news," David told his squad. "Roger is doing smashingly well. He's out of the trauma tube and he'll be back with us tomorrow or the day after."

"What's the bad news?" Alfie asked.

"Get your skates on," Spencer said. "We're off out in twenty minutes. Delta of the Fourth is coming up and we're heading for the river with them, as soon as they get here."

"What about the engineers?" Tory asked. "I thought Delta was minding them."

"Delta's leaving them a squad or two, I guess. Other than that, the engineers will have to watch their own tails for a bit," David said.

"We just going *to* the river, or *across* it?" Alfie asked.

"Across," David said. "And, no, there's no bridge yet. We've got a load of Perry boats down from *Thames*."

"I knew them engineers was useless," Alfie said with disgust. "Just takin' up space we coulda used for *real* Marines."

"I think maybe the admiral agrees," David said. "They're still a mile short of here with their road."

Alfie nodded toward Doug. "Looks like you blokes'll

get yourselves a brand spanking new road leading from nowhere to nowhere.''

Doug smiled. ''Someday we may even need it. If the forest doesn't take it back first.''

''By the time our precious engineers get through, the forest wouldn't *want* it back.'' Alfie was the only one to laugh at his joke.

''Maybe your admiral would let us borrow them for a few years,'' Doug said lightly. ''We could use some civil engineering.''

''Nothin' very 'civil' about our engineers,'' Alfie retorted.

''A few years, maybe they'd finish this road up to the river,'' Jacky added.

''Okay, lads, off your butts,'' Spencer said, coming back from a quick tour of the rest of the platoon. They were all going on this mission. ''Here comes Delta.'' He gestured east at the two columns of Marines moving into the area.

''I suppose they want us to find a path?'' Alfie said.

''Yes, but look at the bright, Alfie-lad, they're going to carry the Perry boats,'' Spencer said.

''That's a surprise,'' Alfie agreed.

Lieutenant Asa Ewing came over to Spencer and the group around him. David saluted.

''We're ready to go, sir. This is Mr. Doug Weintraub, a member of the Buchanan Planetary Commission, one of the men who've been giving the Feddies a hard way to go.''

Ewing extended a hand. ''Glad to meet you, sir. You took out those shuttles?''

Doug took the hand. ''Our only real contribution so far, I'm afraid.''

''That's not the way Colonel Laplace tells it,'' Ewing said. ''You have any ideas where we should hit the river?''

''Unless there are Federation troops hidden between here and there, it doesn't much matter. There are paths aplenty through these woods. And the river, well, down this far, it's all pretty much the same. If you want to hit the river between our towns, we need to head in that direction.'' He pointed just a little south of due west.

Ewing nodded. ''That's the plan, sir. Gives us more flexibility. Past that, depends on what the Feddies do when the other battalions start to move in from the west.''

''In case no one's mentioned it yet,'' Doug said, hesitating, ''most all of our houses have sturdy cellars beneath them.''

Ewing glanced at David. ''Rooting the Feddies out could get dicey in that case,'' he said.

''But if there aren't Federation troops in those cellars, it'll be our folks,'' Doug said. ''Time of trouble, that's where we'd go for safety.''

''We'll be careful,'' Ewing assured him. ''That's the first order of the day, straight from Admiral Truscott himself.''

''I'm glad to hear it,'' Doug said.

''We'll deal with the cellars when and if we have to, Doug,'' David added. ''There are ways to clear a cellar or bunker without doing permanent damage to people or anything else. If worse comes to worst, like if there are Feddies holed *with* some of your people, we can use stun buns—shock grenades—to get in. Makes a bloke feel like hell for a few minutes after he wakes up, but won't hurt him past the immediate shock and discomfort.''

''I'm not sure if I'm relieved or not,'' Doug said.

''I've been hit by one myself,'' David said. ''It's not pleasant, but you get over it in a hurry.''

''Sergeant Spencer, you want to start your people toward the river?'' Ewing said. ''We'll put patrols on the flanks and behind.''

''Aye, sir,'' David said. He looked at the Marines of Delta Company and saw the two dozen Perry boats they were carrying. The plastic inflatables each made a real load for two men, but a Perry could carry fifteen fully equipped Marines.

David quickly deployed his men. Hugo Kassner and third squad were first out. Second and fourth squads were positioned behind and to either side of third. David kept first squad in the center of the wedge. If necessary, his men could provide instant reinforcement for any of the others. If not, they would spell third squad on the point the last half of the distance to the river.

In daylight, the forest posed no hazards of its own. There were no choke points forcing all of the Marines to follow one path, which cut down on the danger of land mines or booby traps. Explosives could be detected by helmet sensors, with a certain amount of attention to detail by the men wearing the helmets. A more insidious danger might be posed by more primitive traps, those that didn't rely on electronics or explosives. Neither sort of defense had been tripped or spotted by any of the patrols out the night before, and it was unlikely that any of the Federation troops could be out laying that sort of trap now, in daylight, so close to Commonwealth positions.

But the Marines remained alert.

David's throat was dry throughout the march, a familiar stress reaction that he discounted as far as he could. One man couldn't look everywhere at once. He had to trust that his comrades would do their jobs properly.

Communication was over helmet complinks. There were more than enough channels available, scrambled to make interception of messages effectively impossible. The Commonwealth forces had no need to mask their presence the way the Federation troops were, so the Marines had more than their helmets to draw on. There were fewer Spacehawks in evidence than there had been the day before, but shuttles orbited over the area to provide surveillance and long-range sensors on the ships overhead contributed to the general intelligence.

"Haven't you any idea at all where the Federation troops are hiding?" Doug asked David Spencer over a private link.

"Not the foggiest," David replied. "Once they turn their helmets off, they're damn near invisible. Same reason they couldn't find your lot—no electronics to give you away, and that thick hide you were ducked out in is almost as good a shield against infrared detection as our field skins."

"That's what we hoped," Doug admitted. "It was all by guess and by God though. We didn't really *know* any of it."

"Last night, *we* didn't see you until you started shooting."

"But you think the enemy must still be in or around Sam and Max?"

"Until we know different for certain, we have to assume that," David said. "There are limits to how far they could have moved on foot without giving themselves away. At most, I'd guess they couldn't be more than fifteen or twenty miles from your towns right now, probably a lot less."

That conversation lapsed. David reported to Lieutenant Ewing and Captain McAuliffe when they reached the half-way point. First and third squads switched positions in the opening wedge, and David put Tory on point, with Alfie and Jacky close to support him.

"Set up a line fifty yards short of the river," Ewing told David. "We'll get the Perry boats inflated then. Set up cover for the crossing and move straight over to the west bank."

"Yes, sir," David replied over the command channel. "Doug informs me that there's little cover down close to the river in any case. Fifty yards back should put us right about the edge of the trees."

"Fine, use that for your guide then," Ewing said. "My mapboard shows the width of the river fairly constant. Any word on the current?"

David checked with Doug before he replied. "Not too bad, sir, no more than two miles per hour. Wide and shallow."

But the crossing would put the Marines out in the open, without cover, for five or six minutes, with nowhere to go in case of attack—except into the water with its muddy bottom. The only counter was to cross in three groups, and bring in a couple of Spacehawks to take on any enemy that showed itself. The Perry boats were equipped with compressed gas to provide propulsion, enough for a short crossing like this one. The Marines augmented the gas jets with oars. I&R platoon went first, with one platoon of Delta Company. As soon as they were ashore on the western bank, and in sound defensive positions, the next group crossed, and then the last. None of them came under fire. Early in the afternoon, even the hippobary offered no obstacle. They were, according to Doug, mostly inert lumps during the hottest hours of the day, resting up for their nocturnal roaming. The animals were easy to avoid, floating with only their backs and the tops of their heads visible, lifting their snouts to breathe once every two minutes or so.

"The Park is a bit more wild than the forest we came through," Doug told David and Ewing. "Besides the native growth, there are a lot of plants that have migrated from our gardens and such. We tried to keep it all native, sort of a memorial for the time when we've taken over the entire area, but there's been some slippage. But the paths are marked better. None of them are paved, but they're packed so hard they might as well be."

David opened up his mapboard and narrowed the scale until it showed only the area between the two communities, down to the edge of the river.

"Where would you suggest that Federation troops might be most likely to hole up?" David asked.

"There's all kinds of secluded nooks," Doug said, pointing out several small clearings on the chart. "A lot of them only have one decent way in or out, with thickets and vines in the trees around them." He chuckled. "Generations of young couples have decided to get married in those out-of-the-way spots. And many have gone a lot farther than a peck on the cheek there. A lot of privacy, a lot of warning if anyone's coming in."

"In other words, a pain in the butt to handle," Ewing muttered.

"We never anticipated the need for military operations in the Park."

"I know, Mr. Weintraub," Ewing said. "It wasn't meant to be a criticism. You can't run normal lives under the fear that someday, somehow, someone might come along and do something like this. There'd be no room for romance in a galaxy like that."

"Works two ways, sir," David suggested. "It may narrow our access to them, but they'll have as much trouble getting at us. Best way to handle the hairy spots would be to wait for dark. Feddies would have to turn on their helmets to spot us then, and we'll know the second they do. We can use what's left of daylight to make contacts in the towns."

"Sounds good to me," Doug said. "We get a chance to talk to some of our people, we may have a better notion where the enemy is hiding."

"Which way do you suggest we go first?" Ewing asked.

"Max," Doug said immediately. He pointed to the northern community on the mapboard. "It's built up a little more. The homes are closer together. Makes it easier for folks to see what's going on around them. And there's this gully, right on the edge, between the Park and the town. That'll give us cover until we're right in town.'' He traced the route. ''There's only water in that gully during the rainy season, and not always then. Not much more than weeds in it now.''

Ewing fiddled with the controls on his mapboard to get a better view of the topography. ''Looks rather obvious,'' he said.

''Ambush?'' Spencer suggested. He pointed at the nearest approaches to the forest on the left of the gully. ''It would have to be along here, if anywhere.''

''Still, we'd have good cover to return fire, if we had to,'' Ewing said. ''The only major danger would be if they got above us, in the gully. They could funnel fire right down into us.''

''How high are the weeds in there?'' David asked Doug.

''No more'n ten or twelve inches, I'd say, and thin. Our rainy season wasn't particularly wet this year.''

''Sir?'' David turned to Ewing again. ''Any Feddies we scare out makes that many less for later. We could send the main body up the pipe. I'd take a squad here, along the edge of the wooded area, back a ways. Anything starts, we'd be in position to set up a quick crossfire. They'd lose interest right fast.''

''The undergrowth at the edge is as thick as it gets anywhere in the Park, brambles so tight a mouse can get stuck,'' Doug said. ''Man sure can't move silently through that, and he can't see far, no matter how fancy his helmet is.''

''Let's do it,'' Ewing said. ''Put a squad on the right too, say thirty yards out, to cover that flank.''

David did everything but hold his breath as he took first squad along the edge of the woods. Thinking about what Doug had said about the difficulty of silent movement in

the thick underbrush, David had told his men to stay absolutely quiet and use their directional microphones to
search for any threat inside the woods. There were animal
sounds, but nothing even vaguely human. But they were
approaching the stretch where the forest came closest to the
dry gully.

Any action will come soon, if at all, David told himself.
Delta's leading platoons, and David's third and fourth
squads, were already level with the patch they had decided
was most dangerous. David's sensors showed no infrared
images of lurking men, no enemy electronics, no human
sounds at all in the trees and underbrush.

He let a long breath out, then took a quick glance at the
columns of men in the gully. They were moving as low as
they could, but the ditch wasn't deep enough to cover them
completely. If there was an ambush, they would find sufficient cover by going flat, but that initial exposure could
do a lot of damage. It was up to David's squad to prevent
that.

Second squad, on the far side of the gully, was holding
back, staying even with David's squad. The plants in the
field they were trudging through weren't tall enough to ob-
scure their boots.

David whispered a command over his squad frequency.
Alfie dropped to one knee, bring his needle rifle up to cover
the danger point. David ordered the rest of his squad down.
They held their positions until all of the men in the gully
had passed the bulge. David expected the shooting to start
at any second. Under tension, an ambush seemed more a
certainty than a possibility. In daylight, they might not even
have the instant of warning that would come from helmet
electronics being switched on.

The seconds passed with an impossible slowness. David
felt a growing urge to spray the woods, but he wouldn't
give in to it. If no answering fire came, his action would

be clearly seen—all the way up to *Sheffield*—as a panic reaction. The thought of certain embarrassment was enough to hold back his twitching finger. For now.

The last platoon moved beyond the bulge. David passed another command and Alfie led the way past the choke point. The men kept their weapons pointed into the underbrush. The shadows beneath the trees were thick. Vines climbed from tree to tree in a chaotic webbing. Even a bird would have to exercise care getting through that tangle.

David walked to the edge of the trees, out of the line of march. He moved slowly, and stared as deeply into the tangle as he could, squinting against the confusion of light and shadow. His sound equipment was still probing for any identifiably human sounds—and getting none. The last of his men moved past him. Jacky stopped and gave him a questioning look. David shook his head and gestured for Jacky to move on with the rest. Jacky nodded and went on, following Sean Seidman. The rookie was performing well. Both of the remaining new men in the squad were. Henny Prinz's death had taken a lot of the newness out of them.

The gully got shallower and wider as the Marines neared its head. After a quick conference on the command frequency, Ewing brought everyone to a stop. The two outlying squads came down into the gully.

"Now we make contact," Doug said when the lieutenant and several sergeants had gathered in the middle of the defensive formation.

"You have any ideas?" Lieutenant Ewing asked.

Doug nodded. "I pull off my helmet, walk up toward that house, and call out to the folks who live there." He pointed at the house, sixty yards from the end of the gully, and off to the right. "If they answer, we've made our contact. If not"—he shrugged—"they're either hiding in the cellar or not home."

"And if your people aren't in there, there might be Feddies in the house," Ewing said.

"Might be," Doug conceded. "If there are, they might take a quick shot at me. That'd give you an answer in a hurry. If they don't, then I guess we'd have to go inside and see what's what."

"You make it sound like a stroll through the garden," David said.

Doug shrugged again. "It all comes down to something like that, doesn't it." There was no question in his voice.

"It does," David agreed.

"Take it one step at a time," Ewing told Doug. "We don't want to lose you."

"If anyone has to go inside to flush the place, leave it to us," David said. "We know the drill back to front."

Doug took off his helmet and met David's look before he nodded. "I'll do that." Then he turned to Ewing. "Any reason why we shouldn't get busy with this right now?"

"Whenever you're ready," Ewing said. He glanced around to make sure that all of the Marines were in position. "We'll give you all the cover we can, if it comes to that. Anything starts, drop flat and let us do the work."

Doug managed a smile. "I appreciate that." He looked at David again for an instant, then stepped up out of the gully.

Doug stood there for a moment. He looked at the house, then looked around him. After taking a deep breath, he walked slowly toward the house, whispering a prayer under his breath. He held his helmet in his left hand, his rifle in his right, both low, at his sides.

He walked to within fifty feet of the back door before he stopped again. There were no lights on inside the house, but that didn't surprise him, not in the middle of the afternoon. Marie wouldn't have a light in the kitchen until she started fixing supper, if life were continuing anything like normal.

They'd be keeping low, even if they're not down in the cellar, Doug told himself. *No reason for them to see me coming in. They might not be looking out.*

He wasn't certain that he believed all of that.

"Elena? Marie? Tom? Jamie?" He called out each name loudly, leaving a short pause between them. Then he started to take a deep breath. He hadn't even filled his lungs before the back door opened, just a little.

"It's Doug," he said, not as loudly as before. The door opened the rest of the way and Tom Genner, Marie's husband, showed himself in the shadows.

"Doug? Is it really you?"

"It's me." Doug took several steps closer to the house. "You have any unwanted guests in there, uniformed guests?"

Tom shook his head. "Haven't seen any of them since yesterday morning, before dawn. They've cleared off, somewhere."

"That's good. I've brought a few friends." He gestured toward the gully. Tom looked that way and grew a worried look. "Commonwealth Marines," Doug said quickly. "They're the reason the Federation bastards took off."

Tom came down off of the porch. He grabbed Doug's shoulders. "The others are down in the cellar. I've been keeping watch. We didn't know if you were ever going to make it back."

"It's not over yet, Tom," Doug said. "Okay if I bring a couple of these chaps up for a powwow? We need information."

"Sure, bring them up. We can go inside, out of sight."

Doug brought his helmet up and spoke into it. "Lieutenant? Sergeant Spencer? Come on up. It's okay here." Then he looked at Tom again. "I hope you've got something to drink, Tom. I've been all this time without a taste."

Tom laughed. "I think we can find a dram or two."

• • •

Neither Marine refused the offer of a drink. Doug went down to the cellar to see his wife and son, and his wife's sister. Tom stayed with the Marines until Doug came back up, ten minutes later, looking much less steady than he had before.

"You okay?" David asked.

Doug's answering smile was painfully weak. "I'll get by. I know my family's safe. That'll do, for now."

"We've been talking," Ewing said. "Your brother-in-law says that as far as he's been able to tell, all of the Feddies moved out of town."

"Southeast, into the forest," Tom said, pointing vaguely in that direction.

"The ones that ambushed us must have been part of that," David said. "Though that was just last night; this morning." He was losing track of time. "They may have moved out of your towns, but at least some of them didn't go very far."

"How certain are you that they all left Sam and Max?" Doug asked.

Tom shrugged. "Not one hundred percent. I've been trying to work up the courage to get on the complink to call around and get more information."

"I've got a lot of men outside to make it safe," Ewing said.

"We can both get busy," Doug suggested. "You've got two terminals here, don't you?"

"Sure, you know we do."

"You take Max. I'll take Sam. Start with the rest of the commission, then whoever you can think of," Doug said. "Let's take back our world."

22

Josef Langenkamp sat in the dark of his cabin, alone. The only light was the pale green glow of the time line at the top of his complink. He had slept for six hours, and counted himself lucky that those hours had passed without nightmares. He hadn't known Seb Inowi all that well, despite the year and odd months they had served together. They had talked in ready room and mess, in the recreation rooms and so forth, the way all of the pilots did, but they hadn't been close. Their associations had run in different circles. Seb had been the squadron commander's wingman. Josef spent his time with Kate, and together they tended to spend their time with other "couples" within the wing.

Now Josef found himself remembering Seb, such chance associations as they had had within the squadron. There wasn't much to build a memory on. That was what bothered Josef most.

What will anyone have to remember me *by?* he wondered. Would anyone in the squadron, other than Kate, have any deeper recollections of him than he had of Seb Inowi? Josef leaned back against the bulkhead that ran along his bed. The wall was cool. It always was.

We're loners, mostly by choice. That's part of what makes us fighter pilots. If we were herd animals, we'd have chosen different careers. In the cockpit of a Spacehawk, a pilot was in a universe of his own, almost as completely as if he were alone in Q-space. All of the radio links and telemetry didn't change that in the least. Those links were no more real than vidgames or comedies. Or tragedies.

The time line clicked over to 1600 hours. Josef stared at it until the next minute ticked over, and the next.

"This gets me nowhere at all," he mumbled. "I might as well do something. Anything." Just getting out of the cabin would be a start. He went into the head for a quick shower. He shaved, cleaned his teeth, and dressed. When he finally left the cabin, he stood in front of his door for more than a minute. He still didn't know what to do, which way to go.

A twinge from his stomach finally headed Josef toward the squadron mess. Combat operations meant that the mess halls were providing meals around the clock. Flyers were going on and coming off duty at all hours. Nearly half the squadron's pilots were in the mess hall when Josef entered. Kate was just going through the serving line. When she spotted Josef, she waved and pointed toward their usual table in the corner.

"It looks like a lot of people needed less sleep than they thought," Kate said when Josef set his tray on the table a few minutes later. "I think most of the others are in the rec room or gym."

"We'll need time for our systems to get used to the new schedule," Josef said.

"Well, we'll certainly have time for that," Kate said.

"You heard something?" Josef asked quickly.

She shook her head. "No, just a feeling. We're going to have more fighting ahead, and one of these days, it's going to be *real* fighting."

"You think the Federation will return." Josef didn't bother to make it a question.

"Next week or next month. They won't write off Buchanan and all the soldiers they left behind. Not so simply."

No more than the Commonwealth would write off hundreds of us.

"Then it makes all the more sense to let us get as much rest as possible while we can," Josef said. "Maybe cut back even more on the number of fighters out at one time. Just put out one flight for ground support. With the escort ships higher in orbit, we'd have plenty of time to scramble to meet any attack on our ships."

"If the admiral cuts back that far on regular sorties, Commander Bentley will have us out on training missions so we don't get rusty."

Josef laughed softly, and Kate managed a warmer smile than before. But then he spoiled the mood. "All the training in the galaxy can't prevent the kind of fluke that got Seb."

"No," Kate agreed. They were both quiet for several minutes.

"I was thinking before, when I woke up." Josef set down his fork and stared directly at Kate. "I really didn't know Seb all that well."

"I was thinking the same thing," Kate said. "All that time working together and he was still almost a stranger. I couldn't even remember if he had close family."

"I never even thought of that," Josef said.

"I had the urge to ask Olive, but I didn't want to make it more difficult for her. Seb was her wingman after all. That's close."

"Don't even think that," Josef said, chilled by the implication. "I don't know what I'd do if something happened to you."

"That last flight, back on Buckingham, when you had to eject." Kate had to stop for a moment. "I froze up completely until you were down. I doubt that I could have overridden my automatics if I'd had to. I was terrified for you."

"We're flyers," Josef said after a long hesitation of his own. "This is what we always wanted to do. I know I never

seriously considered doing anything else from the time I
was ten years old.''

"Me either." Kate stared at her tray. "And civilian flying just wouldn't be the same."

"It's the danger, not just the flying, that draws us."
That's what puts us in the middle of a war. Somehow, war
had always been an abstraction before, even when they
spent virtually every working day preparing for the even-
tuality.

"And what happened to Seb, that's part of the price."
Kate didn't see Josef's nod of agreement.

23

Doug got up from the dining room table and walked out to the front porch. Sunset was near, and he wanted nothing more at the moment than to stand in the open and watch it, without fear of being caught by Federation hunters. He was still at Marie's house, but it was almost like being home. Supper had been something of a celebration, despite Doug's protests that it was premature. Asa Ewing and David Spencer had shared the meal with the Weintraubs and the Genners. The others were still at table, but Doug had felt a need to get away from the festivities.

The sun was a dull red ball, slightly obscured by wispy, distant clouds. Doug felt uncommonly safe, safer than he had felt since the invasion. Commonwealth Marines were stationed around each of the towns. Patrols were searching Sam and Max, guided by local residents who knew all of the places where a few enemy soldiers might possibly hide. And the Marines who had accompanied Doug were stationed around the house, all but Spencer and the lieutenant. But there had been no gunfire, supporting Tom Genner's assumption that all of the Federation troops had left the settlements.

The only nearby place that might conceal any significant number of the enemy was the Park, and *that* would be secured during the night.

"That's the easiest way to do something like this," David had explained. "We'll be using full helmet electronics. To meet us on anything approaching even terms, the Feddies will have to switch on their helmets before they start shooting, and the second they turn on their electronics, we'll know precisely where they are."

"But won't they know the same thing about you?" Doug had asked.

David had shook his head. "They'll be able to tell direction, but without additional sensors to triangulate positions, they'll only have a line, not a point. If that. We really don't know if their helmets are equipped for anything that precise. We just assume that they must have the same fundamental capabilities we do."

"Then if they still had ships here, they'd be able to pinpoint your men just as easily?"

"Most likely," David agreed. "But not necessarily. There are countermeasures we can take to make that more difficult."

"And you assume they have the same sort of defenses?"

David had hesitated a long time before he answered that question. "By the book, the answer would be, 'Until we know differently,' but if they did have that sort of defenses, I can't see why they were so quick to shut off their helmets so completely."

"Or can they hide their electronics so well that you just can't see them?"

David had shook his head violently at that—instinct reacting before he had time to put rational thought to it. "They switched their helmets back on when they ambushed us in the forest. We saw their electronics the second they did."

That discussion had been interrupted for supper. The table talk had been much different. It was a reunion for Doug and his family. They wanted to know what he had done while he was gone, and he asked how they had fared during the occupation. The two Marines had listened without taking any active part.

The sun started to slip below the horizon. On the porch, Doug took a deep breath and looked around at the houses that were close to the Genners' home. Lights were on in every house. Folks were hurrying to get their lives back to normal.

The time that Doug had spent on the complink had provided a lot of information, most of it negative. The one major item of tragic news had been the report of the death of Franz Bennelin. As close as anyone could tell, he had attempted to destroy his complink terminal when the Federation troops burst into his home. He had apparently succeeded. Either that or the terminal had been destroyed when the troops opened fire on him.

"He made it impossible for the enemy to get our population database," Doug had explained to the Marines. Franz's terminal had contained the undeletable master files. The other members of the commission, the ones who had been on the net with Doug at the time, had managed to wipe their copies. "They never knew who was missing." What he still found hard to put into words, even as a thought, was that Franz and the others had made his own escape possible. The Federation soldiers could never be sure how many people were missing, or who.

"Having second thoughts about continuing?"

Doug spun around quickly. He had been so rapt in his thoughts that he hadn't heard anyone come up. David was standing in the doorway.

"You gave me a turn," Doug said. "My nerves aren't what they should be."

"After what you've been through, you're doing terrific." David grinned. "You'd have done the Royal Marines proud. For someone who hasn't had all the training and drills . . ." He shook his head. "Let me put it this way. If one of my lads had been daring enough to launch that MR, and had the foresight to do it, then managed to survive alone in the wild as long as you and your friends did, and finally came back in and knocked out three enemy shuttles without a single casualty, he'd be up for every medal His Majesty's Combined Space Forces have to give. Probably get a King's Cross and cluster, and His Majesty would hang it around his neck himself, like as not.''

''You'll have me blushing,'' Doug said.

''Get used to it. You're a genuine hero, without all the bleeding most heroes have to go through. I've already told your wife and family everything I just told you.''

''I wish you hadn't, really,'' Doug said after a little stammering.

''I didn't mean to embarrass you,'' David said.

Doug made a quick gesture, dismissing the matter, and turned to look at the sunset again. David moved closer to the porch railing and watched with him.

''I'd just as soon forget any of it ever happened,'' Doug said. ''We did what we had to do. I find it rather hard to believe now. It's like something out of a juvenile adventure vid.''

''You *have* done your bit, you know,'' David said. ''Everyone will understand if you want to leave the rest to us. You've got a government to reorganize and such.''

Doug didn't hesitate, shaking his head decisively. ''No. I'll see this through. It's something I have to do. I'm not certain I can explain the why.'' After the last of the sun disappeared behind the horizon, Doug turned to David. ''The first duty of a government is to keep its people safe. Without that, nothing else is possible. I had a lot of time to think while I was hiding in that cave. I had to try to understand why I had done what I had, why I was off hiding like a hermit, grimy, hungry, maybe no more than half-sane.''

"I still say you've done remarkably well," David said softly. "I wish I could be sure that I'd do half as well in similar circumstances."

When David and Doug went back into the house, Asa Ewing was busy on his helmet complink, moving Delta Company into position and coordinating with the other companies that were to turn their attention to the Park. David put on his own helmet so he could follow the discussion. As needed, he transmitted on his noncom circuit to the squad leaders in his platoon. For a few minutes the need to concentrate on two overlapping conversations took all his attention. The snap back from the light society of the dinner table to full military responsibility shut out the civilians completely.

They seemed to sense that. Doug escorted the others back toward the door leading down to the cellar. "Until we see how this goes, you'd better play it safe," he told them.

"You're not going back out there, are you?" Elena asked.

"The job's not finished. I can't quit yet."

"You've done more than anyone could decently ask," Elena insisted.

"I haven't done more than *I* can ask," he told her softly.

After Elena and the others headed down the steps, Doug went back to the two Marines and put on his own helmet. He glanced at a wine bottle on the dining room table. *I'd like one more drink,* he thought, but he refused to take it.

Approaching the Park with David's first squad, Doug felt curiously at ease. He was alert but no longer particularly nervous. Spencer was directly in front of Doug. The squad's two fire teams moved parallel to each other, the men all ten to fifteen feet apart.

I've got to be careful, Doug thought. *I can't be the weak link that hurts any of these men.*

Delta Company and I&R platoon were to cross the Park, north to south, using the main path joining Sam and Max, and establish fire points at primary intersections, leaving a fire team or squad at each. More importantly, they were the decoys being sent in to flush any Federation rabbits who might be hiding. Other units had ringed the greenbelt, ready to intercept any Federation soldiers who tried to flee, ready to move in to assist—or rescue—the men crossing the center of the woods.

Watch yer buns now, Alfie lad, he told himself as he took the point into the forest. *You haven't got yer last convalescent leave yet. Don't go earning another.* He kept his mouth shut. There was enough to concentrate on without useless chat, and even Alfie Edwards knew when to stand mum. He walked slowly into the wood, looking around constantly, using the infrared and sound detectors in his helmet as well as the full head-up display on his visor. Integrating it all was second nature. He never even thought of the complexity. His rifle was a needler, able to spray two thousand high-velocity darts a minute. The darts, each three-quarters of an inch long, could clear quite a swathe, shredding everything in their path until there was nothing left out to a hundred yards.

It had taken Alfie five years to earn the privilege of carrying a needler. No matter what the sergeant or his mates said about Alfie's jokes and carrying on, he knew that he was secure as long as he continued to carry the needler for his fire team.

Occasionally, Spencer passed instructions on the squad frequency. A couple of times, Doug Weintraub provided a detail of information on the terrain they were approaching. Doug's voice was loud on the channel; he hadn't had the proper practice at this sort of drill. The microphones in the helmets would pick up even the softest whisper.

"Off to the right, just a few steps ahead, there's a clearing," Doug said now. "About twenty-five feet from this path, with thick brambles between. There's a smaller path, a hundred feet on yet, that curves around and back to it."

At the front of the line, Alfie whispered a soft "Roger," to show that he had heard and understood.

Bloody fine place for an ambush, Alfie thought, and he moved the muzzle of his needler in that direction, ready for an ambush if it should come.

It did.

Prepared for the possibility, almost anticipating the instant when it came, Alfie was on his way down as the first shots sounded, even before the scattering of red blips appeared on his visor display. He shouted a warning over the squad frequency and opened up with his needler before he hit the ground. Alfie fired in short bursts, clearing a way through the trees and vines, knowing that even in the first seconds some of his needles would reach the enemy positions, though none of the red blips disappeared as quickly as he might have hoped.

Farther back along the path, Doug didn't get his rifle into play nearly as soon as the Marines did. He dropped to the ground sprightly enough, but while the Marines hit the ground already moving into firing positions, it was two separate motions for Doug. And even though his rifle was an autoloader, it wasn't fully automatic like the Marine weapons. He had to squeeze the trigger for each shot.

There wasn't time to get many shots off. One by one, the red blips disappeared from his visor, and as the last one vanished, Spencer whistled softly over the squad frequency and the Marines stopped shooting.

"Tory, take your team in and make sure they're all accounted for," David ordered. "We had seven blips. I want seven bodies, hot or cold."

Tory Kepner and two others got up and trotted toward the connecting path that led back to the clearing. They hadn't quite reached the intersection when there was an explosion just in front of them, and more shooting started as another lot of red blips appeared—this group farther south along the main path.

"We're in for it now," a voice on the squad frequency said. Doug didn't have any idea whose voice it was.

This firefight went as quickly as the first. It ended when another squad of the I&R platoon shot off a volley of grenades that dropped behind and among the red blips, erasing them.

"Hugo, move up past us, with third and fourth squads," David ordered tightly. "Lieutenant Ewing, we need help. I've got casualties."

Doug realized that he had been holding his breath and let it out. He scarcely had finished that thought when David Spencer crawled over to him.

"How do you feel?" David asked. "You in much pain?"

Feel? Pain? Doug stared at his new friend, not comprehending. It took forever before he managed to ask, "What do you mean?" The dreamy, half-conscious slur in his voice shocked him. *I've been hit!* The shock he felt was more surprise than anything else. He didn't feel any pain. He didn't feel anything at all, other than surprise.

"Just let me take care of things," David said, opening Doug's visor. David pulled two med patches from his belt pouch and slapped them on Doug's neck. Then he stuck him with an injector of nanoscrubbers.

I wish I'd had that last drink, Doug thought. *I don't want to die thirsty.* He was only vaguely aware of what David was doing. He scarcely noticed at all as other Marines ran past, jumping over them when necessary, moving deeper into the Park.

And then he slipped into a dream.

David checked Doug's vital signs again. They were weak, but quickly stabilized as the drugs and molecular machines went to work. It was time to turn his attention to the others who had been hit. David was kneeling over Tory Kepner, who had already been given first aid, when Asa Ewing arrived and knelt beside him.

"How bad?" Ewing asked.

"I've got four men injured," David said. "So far, it looks like they'll all pull through if we get them up to *Victoria* in a hurry. One of the wounded is Weintraub."

Ewing whistled. "What's *his* condition?"

"I think his spinal cord's been damaged, maybe severed. He didn't even know he'd been hit."

"That's going to boil some blood," Ewing said softly.

"I know. I was supposed to take special care of him. But he'll be okay. Tory here is in worse shape. He took about a pound of shrapnel."

"We'll carry the wounded around to that clearing the first ambush came from. Medevac will pick them up there. The shuttle's already moving into position. Any wounded in your other squads?"

David had to call the other squad leaders before he could relay the negative to Ewing. "But first squad is gone," David said. "Besides me, there are only two men who weren't hit."

"Turn your platoon over to your number two, Spencer, and I'll rotate them to the rear of Delta," Ewing said. "Take your whole squad up to *Victoria*. We'll finish this go."

"I'll send the others, but I can still run my platoon," David said.

"Forget that nonsense," Ewing said sharply. "Look at your own vitals, man. You're too stressed out to be effective. You'd be like an ox dancing on glass."

David was about to click over to another frequency to appeal the decision to Captain McAuliffe when the captain came on line.

"It was my order, Spencer," McAuliffe said. "Get your men up to *Victoria*. As soon as this patrol is over, I'm pulling the whole platoon. You lads have had the brunt of everything since we landed. You all need a couple of days."

David opened his mouth to argue, but the fight drained out of him then, without warning. "Aye, Captain. Going up."

There *were* seven bodies in the clearing. David counted them for himself, twice, while he waited for the medevac shuttle to lower the first litter basket. A voice from Delta Company passed along the news that there were four more Federation bodies farther along the main path, where the second ambush had come from—four bodies and one badly wounded soldier. He would make the ride up to *Victoria* with the other wounded.

"Bang up job, huh, Sarge?" Alfie asked when Spencer knelt to check on him. "That makes it two convalescent leaves you owe me." The first had been earned as a result of a work accident on Devereaux.

"Anything to get out of an honest day's work," David said lightly. "I'm surprised at you, Alfie. I thought you were turning into a real Marine."

Alfie laughed, but with some difficulty. Despite the pressure bandages across his chest and stomach, and the med patches and all, he could still feel pain, if not so much that he couldn't think of anything else.

"We don't get out of here soon," Alfie said after a moment, "I'll be able to retire off convalescent leaves. That'd fix you up right enough."

"Dream on, laddie," David said, smiling behind his visor. "Dream on."

Part 6

24

Admiral Truscott appeared totally relaxed, as fully at
ease as Ian had ever seen him. They were alone, sitting at
the flatscreen chart table in the admiral's day cabin. Truscott was in his bathrobe, tracking the progress of the mission to clear the greenbelt between Buchanan's two towns.
A speaker provided a soundtrack of the frequencies being
used by the Marines in the woods. Each time a skirmish
occurred, Truscott would close his eyes for a moment. The
view available on the flatscreen was incomplete because of
the trees and the darkness. Infrared could tell him only so
much. An occasional glimpse at the map of the forest to
locate each new group of red blips, to see where the larger
numbers of green blips were positioned, was sufficient to
fuel Truscott's imagination. That gave him a better picture
of the action.

"It still comes down to basics," he whispered at one
point. "Strip away all the technology, and what those men
down there are doing is no different from the first fighting
humans did, tens of thousands of years ago, when the warriors of one tribe went out to bash in the heads of the
warriors of the next tribe with crude axes and clubs."

"Does it ever make you wonder whether we've learned
anything at all?" Ian asked.

"We've learned how to do the job more efficiently.
Mind, I've never been sure if that's progress. Perhaps not,

in the greater sense. I can make the argument either way. The need, real or imagined, for one group of humans to protect itself from another has also led to the development of most of the major innovations that have made our civilization what it is today." He made an airy gesture with one hand, then shook his head.

"Everything turns into fodder for people like you and me, Ian. Example. Ever since we started moving into space, people have talked about how the human diaspora would make major war impossible. At the same time, we created ships like *Sheffield* and *Victoria*, and weapons that we could scarcely have imagined before the diaspora—weapons no one could authoritatively say would ever be needed, or practical. It looks as if the human animal will find a way to fight no matter the obstacles. I've become quite willing to accept the argument that it's hardwired into our genes."

Ian had heard the admiral's lectures on the subject on other occasions. One of the canned talks that Truscott dusted off for his occasional public appearances dealt with the seeming contradictions implicit in the Commonwealth's oft-stated need to prepare for a war that might never come, that might not even be feasible. The Federation's long-standing claims of sovereignty over all human worlds had served many generations of Commonwealth military leaders with every argument they needed to build and maintain the Combined Space Forces and layers of planetary defense systems.

"And you really believe this engagement will turn into something more than it is now?" Ian asked.

"I've a feeling about it, Ian." Truscott held up a hand as a burst of activity sounded on the Marine command channel. Another group of Federation soldiers had been flushed. This fight went as the others had. The enemy had a brief initial advantage, switching on their helmets only as they sprang their ambush, but they quickly lost that advantage, and the engagement.

"We're taking too many casualties," Truscott said afterward. "But unless we can come up with a better way to detect them before they switch on, I don't know of any way to avoid it, other than burning out whole patches like that greenbelt, and we can't do that."

"It could be worse, sir," Ian said. "We could have more killed and fewer wounded. Between field skins and nano-scrubbers, we're saving almost all our people. The Feddies don't seem to have anything to compare."

"Field skins, superior helmet armor, battledress that minimizes penetration, nanoscrubbers that isolate damage and minimize shock and bleeding." Truscott could list factors all night. If a Commonwealth Marine could be kept alive long enough to reach a trauma tube, he was virtually certain to survive, and recover . . . and more Commonwealth casualties made it that far.

"But we've never seen just how far ahead of the Federation we are in this area before," Ian pressed. Technicians were examining every bit of evidence the Marines had managed to collect on the surface—weapons, uniforms, and most importantly, two dozen Federation battle helmets.

"If the situation is general and not just limited to a single battalion sent to occupy a backwoods colony world," Truscott said. "We don't dare accept what we find here as typical. The troops might be a second-rate unit with obsolete equipment. We may find completely different conditions when their reinforcements arrive. Those will likely be the best units the Federation can send our way on short notice."

"How soon do you think?" Ian asked.

Truscott shook his head. "I haven't a clue, Ian, and that's infinitely more worrisome than if I knew exactly when they would show up." He started to add something else, but there was a knock on the door.

"Come in." Truscott turned as Prince William came in.

"Excuse me, Admiral. I just heard that one of the casualties tonight was Doug Weintraub, the member of the planetary commission."

Truscott frowned, then nodded. "Rather a serious injury from the report I heard, but he'll recover. By now, he should be in a trauma tube over on *Victoria*."

"While he's aboard, I'd like a chance to meet with him, if possible," the prince said. "If I could hitch a ride over there before he returns to the surface?"

"No need to thumb a lift," Truscott said. "Take my shuttle. We'll find out how soon he'll be ready for visitors. Ian, you'll see to the details?"

"Of course, sir."

"And perhaps you'd be good enough to escort His Highness," Truscott continued.

"Certainly. I'll put through a call to the chief medical officer now to see how soon Weintraub will be, ah, available."

Prince William left as soon as Ian completed the arrangements. They would leave for *Victoria* just before 0530 hours.

"You might as well turn in as well, Ian," the admiral said when they were alone again. "If you're going to be up and about that early."

Ian chuckled. "Not so much earlier than usual, sir. But, still, I think I will take you up on that offer—if you're certain you won't be wanting me for anything else tonight."

"No, go ahead, go ahead," Truscott said. "I'll be retiring myself shortly. I've just been waiting for *Khyber* to make its first transit." He switched the display on the chart table to show the scout ship's position, course, and speed.

"Should be within the next few minutes," Ian observed. "I can wait, sir. Ten minutes more or less won't affect me."

Truscott laughed. "No, go on with you. I'm not so feeble that I can't tuck myself in."

"Of course not, sir. Good night."

"Good night, Ian." Truscott turned his attention back to the display on his table and didn't hear Ian gently close the door on his way out.

"Miles, I hope you help me pull this off," Truscott whispered, staring at the almost imperceptible movement of the blip representing *Khyber* on the screen. "We're going to need all the reinforcements Long John can scrape together before this thing's over. I feel it in my bones."

Feeling unusually self-conscious about talking to himself, Truscott got up to get himself a fresh cup of tea. He brought it back to the table and stood for several minutes, sipping absentmindedly while his eyes remained fixed on the schematic of Buchanan's system, and *Khyber*.

What's the balance point? he asked himself. *How do I maximize my forces if there are no reinforcements from Buckingham? I certainly can't expect a Federation commander to deploy according to our book standards or convenience.*

"Hell," he muttered. "I've thrown the book out myself coming into Buchanan. It's worse than useless." He growled softly.

If I put my frigates out far enough to intercept an enemy coming in at what the book considers a standard entry vector and distance, I could end up with those ships completely out of range, too far away to take any hand in the battle. But if I keep everything in close, we could be forced into an engagement with no more warning than that Cutter class had.

Finally, Truscott set his cup on the edge of the chart table and leaned forward to watch the last moments of *Khyber* before she entered Q-space. There was nothing dramatic. *Khyber*'s blip simply disappeared from the screen when its Nilssen generators slid it into Q-space.

"That's that, then," Truscott murmured. "Time I was off to bed." But he called the duty flag operations officer first.

"Anything going on I should know about?"

"Operations continuing in that greenbelt, sir. There's been very little activity the last half hour."

"What about casualty totals?"

"We've had three killed and twenty-seven wounded, sir. Federation losses are forty-six killed and nine wounded. Four others were captured after being disabled by stun grenades."

"Thank you," Truscott said before he broke the link. He regained the chart of the greenbelt on his display screen, they keyed in an overlay to show the areas that had been cleared by the Marines.

"Nearly ninety percent secure." He nodded with satisfaction, and then frowned suddenly. "How could they put nearly ten percent of their entire force in a place like that?"

He tapped his fingers against the edge of the table several times. *Was it simply that they had no time to move to better terrain?* That was possible, but it seemed too much to hope for, far too much to *count* on.

Or is that figure so much less than ten percent? Late at night, the latter possibility seemed much more likely. Truscott was shaking his head gently when he finally went into the other room to sleep.

25

Doug Weintraub couldn't recall ever feeling even remotely like he felt lying on his side on a path in the Park. The peculiarity of his sensations was so striking that he could hardly think about anything else. The realization that he had been seriously wounded came slowly, and only as a curious abstraction. He felt remarkably calm, dreamy, almost buoyant enough to float away. There was no pain, no hint of discomfort. Only gradually did he become aware of the intense concern he had heard in David Spencer's voice. More than anything, that was what convinced Doug that he was indeed gravely injured.

Am I going to die? But Doug found it hard to concentrate, even on that possibility. It was almost as if his mind had abdicated any responsibility for, or interest in, his future. Other people were taking care of him. His future was, somehow, *their* worry now. David had seen to his injuries and administered first aid. Another man, a field medical orderly, came along and did more. Doug felt no discomfort even from being rolled over and strapped to a framework of some kind.

"We'll get you right up to the hospital, mate," the second man said. "Not to worry. You'll be all right."

Doug couldn't even summon up a reaction to that. He was still trying to puzzle his way through the words when the anaesthetic finally knocked him out.

His return to consciousness was marked first by an awareness of bright lights. The glare continued even after he closed his eyes again. Bright spots floated across his awareness. He opened his eyes again, just to slits. When he could finally distinguish objects, Doug noted that the lights were beyond a transparent curved panel.

A trauma tube. That impressed itself slowly on Doug's mind. He tried moving, but nothing would budge, not even his head. Only his eyes. He could open or close his eyes; he could look a little from side to side, and up and down. The limited range of movement showed him nothing new.

I'm alive. I'll survive. I'll recover. Those thoughts were separate, cumulative, spread over a timeless time. Eventually, Doug reached his memories of the patrol through the Park, to the burst of fire that had marked the first ambush. There was an immeasurable lacuna to his memories beyond that instant, marked only by dreamlike images that refused to come into focus or identify themselves. He could not recall being hit, or anything about the second ambush.

Seriously wounded. No pain. No movement. In time, or outside it, those data points came together for Doug: a spinal injury. *I could be in this tube for weeks,* he thought. And, somewhat later: *I wonder how much better this tube is than ours?* The newest trauma tube on Buchanan was twenty-five years old.

Doug blinked. He could still do that, if little more. He saw movement at the edge of his field of vision, outside the trauma tube, a moving blur of white and pale blue. He tried to find some way to attract the person's attention, but no exercise of will permitted him to move anything more than his eyes and eyelids. But the transparent panel above him slid away and a face looked down.

"Good morning, Mr. Weintraub. I'm Ahmed Nassir, naval surgeon. Don't try to talk yet. It will be a few minutes before you can." Nassir smiled and reached in to touch

Doug's arm. Doug didn't feel it. "I'll do what I can to anticipate the obvious questions. That will save us a little time. By the time we get through those, you should be able to ask any that I miss." Nassir leaned closer. "I just want a quick look at your eyes now." He produced a small, narrow-beam torch and shined it briefly into each of Doug's eyes, then nodded.

"You're doing quite well," Nassir assured Doug with a wider smile than before. "Your spinal cord was severed, but it was a clean cut, and we had you in the tube in plenty of time to avoid complications. The readouts tell me that the mending process is proceeding precisely on schedule. There've been no flags at all. We should be ready to do follow-up tests in about forty-five minutes, and if those tests come out as I expect them to, we'll release you from the tube shortly after that. There will be no permanent ill effects. In fact, you ought to feel better than you did before you were wounded. The tube is correcting nutritional deficits as well."

Doug realized that his mouth felt dry. He worked his tongue around, trying to tease some moisture into evidence. It was a moment before he realized that he could finally move more than his eyes.

"What time is it?" His voice was hoarse and the words didn't come out easily. They were separate sounds, scarcely coherent. "Dry."

"Yes, of course," Nassir said. "We'll get you a touch of water, straightaway." He turned away. Doug caught a glimpse of part of a gesture. "As to the time, it's, ah, a few minutes before five in the morning, local time."

A nurse came over with a container of liquid and a long, flexible tube.

"We need to take it easy with the liquids at first," the doctor said while the nurse put the tube in Doug's mouth and gave the container a meager squeeze. "Just until you're out of the tube and in the recovery ward. Then, if you want, you can drink until your kidneys float out the door.''

Doug swallowed greedily, astonished at how wonderful such a scant drop of water could taste. He sucked at the tube. The nurse smiled and gave the bottle another squeeze. This time, Doug let the water sit in his mouth for a instant before he swallowed . . . and then sighed with delight.

''More?'' he asked with a hopeful look up at the nurse. His voice sounded more nearly normal now.

''Just a little,'' Nassir said, and the nurse complied.

''There, that should hold you for a time,'' the doctor said when the tube was removed.

''How many others were brought up with me?'' Doug asked. His voice was stronger now that his mouth wasn't desert-dry.

''Quite a few, I'm afraid,'' Nassir said. ''They even sent up a few who hadn't been wounded. None of our lads were killed in that skirmish though.''

That skirmish. Doug noted the qualifier but didn't pursue it. Bad news came too soon in any case.

''Sergeant Spencer?'' he asked.

Nassir smiled. ''Our head nurse had to chase him and two of his lads out an hour or so ago. They were being bloody nuisances, so concerned about you and their other mates.''

Doug closed his eyes for a moment to enjoy the thought of Spencer fussing over his men like a mother hen.

''I hope you'll let them back in to see me,'' Doug said when he opened his eyes again.

''I imagine we can arrange something,'' Nassir said. ''If I can sneak them past our head nurse.''

26

It had taken a direct order from the senior nurse on duty to get David Spencer and his two uninjured men, Jacky White and Sean Seidman, out from underfoot. "Get yourselves back to the troop bays," the nurse, a lieutenant commander, told them, displaying a formal fierceness that was more act than actuality. "You obviously need time for personal hygiene, not to mention hot food and sleep. When we want useless spectators, we'll sell tickets."

David led his men away, reluctantly. "We might as well take advantage of the facilities," he told the others. "Get yourselves cleaned up and we'll see what sort of meal we can scare up."

"This time of night?" Jacky asked. "You going to wake the cook and offer him a tip?"

David managed a smile. "Don't go trodding on Alfie's turf, lad. He'll be back soon enough. No, if there's no one on duty in the troop mess, I'll find someone in the sergeants' mess. Maybe even in officers' country. There's food to be had, and we've got a direct order to get ourselves fed." David knew he could always pop for a meal out of the machines in one of the snack bars . . . but he didn't expect it would come to that. There was always a hot meal to be found aboard *Victoria*, if you knew where to look. And David did.

"How long do you think we'll have before we go back

down?'' Sean asked, his voice quiet as it always was. *'I'll bet he even shouts in a whisper,'* Alfie had quipped. Half of the men in the platoon were already calling Seidman ''Whispers.''

''Not long enough by half,'' David said. ''Unless the rest of our blokes manage to mop up all of the Feddies first.''

''You don't think they will?'' Jacky asked—too quickly.

''My mother didn't raise any optimists,'' David said. '' 'Always look for the clouds,' she told me. 'That way all your surprises will be silver linings.' We're doing well enough, I expect, but it'll be a bloody long road if we have to dig out every Feddie squad the way we did those to-night.''

''We got off lucky tonight,'' Jacky said. ''That could have been even worse than the first ambush.''

''We were lucky,'' David agreed. ''But part of that luck is made by good men honed by first-rate training, protected by the best gear available. Think of those Feddies. Look at the ratio of killed to wounded. I'd hate to be one of their lot.''

With two-thirds of her Marines dirtside, *Victoria*'s troop section seemed even emptier than it had during the trip from Devereaux to Buckingham. And in the early hours of the morning, nearly all of the Marines who *were* still aboard were asleep, adding to the sense of emptiness. David took his time showering and changing to a fresh uniform. Not having on the field skin was a holiday in itself. For all the good a field skin did in the field, he always had a sense of confinement wearing one, and a need to scratch all over when he took it off. David's exhaustion retreated a little with the shower and clean clothing. He was still tired— sleeping the clock around twice would scarcely cure that— but hunger was more immediate. Before he left his cabin, David called the sergeants' mess.

"This is Sergeant Spencer, First Battalion. Can you fix up three hungry men?" he asked the mess steward who answered the complink.

The steward grinned and nodded. "Three or thirty, Sergeant?"

"We may eat like thirty," David said. "We've had a busy couple of days."

"Whenever you get here," the steward said.

Jacky and Sean were almost ready when David got to the troop bay. Sean was still dressing. Jacky was dressed, except for his boots, and lying on his bunk. But he got up as soon as he saw Spencer.

"Thought you'd skipped out and forgot us," Jacky said.

"Had to make the arrangements, lad," David said. "I figured that was easier than doing a forced march from mess hall to mess hall."

"Got the Christmas goose waiting for us, have they?" Jacky asked.

"One wiseacre in a squad is more than enough," David said with a smile. "We've got a hot feed coming up. Count yourself lucky and let it be."

"Admiral's table?" Sean asked with a nervous grin at Jacky.

"I give up!" David threw both hands up. "When we get back to the medical department, I'm going to ask for a vaccine. This must be contagious."

The others started laughing. "Get that under control before we get out in the passage," David told them. "Don't want to wake the rest of the regiment, the ones who don't know there's a war on yet." It took quite an exercise of willpower for David to keep from joining in the laughter.

The duty cooks and mess stewards were eating a meal of their own when David and his men arrived. It wasn't quite time for the staff to start preparing breakfast for the units of the regiment that were still aboard *Victoria*. The steward David had spoken to over the complink got up from the table.

"You're in luck, mates," he said. "You got here in time to share *our* fare." It was an article of faith among serving Marines that the mess staff aboard ship ate better than anyone else in the CSF.

"You've been down below, then?" one of the other stewards asked.

David nodded. Jacky said, "Been down? We've been most of the whole bleedin' show, mate. I&R platoon, H&S Company, First Battalion."

The curious steward whistled. "We been listening to the complink traffic, mates. Sit yourselves down. We'll bring your tucker out. You blokes done enough work."

"Thanks," David said, sitting at the table next to the cooks and stewards.

"A lot of your men hurt?" one of the cooks asked.

"Too many," Sean said when the sergeant showed no inclination to answer. "One killed and the rest of our squad in hospital, all but the three of us. The whole platoon's been hit hard. They're being brought up for a breather."

"But we've taken full payment," Jacky said grimly.

"Not full yet," David said, his voice little more than a whisper. "Won't be full payment until we've cleaned Buchanan of Feddies."

Three stewards marched out from behind the serving line with trays heaped with food. A fourth steward wheeled the tea cart over from the sergeant majors' table in the corner.

"You want more of anything, just give a shout," one of the stewards said. "On the house, so to speak."

David looked at the tray in front of him and grinned. "We eat any more than this, you'll have to call the medical orderlies. We'll explode."

"That's okay," the steward said. "It's time for us to get

back to work anyhow, so we'll be out of the way." His mates burst out laughing.

A half hour later, there was little food left on any of the trays. David and his companions had declined refills, except for tea, coffee, and juice. With his stomach full, David felt too lethargic even to push back from the table. He continued to pick at the serving of chips on his plate, even though they had long since gone cold.

"Three o' these a day and soon enough we couldn't even get into field skins," Jacky said. He had given up trying to finish the food on his tray.

"It's a good job we've got a day or two before we go back down," David said. "We wouldn't be able to move worth a damn today."

Sean was still eating. Almost as short and thin as Jacky, Sean was drawing stares from his companions. Once, Jacky even leaned to the side to make sure that Sean hadn't dumped a portion of his food on the deck.

"Where the bleedin' hell you puttin' all that chow?" Jacky asked finally. "It ain't normal."

"When I'm hungry, I eat," Sean said.

"We get back to Buckingham, we're going to enter you in the eating contests," Jacky said. "You'll make the whole squad rich. Your size, we'll get good odds and clean up."

"First, we've got to get back to Buckingham." Sean set his fork on the tray and leaned back. His appetite was, quite obviously, gone.

"You all right, lad?" David asked, very softly.

"I don't know, Sarge," Sean said. "I really don't know." He stared at Jacky for an instant, then looked back to Spencer. "I was just getting over being scared."

"We all get scared," Jacky said, before David could say the same thing. "Be unnatural not to get scared with all that hell goin' on."

"He's right," David said. "I've been in the RM for fifteen years, and I still get scared, every time we go into combat, whether it's Feddies or half-armed farmers."

"How do you deal with it?" Sean asked. "Down there, I was sure I was going to freeze up, almost any second."

"But you didn't" David said. "That's what's important. Deal with it? I don't know that there's anything anyone can tell you about that. We all have to find that inside ourselves."

"I can tell you one thing," Jacky said, and he waited until Sean turned his eyes toward him before he continued. "That fear, that's why we spend so bleedin' much time trainin'. The RM wants to make sure that the drill is etched in our heads so deep that we can do what we're supposed to do even when we're too scared pissless to think it out."

David stared at Jacky through that speech. "Instead of going back to civie street, Jacky, you should be thinking about a career in the RM."

Jacky shook his head and wouldn't look at David. "Not me. I'm too much a civilian at heart."

"Humor me, lad. Give it a thought. You do have the makings."

27

The crew of the admiral's gig was already aboard when Ian escorted Prince William to the hangar bay. The shuttle was housed well forward in *Sheffield*, only a short walk from flag country. This hangar was just large enough for the one boat.

"Morning, Your Highness, Commander Shrikes," Lieutenant Miko Balaski said when his passengers boarded the shuttle. Miko had been Admiral Truscott's pilot longer than Ian had been on staff. "We're ready to go as soon as you're strapped in. Sorry to rush you, but if we don't get out of here double quick, we'll have to wait until after the next launch and recovery of Spacehawks. That could hold us up for a half hour."

"Then, by all means, let's be off," Prince William said.

"We can see to the strapping in," Ian told the pilot. "Give us forty-five seconds and we'll be ready to go."

"As you say, sir." Balaski checked to make sure that the hangar crew had secured the hatch and retracted the ramp. Then he moved forward to the cockpit.

Ian gestured the prince to one of the plush seats. "I assume you remember the drill?"

"Quite," William replied. He dropped into the nearest seat and pulled out straps, connecting the harness with the ease of long familiarity.

Ian sat across from him and did his own buckling. He

was sure that it was less then forty-five seconds before he flipped an intercom switch and said, "All secure back here."

"We're on our way then," Balaski replied from the cockpit.

Ian sat back and looked out the porthole on the far side of the cabin. A large section of the hangar's outer bulkhead rolled out of the way, exposing the shuttle to open space. Two telescoping pistons moved the shuttle out of its hangar, clear of the ship, and the shuttle passengers lost *Sheffield*'s gravity. Ian adjusted his seat straps the final little bit to keep him securely in place.

With quick blasts of compressed gas, the shuttle was pushed farther away from *Sheffield*'s hull. The launching booms were retracted. The hangar door slid shut.

"On our own now, gentlemen," Balaski said over the intercom. "There'll be a short delay while we do our farewell dance."

"Our *what*?" the prince asked softly.

"Lieutenant Balaski fancies himself a comedian," Ian said. "He's talking about using attitude jets to get clear of the hull before he fires the main rockets."

"Is it just our pilot or has the slang changed that much since I served?" The shuttle was already moving, dropping below and falling back along *Sheffield*.

"I think it's mostly Balaski," Ian said. "He tries to find a different way to say it every time we go out. The admiral gets a kick out of it. Usually."

William laughed. "Yes, I can imagine that there would be times when such levity would be less than welcome."

Ian chuckled. "Now and then. If I get a chance, I try to give Miko a little warning. But when the admiral's in a mood, I don't always have a chance." The shuttle turned and pointed toward *Victoria*. There was a short pause before the shuttle's main rockets came on, initially at minimum power, building gradually for a short time, then cutting out as the shuttle rotated into the proper attitude for docking with the second ship.

Prince William pressed the intercom button. "Lieutenant Balaski, could you rotate us a little so we can see the surface?"

"Port or starboard, sir?" Miko asked.

"Er, port, if you would." The words were hardly out of his mouth before the shuttle started to rotate. Miko stopped it at precisely the right moment to give the prince a clear view of the settled area of Buchanan, not that anything was really visible of those settlements.

"The clear weather is ending," Ian said. There were thin clouds showing against the first light of morning, and a glance to the west, out over the shore and ocean, showed heavier clouds moving into the area. "The Marines might get wet before the day's done."

"Shouldn't make all that much difference," William said. "I've tested the field skins they use." He stopped talking when he saw the look of surprise on Ian's face. "It's not all affairs of state and fancy dress balls, you know. Between the skins and their helmets, it wouldn't much matter if the Marines had to operate underwater."

"Until one of them raised his visor to scratch," Ian suggested, and the prince laughed.

"Does the admiral insist on comedians for all his staff positions?"

"He blames the first lord of the Admiralty for that," Ian said, keeping a straight face. "He swears that Sir John sends him nothing but misfits and comedians. But have a guess who gave everyone on staff bath talc laced with itching powder last Boxing Day."

This time, the prince fetched up against his seat straps, he laughed so hard. "You did it again. You set me up for that one."

"I beg to differ," Ian said, struggling to keep from laughing himself. "You were the one who asked about comedians."

Prince William took a deep breath, then another, fighting the urge to start laughing again. "I really must find a way to show my, ah, appreciation, Shrikes. Perhaps I should ask my brother to appoint you his naval attaché. He could use a wit like yours around the palace."

"Well, half a wit is better than none," Ian said, and that was too much. This time he couldn't hold back his own laughter. "I'm sorry," he said when he could talk coherently again. "It must be your fault though. I don't get like this most times. My wife says I have no sense of humor at all."

"Perhaps you should spend more time at home," William suggested.

That was enough to sober Ian's mood. "She says that too." He shrugged. "But you know how it is for a serving officer. I've been home more than usual since I became Admiral Truscott's aide, but even so, there have been inspection trips and so forth. And now this."

"Ah, yes," William said. "I do know what it's like. At times, duty is more a shackle than a badge."

Victoria had been briefed to expect them. Captain Reya Naughton came to the shuttle bay to welcome Prince William aboard, omitting the full court honors they would have been forced to suffer through if he had been making an official visit as a member of the Privy Council.

"Can I offer you breakfast, sir?" Captain Naughton asked after Ian performed the introductions.

"No, thank you very much, Captain," William said. "We ate before leaving *Sheffield*. We're just here to visit a patient in your casualty ward."

"The local man?"

"Doug Weintraub, a member of Buchanan's Planetary Commission," the prince said, emphasizing the title. "Not to mention being a genuine hero for his deeds in defense of his homeland."

"As you say, sir," Captain Naughton said, needing an instant to cover her irritation at being corrected.

"Ah, Captain," Ian said, recognizing that it was time for him to act as a buffer. "We really don't want to put you to any trouble. If you could have someone escort us to the Marine casualty ward, we'll be out of your way as quickly as possible."

The look Captain Naughton gave Ian wasn't quite relief, but Ian decided that it would do.

Dr. Ahmed Nassir greeted them when they reached *Victoria*'s hospital. "Mr. Weintraub has just been moved from a trauma tube to a recovery bed. The nurses are getting him situated now. A matter of a few minutes?"

"Of course, Doctor," William said. "We have no desire to interfere with Mr. Weintraub's comfort or treatment. You've been quite occupied, I take it?"

"Quite," Nassir said. "But we're on top of it all, sir. Once we get a patient into a trauma tube alive, he stays that way."

William nodded affably. "No one has any doubts about the treatment patients receive in a naval medical facility, Doctor. You do know that His Majesty has always insisted that his personal physician be a naval surgeon?"

"I did not know that, sir," Nassir replied, his voice a trifle softer, "but I am pleased to hear it."

"If we have time after our chat with Mr. Weintraub, I'd like the opportunity to speak with some of the Marines you've treated after the night's action—with your permission."

"Certainly, sir."

"I'll do my best to avoid getting in the way, Doctor. If I do, you and your staff should feel free to tell me to get my bloody arse out of the way."

Nassir blinked several times, clearly put off stride by the mild vulgarity.

"He means that, Doctor," Ian put in. "We're here completely at your sufferance. And *that* is a direct quote from Admiral Truscott."

"I'm certain we can accommodate you, sir," Nassir said, nodding to the prince. "Mr. Weintraub should be settled now. If you'll come with me?"

Doug Weintraub was busy scratching at areas he had been unable to reach in the trauma tube. The other wounded Marines of Spencer's first squad were all watching him, laughing and making comments, instead of providing the distractions that might have eased the need to scratch. The arrival of visitors stopped the laughter, and the new attraction allowed Doug to stop scratching, for a moment at least. Dr. Nassir was the only one of the three men that the patients recognized.

"Mr. Weintraub, this is His Highness, Prince William Albert, Duke of Haven," the doctor said, introducing him formally. "And Commander Ian Shrikes, aide to Admiral Truscott, the task force commander. Gentlemen, Mr. Doug Weintraub of Buchanan." Doug pushed himself up a little higher against his pillows.

"Thank you, Doctor," William said. "We'll do fine now. Don't let us keep you from your work."

"I'm available if you need me." Nassir nodded to the prince and left.

"Mr. Weintraub, I've been waiting for a chance to meet you since I first began to hear of your exploits," William said. "I regret that it has to be under these circumstances."

"You can't possibly regret it more than I do," Doug

said, earning a quickly stifled laugh from the Marines around him.

The prince chuckled as well and glanced at Ian.

"Not my fault at all," Ian said quickly.

"Fault?" Doug asked.

"Nothing at all," William said, smiling as broadly as he could. "Commander Shrikes has contrived to surround me with comedians, I think. It has put me quite off my pace. I apologize, sir."

"I'm still not sure I have any idea what's going on," Doug said. "But then, I've never been around royalty. I have no idea what the proper etiquette is."

"Etiquette is best reserved for proper stuffy formal occasions," William said. "Patients in hospitals never have to worry about it. Sometimes I envy that freedom."

"He's a right bloke, ain't he?" one of the Marines whispered. Ian took a quick glance but couldn't decide who had said it. Prince William overheard the comment though.

"Thank you," he said, smiling at the group of Marines on that side. "I take that as high praise from men such as yourselves."

"They're all good men," Doug said. "Wasn't for them, I might not have made it tonight."

"I meant what I said," William assured him. "Just because my father was king of the Second Commonwealth doesn't mean I have to be six kinds of bastard."

"You're egging them on now," Ian told the prince in a stage whisper when the Marines started laughing again.

"It's contagious, I told you," William reminded Ian. "And I'm afraid we're giving Mr. Weintraub the wrong impression."

"I haven't the faintest idea what to make of you," Doug said, not hiding his bewilderment. "It makes me wonder if they haven't stuck me in Bedlam instead of a casualty ward."

"A little levity can work wonders," the prince said. "It's just hard to measure it out properly at times." He shook his head. "And I fear we're starting out on the wrong foot."

"It might help to have a seat," Ian suggested. He moved a chair around for William, then hooked a chair for himself.

"Right, that saves the stiff necks," William said. Then he shook his head. "There I go again. I'd best start from scratch." When that elicited more laughs, he looked genuinely bewildered. He chose to ignore the response.

"There were a couple of reasons for this visit," William said, taking a deep breath to settle himself. "One is purely personal and unofficial, the other rather more official. As to the first, I simply wanted to meet you. Any man who does as much for his homeland as you have is a man worthy of all the respect in the universe. To have the daring and foresight to send off that message rocket the way you did was an achievement by itself, one that will have such far-reaching consequences that we can scarcely imagine them at present. But that was merely your starting point and not your grand finale. You are indeed a hero, sir, and a patriot in all of the best senses."

Doug needed a moment to find his voice. The prince had spoken levelly, leaving Doug no doubt about his sincerity. "Thank you," he said, barely in a whisper. "But I can't say that there was any great heroism in it. Buchanan is my home. Doing what I could to protect it was really nothing more than some primal instinct. Had I thought before I acted, I doubt that I would have done any of it."

"That doesn't lessen the value of the act, but I won't press the matter," William said.

"Uh, you said there was also an *official* reason for your visit?" Doug prompted.

"Ah, yes," William said. "I'm here to make an offer to you, to the government of Buchanan, that is. An offer, not

a demand. I want you to be absolutely clear on that. I'm
not here to state a price for our assistance, or to pressure
you into doing anything that you and your compatriots
don't honestly believe is in your own best interests. It might
even be better if you don't formally consider this offer until
the Federation has been completely suppressed or evicted.
The offer is for Buchanan to join the Second Commonwealth as a full member world, with all of the rights and
duties that implies. Membership in the Commonwealth is
only achieved through the unforced desire of the population
and government of a world. We make no claim of sovereignty after the fashion of the Federation. We're a voluntary
association of sovereign worlds, banding together for security and mutual benefit." He managed an embarrassed
smile. "Sorry if that sounds like memorized electioneer-
ing."

Doug stared at the prince for a moment before he spoke.
"We have little of value to offer."

"That never enters the equation," William said. "As a
member world, you would have access to those who can
help you develop your world as you see fit. The Commonwealth imposes no special burdens. It doesn't demand trib-
ute or taxes. By the strictures of our constitution, the
Commonwealth can levy no more than one-tenth of one
percent tariff based on the difference between cost of pro-
duction and the sale price of goods and services transported
between member worlds. But if you're looking for additional settlers, there is a moderately large pool of colonists
available—*at your discretion*. You would have easy access
to markets for whatever products or services you have to
offer. Somewhere, there is a market for virtually anything,
and there are merchant specialists who can come in to help
you develop your trade potential. Not all worlds are as ideally furnished for human residents as Buchanan."

"You realize, of course, that I'm but one member of our

planetary commission,'' Doug said. ''And for a step of this size, we would certainly defer to a referendum of the entire population. The commission is rarely called upon to make any decisions more important than the dates of our public festivals.''

''The method is entirely your choice,'' William said, ''and I neither expect, nor particularly desire, any reply now. If the commission prefers, you can even put off any consideration until after this fleet has gone home—or decide not to formally consider the offer at all.''

''You can believe him, mate,'' one of the marines said, his interruption catching everyone by surprise. Ian thought it was the same man who had made the earlier sotto voce comment, but he wasn't positive. ''I'd have never enlisted in the RM if they was using us to make slaves the way the Feddies do.''

Like the others, William turned to stare at the man. ''Sorry, sir,'' the Marine said.

''No need to be sorry, Marine,'' the prince told him. ''I feel as strongly about it as you do. What's your name, lad?''

''Edwards, sir, Private Alfie Edwards, H&S Company, First Battalion, Second Regiment. I didn't mean to interrupt, sir, really I didn't.''

''Maybe you should have made the speech instead of me, Edwards,'' William said. ''You sound more sincere.''

''*Speech,* sir? *Me,* sir?'' Alfie sounded nearly hysterical at the thought.

''Not to worry, lad. You did fine. You're a credit to the Royal Marines, and to all of us.''

''T-thank you, sir.'' Alfie's face was red. He looked ready to dive under his blankets for cover.

''You marked that man's name and unit?'' the prince asked Ian when they were back in the shuttle for the return to *Sheffield.* "Private Alfie Edwards, H&S, First of the Second?"

Ian nodded cautiously, waiting to hear what the prince had to say.

"Do you suppose the admiral would think I was far out of line if I wrote a personal letter of commendation for that man?"

"I don't think he would object at all," Ian said. "That man's the best advertisement for the CSF I've seen in ages."

28

Eleven Spacehawks of *Sheffield*'s fourth squadron, the six fighters of white flight, and the remaining five from red flight, nosed back into their slots after an uneventful four-hour mission. Ground operations had ended in the greenbelt between the two communities on Buchanan. There had been no call for fighter support on that, and the perimeter surrounding the settlements had remained quiet.

The pilots trudged back to their ready room following short after-mission discussions with their crew chiefs. The Spacehawks had seen considerable use during the past days, with little time for routine maintenance, and small problems were beginning to surface with some of the fighters. So far, the only problem Josef had encountered was in one of his radio frequencies, a light static that seemed to reduce the volume, but only on the single channel.

"If I boost the gain to compensate," he told Andy Mynott, "then the other frequencies threaten to blast me clean out of the cockpit."

"Leave your helmet with me, sir," Andy said. "Problem's most likely in that. I'll get Meckli to run the diagnostics and fix it up if it is the helmet. If it's not that, I'll start looking for gremlins in the bird."

On his way to the ready room, Josef reached up to touch the spot behind his left ear where the helmet plugged into his neural enhancer. The permanently depilated circle around the plug felt cold. Josef had thought of another possible explanation for the radio difficulty. The glitch might be in his implant. If it were, it would almost certainly mean getting a replacement—three hours in surgery, and twelve hours or more of tuning afterward. Josef had gone through two replacements in the years since he received his first implant at the beginning of flight training. It wasn't a pleasant procedure. A new implant meant hours of disorientation and malaise during the tuning process, as if the brain itself were being retrained.

"Something wrong?" Kate asked as they neared the ready room. That it took her so long to broach the subject reflected her own growing exhaustion and concerns with her fighter.

"Nothing major, I think." Josef mentioned the communications problem, but not his suspicion as to where the problem might lie.

"At least it's not your hydraulics again," she said— dully, not as a joke the way it would have been before Seb Inowi had his Spacehawk blown out of the sky.

The debriefing was short. Olive Bosworth seemed as lifeless as everyone else, stepping through the formalities. "Let's try to catch up on sleep," she said before she dismissed her pilots. "We're all getting too ragged to be very efficient."

The dull atmosphere continued into the squadron mess. It wasn't just the hours of flying. Morale had been deteriorating since Seb's loss.

"We need an excuse to cut loose and let everything out," Kate said after she and Josef had their food and were sitting at their usual table. "A chance to let go and get the energy levels back up."

"The only way you'd get a party organized now would be at gunpoint," Josef said.

"That's the problem. We're turning into a flock of zombies."

They ate in silence for several minutes before Josef said, "I wonder where *Khyber* was going in such a panic. They tore out-system as fast as that Cutter class did."

"They certainly weren't running *from* anything, so they must have been running *to* something," Kate said.

"Back to Buckingham?" Josef answered his own question with another. "It could hardly have been anywhere else, could it?"

"Something's up we don't know about," Kate said. "The admiral certainly can't be sending a 'mission accomplished' message yet. Not just a progress report either with *Khyber* zapping out that soon. But we haven't seen any Feddie ships coming in-system."

"Doesn't leave many real possibilities, does it?" Josef asked. Any distraction was welcome. This one seemed tailor-made. "Did an MR come in before *Khyber* left?"

"Not that I know of. I heard that a couple went *out* just before *Khyber* left."

"Can't be certain there wasn't one though," Josef decided. "Maybe *Khyber* picked one up out near its station."

"Truscott must have called for reinforcements." Kate dropped her fork onto her tray. It clattered noisily. "That's the only thing it could be. He wants more ships."

"To take care of the few Feddies on Buchanan?" Josef asked skeptically.

"No, to take care of the Feddies that Cutter class fetches back," Kate said. There was utter certainty in her voice. "There's no other possible explanation. The admiral figures we've got more grief coming and he wants to get help as quickly as possible."

29

Stasys Truscott found himself doing something he almost never did, whistling while he worked. He had been broken of *that* habit as an eighteen-year-old cadet in his first term at the Naval Academy. His surprise was so great that he stopped working for a moment. Then he chuckled and shook his head.

"I must be losing my mind," he whispered. Talking to himself was more habitual. He had spent a lifetime doing that. "You'd think we'd just won the whole bleeding war."

The news from the surface of Buchanan *was* good, but only in a limited, tactical fashion. The greenbelt between the towns had been secured. There were no Federation soldiers remaining within the Park or the two towns. From east of the river out past the spaceport on the west, Commonwealth Marines had a secure perimeter with dug-in fire points and remote sensors that would make it impossible for anything larger than a mouse to enter without being detected—and intercepted, if necessary.

But there was disquieting news as well. The actions that had taken place so far accounted for no more than ninety Federation soldiers, which left perhaps six hundred or more at liberty, *somewhere* on the world below.

"I suppose we can narrow that down considerably," Truscott mumbled. He zoomed the map of Buchanan on his chart table out to show the entire planet.

"It's inconceivable that they moved to either of the other continents, or to any of the large islands." He zoomed the map in to cover just the one continent, eliminating two-thirds of Buchanan's land area and 90 percent of its total surface area.

"Since they didn't use aircraft or motorized ground vehicles to disperse after we arrived, we can narrow the possibilities even more. Four days, no more than forty miles a day, even if they pushed themselves." That provided, Truscott thought, a healthy margin of error. Under the conditions of terrain and exposure, twenty-five miles a day would have been extraordinary. He made more adjustments on the map. A circle centered on the Park and with a radius of 150 miles appeared. To the west, much of that area was ocean.

"Little cover to the west," Truscott said, examining the topological features more closely. "We'd have spotted organized movement of any large groups. Perhaps even individuals." He shrugged and shook his head. "No good making assumptions that iffy." But the ocean could be eliminated. He made more adjustments. The circle became an ellipse, and the scale improved a little more.

"Today, we start looking for the rest of them." He brought up a notepad window at the corner of the map to start outlining orders.

Search patterns: shuttles and Spacehawks. The shuttles could conduct more refined detection operations because they could hover and operate at minimal speed. But they needed fighter protection. They would be sitting ducks otherwise. "Like that Spacehawk we lost," Truscott muttered. Finding enemy troops who were operating without electronics was a classic training problem—many of the colonial affairs that the Navy had been involved in were against irregulars who didn't possess advanced helmet technology.

But even the best solutions to that problem were less than satisfactory.

Ground sufficient shuttles to carry Marine response teams to engage any Federation soldiers located. The admiral hesitated over that. When, if, the recon shuttles found Federation troops, someone would have to go in and neutralize them before they had a chance to escape and find new cover. But Truscott was uncertain how many troops to assign to that, so he added a second-level note to confer with Colonel Laplace before finalizing that order.

"Might as well get it done now," he said. He looked around, but Ian hadn't returned from his trip to *Victoria*. Truscott was unused to his aide's absence. "Do me good to do for myself once in a while," he said. He keyed the call to Colonel Laplace. Their conversation lasted less than three minutes and ended with an agreement to assign two line companies to the response duty.

"We can always put more men on it if we have to," Laplace reminded the admiral. "Ground more shuttles if you think that will help. Or use companies from Fourth Battalion and we can dispatch them directly from *Victoria*. Give them something to do besides rust."

Truscott nodded to himself while he finished polishing the orders. Then he signed and dispatched them.

"That's the immediate business," Truscott said softly. He leaned back in his chair and stared at the ceiling then got up and paced around the table several times.

It's not enough, he thought. *We're doing everything we possibly can here, and it's still not enough.* He knew why he wasn't satisfied. He was still doing nothing more than reacting to the original Federation invasion. And that was little better than maintaining a defensive holding pattern.

"How do we get ready for the next wave?" He stopped pacing at the tea cart and fixed himself a cup of tea, then took it back to the chart table. He clicked off the surface map and replaced it with a chart of the entire system, with markers for each of his ships.

Limited resources. Truscott's thinking was never "If the Federation returns," but always "When the Federation returns." And they would certainly return, in larger numbers, prepared for a fight. They would have the report of the troopship on the size of the Commonwealth fleet. From that, their command would be able to deduce, very closely, the opposition they would have to face.

Truscott sipped at his tea but kept his eyes on the system chart. When the Federation returned, they would have an element of tactical surprise. Truscott had no way to know exactly when and where they would emerge from Q-space, flaring in at high speed, ready to launch an attack before his ships could react.

They know our size, and they can make good guesses at where we are, especially Sheffield *and* Victoria. *They're certain to assign forces they think will be sufficient to do the job.* Truscott was too good a commander to ignore reality just because it might prove unpleasant.

There has to be a way to maximize what we have. Options flowed through his mind, scenarios from texts and past fleet maneuvers. There were also alternatives he had dreamed up himself over the years but had never had the opportunity to test. Most of the possibilities could be disregarded without much thought.

"I know what I'd like." He set his cup down. "I'd like a way to hide my ships." *If only there were some way I could hold part of the fleet in Q-space and bring them out at precisely the right time to catch the Federation with its pants down.* But there was no way to communicate between Q-space and normal-space except by coming out, and if the fleet was hiding in Q-space, they would have no way to know when the Federation forces arrived.

Truscott leaned forward and stared at the map. After a

moment, he narrowed the scope of the chart, centering the image on Buchanan and extending it only as far as the next planetary orbits, in and out. Then he narrowed the image even farther, three million miles to a side, still centered on Buchanan.

A way to hide my ships. This time he narrowed the portion of the system shown on the chart to a 700,000-mile diameter. The admiral smiled as he spotted the one possibility the system offered. He hit two keys and put the chart into a high-speed simulation of the orbits of the planet and its two moons. He watched the display for five minutes, hardly blinking as the screen showed him the equivalent of three full days of motion.

He kept his eyes on the display while he initiated another complink call. A holographic image of Captain Harris Murphy of *Repulse* formed across the table from the admiral.

"Link to my chart table, Captain," Truscott said, bringing the display back to the present and real time.

"I've got it, sir," Murphy said after just a few seconds more than the speed-of-light delay for two-way communications between the ships.

"Bear with me on this," Truscott said. "I've been looking for a way to come up with a few surprises for the Federation when their navy returns. They're certain to know . . ."

"I think we've all been doing that, sir," Murphy said, interrupting. The start of Truscott's last sentence hadn't had time to reach *Repulse*. The admiral waited to be sure that Murphy had finished before he resumed.

"They're certain to know how many ships we have. At least, they'll know how many we had when their ship scrambled out of the system. They can make decent guesses as to where we'll be deployed. An imbecile could judge where *Sheffield* and *Victoria* need to be to support ground action. On that basis, they'll have the same sort of tactical advantage over us that we had over their single ship before. You follow so far?''

"Yes, sir. My staff and I have been going through these same points, at some length. We haven't come up with any brilliant schemes to offset those advantages though. I take it you have?''

"Only time will tell how brilliant they are, but I may have a way to give us a little tactical surprise of our own.'' He paused and leaned back, giving Murphy a chance to respond.

"We're ready for anything, sir,'' Murphy said.

"This is going to require considerable maneuvering,'' Truscott said. "Let me direct your attention specifically to Buchanan's smaller moon, the one nearer the planet. What do they call it, the Pebble?''

"Yes, sir. And the other is the Boulder,'' Murphy volunteered.

"Yes. In any case, the Pebble has an orbital period of just over fifteen hours.'' Truscott paused, but Murphy had no additional comments.

"I want you to conceal *Repulse* on the side of Pebble facing Buchanan. Hold position as close to the surface as you can without actually landing.'' Truscott made an impatient gesture with one hand. "I want you to maintain station there from the time Pebble is 120 degrees east of the settlements until it's 120 degrees west, on every orbit from now until the main battle is joined and I call for you. When Pebble gets 120 degrees west of the settlements, you will reverse course and accelerate to rendezvous with the moon again when it gets back to the starting point in the east. I'd leave you in position all the way around, but your response time from the far third of the orbit would be unacceptable.''

Truscott watched Murphy's image carefully through his explanation. *Repulse*'s captain started with a deep frown. It eased a little by the time Truscott finished, but it didn't disappear completely.

"I see the point," Murphy said after a pause that was much longer than that imposed by the distance between *Repulse* and *Sheffield*. "Ten hours out of every fifteen, there would be at least a possibility that an arriving Federation fleet wouldn't see us immediately, would perhaps assume that we had been sent elsewhere. Then, assuming that we were within reasonable striking distance, we could hit them from behind, perhaps do significant damage before they could react to us."

"If it looks as though I'm grasping at straws, you're right," Truscott said. "I'm looking for anything at all that might improve our chances by even the slightest percentage."

Murphy nodded. "May I ask if you have similar plans for *Lancer*?"

"I haven't made a final decision on *Lancer* yet. The other moon is farther out and I'm not certain that posting *Lancer* that far out offers any benefit. In any case, I have something else in mind for her first, once I finish tying the loose ends together."

That was, to say the least, an overstatement. The ends of Truscott's plans for *Lancer* were loose all the way to the center. All he really had was a notion that he had to do something unorthodox, and preferably *outrageously* unorthodox, with his second frigate. *Repulse* was the cautiously unorthodox experiment. *Lancer* . . .

"I think that's all for now, Captain," Truscott said. "I want you in position on this orbit."

"Aye, aye, sir," Murphy replied. "I've already got my navigator laying in the course."

Outrageously unorthodox. Truscott rolled the phrase around his mind. He liked the sound, so he said it aloud.

An officer in the CSF didn't reach flag rank by being outrageously unorthodox—not in peacetime. There was no precedent for wartime. The sporadic colonial skirmishes that were all the CSF had ever been called on to fight didn't count as *war*.

The question was as simple as it was difficult to answer. *What do I do with the limited forces I have available?* Truscott knew that he couldn't be so outrageous that he would risk either of his capital ships on a madcap gesture, not unless his position became extremely desperate, and there was no need to classify the fleet's current position that way.

Yet. We may come to it though, he reminded himself.

Brilliant ideas didn't come swarming. For a considerable time, there were no ideas at all. He got up, paced some more, and went back to the tea cart for a refill. He walked out to the flag bridge to ask after updates from the ground and from the other ships. He walked back to the wardroom to get a bowl of fruit cocktail, and sat there to eat it. He even considered going to the gymnasium to work out for a half hour, reprimanding himself for failing to keep up with his normal physical regimen through the time that this mission had already taken.

You're stalling, damn it, he told himself. He forced himself to return to the chart room of his day cabin. He sat down and used the screen to tour the Buchanan system repeatedly, zooming through and coming back from a variety of positions, varying scales occasionally, trying to spark ideas.

"The answer's just not here," he said eventually. He pushed his chair back from the table. "Not *here*," he repeated. That gave birth to the idea that had been eluding him for hours. "If I can't come up with a better way to meet the Federation forces that come to Buchanan, I need to keep them from coming." Since there was no way to detect or intercept ships in Q-space, there was only one way to affect ships heading towards Buchanan's system.

"I have to send *Lancer* to Union." Union was the capital world of the Federation, one of the first worlds settled when men started the serious waves of emigration from Earth seven hundred years earlier. "A quick smash and run, back here at the double. Cut corners all around." It sounded so simple and elegant, despite the risks. Truscott's smile was very tight.

"No telling what sort of hell you'll unleash," he told himself with grim relish.

Once he had the outline, it was the work of no more than a few minutes to fill in the essential details. He called up a chart of Union's system on his flatscreen, then brought back his notepad window at the corner, wrote and rewrote. This order had to be worded just so. It was likely to become a document of some notoriety. "After all," Truscott muttered under his breath, "if this is to be the star exhibit at my court martial, I want it to be properly phrased."

The order was ready, and the admiral was about to put through his call to *Lancer*, when there was a knock at the door. Ian and the prince had returned from *Victoria*.

"Ah, there you are," Truscott said when his aide entered the cabin. "It's about time you reported for duty." When Prince William came in as well, Truscott nodded to him. "I trust your visit went well?"

William smiled. "It was an experience, sir."

Truscott nodded absently, missing the hint of humor in the prince's voice and the sudden grin on Ian's face.

"Ian, would you get Captain Rivero on the line for me, full holo?"

"Yes, sir, right away."

Prince William excused himself and left.

"I noticed that *Repulse* is moving," Ian said while he put through the call.

"I'll brief you in a few minutes. *Lancer* will be moving

as well. You'll hear about that while I brief her skipper.''

"Yes, sir.''

A holographic image of Arias Rivero appeared across the table from the admiral, where Captain Murphy's image had been earlier.

"I have a job of work for you, Captain,'' Truscott said after cutting short the greetings.

"We could use it,'' Rivero said.

"You may not think so when you hear what it is.'' Truscott laid out the outline. ''I want you to take *Lancer* out of Q-space as close to their high port facilities as possible, on a course that aims you toward the horizon. Immediately on exiting Q-space, you will take every target within range under fire, expending a maximum amount of ordnance. Feel free to launch missiles toward the government complex in their capital city as well. Then you will transit back to Q-space to return here. I don't want you in normal-space in Union's system any longer than ninety seconds.''

"Ninety seconds between exit and reinsertion to Q-space?'' Rivero asked, disbelief overwhelming any objections he might have to the mission.

"Ninety seconds,'' Truscott repeated. ''Not one second longer. That means you'll need to have your provisional insertion calculated before you arrive, and you'll make the second transit the instant your Nilssen generators have cycled through from the previous jump.''

"It's never been done, sir. Nothing even close to that has ever been attempted.''

"It's never been necessary before. Here are your written orders.'' Truscott hit a key to transmit them. ''Unless you feel that you are incapable of the required performance?'' Truscott said with a deceptive lightness.

"There's no call for that, sir,'' Rivero said, straightening up. ''*Lancer* will perform her mission.''

Truscott nodded. ''You will also note that I expect you

there and back within seventy-two hours, which will permit a lot less leeway between all jumps than the book calls for, though not nearly the minimum margin of the one jump in and out of Union's space. We *are* learning about those margins, Captain, and mostly we're learning that they're unnecessary. Before this war is over, ninety seconds may well be the standard separation."

"Yes, sir," Rivero said, but he had to swallow hard first.

"I want *Lancer* under way immediately, Captain. Good luck and good hunting."

After Rivero's image disappeared from the room, Ian whistled softly. "An attack on Union. I never would have dreamed of something that bold, sir. I wouldn't have dared."

Truscott turned in his seat and looked up at his aide. "It's a big gamble at long odds." He shrugged. "It's not *Lancer* that I'm concerned about, not particularly. I am, as they say, ninety-nine and nine-tenths percent confident that it's safe to make Q-space jumps that close together, and *Lancer* won't be in Union's system long enough for anything to target them but energy weapons. Her hull is hardened enough to withstand beamers for that long. They'll be back in Q-space before any missiles or cannon can touch them."

"You hope to keep the Federation from sending reinforcements here?" Ian asked.

"I'll settle for a delay just now," Truscott said. "It's still a long shot. They might have a fleet on its way before *Lancer* shows up. They could even have ships here by the time *Lancer* sends in her calling card. But if they *haven't* dispatched that fleet yet . . ."

"They'll need time to recognize the attack as a one-ship raid," Ian supplied. "The politicos and Ministry of Defense will have to rethink their own defenses, perhaps make them hold back on sending any sizeable forces anywhere immediately."

"Perhaps. That's partially why this is such a long shot. But the real danger is that *Lancer* will simply make them madder than hell. One frigate isn't going to inflict any serious damage on Union in ninety seconds. In trying to take the pressure off us here at Buchanan, I may only make the war longer and more bitter. I may even be stirring up something that will take generations to mend."

"How do you think it will be received back on Buckingham, sir?"

Truscott permitted himself a mirthless chuckle. "That depends entirely on the results, Ian. My orders give me the latitude, and responsibility, to take all measures 'necessary and proper' to liberate Buchanan. All the rope any man could need to hang himself. But I'll know I've done my duty to the best of my ability, whatever comes of it."

30

David Spencer had taken to eating his meals with the rest of his platoon, forgoing the slightly better service of the sergeants' mess. It had been two-and-a-half days since the ambushes in the Park had put the platoon out of action. This lunch would be their last meal aboard *Victoria* for an unspecified time. The last of the wounded had returned to duty, and the platoon would be returning to the surface shortly after the meal ended.

"Eat hearty," David told his men when some of them started to slow down. "You can't tell when we'll get our next decent feed."

"*This* is decent?" Alfie asked, his mouth full.

"Obviously close enough that *you* can't tell the difference," David shot back.

"It looks as if most of the work's been done down below," Doug Weintraub said. He too had chosen to eat with the Marine other ranks, even though he had open invitations to dine in the Marine officers' mess and in the naval wardroom. "There's been precious little activity in the last day, and there don't seem to be any Federation soldiers anywhere near Sam and Max."

"They're still down there somewhere," David said. "Six hundred or more. We have to account for all of them before the job's done." He spoke softly. "Unless the brain-boys in command come up with a better way, it could all be like that lark in the Park, maybe a hundred times." David could see the effect he was having on his men, but he wouldn't lie to them.

"There are special shuttles looking for pockets of the enemy," David continued. "There's some hope that they'll be able to find any concentrations of Feddies even with their electronics switched off." He shrugged. "But they've been looking since the morning after our little soiree and haven't found any. It may be that they just haven't searched the right places, but I don't think we can count on the shuttles doing our work."

"We can't cover this entire world one foot at a time," Roger complained. "Not even one continent. We'd all be due retirement before we had ten percent of it done."

"I hear, unofficially, that the admiral sent for reinforcements," David said. "I hate to spread rumors, but the scout ship's been gone quite a time, and one of the frigates has gone off as well now."

"Maybe I should ring up the prince and ask," Doug said, making it light.

"Don't bother," Alfie said. "I'm happier with a rumor. It makes the work that much easier to bear."

The others initially assumed that Alfie was making a joke. There were a few halfhearted smiles, but the look on Alfie's face convinced his mates that he was serious for a change.

"Too much information can be worse than too little, at times," David said, nodding. Doug looked from Alfie to David.

"I guess I'm still not used to thinking like a soldier," Doug said. "I've been at the other end of the data chain too long."

"If you do ask His Highness about it, please don't tell us, one way or t'other," Jacky said.

"Unless the rumor's right," Alfie chipped in brightly,

and this time he did earn a laugh.

"You're a strange lot," Doug said. "Sometimes I think I don't understand you at all. I *know* I don't understand why I decided to stick with you until the job's done. But I will. You seem to understand what this is all about better than most of the people who live here."

"When we fight, we still meet the enemy right up close," Jacky said seriously. "It's not all blips on our visors. We hear the screams. That's the worst part. They stay with you, sometimes forever."

The platoon filed back to their barracks compartment and started dressing for the field. The light mood had evaporated before they left the mess hall, leaving the Marines all business now. They had run diagnostics on their helmets that morning, and the armorers had gone over their weapons. Once the men were dressed, they stood in line at the armory for weapons and ammunition. Doug drew a Marine-issue automatic rifle and an officer's pistol, a compact needler. Over the past day, David had been giving him lessons with the weapons, including two long sessions on *Victoria*'s firing range.

"You're still a rookie at this business," David told Doug, softly, away from the rest of the men. "You've proved you've got the instincts, but you haven't had the training. You haven't had an old hand like me screaming at you twenty-four hours a day forever either. Just stick with our old-timers, and if one of us screeches for you to do something, do it. Save the questions for later."

"Whatever you say," Doug said. "I know how new I am at this."

"We'll get through it, one way or another," David said. "We've still got all the advantages."

When the last of the troops filed away from the armory, David whistled and told them to form up.

"Just like a drill," he said as the men started toward the shuttle deck. "We've been through this too often for any muddling. Right through to the shuttle, lads. The holiday's over."

There was no idle chat on the shuttle. A few men sat with their visors up, but most had them down, closing themselves off into the solitary confinement of their thoughts. The only man in the shuttle who hadn't gone through this routine at least once was Doug.

I am the amateur here, he reminded himself. There had been little chance for nervousness before, but now a knot in his stomach churned and finally seemed to congeal his lunch. He gritted his teeth at a sudden cramp.

Why am I here? Doug was suddenly full of reasons why he should have withdrawn gracefully while he had the opportunity. None of these people had expected him to remain with them. After all, he was a member of the Buchanan Planetary Commission, a leader, a politician of sorts. He was too old. He wasn't trained for combat. But he had made his choice, and—once he forced himself to discard the nervous excuses of the moment—he knew that he had made the only choice that was possible . . . for *him.* "Live or die," he mumbled under his breath, and only then did he remember to make sure that none of his complink channels were open.

David sat with his visor down, looking at his men, alert to any clue that might mean that someone had problems they hadn't told him about. He also had information coming in over two complink channels, listening to the traffic between the pilots working the search pattern and the Combat Information Center on *Sheffield.* He was also monitoring Captain McAuliffe's command channel.

Seems fairly quiet, David assured himself. *No firefights going on.* But the quiet didn't last. David heard an excited voice, one of the shuttle pilots, reporting to *Sheffield's* CIC.

"Bingo! We have fifteen to twenty targets on the ground, helmets inactive." A string of map coordinates followed. David pulled out his mapboard and unfolded it. Almost as quickly as he located the site, a small blue circle appeared on the board as CIC updated it. The shuttle climbed to a wider orbit around the location, putting more room between it and possible surface-to-air missiles. The shuttle's crew worked to keep track of the fuzzy targets, sticking around to make sure that the troops didn't sneak off, and looking for more of them.

Less than a minute later, David had a call from Captain McAuliffe. "You're going straight into action, Spencer. The search shuttles just located a pocket of Feddies, twenty miles southeast of our position."

"I've been monitoring the traffic, Captain," David said.

"You'll be dropped in a mile and a half south of the sighting. A Spacehawk is moving in now to provide backup, and the search team is looking to make sure that there aren't any surprises between the drop zone and the located targets. You've got three minutes before you go in. Good luck."

David switched to his platoon frequency to warn the men. He gave the order to load weapons. "We'll be going down the ropes in three minutes." He then clicked over to the squad leaders' frequency and had them slave their mapboards to his. There wasn't time for much more. The pilot broke in on David's briefing to set up the drop schedule, then it was time for the ropes.

There was a good clearing for the platoon to jump into. They scarcely needed the ropes. The shuttle hovered within ten feet of the ground, rock and scrub grass under them. If it hadn't been for the rocks, perhaps a third of the men *would* have jumped. Adrenaline and the shock-absorbing abilities of their boots and field skins would have sufficed for that distance. But not over rocks.

Alfie Edwards was the first man on the ground. He moved out from under the shuttle and went to ground, taking the best position he could and aiming his needler in the general direction of the distant enemy. He was ready for instant action, even though the needle gun's effective range was only a hundred yards and the known enemy positions were a mile and a half away. His throat was dry, but he had seen enough action to pay that no mind. *Our bodies are smarter than we are,* an instructor had once told a group that Alfie was in. *They know full well the folly of combat, the possible outcome. But you can—you will—learn how to override your body's signals when you have to.*

"An' it's even worse just comin' out of hospital," Alfie told himself as his eyes searched the terrain in front of him. He was only vaguely aware of his mates coming down and moving into position, forming a defensive circle around the drop zone. This was a basic maneuver. Even Doug Weintraub found his place in the ring without any difficulty, right next to Alfie.

"Nobody told me about shinnying down ropes," Doug said when he took his place on the ground. His visor was up. Alfie reached over and slapped it down, none too gently, the way a drill instructor would have done it in boot camp.

"Keep that down unless you see me or the sergeant with ours up," Alfie said, clicking off his radio and speaking loudly enough for his words to carry to Doug. "An' even then you're better off askin' first."

By the time the shuttle pulled away from the drop zone, David had his squad leaders together, looking over the same mapboard while they talked over their private complink frequency.

"We know exactly where the enemy is, but not how

they're deployed. Assume it's an efficient defensive position. We're going to have to go for maximum quiet moving in. We don't have dark to cover us." He looked around at the others. The visors left their faces in shadow, vague.

"We'll put the horns on them." David held his right hand out with the index and little fingers extended. "First and third squads on the flanks, second and fourth coming up the middle. We'll do it the easy way, stop a hundred yards out—sooner if we come under fire—and put grenades in on top of them. As soon as the action starts, the shuttle will move back in to keep track of any Feddies who try to duck out, and the Spacehawk will be on tap if we need it." David looked around at the squad leaders again. "And remember, we've still got a novice with us."

The squad leaders moved to gather their men. While the flanking squads moved off to the sides and started to pick their way into the forest, the others provided cover, then got up and started north between the horns, spreading out into a skirmish line as they advanced.

"Stay close and stay quiet," David told Doug, breaking in on a private channel. "This could get touchy if they hear us coming."

Doug nodded. David nodded back and kept going.

The forest was different here than it was close to the towns and river. The soil was loose, sandy. Trees were farther apart, allowing for patches of scrub brush and irregular clearings. The animal paths were less clearly defined, but there was less need for them in the more open terrain. The Marines had no trouble maintaining a coherent skirmish line across the base of their formation, and the horns had little difficulty maintaining their positions to either side.

When the terrain didn't close up, David revised his initial plan. "We stop at a hundred fifty yards," he advised the other squad leaders. The horns were moved farther out to the sides. The base held up for a couple of minutes, then spread out to cover the wider gap.

The Marines crawled the last fifty yards, then snaked their way into position on their stomachs, using every possible bit of cover. David squirmed down into the loose soil when he finally stopped the platoon's advance. There was just a little give to the sandy dirt, enough to allow him a little extra security.

"All grenadiers," he whispered on the platoon frequency. "Five rounds apiece into the enemy position. On command." He hesitated long enough to give the eight men who carried the grenade launchers time to get the weapons into position.

"Fire!" David raised his voice but didn't shout. Then he pressed himself into the ground with all the force he could muster. Less than six seconds passed before the mayhem erupted.

The first eight grenades all exploded within a tenth of a second. In less than twelve seconds, all forty of the ordered grenades had burst within the same hundred-foot circle. The blasts blended into one continuous assault of sound. As the explosions ended, the Marines could hear the lesser sounds of trees falling and the crackle of flames.

"On your feet!" David shouted over the platoon frequency. "At the double. Close the gap."

David moved as he gave the order, running toward the positions of the Federation soldiers. He had the safety off on his rifle, and his finger was on the trigger, ready to spray any hint of movement. The smoke of the grenade explosions lifted. Before he got to the circle of complete destruction, David slowed his run . . . and then stopped. There was no hurry, not now.

"Check the perimeter," he ordered over the radio. He forced himself to walk forward again. Doug stayed right with him, his rifle lowered until the barrel was pointed at the ground by his side.

"Oh, my God!" Doug said. His hand came up to lift his visor before he remembered what Alfie had said. But the warning meant nothing to him just then. He had to lift the visor, quickly. He had scarcely gotten it up before he had to lean over and vomit—at considerable length.

It was difficult to differentiate among the individual bodies in the newly created clearing, impossible to get a quick count on the Federation dead. Bits and pieces had been blown off and mixed like chunks of ham in the tossed salad of the shredded circle of forest.

David forced himself to look. "That's the easy way," he mumbled, before realizing that he had the platoon frequency open on his complink. Several of the men turned to look his way, but no one replied. One way or another, every one of them shared the same thought.

It could have been us.

Part 7

31

Frigates of the Second Commonwealth's Essex class, like *Repulse* and *Lancer,* were the smallest naval vessels equipped with Nilssen generators sufficient to make Q-space transits on their own. Essex class frigates were designed as fast, maneuverable weapons platforms, their primary mission to protect the Royal Navy's larger vessels. Among the designated secondary missions were battlefield preparation and raiding enemy fleets, facilities, or bases. While the mere arrival of a Commonwealth frigate overhead had occasionally been enough to end a colonial dispute, none of them had ever actually been employed as solitary raiders prior to the start of the war with the Federation.

Captain Arias Rivero was well aware that he would earn a line or two in the history of naval tactics as *Lancer* prepared to make its final jump en route from Buchanan to Union. Only the nature of that entry remained to be determined. The first two jumps had gone without a hitch, even though Rivero had permitted only a two-hour delay between them. He wanted to save as much time as possible for the interval between the second and third transits, the last before jumping into the Union system.

During that final interval before jumping into enemy space, Rivero gathered all of his department heads in *Lancer's* wardroom.

"You've all had plenty of time to come up with practical objections to our mission," Rivero said. "Forget them. Don't bother telling me that we can't do this for one reason or another. We have our orders. We will carry them out. Come up with work-arounds if you have to." He didn't give anyone a chance to interrupt before he went on to specifics.

"Navigation, I want the preliminary program for the jump *out* of Union space in the computers before we jump *into* that space. You'll have exactly ninety seconds turnaround in order to make any necessary corrections. Remember that figure, *ninety seconds*, not one second more. At that point, we reenter Q-space, ready or not, and if we have to waste time finding out where we are after that jump, your neck is on the chopping block, right next to mine.

"Weapons. Those ninety seconds in Union space are yours. I expect to see munitions being expended during eighty-eight of those seconds. That means everything you can put on any target within range. Start with the first available targets, regardless of what they are. Maximize target selection as quickly as you can. As possible, get missiles out toward the surface targets the admiral indicated. You will also be our snowplow. Blast anything out of our path. I don't care if its a comsat, or their main construction docks. We won't have time to detour around obstacles. Use whatever you need to open the way."

The weapons officer nodded, but weakly. He hoped, most fervently, that there wouldn't be anything even one-tenth the size of a construction dock in the path of *Lancer*. A concerted volley of all of the ship's weaponry might not suffice to open a lane large enough for *Lancer* to clear it at speed. For the rest . . . it would be hectic, but he was only being asked for a *volume* of fire, not highly effective, coordinated assaults on specific targets. Spectacular results would be a bonus. *Lancer* wouldn't be in-system long enough for textbook engagements, or for damage assessment.

"Damage control," Rivero continued. "We shouldn't be in normal-space long enough for Federation forces to take us under fire, but be ready. We might pop up in front of a dreadnought starting target practice. Remember, we have one imperative. Get out of normal-space exactly ninety seconds after we enter. Unless our Nilssens are gone, any other repairs will have to wait until we jump back to Q-space.

"Engineering. Make bloody certain that the Nilssens don't go south. I want a thorough inspection and diagnostics performed now. You've got the next six hours to find and correct anything that *might* conceivably go bad in two more jumps. The same thing goes for life support systems. Do whatever you have to do now to make sure they don't give us difficulties at the wrong time later." Rivero paused and looked around at his officers.

"I don't want anyone coming to me while we're in Union space and saying, 'We can't jump out on schedule,' for any reason. If we don't make that transit, we're all dead. Period.

"Questions?" The belligerent tone Rivero used for the word insured that there would be none. "Very well. Get busy. Get us ready for Union."

Arias Rivero retreated to his cabin after leaving the wardroom. The tension that had gripped him when Admiral Truscott gave him his orders hadn't eased. It was more a result of Truscott's unwarranted insinuation that he might not be equal to the assignment than the risks of the mission itself.

What did I ever do to earn such a slur? Rivero asked himself again. It still stung enough to warm his cheeks. *Nothing! The admiral must be losing his grip to snap so quickly, so unjustly.* That didn't ease his embarrassment, his anger. And anger was no better a mate to take into combat than tension.

Rivero sat on his bunk and leaned back against the bulkhead. He stared at the room's single decoration, a framed letter on the opposite wall. After a time, his tension started to ease. Eventually, he managed to smile. That letter was a commendation from the governor of Dorado, his homeworld, for being its first citizen to be accepted for the Commonwealth Naval Academy on Buckingham. At the ripe old age of eighteen, Arias Rivero had been the celebrity of the moment on Dorado. His photograph had been in the news, there had been interviews, public affairs, enough to turn the head of anyone, let alone the rather naive son of a systems technician in a nanotech factory. Five years later, when Ensign Rivero came home on his graduation leave, there had been a similar to-do. *Our whole world is proud of you,* he had been told—repeatedly. The welcome could hardly have been greater if he had just been named first lord of the Admiralty. But by that time, Arias was much less naive. His years on Buchanan had shown him just how provincial Dorado was. The celebration on his return was almost embarrassing, a distraction from the real purpose for his visit, to marry his adolescent sweetheart and take her back to Buckingham. They had only been home twice in the seventeen years since. But that first letter of commendation was still his most prized possession.

Feeling the first bit of relaxation he had known in the hours since his conference with Admiral Truscott, Arias stretched out on his bunk. He took a series of deep breaths and focused his mind on the image of his wife, an image that remained as fresh as that of the letter on the wall. Teresa and their four children, one son and three daughters.

Thirty minutes, Arias thought. *I can afford to sleep for thirty minutes.* Within seconds, he was asleep, certain that he would wake on his own when the half hour was up.

• • •

Every position on the bridge was manned before the call to quarters. The corresponding backup positions in the secondary command station were also manned, ready to take over in an instant if that became necessary. Rivero sat in his chair overlooking the bridge stations and looked around—nervous, but satisfied that *Lancer* was as prepared as she could be. A few minutes earlier, Rivero had broadcast a message to the crew, laying out for them exactly what they were going to do, giving such reassurances as he could. "Naval warfare will never be the same after today," he had told them. "What we are about to do will set the standards that other ships and crews will seek to match in the months and years ahead."

A message rocket had been launched just before that, aimed back to Admiral Truscott, programmed to make the journey in two jumps, ending up three hours' normal-space travel from the flagship. The entire message was:

WE ARE ABOUT TO TRANSIT TO UNION.

LANCER

Give the old bastard something to think about, Arias had thought—with more than a little satisfaction—when he keyed in the message.

"All stations report ready for Q-space transit, ready for combat," the first officer reported.

Rivero nodded. "Set the countdown for Q-space insertion."

Thirty seconds. The standard announcement sounded. Arias focused his attention on the countdown numbers on his complink screen. He was breathing shallowly, already keyed up for combat. There would be little time to relax until after the engagement was over . . . one way or the other. The rapidly elapsing seconds now, perhaps three minutes in Q-space, and then the hectic ninety seconds over Union. After that? Arias scarcely dared to think past that point. If all went well, they would be back in Q-space, feeling a need to celebrate. If things *didn't* go well, they might not feel anything at all.

At least give us a clean ending, Arias thought, scarcely recognizing that he was praying.

"Q-space insertion," the navigator announced. The exterior monitors showed a featureless gray replacing the star-speckled blackness of normal-space.

"All systems nominal," the first officer reported. "Nilssen generators show no strain. All departments report ready for action."

"Navigator?" Rivero asked.

"Exit Q-space in seventy-three seconds. The plot for the next transit is already laid in. I'll key it as an action command the instant we enter Union's space. We'll have any necessary updates integrated within forty-five seconds . . . provided we're within a million miles of where we're supposed to be off Union."

"I want exterior recorders up and running now, before we exit Q-space," Rivero said. *We'll have something to show the admiral, if we make it back to Buchanan,* he told himself. *I hope he enjoys the show.*

The thirty-second countdown started. "On your toes," Rivero said over the all-ship channel. "Remember, when we come out over Union, we only have ninety seconds to do our damage. Good hunting."

Once *Lancer* emerged in Union space, Arias found himself effectively no more than a spectator on his own bridge. He watched the monitors. He listened to the reports of his bridge officers. He sweated. The ninety-second limit meant that there was little he could do to affect the operation of his ship during that time. There would be no relaying of target sightings for him to pick and choose and then direct the weapons officer as to which he should aim at. There were no navigational commands, no firing of attitude rockets to improve the ship's course. Nothing.

Lancer emerged from Q-space almost precisely on target. The main construction docks were ahead, above, and slightly to the left of the ship. There were four ships, one Cutter class troopship, two dreadnoughts, and one frigate docked in line aft—west—of the docks. There were a few small craft visible as well, but none were particularly close, or directly in *Lancer*'s path.

The decks and bulkheads of *Lancer* started to vibrate as the weapons stations began unloading munitions as rapidly as they could aim and fire. A time line on every complink screen clicked down the time remaining before the escape transit. The bridge lights dimmed by 10 percent, briefly, as the ship's generators took up the strain of maintaining maximum fire rates.

Captain Rivero tried to keep track of the rate-of-fire indicators on his command console, but the numbers cycled too rapidly. At the same time, there was really little of interest to see on the exterior monitors. Through most of the ninety seconds, only energy weapons—those that raced through the vacuum at the speed of light—were engaging enemy targets, and military targets were especially hardened against that sort of weapon. It was only in the last few seconds that *Lancer*'s missiles started meeting defensive weapons, and targets.

There was one magnificent blast, from a ship in the center of the construction docks, that started to blossom in the last three seconds before *Lancer* poked its way back into Q-space.

Arias could hardly keep from joining in on the cheers that sounded on *Lancer*'s bridge. He took a deep breath and closed his eyes for an instant as the reassuring gray of Q-space surrounded his ship.

32

"It'll take a while to rebuild the barn," Doug said, pointing out the wreckage to David Spencer and his other guests. The men of I&R platoon had their rifles slung. Most carried their helmets and had the hoods of their field skins pulled back off of their heads.

"Was that foundation plascrete?" David asked, looking at the molten and fused remains of the structure.

"The best we could make, foundation and beams," Doug said, somewhat ruefully.

David turned and looked at the scorched roof and siding of the house. Doug's wife and son had moved back in, finally comfortable with assurances that there were no Federation soldiers near enough to pose a threat. Elena continued to use the return as an inducement to persuade her husband to remain with them but, so far, Doug had resisted.

"It's a good job the house wasn't a few feet closer," David said. "You might have lost that as well."

"I know." Doug turned to make sure that Elena was out of earshot. "If there hadn't been such a damned rush, I doubt I'd have had the nerve to do what I did. Elena and Jamie were in the storm cellar."

"If you hadn't sent off that MR the way you did, you might never have had help." David walked toward the barn. Doug followed. The rest of the platoon was scattered around the yard, many already inside the ruins. "Given enough time, the Federation could have established itself so firmly you'd never have a chance to get free. Bring in enough settlers to make your lot a minority. Something like that. They've done it before."

"I still can't see why they came here in the first place," Doug said. "It's not as though we made anything of importance."

"Buchanan is a prime world," David said. "It's fully suitable for human settlement, as good as any and better than many. That's lure enough if you're looking to expand. It wouldn't have taken much time for the Feddies to settle their own people and a docile government here. You'd be safer if you had ten times the population you do, safer still with a hundred times."

"Sounds like you're making a pitch for us to join the Commonwealth," Doug said.

David shrugged. "I'll leave that to His Highness, but I believe in the Commonwealth, or I wouldn't have spent fifteen years in the Royal Marines. I'm certainly not in it for the money."

Doug walked on a couple of steps before he said, "I think some folks here might be bothered by the idea of a monarchy. That's something that belongs to Earth, to the old times."

"Not necessarily," David said. "The Federation, for all its symbols, is more despotic than the Commonwealth has ever been—all the forms of democracy but none of the meat. They claim an inalienable right to rule every world settled by humans, no matter where those settlers came from or what they want. The Commonwealth has royalty and nobility, but His Majesty's government are popularly elected, and the King has very strictly limited powers."

"Or is that merely form as well?" Doug asked.

"Not the way I see it," David said. "And I've seen quite a bit of it."

Once they reached the barn, both men were more interested in examining the remnants than in continuing the political discussion.

"Would you mind if I cut loose a chunk of this for our lab boys to examine?" David asked after getting his head down as close to the fused plascrete as he could.

"Take as much as you like," Doug said. "But whatever for?"

"Intelligence and reconnaissance." David laughed. "That's supposed to be our job. I doubt that anyone's ever put a lens on plascrete that's been fused in atmosphere by a transit to Q-space."

"You don't think this was caused by just the rocket blast?"

"Not likely," David said. "You had an old MR. Like as not, its firing chamber was *lined* with plascrete."

"I didn't know that," Doug conceded.

"There's newer materials now, but that's what they all used to be lined with. Not just MRs either. A lot of high-temperature chambers were routinely lined with plascrete."

"Take the whole lot if you want," Doug said. "I must admit, I'd be interested to know what your lab people figure out . . . if I could understand it."

"Right now, I'm not sure *they'll* understand it." David laughed. He pulled out his sheath knife and tried to chip out a piece of the fused material, without success. "You have, perhaps, a sledge and a sharp chisel?"

"Look around. If they survived, they're in here."

David took a quick look around, for form, then said, "I see what you mean. I'd hate to call in help. Whoever came would take all the credit."

"Should have a power saw in the house," Doug suggested.

"Unless it's got diamond-tipped blades, or something

even better, I don't think it would work, not if my knife didn't," David said.

"I don't have the faintest idea," Doug admitted. "I'll go have a look."

"Uh, don't bother. We've got something better, if a trifle messy."

"What?"

David raised his voice and shouted at one of the groups of men. "Roger? You got the beamer?"

"Aye, Sergeant." Zimmerman ran over, unslinging the weapon on the way.

David held his hand out and Roger gave him the gun. "All right, you lot," David said, very loudly. "Clear out of the barn for a few minutes and put your helmets on, visors down." More softly, primarily for Doug's benefit, he said, "I don't want any accidents. I'm going to try to burn loose a chunk of this stuff."

"You think that'll work?" Doug started to pull on his helmet. Two steps away, Roger was putting on his; he hadn't hurried out of the barn with the others.

"It's worth a try." David noticed Roger standing by. "What are *you* waiting for?" he demanded.

"You have my weapon, Sergeant. My weapon, my responsibility. I'll be happy to do the cutting. I might be able to coax a little extra power out of it."

Spencer stared at Roger for a moment, then nodded. "You might at that, lad," he admitted. He handed the beamer back, then donned his own helmet. "I'd like about ten pounds, but I'll settle for whatever I can get."

"If you and Mr. Weintraub would kindly step out of the way, I'll see what I can do," Roger said, his expression and tone hidden by the lowered visor over his face.

David led Doug halfway across the remains of the barn. *Even this might not be far enough,* David thought, but he wanted to see what happened.

"Darken your visor, Doug," he said, "to the maximum." He wiggled his fingers to set the polarity control of his own helmet. Doug, unpracticed, needed longer.

"Whenever you're ready, lad," David told Roger over a helmet circuit.

Roger aimed his beamer at the edge of a section of the fused material where there appeared to be the hint of a seam. His first squeeze on the trigger was short, testing, aimed at a shallow angle across the surface. The brilliant blue-white beam sparkled off of the fused plascrete. When the glare died, Roger lifted his visor to take a close look at the target.

"This stuff's tougher than mess hall pancakes," he reported, "but I think I can get your sample."

"Do what you can," David said.

It wasn't a quick operation. Roger ran the power charge completely down on his beamer, and the second battery pack was low before the hunk of fused plascrete finally fell free of the warped foundation. Roger set his weapon down carefully, leaning it against another section of the foundation. Then he lifted the visor on his helmet. David and Doug were already bending over the chunk that Roger had cut free.

"I wouldn't touch that yet," Roger warned. "The surface temperature must be two hundred degrees."

David took off one of his gloves and held his hand over the chunk of plascrete, moving it gradually closer. After only a slight hesitation, he laid his hand right on the cut edge.

"Not much more than body temp. Didn't hold the heat at all." He stood and looked at Doug. "I'm more certain than ever that the lab boys will want to look at this stuff."

Roger took off both of his gloves and picked up the chunk. "I think it's a bit more than ten pounds, Sarge, maybe closer to twenty."

"In that case, lad, I'll let you carry it," David said with a laugh.

Two hours later, David was in Captain McAuliffe's command bunker a mile east of Sam. First battalion had been moved, and turned around, facing out instead of in. Most of Second Regiment's committed units were concentrated on the eastern half of a perimeter that enclosed Sam, Max, and the spaceport. The western half of the perimeter, consisting mostly of open terrain, was manned more lightly, relying on automated sentry systems and fire points. Any enemy movement in the open country on that side would be seen soon enough to bring reinforcements around, or to call in Spacehawks. It was in the forested areas east and southeast of the towns that heavier manpower was needed.

"Your men ready to move?" McAuliffe asked when David entered the bunker.

"Yes, sir. We're getting to the point where a little action might be welcome, depending on what sort of action it is."

"It's not liberty in Westminster," McAuliffe warned.

"We don't expect that, sir."

"We're going to try something different to clean out the last Feddies. It involves all the I&R platoons."

"In other words, a particularly nasty job of work?"

"Not necessarily. It just requires I&R expertise. Each I&R platoon will be backed by two line companies. You'll be dropped beyond the line that intelligence has decided is the farthest the Feddies could have gone, along the most likely routes. Your job will be to move back this way and either engage and destroy the enemy or flush them out so the mobile response teams can get them."

"How much support will we have? I mean, sir, will the recon shuttles be operating in front of us?"

"A shuttle will work with each group. There will be two or three crews rotating duty, so you'll have just brief intervals without cover. And Spacehawks will be available if necessary."

"And if there's time for them to get into it," David said. The way most of the engagements had gone on Buchanan, the Spacehawks had rarely arrived until the fighting was over.

"You'll be working with our Alpha Company and with Delta of the Fourth. You seemed to mesh nicely with Delta on that other business."

"Lieutenant Ewing and his lads seem to know their business," David allowed.

"Ewing will be in tactical command of the combined group. You know his lead sergeant?"

"Bandar Jawad? Sure, I've known him forever. You mean the engineers let loose of him?"

"Not willingly, I understand. But Delta is back together again. I hope you won't have any trouble working with Ewing and Jawad."

"I wouldn't expect so, sir. They're both top-notch Marines. Like you and me."

McAuliffe allowed himself a soft laugh. "Maybe they can handle your softsoap better than I can."

The engineers had finally finished their road between the river and their original landing zone five miles east of it, and there were actually trucks down and running along it. David managed to commandeer transport to carry his platoon east. Delta of the Fourth and Alpha of the First had already moved to the landing strip. *They* had walked.

"They give us lorries, it must be a real pisser coming up," Alfie said as he climbed aboard.

"The lorries were my cadge," David told him. "It just means we're going to get our quota of walking later. You heard the briefing, unless you had your fingers in your ears."

"An' we're goin' in first, right?" Alfie squirmed to get himself a little more room in the back of the van.

"That's our job, Alfie-lad."

The ride to the landing strip was short. Four shuttles were on the ground, with more circling to the north, ready to land and load as soon as there was room. Lieutenant Ewing was waiting for David. This time, Lead Sergeant Jawad was with his company commander.

"You'd better be careful or they'll transfer you to the Fourth permanently," Ewing said.

"No way, sir. Captain McAuliffe would never permit it," David said. "Hello, Bandar. I see you finally escaped the engineers."

Bandar's smile was characteristically tight. "None too bloody soon. You learned how to keep your arse down in a fight?"

"At least I can still get mine out of the way, not like that corporation you're carrying around."

"You spend as much time at a desk as I have to, you'll balloon out too, mate," Bandar said. "You seen where we're going?"

"Just on a mapboard. But we'll go in first and have a look-see so your lads don't get lost."

"You'd best hurry or you'll miss your shuttle," Ewing said, jumping back into the conversation. "Your men seem to be aboard already."

"I think we've got a good drop zone for you, Sergeant," the shuttle pilot told David just after take-off. "Matter of fact, we can put you down close enough to step out."

"That's the way I like them, sir. How far from cover will we be?"

"About a hundred feet to the northwest. But I doubt there's any Feddies within eight to ten miles."

"Don't remind me how far we've got to walk," David

said. "Still, better safe than shot."

"No argument from me," the pilot said, and David returned to his seat.

There was no hint of opposition to the landing. David got his platoon on the ground and into a defensive perimeter. Then the line companies came in, two platoons at a time, and took over the protective formations.

"Take your men out and find us a good place to spend the night," Ewing told David as the last of the transports cleared out. "We don't want to march too far today, so try to find a spot within two or three miles."

Five minutes later, I&R platoon was on the march, working its way through the forest.

"You realize that it's entirely likely no human has ever walked this path," Doug told David early on the march.

David nodded. "At the moment, the only humans I'm interested in are Feddies. "I'll be happy if none of them have walked *any* of the paths we do."

This was the sort of special operations mission I&R platoon was trained for, operating in front of other units. Although they had been assured that there couldn't possibly be any Federation troops within ten miles, none of David's men took their safety for granted. They spread out in two skirmish lines, one in front of the other, leapfrogging frequently, providing cover for each other.

David had spotted three potential bivouac sites on his mapboard. It looked as if any of them might make acceptable positions for two companies and an extra platoon, but he wouldn't be certain until he had seen at least one of them on the ground. If the first was acceptable, he wouldn't insist on investigating the others. There was no need to comparison shop, not for one night.

Doug kept an eye on his helmet sensors, but realized that the Marines would almost certainly spot any threat long before he could. The overlays on his visor display were still confusing. He also paid as much attention to the flora and fauna as he could. This was a part of his world he had never seen before, like more than ninety-nine percent of Buchanan's land area.

Less than two hundred miles from home and it's almost a different world. In the first hour of this trek, he counted a half dozen new species of trees, plus several new sorts of birds and small animals. As he had many times before, Doug wished he had more time simply to explore, but exploration had never been high on the list of priorities. The area the original settlers had chosen for their colony had served generations well. Several times, Doug knelt to grab a handful of dirt and let it sift through his fingers—light and sandy. It didn't look particularly suitable for intensive cultivation, but it supported a lot of healthy trees and occasional patches of underbrush.

"Any idea what sort of animal might have made these paths?" David asked during one of the platoon's brief rest stops.

Doug shook his head. "They might be blue-capped deer like we have around the settlements, or something we've never seen. I think we can safely rule out hippobary though. They never get more than a couple of hundred yards from water, and there's nothing deep enough for them around here."

"Your people have never made any systematic investigation?" David asked in a very casual tone.

"No. It's something that's always been a step or two down the list of jobs to be done. You know, 'We'll get around to it when we have more time.' " Saying it was worse than simply thinking it. Out loud, the words brought a sense of guilt.

David nodded. "I know. Things you'd like to do but that aren't so critical that you can put other things on hold while you do them."

"Once this is over, I think we'll have to find the time, particularly if we decide to join the Commonwealth."

"You think you will?"

Doug shrugged. "If it were up to me, I'd say yes now. I think it's likely. Depends on how the rest of this war goes, I suppose.

"Yeah," David said noncommittally. *Like whether we win or lose.*

33

Stasys Truscott had effectively locked himself in his day cabin. The Marine sentry outside had orders to admit no one, under any excuse. Even Ian Shrikes had been excluded. The admiral hadn't communicated with anyone since shortly after 0700 hours, when he had informed the duty officer that he wasn't to be disturbed for anything less than total disaster . . . or the return of Federation naval forces, whichever came first.

Unexpectedly cut loose from his normal duties, Ian had gone to the flag bridge for a time, but without the admiral he was a loose cog and didn't stay very long. He kept getting the same question: "What's wrong with the old man?" Even Captain Hardesty came back to ask that question. Ian retreated to the flag wardroom with Prince William, but even that proved insufficient. Still, officers stopped to ask about the admiral. After the third or fourth interruption for the same question, the prince offered an alternative.

"Why not retire to my cabin? We could play a game of chess."

"Looking for an easy mark, are you?" Ian asked. "Sure. I may not be able to concentrate, but your cabin may be the one place where I can get away from all these questions."

The prince already had a chess board set up in his cabin,

an actual set, marble and onyx pieces and board, rather than just a holographic projection. When Ian sat down at the board, he picked up the black king and inspected it closely. And whistled.

"This is quite some set." Ian set the king down and picked up the queen. "I can't even recall the last time I played with solid pieces."

"It's always seemed incongruous to me to play such a venerable game any other way, though I do often enough," William said. The two men had played several games already on this voyage, always on a complink holo. "This particular set was a gift to one of the men I was named for, the Prince Albert who was consort to Queen Victoria. That was about eleven hundred and fifty years ago."

Ian set the queen down very gingerly and edged his chair away from the table. "You actually dare to *play* with it?"

William chuckled. "Regularly. It's always been my favorite."

"It should be in a museum someplace."

"Nonsense," William said. "The craftsman who carved this set intended it to be used by players who enjoyed the game, not to sit behind glass in a museum cabinet. The black king is supposed to be Napoleon Bonaparte, and the white the Duke of Wellington, the man who defeated him. The other major pieces are also supposed to represent actual historical figures from England and France. I can't answer for the faithfulness of the images, and there are some I've never been able to identify. The original letters of provenance disappeared before my ancestors left Earth."

William sat down across from Ian. "If you'd rather, we *could* play on the link."

Hesitantly, Ian shook his head. "I may never get another chance to play with a set like this. I just hope I don't break anything."

"Don't worry about it."

Both men stuck to simple opening patterns. None of their games had been marked by startlingly daring tactics. As this game got under way, William kept an eye on his opponent, and noticed that he seemed to be relaxing as he got into the game. But after the eighth move, Ian suddenly pushed his chair back from the table.

"You know what really gets me?" he asked, rather loudly.

William looked up and waited.

"I really don't have the foggiest idea what's gotten into the admiral. There's been no news to put him in a funk. Everything is progressing smoothly on the surface, and nothing's come in from out-system since we got the MR saying that *Lancer* was about to make the final transit to Union."

"Perhaps that's it," William said. "Is he that impatient for the return of *Lancer,* or for some reply from Buckingham?"

"*Lancer*'s not due until tomorrow, and there hasn't been time for word from Buckingham, certainly not time for significant reinforcements to arrive."

"What else could it be? I can't think of anything, unless he's having health problems."

Ian hesitated, then shook his head. "No, he's never hesitated about yelling for the chief surgeon the second he notices anything that might be even vaguely uncomfortable."

"He's never done anything like this before?"

"Not since I've been on his staff." Ian stood and turned away from the prince. "Unless he gave secret instructions to either *Khyber* or *Lancer* that I don't know about."

"That's possible, isn't it?"

"Certainly, it's possible. He doesn't tell me everything. But what kind of instructions? Why would they have him hiding in his cabin? This just isn't like him."

"We can't simply barge in and demand an answer," William said. "I doubt that Marine sentry would step aside even for me—and he would likely be guilty of a court-martial offense if he did."

"I should let the duty officer know where I am so he can find me when the admiral decides he's ready to come out of his hole," Ian said.

Oblivious to the questions his self-imposed isolation had raised, Truscott had long since lost track of time. He was too busy to give much thought to anything but the work at hand. Since chasing Ian out, Truscott had, in effect, completely rewritten *The Book* on space navy operations. That hadn't been his original intent, but his thinking was too acutely focused for him to miss the evolution occurring on his notepad. Page after page was saved to file, keyed to figures constructed on the flatscreen.

He had started by simply making notes on various contingency plans for the defense of his ships and the Marines on the ground. The operations staff had run hundreds of simulations of possible encounters between the fleet and the expected Federation reinforcements. Truscott had gone through them all, gradually eliminating many from consideration. For the situations that remained, he drastically changed the tactics proposed by his operations chief.

In Truscott's first revisions, he assumed that he had only the ships he had brought to the Buchanan system, or the ones remaining after sending *Khyber* and *Lancer* on their missions. He tried to devise novel methods for meeting a Federation response of varying strength, from a single three-ship battle group to a grand fleet of as many as a dozen capital ships with a full complement of escorts and ancillary vessels. Fundamental to every potential response was a drastic curtailing of previous limits on Q-space travel. Cutting the interval between transits from days to minutes changed virtually everything about warfare in space.

Once he had covered the immediate possibilities, Truscott expanded his thinking to cover other contingencies—such as receiving reinforcements from Buckingham in different strengths.

After going through the scenarios his staff had prepared, Truscott needed little more than two hours to outline another thirty possibilities. He had spent the rest of his time devising new responses to each of those scenarios, starting with outlines and gradually fleshing them out, the way he drafted and polished orders. During the hours of work, he had emptied his tea cart of both tea and coffee, and had finally switched to fruit ades, just keeping something—*anything*—at hand to drink.

And then it was finished.

At first, Truscott simply stared at the last page of writing in his notepad window. *What have I forgotten? What's left to do? There must be something more.* He blinked several times. Nothing came to mind, and the ideas had been coming so quickly all day that, at times, he had struggled to keep up with them.

"Nothing. I can't think of a thing." There was amazement in his voice, but he didn't start to celebrate. Instead, he jumped back to the first pages of his notes and plans, and went through everything he had done, scanning each chart and animated sequence, reading each page of descriptions and the glosses he had added—copious notes, sometimes longer than the sections they were meant to explicate.

Noticing the time was accidental. Truscott looked up from his review and his gaze came to rest on a clock. At first, he merely blinked and thought that the clock had to be wrong. It showed 1650 hours.

"It can't be ten hours since I started." Even as the words came out, he realized that it could.

He saved a copy of his work to his private files, sent another to his flag operations officer, a third to Admiral Greene on *Victoria,* and a final copy to Ian's document file. There were no covering letters. If and when Truscott's new "Operations Bible" was read by the addressees, the questions would come. He smiled. There would be some lively moments ahead.

Truscott stood and stretched. He was tired, but the exhaustion felt uncommonly good. *I've earned my pay today,* he decided. He went to the door and opened it, half expecting to see a line of people waiting. But only the Marine sentry was there. He snapped to attention.

"Would you go to the wardroom and have them fix a tray for me, Sergeant?" the admiral asked. "And ask Commander Shrikes to come in."

"Yes, sir."

The Marine sergeant hurried down the passageway. Truscott watched him for a moment, then stepped back into his cabin.

"Ian's slipping. I'd have thought he would have busted in here four hours ago." He chuckled and made a quick trip to the head. He had been drinking a *lot* of fluids.

"Come in. Have a seat." Truscott was making deep inroads on the tray of food that had been delivered minutes ago, and had already ordered seconds. The tea cart had been taken off by the mess steward to be refilled.

Ian sat and leaned back, holding his questions. The admiral was eating with more appetite than Ian had ever seen him display. Whatever Truscott had been doing locked away for the entire day, he hadn't been hiding in a funk. The admiral slowed down for a moment as he neared the end of the food on his tray.

"There's a new file in your chronology of documents," Truscott said. Ian's duties included compiling an official bibliography of the admiral's papers. "You might have a look. By the way, have you eaten?"

"I ate with the prince," Ian said. "A new file? I take it that means you've been working all day?"

"Naturally. What did you think?"

"You wouldn't want to hear some of the rumors that have been circulating, Admiral," Ian said. "When the commanding officer locks himself away incommunicado while the fleet's in a combat zone, people get nervous."

Truscott looked astonished. "I simply had to work without interruption."

"We don't have any mind readers aboard," Ian said drily.

The admiral shook his head. The mess steward came in with the recharged tea cart and another food tray. After he was gone, the admiral shook his head again.

"Is morale really that uncertain?" he asked.

"It appears so," Ian said.

"Have a look at that file. I haven't given it very wide circulation yet, just to Paul Greene and our ops people." He refused to comment any farther. "Just read the file," he repeated, focusing on his second supper tray.

Ian did as he was told. He sat at the chart table and called up a directory of the admiral's official documents. The new entry was obvious, and imposing in its length.

"All that in one day?" Ian asked, but the admiral didn't respond.

Ian made himself comfortable and started to read. He didn't try to commit it to memory but merely scanned, stopping for a close reading only occasionally, and he zoomed through the animations at high speed. Ian was a fast reader, but the admiral finished eating long before Ian finished the file.

Truscott watched the changing expressions on his aide's face. He felt comfortably sated, and he allowed himself to feel amused at the play of emotions Ian displayed. *It's a good day's work,* Truscott assured himself.

"All that in one day?" Ian asked again when he finished the file.

"It's amazing the work one person can do if he shuts out all interruptions."

"Are you going to send this to Sir John?"

"I thought it would be best to get some local reaction first. That's why I copied it to Greene and our ops." He shrugged. "Of course, I didn't bother to emphasize that to anyone."

"Should I?" Ian asked.

"What's your reaction to it, Ian?" Truscott asked softly.

Ian took a deep breath. He knew the admiral expected nothing less than a completely honest opinion. Truscott had made it clear from the start that he had no use for yes-men.

"A month ago, I might have suggested that you schedule a medical evaluation," Ian said carefully. "And I would have had a few words with the surgeon in advance. But that was before we received that MR from Buchanan, before all the other, ah, experiments." Ian watched the admiral's reaction, but Truscott showed nothing but a bemused smile.

"And now?" Truscott asked, as softly as before.

"Now it appears to be a reasonable set of contingency plans. If we have the opportunity, and the need, to use any of these here, we may obtain the objective evidence that the Admiralty would doubtless require before accepting them for general implementation."

"*Lancer* should provide proof of the basics, Ian," Truscott reminded him. "Barring disaster, we should know by morning how workable this is. Once you get past the practicality of making Q-space transits ninety seconds apart, there's little that can be considered particularly revolutionary about the rest. Once I have *Lancer*'s log for its current mission, I will undoubtedly add a postscript to the file. Certainly before I forward it to Long John.''

"You might put these ideas out for the captains to comment on, sir,'' Ian suggested. "If nothing else, that will insure that they're familiar with the concepts before a situation arises where they might have to implement them.''

Truscott nodded. "Would you do that for me, Ian?''

"Of course, sir.'' Ian did it immediately. "I would imagine that you'll have reaction by morning, if not long before.''

"I think I'll retire early tonight,'' Truscott said. He stood and stretched. "I've had an uncommonly full day.''

"So it seems, sir,'' Ian allowed with a chuckle. "If you were to put out this volume every day, we'd soon have to add memory to the ship's datanet.'' He got up. "Will you need me any more tonight?''

"I don't think so. You might lay some of those rumors to rest if you get the chance. I'll see you in the morning.''

"Yes, sir.'' Ian was on the way to the door when the message came from the flag bridge.

"*Lancer* is back, sir. She's about three hours out, decelerating at full thrust.''

Truscott laughed out loud. "Stick around, Ian. It looks like the day isn't over for us yet. Get Captain Rivero on a holo hook-up and we'll see what he has to say.''

34

It was almost possible for Doug to forget that there was a war going on, that Federation invaders remained on Buchanan, perhaps within a few miles of where he sat. This sort of wilderness trek wasn't completely new to him. He had occasionally taken hiking trips with friends. It was enjoyable, a way to get away from the workaday routines of farming and the commission. Usually.

This time, the four-hundred armed Marines of the Second Commonwealth with him spoiled any illusion of normalcy. They were bivouacked for the night now, in three separate camps. There were sentries posted and, in a circle farther out, microphones and remote-controlled mines. Delta Company was to the left, south. Alpha Company was on the right. And the I&R platoon was between and west of the others.

"I'm still not certain I see the logic of this," Doug said while he and David were sitting over their field rations. "You kept saying that you couldn't possibly clear Buchanan by walking it foot by foot, but here we are, walking through the woods hoping to stumble on Federation soldiers."

"Logic? In the Royal Marines?" David shrugged. "I guess it's a matter of combining tactics. The object, as I understand it, is to get the job done as quickly as possible. The close air searches have been only partially effective.

So we choose the most likely escape routes for soldiers who don't want to be seen and put men across them as well.''

"How do you choose likely routes, and what's to stop the enemy from ducking out of the way and moving back after we pass?"

"We have very detailed maps for this part of your world. We can pinpoint anything as small as four inches in diameter that's visible from the sky and not damn well camouflaged. We assume the Feddies are aware of the air search and don't want to be found, so they'll stay low, in heavily forested areas or in caves, places where they have some chance of hiding as long as they keep their electronics off. Whether they're going to ground or trying to put more distance between themselves and your settlements, there are only a limited number of prime routes. Intelligence picked out the places for us to search. As for ducking aside and coming back later, well, we'll make that a little more difficult.'' He looked around, then called to Sean Seidman.

"Bring me a doughnut cutter and a snoop."

Sean quickly dug into his pack, pulled out two objects, and brought them across.

"We'll plant a lot of snoopers across the terrain." David showed Doug the circular cutter. There were two concentric metal cylinders, held together at the top, with separate plungers and a solid handle.

"We find a likely spot and stick one of these in the ground. Give it a twist and it pulls out a plug of earth. Hit the center plunger to empty the smaller cylinder, switch on a snoop, stick it into the cutter, then plug the cutter back into the hole and hit both plungers. That leaves the snoop in place, concealed and ready to operate, without leaving much evidence of our, ah, gardening.''

Doug took the cutter and looked at it. He hit the plungers, then handed it back. "What about these snoops?"

David held it up. "Eight inches long, three wide at its

widest. In place, only this one-inch knob shows. It has a listening device that can pick up the heartbeat of an insect sitting on it, and a camera that takes a full panoramic view, 360 degrees around and 160 degrees over the top, one frame a second. When the microphone picks up a sound, the camera starts snapping until it determines that the sound isn't something we need to know about.''

''It makes its own decisions?'' Doug asked.

''Within limits,'' David said. ''There's considerable expertise built into its control circuits. In a questionable case, the data is relayed to CIC for further examination. These snoops each send their data up in bursts, and the big computers process everything double quick.''

''Telltales,'' Doug said.

David nodded. ''And there's no way the Feddies can disarm them without giving themselves away. By the time they spot anything so small, they've got to be close enough to be heard and photographed. After that, it doesn't matter. We've got a lock on the position.''

''But what if they go around our route? They've got to come fairly close to one of these telltales to show up, don't they?''

''Part of our job is to make it difficult for them to go around. We'll be ranging from side to side, putting these well out on the flanks. The line companies will plant them across the middle, behind them. It's odds-on that anyone coming in this direction will pass within range of at least one of the little buggers.''

Later, Doug used his helmet to link through *Victoria* to Buchanan's public net. That was one of the tricks David had taught him. Doug talked to Elena and Jamie, then had Elena patch him through to a conference with the other members of the planetary commission.

The six of them—there hadn't been time for an election

to replace Franz Bennelin—talked longer than Doug had talked with his wife and son. There had been several short meetings since the liberation of Sam and Max, but those had dealt with immediate necessities. Now, for the first time, they had a little leisure to discuss the future.

Ehud Novack wanted only one thing. "I'll be glad when we can get back to the way life was before all this started, when *all* the outsiders are gone." But even at the outset, he was a minority of one.

"We can't go back," Oscar Patterson countered. "If we try to go it alone, the Federation will be back, sooner or later, and if we turn the Commonwealth away now, they won't help us the next time."

"The Prince suggested that we don't even consider the offer until after the crisis," Doug reminded the others, "but I don't see any reason to hold off. Joining the Commonwealth is really the only way we can protect our sovereignty."

That opinion came close to carrying the meeting, but Ehud managed to stall any decision, though he harbored few illusions that he could affect the final choice. "At least we should have everything spelled out clearly before we join," he told the others. "Get firm commitments on what the Commonwealth offers, and find out exactly what it's going to cost us, now and in future."

"I have no argument with that," Doug said. "It's the prudent course." The others agreed, eager to avoid a continuation of the argument, and Doug was appointed to continue his talks with Prince William.

"It may take awhile," Doug warned the others. "I don't know how much chance I'll get to talk with him until we finish this mission. But then we'll have time to spare. I think."

Still, he placed his call to the prince as soon as he said good-night to the other commission members.

35

Three Spacehawks of fourth squadron's red flight climbed toward patrol positions above *Sheffield, Victoria,* and *Thames.* The squadron's white flight was also moving toward defensive patrol areas around the capital ships, leaving only two fighters of red flight to carry out ground support operations—the Marines had been requesting little air support. This was the new spread that Admiral Truscott had ordered, just a few hours earlier. No matter what direction an enemy force might appear from, either fighters or one of the frigates would be in position to intercept. *Lancer* was back and had taken up position above and west of the capital ships.

Josef closed his eyes briefly. There was a throbbing in his head, roughly focused around his implant. The ache had been growing for two days, getting worse while he was wearing his helmet, fading only marginally when he got out of it. Kate had started nagging him to see the flight surgeon, but Josef had stalled, trying to ease the ache with tailored endorphin stimulators. "I can get by," he had told Kate. He didn't want to stop flying, even though the schedule was wearing on him as much as it was on any of the others. *Red flight is already short one pilot,* he told himself. *I don't want to make things even rougher for the others.*

The last several sorties had been as routine as they could possibly be. Slowly, the Marines were uncovering pockets of Federation soldiers, but while red flight was on call at least, the Marines had always handled the Federation troops without help. And no enemy ships had challenged the Commonwealth fleet.

Olive Bosworth's fighter was ahead and to the left of Josef's. Kate was behind and to the right. Since Seb's loss, they had been flying a three-fighter formation.

"Red three, are you having problems?"

Josef blinked at the sound of Bosworth's voice.

"No problems here," he replied after a quick scan of his monitors. "Why do you ask?"

"I'm seeing rather large fluctuations in your biologicals."

"It must still be that glitch in my helmet, Commander," Josef said. "Andy hasn't been able to isolate the problem yet. But I'm fine."

"If your crew chief can't chase down the problem, I want a new helmet on your head before we come out again."

"Roger, Commander." Inwardly, Josef groaned. Once it became apparent that the problem wasn't in his helmet, he would have no choice but to report to the flight surgeon. Then there would be that new implant. The thought of that made Josef's headache worse.

Once the three Spacehawks reached their patrol area, they killed extra velocity. For the next three hours, they would maintain station, ready to intercept any incoming Federation ships. Josef scanned space through his cockpit bubble, looking for movement that was too fast to be natural. He moved his eyes from that to his control displays, then back. The routines of flight. When the pain in his head flared, he closed his eyes and concentrated on resisting it. Occasionally, he had to lift his visor to rub at his left temple or press his fingers against the side of his head before he could ease the ache.

By the time red flight headed back to *Sheffield*, Josef's hands were trembling from the effort.

"Langenkamp, report to the flight surgeon immediately," Commander Bosworth told him as soon as they emerged from the LRC.

"But, Commander . . ."

"None of that crap," she snapped. "I've been watching you through this entire flight, running diagnostics. There's not a damn thing wrong with your helmet. It's either in your implant or deeper, and I won't have you flying until the surgeon clears you. Should have had that implant replaced after you ejected on Buckingham."

Josef stood there for a moment, head down. "Yes, Commander. I'll go immediately after the briefing and lunch."

"You'll go now. I want you back fit for duty as soon as possible."

"Aye, aye, Commander." Josef finally allowed himself to raise his hand to rub at his head near his implant.

"I'll see that he gets there," Kate said. "I tried to get him to go yesterday."

"We'll talk about *that* later," Bosworth promised, and then she turned and walked off.

"See, all you did was get yourself in trouble," Josef said weakly.

"You can hardly navigate," Kate said.

"Nonsense. It's just a little—" He didn't finish. When he tried to walk, his knees buckled and he slumped to the floor.

Implants required more than an ordinary trauma tube. The replacement of a neural implant was a complicated procedure, beyond the scope of the molecular factories in the usual medical apparatus. Although the operation itself was carried out by computer-controlled "hands," the flight surgeon was at the console directing the work. After so many years, it was a routine operation, even aboard ship, and despite the emergency nature of this case, the surgeon foresaw no complications. Josef, like all serving fighter pilots, was in basically excellent physical condition. The old implant was removed and set aside for thorough inspection. The open socket was flooded with nanoscrubbers to clean the organic connections inside Josef's brain. After the maintenance molecules finished their work, they were flushed and the new implant was inserted, along with the erector molecules that would connect the new implant, run the first diagnostics, and begin the process of tuning implant to brain.

Three hours after Josef was sealed into the surgical tube, the procedure was finished and he was transferred to a recovery tube for postoperative observation. Then technicians took over, to complete the tuning of Josef's new implant.

"You'd better get some sleep or you won't be fit for duty on our next shift either," Commander Bosworth said. Kate Hicks was standing next to Josef's recovery tube. She spun on her heel. She hadn't heard Bosworth come into the room.

"I had to be sure that he's okay first," Kate said. "I couldn't sleep otherwise. I'm still not sure I'll be able to."

"If you're not sure, have the flight surgeon give you a sleep patch. We've got new orders to pick up the pace again. Three hours on ready alert, three in flight, six off. The admiral is getting antsy, expecting Feddie ships to show up."

"Is he really that certain trouble's coming, or is he just nervous?"

Commander Bosworth shook her head. "If I knew things

like that, I'd be C in C of fighter ops back at the Admiralty.''

''Do *you* think they'll be back?''

''Never second-guess an admiral, Hicks. There's no future in it.''

36

Admiral Truscott presided over breakfast in the flag wardroom for the first time since coming aboard *Sheffield*. Coming out for this meal had been Ian Shrikes's suggestion, to counter the worries that had arisen because of the admiral's isolation the day before. There was nothing forced about Truscott's ebullient mood at breakfast. Since viewing the action reports on *Lancer*'s raid on Union, he had been ecstatic. After sending Ian off to bed the night before, Truscott had scarcely been able to sleep for his excitement.

Most of the staff members started breakfast rather tentative in their reactions to the admiral's presence, but his buoyancy quickly cut through that reticence and the meal took on something of a celebratory nature.

"It's not over yet," Truscott cautioned at one point. "We've likely not even seen the worst of this campaign. But we now have striking confirmation of the efficacy of our newest tactics. If and when a Federation fleet arrives, we'll have a few surprises for them."

Details of the admiral's revolutionary new operations manual were just beginning to circulate, even among his own staff. To the best of Ian's knowledge, the only member of the staff who fully knew what *Lancer*'s return meant was Captain Alonzo Rinaldi, flag operations officer. Rinaldi had wakened Ian at four that morning, after reading through the new operations manual and *Lancer*'s after-action report.

"Is this for real, Shrikes?" Rinaldi had demanded.

Ian, fighting his way out of sleep, had been slow to respond. "It is," he managed. He sat up and yawned. "It's what he was at all day yesterday, and *Lancer* is the proof that the new tactics can work."

"He means to put these into general use?"

"I expect he'll use them when the Federation returns. I have instructions to get the manual and *Lancer*'s report to all of the skippers this morning. I think you should start building contingency plans based on ninety-second transit intervals."

"I'll have nightmares for a month," Rinaldi had complained before breaking the link.

Good for you, Ian had thought as he flopped back on his bunk. *Spoiling my sleep like that.*

After breakfast, Truscott called Rinaldi aside. "I want you to make sure that my notes get full circulation throughout the fleet, along with *Lancer*'s action report and all the video and other telemetry she brought back. Get together with the ops officers and navigators, and start building your procedure files. When we go into action, I don't want any failures because people haven't figured out what to do."

"I've had people working on it since four this morning, Admiral," Rinaldi said. "But it affects more than ops and navigation. These measures will touch everything from engineering to weapons."

"Push it, Alonzo, right down the line," Truscott said. "There's no time for drills, so everyone will have to get it right the first time."

"Yes, sir." Rinaldi didn't look happy as he left the wardroom.

Truscott invited Prince William to join him and Ian in his day cabin for coffee.

"I haven't seen it yet, but I understand you've rewritten the Admiralty's *Fleet Operations Manual,*" the prince said when they were sitting around the chart table.

"Significant sections of it," Truscott admitted. "It may give us a real chance against the Federation forces, even if Long John doesn't get reinforcements to us in time."

"Are you going to send him a copy?" William asked.

Truscott nodded. "This morning, along with all of the documentation that *Lancer*'s raid provides. Of course, he's had some warning by now that we're up to something devious out here. *Khyber.*"

"I would dearly love to see the reactions on Buckingham, but not so much that I would forgo the opportunity to see what happens here," William said.

"There's the barest chance that the Federation will hold back on returning to Buchanan, at least for a time, because of *Lancer*'s raid," the admiral said. "*If* they hadn't dispatched a fleet already. But I can't assume that. There's every chance we could find ourselves in action, almost any minute now."

"You seem rather, er, at ease if you really think that's the case, sir," the prince said.

"It wouldn't help a bit for me to run around like a chicken with its head cut off. After the way everyone reacted because I took a few hours to myself yesterday, what would happen if I started acting like a berserker? I've done my worrying, and gone ahead and made what plans I could. I've done everything I can for now. Anything more would muddy the water. The best I can do for the men and women in this fleet is to show them that I have every confidence in them and in the new tactics."

"I had a long chat with Doug Weintraub late last night," William said after nodding agreement with Truscott's explanation. "Buchanan's planetary commission has already begun to discuss the offer of Commonwealth membership and they want more detailed information.''

"Sounds promising," Truscott said. "Are they down to dickering for terms?"

"I don't know that it's that sort of thing," William said. "It's more that they want to know precisely what may be involved, what they'll get from membership, what it might cost them."

"Were you able to ease his mind?" the admiral asked.

"This isn't something that can be easily handled over a partial link, Admiral. Mr. Weintraub is still out with that Marine detachment, part of the sweep southeast of the towns."

"Then there's not much you can do until he's back, right?"

"Not necessarily." William drew the words out. "I *could* go down and have a chat with him in the field."

"During combat operations?"

"With your indulgence, sir. I realize that this must be entirely your decision. But the sooner we put their minds at ease about the Commonwealth, the better all will be, diplomatically. As for combat operations, I believe I am fully capable of meeting the demands of the situation. I know Marine combat operations and equipment, and my physical condition is the equal of any man in the field. Again, with your permission, I *would* like to talk with Mr. Weintraub as soon as possible."

"We could give Mr. Weintraub a lift home, or bring him up here," Truscott suggested.

"I mentioned those options, but he remains adamant about taking a full part in the military operations to liberate his world. He wants to stay in the field with his new Marine friends. Anyway, those Marines may be the best argument we have to convince Mr. Weintraub to support bringing Buchanan into the Commonwealth. Their, er, testimony while he was in hospital on *Victoria* was quite moving. Mr.

Weintraub appeared extremely impressed.''

Truscott's silence went on for several minutes. ''I'm really not certain that I dare risk your life like this, Your Highness,'' he said at last. ''Your brother would have my head if I let anything avoidable happen to you.''

''The risk is mine, Admiral, freely accepted. And, on another level, if a Federation fleet does suddenly appear close by, I might be safer on the ground than aboard *Sheffield*. We have clear superiority on the ground. If a Federation fleet shows up, we will likely not have clear superiority in space until your new tactics have time to operate.''

''It will certainly show the Buchananers how much we value them,'' Ian offered. ''This Weintraub clearly places a great deal of importance on taking personal part in the liberation of his world. If His Highness shows that he's willing to share his risks, it must count for something.''

''Ian, you did a tour at commando school, didn't you?''

''Yes, sir,'' Ian said, seeing what was coming. ''Nine years back.''

''If His Highness goes down, you'll have to go along as his minder. Sorry, sir, but if you go, I must insist on *some* precautions.''

Prince William nodded. ''As you say, sir. Ian, are you willing to take a few chances?''

Ian did hesitate before he nodded. ''I'm willing.''

''I'll want you both in full battle kit, of course,'' Truscott said. ''And you'll have to take along enough men to make sure you don't bollix up the normal operations of that Marine team.''

''A squad from *Sheffield*'s Marine complement?'' Ian suggested.

''That will do. Check with their commander. You'll want the best commando squad they have.''

''Yes, sir.''

The admiral stared at Prince William for a moment. "I assume you want to get about this lark as soon as possible?"

"I think it would be best, sir," William said.

"Very well. You've both got things to do then. I'll be on the flag bridge. Check with me when you're ready to go."

"Aye, aye, sir," Ian said.

The prince stood and gave the admiral a formal salute. "Thank you, sir."

37

David Spencer's platoon was operating in two sections. David had the first two squads on the right flank. Hugo Kassner had the rest on the left. Between them, the two line companies moved along a mile-wide front, covering as much of the terrain as they could. They were all moving northwest, toward Sam and Max, 150 miles away. The Marines averaged under two miles an hour. I&R platoon covered considerably more ground, zigzagging back and forth, planting snoopers out to the sides, plotting their courses as much by the intuition of their sergeants as by any set plan.

"I look for spots where *I* might go to ground if I was on the other side," David explained to Doug. "And we check any areas that the search shuttle reports are too densely wooded for its instruments to say for certain that it's clear."

"Even out here where you don't think they could possibly be?"

David nodded. "Just in case the estimates are wrong. If the Feddies had a real bug up their backsides, they might have gone a lot farther and faster. I know *we* could have. If it had been this platoon, we could have been another thirty miles out."

"Then are you worried that there might be enemy soldiers *behind* us?"

"Worried? No, not particularly. But aware. It's possible,

but not too likely,'' David said. ''We haven't seen any trace of anyone this far out, and the combination of speed and stealth is the most difficult there is.''

During that conversation, a snooper was planted and the core of dirt scattered. ''That's another disadvantage they put themselves under, operating without electronics,'' David explained. ''A good helmet would spot a snooper long before a man could see it without help.''

This time, the team stopped for their rest fifty yards from the snooper, and discipline was tight. When they left, Doug could see nothing to give away the fact that men had ever been there, even briefly.

''Camouflaged ghosts,'' Doug whispered as they moved off through the woods again. His radio transmitter was off, so no one could hear his comment. ''The ultimate invisibles.'' His reaction to that image surprised him, an eerie feeling that seemed to crawl up and down his spine.

''We're what?'' David said into his microphone when Lieutenant Colonel Zacharia gave him the news.

''You're going to have visitors,'' Zacharia repeated. ''Prince William, along with Commander Shrikes, the admiral's aide, and a squad of Marines off *Sheffield*.''

''How can we complete our mission with them along?'' David asked. ''This isn't supposed to be a tea party.''

''No, it's not,'' Zacharia agreed, ''and it won't be. His Highness and Commander Shrikes have both gone through our commando school. So have the Marines who'll be down with them. Don't expect any less from them than you would from your own men. This is political, Spencer. Your Buchananer requested more information about joining the Commonwealth, and His Highness is coming down to talk with him.''

''Can't you head this off, sir?'' David pleaded. ''We'll

need a month to work our way to the towns with extra baggage.''

"Nothing I can do, Spencer. This comes directly from Admiral Truscott. And do try to be civil. Prince William has a smashing opinion of you lot. He's already written a personal commendation for one of your lads. Don't sour his impression. He's on the Privy Council, and that means he has a finger on the purse strings for the RM.''

"Yes, sir. We'll do what we can.''

"The quicker you can make time for them to talk without jeopardizing your mission, the quicker the prince will be able to return to *Sheffield,* if you catch my drift.''

"Aye, sir,'' David said. "When will they be coming in?''

"As I understand it, they're leaving *Sheffield* now. Alpha Company is securing a landing zone. You'll have to collect them after they touch down. Lieutenant Ewing will contact you when he knows how soon.''

I can hardly wait, David thought, but he merely acknowledged the information and switched channels. Ewing was waiting to hear from him.

"The shuttle will be on the ground in thirty minutes.''

"I'll be there to collect them, sir,'' David promised.

"Tory!'' David called over the squad leaders' frequency. "Take over the squads. I've got to go back and pick up visitors.''

"Visitors?'' Kepner asked. "Who's coming?'' And after David told him, his only comment was, "Tell me you're joshing!''

"I wish I could,'' David admitted. "I'll take Doug with me. We'll collect them and get back as soon as we can.''

"This wasn't my idea, David,'' Doug said as he hurried to keep up on the way to the rendezvous. "I had no idea the prince was coming until twenty minutes ago. I never dreamed he'd think of something like this.''

"Royalty," David said. "I guess they're just like officers, only more so. Trust 'em to do the most inconvenient thing possible, give you a mission and then make it more difficult.''

"They must have considerable faith in you and your men, or they'd scarcely risk your king's brother out here.''

That mollified David, but only briefly. "Not necessarily. Prince William is so far removed from the throne that he might be considered expendable.''

"That seems rather a . . . a cavalier attitude.''

David shrugged. "Man's got a right to his opinions. It's just a bloody nuisance, having people like that to nursemaid.''

"Or people like me?" Doug asked, and David stopped walking.

"You're different. You showed that you've got the instincts.''

"But not the training," Doug reminded him. "You said that yourself. I was told that the prince and the other officer *have* had the training.''

That stopped David. "Okay, you're right. I'll reserve judgement. Perhaps they *can* find their way between two trees.'' He shook his head. "Old habits die hard. The prince seems a right sort, from what you and the others who met him told me.''

"That's the impression I had," Doug said. "I took to him straightaway.''

"Okay, let's collect them," David said, setting off again. "The sooner we get you folks together, the sooner you'll finish.''

Ten men came off of the shuttle at the double, all armed and in full battle kit, moving as if they were the first forces down in a hostile zone. There was no way to tell who was who among them. *That's a good sign,* David allowed as he waited at the edge of the clearing.

Two men separated themselves from the rest after the entire group was far enough away from the shuttle to let it take off. David tilted his visor up and walked toward them. Doug followed, raising his visor only after he saw David with his up. The two men from the newly arrived group also lifted visors.

"I certainly didn't expect to see you again so soon," Doug told Prince William, "nor in quite these surroundings."

"No call to put these things off indefinitely," William said.

"This is Sergeant David Spencer," Doug said.

"Your Highness," David said with a nod.

"And this is Commander Ian Shrikes," William said with an equal bow. "Sergeant, I met some of your lads in hospital the other day. Good men, all of them."

"I think so, sir," David replied.

"We'll try to avoid causing you problems, Sergeant," William said. "We might even manage to be of some assistance. Commander Shrikes and I both survived your Marine Commando School, as have all these lads the admiral sent along to be our minders."

"I hope you've kept in tiptop shape, sir," David said. "We move rather rapidly in I&R. Have to, since we cover more ground than the rest."

"We'll do our bit," William assured him. "And if it comes to a fight, we do know how to use our weapons."

David had already noticed those. Both men wore needle pistols at their waists and carried rifles of the same sort.

"Very well, sir. If you're ready to go?"

"As you will, Sergeant. By the way, I believe I should introduce our senior minder, Sergeant Chou of the First Regiment."

"Gaffer Chou?" David asked, looking toward the Marine who had moved up toward the prince.

"How come you're not regimental sergeant major yet, David?" Chou asked, raising his visor.

"I don't know. How come they haven't retired you?" Chou had earned the nickname Gaffer when he was an eighteen-year-old in boot camp. His squad mates had accused him of being an old man in disguise.

"I couldn't stand the strain of retirement," Chou replied. "I'm too used to showing up young pups like you."

"You'll get your chance on this stroll," David promised. "Real dirt under your feet even."

"Dirt's softer than a ship's deck, in case you've forgotten."

"Shouldn't we be going?" Doug asked.

"Yes," David said. "If you've got wind for conferences along the way, use auxiliary channel three." He turned to the prince. "Your Highness?"

"Auxiliary three," William said with a nod. "Very well, Sergeant. You're in charge."

David pushed the pace as he led the new group to join the first two squads of his platoon. There were no complaints, no sign that the pace was overtaxing any of the newcomers. The Marines from *Sheffield* moved professionally into field discipline, weapons ready, their own senses and the augmented sensors of their helmets tuned to the forest. Even the prince and Ian seemed to fit into the routine.

Maybe it won't be so bad after all, David conceded as they neared the latest position of the first two squads. He got on the squad leaders' frequency to alert Tory Kepner of their arrival.

After a short break, the three squads were ready to move again.

"The numbers are going to make this awkward," David

told Chou. Prince William, Ian, and Doug were on the channel as well. "We'll continue normal operations. You follow along behind us. If we get into a jam, you'll be in position to act as a reserve. You can jump in and be the heroes."

"Whatever you say," Chou replied. "We can save ourselves a few steps in the process." He bowed to David.

"Doug, you can stick with them and carry on your chat if you get the chance. Not too loudly though, please."

"I'm learning," Doug reminded him. And, David had to admit, he was.

"If we get out of line, just give us a shout," William said. "We'll fit in our discussions as and when possible."

"Yes, sir," David said, still not totally convinced.

The forest gradually became more dense as the Marines worked their way northwest. The soil became darker, richer; the trees were closer together, with thick patches of underbrush, even brambles. The ground became more irregular, with poor footing. There were occasional creeks, but rarely more than a thin trickle of water.

As the forest became thicker, there were fewer paths to choose from. Any restriction of options made David nervous. It increased the odds of walking into a Federation ambush. The zigs and zags of David's squads came farther apart and became more erratic. The pace slowed for the entire Marine detachment. Periodically, David pulled out his mapboard to check references. An empty blue diamond marked his position—more accurately, the position of his mapboard. A filled blue diamond marked the position of Hugo Kassner's mapboard on the other flank. A thin blue line connected the positions of the mapboards active in the two line companies that were coming along behind and between the I&R advance. David had suppressed the display of blue dots that would have shown him each of the helmets on line.

Doug, Ian, and Prince William were in the middle of the squad of Marines from *Sheffield*. Their conversation was irregular, spaced as conditions permitted.

"I feel somewhat like a huckster at a fair," William said at one point, "trying to get folks to come in for the freak show. I suppose the only real difference is that I believe in what I'm trying to sell."

"We're a cautious lot here," Doug said a few minutes later. "We've been mostly alone since our ancestors first came to Buchanan. We're all original families, which carries its own dangers, or will before many more generations pass. I think we're all ready for more regular contacts with the rest of mankind. But we're not much on buying next month's eggs, if you know what I mean."

"I think so," the prince said. "But, in a way, more than half my job has already been done. You've seen how the Federation operates."

The prince talked about the Second Commonwealth, its foundation, the basics of its government, the relationships among worlds, and so forth. Occasionally, Ian Shrikes added a comment, and—rather more frequently—the two men answered Doug's questions.

"It still sounds like getting a lot of something for not much of anything in return," Doug said during a mid-afternoon break. "Too good to be true."

"The economics are there, Doug," William assured him. "It's the scale that makes it seem so odd. We can download solid examples to your datanet if you like, enough statistics to burn out a score of economists."

"On Buchanan, an economist is merely someone who can figure out how many pounds of pork equal a barrel of ale." Doug laughed soundlessly.

"And on an interplanetary scale, it might come to

something like how many tons of nanotech installations equal the annual rent and maintenance for a Commonwealth University scientific observation station. All the same, one way or another.''

"Or how many colonists equal a local shuttle operation," Ian added.

"I don't imagine any of us would care to be flooded with umpteen thousands of new settlers, all at once," Doug said.

"Of course not. A flood of people would drown your resources, spin you into chaos," William said. "The way of that would be to start small, slowly. As each group of new arrivals is integrated into your existing society, you'll find you have the means to accept that many more the next time, and so forth, at whatever rate, and to whatever limits, you care to accept."

And on, and on.

The next morning started out the way the previous afternoon had ended, with the Marines marching through the forest. Everyone fell easily into the routine. Early on, there was little conversation between Doug and the prince. And then . . .

There was no warning from their helmet visors or from the search shuttle that had passed overhead minutes earlier. There was only a burst of gunfire and a rain of grenades. The gunfire came first, by perhaps two seconds. That lack of coordination between rifles and grenade launchers saved most of the Marines. The gunfire sent everyone diving for cover, off of the path, behind trees, or into the thickest underbrush they could find on the instant.

Prince William's escort pulled him and his companions down, and covered them—partially with their own bodies. It cost two of the Marines from *Sheffield* their lives, but the three men they were charged to protect weren't even wounded.

Surprise was the only advantage this group of Federation soldiers had. They never switched on their helmets. It was daylight, so they could see, but they had no way to coordinate their actions.

The Marine response was immediate and overwhelming. The trajectory of the Federation grenades had been tracked by Commonwealth helmets, which gave the Marines a fix on the enemy positions. They returned grenades ten for one. Four needlers hacked through the underbrush while automatic rifles hurled heavier chunks of metal at the ambushers.

David's second squad concentrated on dumping fire into the Federation position. He split the fire teams of first squad and sent them around both sides. The remaining Marines from *Sheffield* supported second squad.

There was no more fire from the Federation soldiers.

"Move in," David ordered. "Keep your eyes open. Make sure the ambush isn't two-tiered." He switched channels to get the search shuttle to come back for a closer scan. "I want an inch-by-inch check," he said. "I've got dead and wounded, so we need a site for medevac as well."

There was a muffled "Oh, my God!" from the shuttle pilot that startled David by the horror in it. Before the pilot could say anything else, David got a call on the regimental command frequency.

"Enemy ships converging on our fleet. Find defensive positions and dig in . . . *fast!*"

Five seconds later, there was an explosion overhead as the shuttle was destroyed.

Part 8

38

Stasys Truscott kept busy all morning, but this time he made sure that people could see him. He held conferences with his captains and operations officers, explaining his new tactics. "We won't have time to run drills," he told them. "Unless the Federation stays away, we'll be going into combat with the new maneuvers first time." Nearly everyone had complaints about that. A few voiced them at length.

"It works," Arias Rivero said during the holographic conference. "I didn't much like the idea when the admiral gave me my orders either, but damn it, it works. I've gone back over every bit of control data for *Lancer*. We entered and existed precisely where the navcomps said we should be. The Nilssens showed no strain, and we've had no fault-prediction alerts since." Suddenly self-conscious about the way he was carrying on, Rivero stopped and looked around. "Sorry, Admiral."

"Not at all." Truscott grinned. He had been watching the faces of the other officers during Rivero's talk, enjoying himself tremendously.

"We've all had it pounded into our heads from the day we took the king's shilling that there were certain important limitations to our use of Q-space. You can't do this. You can't do that. So little was known about the theoretical limitations of Q-space and the technical limitations of our Nilssen generators that we didn't dare press our luck, even with unmanned drones or MRs. Our planning commissions, the Matériels Board, even the Admiralty took those initial fears—born when Q-space was a brand-new discovery—and fossilized them into Unquestionable Creed. Then one frightened and desperate man took a chance that no one in authority at the Admiralty would have *dreamed* of taking and catapulted an antique MR into Q-space directly after launch from his backyard. He didn't destroy his world or the MR. He didn't rip a great gash in the fabric of space-time or any of the other rot the naysayers have been vomiting out for generations.'' Truscott paused to scan the holographic images around his chart table.

''The rest followed like gas after a spicy meal.''

When the meeting ended and the last holographic image had faded, Truscott leaned back and took a deep breath. ''You're getting too tense,'' he told himself. ''You'd think you were already defending yourself before an Admiralty Court of Inquiry.'' He grunted then, aware that it might come to that.

He got up and fixed a cup of tea, then went out to the flag bridge.

''Any word from Ian or His Highness?'' he asked Gabby Bierce.

''No, sir, not a word. The Marines are still moving.''

The admiral nodded, then took a long, slow sip at his tea. ''I can't help but wonder just how much of the rough life our guest will take to. The Marines won't make it any easier for him than they have to.''

''Likely not, sir.'' Gabby grinned. ''I imagine they're pretty ticked at having outsiders stop by for a natter while they're looking for Feddies.''

''Is Miko ready to go down and pick them up when they call?''

''He's been waiting since first thing this morning, sir. I

think there's some sort of pool over how long His Highness will stay on the ground.''

''I didn't hear that.'' Truscott put a stern look on his face, then relaxed. ''I hope you got your money down on a good time.''

''I think so, sir,'' Gabby said, but the admiral was already on his way to the door.

It took Truscott less than a minute to walk the forty feet to his day cabin, but that was enough to change the situation completely. ''Call to Quarters'' sounded as Truscott reached for his doorknob. He hesitated, hand on the knob, then pushed the door open. His complink was buzzing madly. He crossed to it just long enough to say, ''I'm on my way back to the flag bridge.'' He didn't wait for an acknowledgement.

''Federation ships bearing in at attack speed,'' Commander Estmann reported when Truscott reached the flag bridge.

''What's the layout?'' the admiral demanded.

''Nine ships so far, in a skirmish line, from forty-five degrees north of the ecliptic, heading directly toward us, no more than thirty miles higher than *Victoria* and *Sheffield*. The initial scans show five dreadnoughts and four escorts.''

''What's the closest match with the new ops plans?'' Truscott adjusted a monitor to show the essential portions of Buchanan's system.

''C-4'' Estmann replied after a second's hesitation. ''We show two more escorts now, on their flanks.''

''Make to all ships, 'Execute C-4 instantly,' '' Truscott said.

''A report from below, Admiral,'' Gabby said. ''That lot of Marines the prince is with just walked into an ambush. Fighting going on now.''

''Keep me posted, Gabby,'' Truscott said. ''Get Captain Hardesty on link.''

"Two more escorts, Admiral," Estmann reported. "These are below us, almost atmospheric. C-4 is still the best match."

"Admiral?" A holo of Captain Hardesty appeared in front of Truscott's command console.

"Launch the alert squadron to take the escorts below us under fire. Direct the Spacehawks that are already out to go after those two as well. Any weapons you can bring to bear on them in the next thirty seconds. Then jump us to *Sheffield*'s first C-4 alternate."

"Aye, sir." Hardesty's image disappeared.

Victoria, Sheffield, Thames, and *Lancer* jumped to Q-space within twenty seconds of one another. *Repulse,* concealed from the main Federation formation by Buchanan's smaller moon, waited longer before moving.

The classic scenarios of space combat were like graceful ballets in slow motion, with engagements requiring hours—even *days*—to be joined, fought, and decided. There was time for admirals to micro-manage the fight, running alternatives through Combat Intelligence Center computers at great length. Truscott's wholesale rewriting of combat procedures made that impossible. The battle arena became too fluid.

Repulse made what was almost certainly the shortest Q-space transit in history. It entered Q-space five hundred yards above Pebble and exited 150,000 miles away, slightly above and behind the center of the Federation line, effectively between two of the five dreadnoughts. For ninety seconds, *Repulse* bombarded those two ships with every weapon she had. The dreadnoughts had scarcely had time to begin returning fire before *Repulse* was directly between them, limiting the firepower the enemy could bring to bear without risking damage to its own vessels.

Then *Repulse* returned to Q-space. The dreadnought to

her left was close enough to be touched by the bubble of Q-space that *Repulse* generated.

Repulse had no opportunity to see the damage she caused, but *Sheffield* was back in normal-space by that time, and her cameras caught the explosion as the dreadnought's starboard bulkheads were torn and twisted. Debris was sucked through the space-time vacuum created by the Q-space maneuver, hurtling large chunks of shrapnel toward the next dreadnought in the Federation line.

The second dreadnought survived only by turning its weapons on the approaching debris, vaporizing the most dangerous chunks. All of its attention was focused on that threat when *Lancer* passed through the Federation line on the other side at a ninety-degree angle, aimed directly at the surface of Buchanan. Like *Repulse, Lancer* only remained in normal-space for ninety seconds. Though *Lancer*'s results were less spectacular, she still scored telling hits on the nearest Federation ships before she reentered Q-space.

By that time, *Sheffield* had completed her first interchange with the two escort vessels that had been the last to arrive. Coming up from directly astern, *Sheffield* was shielded from many of their weapons while she launched her Spacehawks and opened fire on the Federation ships. Then *Sheffield* was gone through Q-space, out of reach.

The first hit that either Federation escort scored wasn't even against any of the ships or fighters in space. One of its beam weapons scored a hit against a shuttle operating low over the forest below.

Victoria and *Thames,* the most lightly armed of the five Commonwealth ships, made the longest jumps in the original dispersal. *Thames* jumped out of the ecliptic, taking her position over the sun's north pole, far from any of the action. *Victoria* hopped to the far side of Buchanan to launch its shuttles with the remaining companies of Marines. The shuttles landed out of direct observation by the Federation ships. And although the Marines disembarked and set up defensive perimeters, they remained ready to board their shuttles again to return to *Victoria*, or to move closer to the action. After the last Marine shuttle had been launched and was well clear of the ship, *Victoria* went back into Q-space and emerged in normal-space well behind the Federation ships, too far away to be in immediate danger from any enemy weapons.

The battle progressed considerably during *Victoria*'s absence.

Admiral Truscott leaned forward in his seat on the flag bridge. He kept his eyes on a holographic projection of the engagement. The projection was visibly disturbed each time one of the Commonwealth ships providing the video jumped back to Q-space to regroup and return. The repeated and sudden shifts in the time the signals needed to reach *Sheffield* taxed the computer that maintained the projection.

"One Feddie escort definitely degraded," an enemy damage assessment officer from CIC reported. "The shift in her power emissions is clear."

"We're ready for our next jump," Mort Hardesty reported immediately after that. "No difficulties with the Nilssens."

"Very well, Captain, shift to our next position as soon as you're ready," Truscott replied.

"Q-space insertion in thirty-one seconds, sir." Then Hardesty was off the link. Truscott focused on the holo display of the battle again. *Repulse* and *Lancer* were attacking the main enemy formation simultaneously now, one from either end of the line. *Repulse* veered off above the enemy ships. *Lancer* ducked below. They made the transit to Q-space simultaneously, but Truscott had no chance at the time to see if that caused any damage to the Federation dreadnought between them because *Sheffield* made her jump before those images had time to reach the ship.

The concealing gray of Q-space formed around *Sheffield*, but only remained there a little more than the minimal ninety seconds that the Nilssen generators needed to recycle. This time, the ship emerged directly in front of, and slightly above, the two low-flying enemy escort ships, and the weapons officer concentrated on the already damaged ship as they approached on a near collision course. Near the rear of *Sheffield*, a pattern of mines was deployed. While *Sheffield* remained in normal-space, her bulk would hide the mines. When she exited to Q-space, the enemy escort ships would be too near the mines to effectively maneuver away from them. *If* the plan worked.

Arias Rivero was shocked when he saw his face in a chance reflection from a complink screen. His teeth were bared in a fierce grin, the heady aggressiveness of a successful predator. There was something exhilarating about this sudden stooping to the attack, assaults that were broken off before they could become *too* dangerous, to be resumed from another direction minutes later.

After *Lancer*'s second pass at the main Federation battle line, she jumped ninety-two light-seconds away, reemerging in normal-space just as the images of the end of the attack were reaching that position. As *Lancer* and *Repulse* disappeared from their own screens, one of the remaining Federation dreadnoughts suddenly twisted ninety degrees out of line. Its momentum continued to carry it forward, but its rockets were pushing it toward the surface. Attitude rockets were fired and slowly started to correct the ship's alignment. The maneuver hadn't been completed before it was time for *Lancer* to duck back through Q-space for her next attack.

This time, *Lancer* appeared precisely where she had disappeared the last time, below the center of the Federation line, but on a different heading, pushing up through the line, next to the dreadnought that was still attempting to return to its initial course. *Repulse* appeared on the other side of the massive Federation ship, and both of Truscott's frigates opened up on the one ship ... while taking other targets under fire on their opposite sides.

It wasn't coordination, it was merely luck. Missiles from *Lancer* and *Repulse* hit opposite sides of the Federation dreadnought at virtually the same instant, both far back along the final major segment of the twelve-mile-long ship. The final eight hundred feet of the dreadnought were blown loose, taking down the ship's main propulsion units. By the time the two Commonwealth ships blinked back to Q-space, the dreadnought was obviously out of commission, falling behind the other ships in the line.

Seven Federation ships changed course, climbing higher, away from the planet. The three dreadnoughts and four escorts spread out their line, the wreckage of two dreadnoughts remaining behind. The ship that had been caught by the Q-space bubble had been shattered. There were no life support systems operating. The other dreadnought had lost its main propulsion module, but the rest of the ship remained intact, gastight. Life support systems were still functioning. The ship was using maneuvering rockets, trying to achieve a stable orbit; it no longer had the power to climb away from the planet.

The two Federation escorts that had come in separately from the rest of the fleet appeared to be in worse condition. The one that had been damaged first had taken more serious damage on *Sheffield*'s second pass. Then it hit two mines. Its companion had escaped damage the first time around, but this time it suffered several missile hits, then struck a mine. It was without power, and its orbit was degrading. Unless its crew managed to restore power, the ship would be atmospheric in three hours. That would spell the end of it.

"Take five," Truscott whispered to himself as he viewed the latest conditions. "Give them a little longer to stew." It was part of the plan he had ordered to meet this attack. Blitz quickly, then pull away, long enough to communicate among the ships of the fleet and, more importantly, to run more detailed diagnostics of critical on-board systems, particularly Nilssen generators.

It was mere proximity that brought *Sheffield*'s reports to Truscott before news came from the other ships. "The Nilssen generators are running about a tenth of a degree hotter than normal, but cooling quickly," Hardesty reported. "We've sustained no detectable damage."

Victoria and *Thames* also reported no damage. Since they had stayed clear of the fighting, that was no surprise. *Repulse* reported damage to one maneuvering rocket, but no degradation of operating ability. *Lancer* hadn't taken a single hit.

Truscott got all five captains together on a holographic link. "We're doing fine so far," he assured them. "We've already put a force greater than our own out of action, and the rest of the Federation fleet has to be reeling. Stay alert though. They may have somebody bright enough to figure out a way to counter what we're doing. With those two escorts away from the main fleet out of action, we'll switch to the C-3 schedule. *Sheffield,* move in to recover your Spacehawks, then we'll rendezvous with *Lancer* and *Repulse* for our next go. That dreadnought that's lost its tail still has a sting. Let's finish it off."

"Why don't they pull out to regroup?" *Lancer*'s first officer asked, only half turning toward the captain.

"I've been wondering that for five minutes," Captain Rivero replied. *Lancer* was back in Q-space, heading for its next attack. "Either that first dreadnought was the flagship and they haven't sorted out their command and control yet, or there's some overriding reason for them to stay in reach."

"Transports coming in behind them?" the first officer suggested.

"That's the obvious thought," Rivero said. "Another flight of ships in any case, transports or another battle line. Could be their mission is simply to keep us engaged for another fleet to box us in."

"Except the box has too many holes."

"We hope," Rivero said as *Lancer* came out of Q-space.

Sheffield and the two frigates came out of Q-space together this time, *Sheffield* over and behind the center of the Federation line, *Lancer* to the far left and *Repulse* to the far right. Return fire was heavier this time than before, but still uncoordinated, scarcely effective, unable to overwhelm the defensive systems of the Commonwealth ships.

The Federation escort ship nearest *Repulse* started to maneuver away from the fleet line, half of its propulsion systems suddenly inactive. *Repulse* delayed her return to Q-space by ten seconds to pump another volley of missiles at the wounded Federation ship.

The ten-second delay meant that *Repulse* was the last of the Commonwealth ships to spot the five Federation Cutter class troopships that emerged from Q-space on a low approach to the settled area of Buchanan. The first shuttles were already being launched from the enemy troopships when *Repulse* identified the new targets.

39

It had been a miserable twenty-four hours for Josef Langenkamp, even before the arrival of the Federation fleet. When the trauma tube let him regain consciousness after surgery, he felt overwhelmed by the familiar nausea and disorientation—and this time seemed much worse than he remembered. The process of tuning the new implant took two technicians seventeen hours, and that too was extraordinary. A large, specialized, imaging apparatus was connected to Josef's neural implant. The computers that collated the data would be able to account for the firing of virtually every neuron in his brain for the entire time. There was no *physical* pain, but the process was uncomfortable.

By the time the technicians pulled Josef free of the equipment, he felt so nauseated that he held both hands over his stomach. He felt weak, almost unable to keep his legs under him long enough to transfer from the lab table to the wheelchair that was waiting to take him to the convalescence ward.

"Easy, Lieutenant," one technician said. "Let us do the work. You'll come out of it soon enough. A little broth when you get to your bed, and you'll be ready for a real meal in two or three hours."

"I don't believe it," Josef said. "I don't think I'll ever be ready for food again." *And I don't ever want to go through* that *again.*

"Sure you will," the technician said. "We issue a brand-new warranty every time. There's not a thing wrong with you from the neck up."

"At least nothing physical," the other technician added with a laugh.

The horrible feeling passed as quickly as the technicians promised. In two hours, Josef was hungry. A meal was brought in, high on proteins and carbohydrates, twice the calories of a normal dinner. He ate every bit and considered asking for more, but settled for an extra glass of citrus juice.

He didn't taste the sedative that was added to his juice. And when he woke eight hours later, he never even considered the hows and whys of his long, restful slumber.

"When can I get out of here and back to duty?" he asked the nurse as soon as she came in. "I'm just taking up space here."

"I'll agree with that, but you know the rules, forty-eight hours after coming out of the box before we can release you."

"Peacetime rules," Josef countered. "This is wartime. Everything's rush rush now."

"I'll ask the flight surgeon," the nurse said. "I expect he'll have your answer tomorrow night."

Josef didn't doubt her for a moment. Even when the flight surgeon, Lieutenant Commander Shai Jupa, came in later than morning, Josef wasn't prepared for the answer he got when he repeated his question.

"How do you feel right now?" the surgeon asked.

"Ten thousand percent. And that's on an empty stomach."

"We'll run a few tests and see what the black boxes say," Jupa told him. He called up Josef's file on his portable complink. "You were rather beyond the usual replacement parameters. You should have been in for your replacement a week ago."

"Wartime necessity," Josef said.

"That's not the way your squadron commander put it," Jupa replied. "She insinuated that we should have done a preventive replacement after your last, um, misadventure."

"It was my fighter that was leaking, Doc, not my head."

"You'll have to take that up with Commander Bosworth. I have no desire to get in the middle of *that* discussion."

"Just get me out of here as fast as possible."

"We always get our patients out of here as quickly as possible, and not one second sooner."

Josef still got out sooner than he expected.

When "Call to Quarters" sounded, Josef didn't wait for orders. He got out of bed and started pulling on the clothes he had been wearing when he was brought to the hospital. Everything but his flight suit was in the cupboard by his bed. The flight suit had been taken back to the squadron. Josef was slapping down the clamps on his boots when Dr. Jupa came in.

"What is it?" Josef asked.

"Federation ships," Jupa said. "You still feel fit?"

"Ready to go," Josef assured him.

"Then get back to your squadron in a hurry. We're going to need every pilot we have in the next few hours, I think."

Josef didn't wait to be told twice. "Thanks, Doc." He was already out the door, hurrying along the passageways toward the squadron's section of the ship, a mile away. During long straightaways, he even ran, exulting in the fact he didn't feel the slightest dizziness or pain. Gastight bulkheads slowed him since he had to stop to open the hatches and then shut them again after him. Under general quarters, each section of the ship was sealed off from the rest to localize damage. With the frequent stops, Josef needed fifteen minutes to reach fourth squadron's ready room.

"The flight surgeon release you?" Commander Bosworth demanded.

"Yes." Josef sucked in a deep breath. "He said we're under attack."

"We are. Get into your flight gear. I'll notify your crew chief. We're the only squadron left aboard, and we've just been placed on ready alert. Hurry it up."

Kate and another pilot helped him suit up and asked how he felt.

"Brand new," Josef assured them, particularly Kate. She smiled and gave his arm a squeeze. "What's the opposition look like?"

Kate gave him a quick rundown. "We launched the other squadrons, then jumped to Q-space. We're jumping every ninety *seconds*. The whole fleet is."

"What's the rest of the wing doing?"

"Harassing two Feddie escort ships operating low."

"Any sign of transports?"

"Not yet."

The pilots kept their eyes on the complink monitors, watching the battle as best they could, cheering when a Federation ship appeared to be damaged, clutching the arms of their chairs nervously when one of their own ships came under fire. *Sheffield* remained untouched through several passes.

Then the Federation transports arrived and started disgorging shuttles. It took less than a minute for orders to arrive for fourth squadron.

"Listen up," Commander Bosworth called out. "We're going to our fighters, ready for launch. Our mission is to splash as many shuttles as we can. It looks as if the Feddies want to land a regiment of their own. Let's keep the odds down for our Marines."

"Gang launch?" someone asked.

"With only ninety seconds in normal-space at a time?"

Bosworth said. "Of course we're going out in a gang launch."

"You feeling right, sir?" Andy Mynott asked as he helped Josef into the cockpit of Red Three.

"Right as rain, Andy."

"You mind yourself out there, sir. This time it's a proper fair."

"I'll keep that in mind. You mind yourself as well. Skipper's using *Sheffield* like a Spacehawk."

"I know. I've been worrying about that."

Locked into his fighter, Josef turned his attention to the battle again. *Sheffield* made another Q-space transit. When she returned to normal-space, she was coming in on the Federation transports while the frigates continued to engage the enemy's main battle line. The LRCs were extended and the Spacehawk pilots were hurled out into space. *Sheffield* vanished almost before Josef had time to adjust to the tactical situation.

The transports tried to take the Spacehawks under fire, but it was uncoordinated, and limited by the need to avoid endangering their own shuttles. The shuttles themselves were defenseless, and so much slower than the Spacehawks that they were virtually standing targets. The first thirty seconds it was a duck shoot.

Then one of the Federation escort ships came close enough to bring its weapons to bear and the Spacehawks had to divide their time between shooting down shuttles and gyrating through random evasive maneuvers. For ninety seconds, the only ships visible over Buchanan were Federation. During that interval, *Sheffield*'s Spacehawks took the brunt of all the enemy's weapons.

Josef and Kate each logged two solid kills on shuttles. Altogether, the fighters hit half of the three dozen Federation landing craft in the first minute. Then the fighters were deluged by missiles from the enemy ships. For a time, escaping that deadly shower took all of their attention, taking them out of position for continued strikes on the shuttles.

"We might as well get in a few blows against the ships," Commander Bosworth decided. "We need the altitude anyway."

The five fighters of red flight took up an intercept course for one of the Federation escorts. They still weren't in optimum range when the Commonwealth ships returned—*Sheffield* and *Victoria* taking the transports under fire while *Lancer* and *Repulse* concentrated on the battle line.

Up to a point, Spacehawks could maneuver automatically to evade incoming missiles, but when the fire was too heavy, the pilot had to be ready to take over. Even plugged directly into the fighter's circuitry, there were limits to his ability as well. Josef saw the missile coming, and he clearly saw that he had no avenue of escape.

"Here I go again," he said over the radio just before the missile took off his fighter's left wing and sent him spinning over the other Spacehawks of red flight. The blast stunned him for a moment. Then he blinked, astounded to find that he was still alive.

"I'm going down," he reported, so calmly that he didn't believe it himself. "I'll hold off as long as I can before I eject. I hope there are friendly faces down there to collect me."

"Roger," Commander Bosworth said, too occupied to spare more words.

A few seconds passed before Kate managed a quick "Luck, Joe."

Josef calmly went through his emergency checklist, making sure that his escape pod retained full integrity. He wanted to hold off ejection until he was below twenty-five thousand feet.

He just happened to be facing the right direction to see a missile take the nose off *Lancer*.

The Nilssen generators couldn't adjust instantly. When the missile struck *Lancer*, it shifted the ship's attitude immediately. The propulsion units continued to power the ship, working at an angle to the ship's momentum as it did a slow backflip. Throughout *Lancer*, those crew members who weren't strapped in or firmly hanging on were thrown down or around, adding to the confusion.

"Damage control, what's our situation?" Arias Rivero shouted. "Navigation, get us stabilized." He quickly noted that almost a minute remained before they could shift back to Q-space—if they were still able to.

"Engineering. Generator status!"

"We've lost the first three compartments forward," the first officer reported. "That's the nose off all three hulls. Behind that point, our integrity remains intact. No word on casualties yet."

The ship's remaining maneuvering rockets started slowing *Lancer*'s cartwheel spin. But the ship was finally stabilized not by her own efforts, but by the impact of another missile exploding far aft. That blast put *Lancer*'s Nilssen generators out of commission. With the Nilssens gone, *Lancer* lost its artificial gravity as well as the ability to transit Q-space.

"Weapons, keep putting out everything you can," Rivero said. "Engineering, can we get our Nilssens back on line?"

The weapons officer acknowledged immediately. A third of the ship's weapons systems were out of action, or gone, but everything else was still operating. Engineering didn't respond. Rivero repeated his question before the first officer gave him the news.

"Main engineering station is gone, Captain."

"Get the secondary station. I need to know if we have anything left," Rivero told him. The first officer nodded and went to work.

Rivero put in the call to *Sheffield*. In four quick sentences, he alerted Admiral Truscott to their condition and immediate prospects.

"Your course is carrying you away from the action," Alonzo Rinaldi told Rivero. "We're holding in normal-space for an extra thirty seconds. *Repulse* will be out and back in on schedule. We're pulling all of the Spacehawks out to divert the Feddies in the interim. If you can't get your Nilssens back up, we'll have *Victoria* come in to evacuate as soon as you're clear of the Feddies."

Rivero's first officer returned and shook his head. "The Nilssens are gone, completely."

"It looks as if we'll need *Victoria*," Rivero told *Sheffield*. "Our Nilssens are gone."

"Right, *Lancer*. We'll have *Victoria* rendezvous with you. Twelve minutes. That will put the Feddies far enough away to let the transfer proceed."

Twelve minutes.

Two more Federation missiles hit *Lancer* during the first of those minutes, but only one penetrated the outer hull, damaging two more compartments. Rivero and his crew started preparing to abandon ship. Wounded crew members were given first aid. It was too soon to start numbering the dead, but Rivero wanted to be absolutely certain that no living crew member was abandoned with the ship.

"Let's expend all the ordnance we can before we go," Rivero told his first officer. "We might as well not waste it."

He closed his eyes then for a minute, overcome by the difficulty of maintaining a calm exterior while he was screaming inside. *My ship. My people.*

• • •

It was an act of rebellion, but Josef took his helmet off before he blasted the escape pod free of his crippled fighter. "I'm not going to go through another implant *this* soon," he swore.

He plotted his landing zone and updated the memory modules in his helmet. He would need the radio links in the helmet once he was on the ground. And he could project maps onto the visor to keep track of his location. It brought a chill when he realized that he might have to walk all of the way to the settlements on Buchanan, especially when he realized that he would land 125 miles away from them.

"If we lose the battle, I might have to walk all the way back to Buckingham," he whispered. The thought of being stranded, perhaps permanently, was more frightening than the thought of a dozen replacements of his neural implant.

Braking rockets. First parachutes. And on. Josef held his helmet tightly against his chest. He didn't want it caroming around the cockpit like a billiard ball when the pod hit the ground.

"I've got to be able to walk away from this if I'm going to make it," he reminded himself.

Then his pod was smashing into the trees, the endless trees.

40

David Spencer and Tory Kepner were still working with the wounded when Lieutenant Ewing brought up the line companies. David's third and fourth squads had already come across to reinforce their mates.

"Laager up, Bandar," Ewing told his lead sergeant by radio. "We'll stay here to take care of everyone, then find a better defensive position."

"We've got four dead and six wounded, Lieutenant," David reported. "Three of the dead and two of the wounded are from the squad off *Sheffield*."

Ewing looked around and was relieved to see that the VIPs appeared uninjured. "How serious are the wounds?"

"Well, if we get them into trauma tubes right away, none of them are in danger. Sergeant Chou is hurt worst. The others will be able to walk, at least for awhile. Gaffer's legs are both hit—bad. We had to tourniquet both of them."

"I don't think we can count on pickup anytime soon, even for wounded," Ewing said. "Commander Shrikes, you're senior serving officer here. I don't think earlier conditions prevail any longer."

Ian exchanged glances with the prince. "I'm not a serving officer," William reminded him softly, and Ian nodded.

"Lieutenant, you know your men far better than I do. For the moment at least, I won't interfere with your tactical command. I'll simply play admiral and let you do the skippering."

"Very well, sir."

"I'll contact *Sheffield* and get what guidance I can," Ian continued. "That may take some time if Admiral Truscott puts his new tactics into operation. How good is our position here?"

"It'll do for a bit, sir," Ewing said. "There's better to be had."

"Find us a good spot, Lieutenant, and let me know when we're ready to move," Ian told him.

"Aye, sir." Ewing started talking into his helmet radio, calling for Bandar Jawad to meet him, and unfolding his mapboard as he walked to confer with his lead sergeant.

Ian knelt next to David, who was still working with Gaffer Chou. "Sergeant, you've had more opportunity to work with Ewing and his men. How good are they?"

"I've known Bandar Jawad forever, and Ewing has had him to bring him along. They'll do quite well, I'd say."

"Good. I'll trust your judgement. I know something about *that*."

"Thank you, sir." David hesitated. "I hope that you and His Highness haven't completely forgotten what you learned in commando school."

"So do I," Ian replied, and Prince William nodded his agreement.

"We may get down to the same fix the Feddies have been in since we arrived," David said. "That kind of go is rough on everyone."

Ian shook his head. "No, that's not the way for us. Worse comes to worst, we head back toward the towns. If we can't act as a cohesive military force with some real hope of holding out, we surrender."

"Surrender?" David asked.

"What good does it do the Commonwealth to have its

best men fight to the death in a hopeless exhibition of bra-
vado?'' the prince asked. ''In any case, we can cause the
Federation more trouble as recalcitrant prisoners of war
than we can as a few ragged guerrilla bands if they come
out of the battle overhead with the sort of supremacy we've
had until now.''

''I hope it doesn't come to that, sir,'' David said, getting
to his feet. ''If I might be so bold, all of our I&R platoons
are on the ground. We've got the training and experience
that could give us a chance to be effective, even if the
Feddies do own the skies after today. It's part of our training, sir, part of the job description, you might say.''

''Let's stick with 'I hope it doesn't come to that,' '' Ian
said.

''Aye, sir,'' David said.

''I'm not about to meekly turn myself over to the Federation in any case,'' Doug said. He had been sitting off to
the side, unsettled by everything that had happened in the
last half hour. ''I won't simply let them take over my world
again without every bit of fight I can give them.''

''Let's not get so far afield,'' Prince William suggested.
''With the admiral's new operations book, I don't think it
will come to that pass. And we still haven't heard from
Buckingham.''

Thirty minutes later, the force had moved a mile and was
digging into defensive positions on a low, heavily wooded
hillside. But even that routine operation was interrupted
when Lieutenant Ewing received a call from *Sheffield*.

''We have a pilot down, twelve miles northwest of your
position. Marked by the green cross on your mapboards.
Can you pick him up?''

''We'll try,'' Ewing replied.

''There's another problem. The Feddies have managed
to land troops. They have at least a full battalion of fresh

troops on the ground and together, nine miles the other side of the pilot, on a direct line from you through his position.''

"We'll keep our eyes open," Ewing said, noting the red blips of Federation helmets appearing on his mapboard. As soon as the link to *Sheffield* was broken, Ewing turned the information over to David Spencer.

"Your lot is best equipped for this sort of work," Ewing said, and David nodded.

"Part of the job, sir." He pointed to the green cross on the mapboard. "With a little luck, we can reach him in well under four hours. Should we come back this way, or wait for you to join us?"

"Neither. We'll rendezvous here." Ewing brought his finger down on the mapboard. "That'll give you another three miles to walk after you get the pilot, and it'll put us ten miles closer to Sam and Max. Hilly ground. Should give us good defensive positions." He expanded the mapboard's scale and called Doug over.

"Do you know this area at all?" Ewing asked, returning the map briefly to its earlier scale then zeroing in again.

"I've never been there, if that's what you mean. You suspect Federation troops are there?"

"No. Unless you know some reason not to, that's where we're heading. The I&R folks have a pilot to pick up and we'll rendezvous there."

"No reason I know of," Doug said, turning his attention from Ewing to David. "How far do we have to go to pick up this lad?"

"Twelve miles," David said. "But this is one march you'd best forgo. Stay with the companies. We'll be pushing ourselves hard."

"You're afraid I'll slow you down?"

"On this go, yes." David said. "It's all speed. Twelve miles of heavy forest in four hours. With Feddies coming in from the other side. They may try to get to our pilot before we can, and they're three miles closer.''

Doug hesitated for only an instant. ''In that case, I'll stay. I don't want to be the cause of one of your men being captured.''

Sheffield and *Repulse* continued to harass the main Federation battle fleet, driving them farther away from the crippled *Lancer*. A dozen Spacehawks added their stings, while the rest of the wing continued to attack the transports and made occasional dives to fire at the shuttles and troops that had already landed. For the time being, the crippled dreadnought was left to its own problems. *Lancer* was drifting, but at escape velocity, so there was no immediate worry that it might crash on Buchanan. *Victoria* came out of Q-space and matched course and speed with *Lancer,* moving carefully closer to shorten the time of exposure to enemy weapons as it launched shuttles to rescue the frigate's survivors.

Captain Rivero remained on the bridge of *Lancer* with most of the regular bridge watch. The conversations were subdued. Several of the men showed signs of injuries sustained when the ship had lost its artificial gravity, cuts and bruises. But there was no hint of panic.

''Double-check the integrity of the seals at the docking ports,'' Rivero instructed. ''No telling how badly the hulls have been warped.''

Two minutes later, the first officer relayed the report. ''Three ports are all we have, Captain.'' Three left of twelve, no change from the first reports. ''We have shuttles mating with all three now. The pilots know what they're getting into. They'll run their own checks on the airlocks.''

Rivero nodded. He squeezed the top of his nose, trying to clear a dull pain between his eyes. ''How many people have we lost, Mel?''

''Forty-two,'' the first officer replied.

"Out of a complement of a hundred and eighty-seven."

"We did a lot of damage first, sir," the first officer said. "Union and here. *Lancer* made her mark."

A report came over the speaker. The first three shuttles were loading people. Three more shuttles were waiting to dock. That was all it would take to remove the last survivors.

"We've done our job here," Rivero told the others on the bridge. "Let's make our exit with what dignity we can."

"You'll be wanting this, sir." The first officer handed a flat object to Rivero. The captain needed a moment to recognize his framed letter of commendation from the governor of Dorado. He took the letter, fondled it for an instant, then looked up.

"Thank you, Mel. I forgot all about it."

"I knew you'd miss it later, sir."

"One last check, Mel. We don't want to leave anyone behind."

"Aye, sir. I figured we'd do that ourselves." He gestured at the bridge staff. "We'll meet you at the number two airlock."

David pushed himself and his men. He had spoken to the pilot over the complink, to tell him how long it would take the rescue party to reach him and to take what cover he could. "We've got a relay on your helmet beacon, and you'll be able to track us as we come in. Keep your head down. If those Feddie blips get too close, turn your helmet off and move due east. We'll find you."

"Will do, Sergeant," Josef Langenkamp replied. "I've grown very attached to my head." *More than you can guess.*

The I&R platoon moved in two lines roughly thirty yards apart. No matter how rapidly they hurried, every man in the platoon remained alert for any hint of an ambush. Fingers rested over trigger guards, ready to move to action in less than a heartbeat. There was a measure of fear as well, but fear was merely another tool to be used, not an enemy to be hidden from.

A third of the way to the flyer's position, David stopped his men for a very short break. He linked back to Lieutenant Ewing to ask how the sky battle was going.

"Fluid," Ewing reported. "Not as much activity as before. Looks like the Feddies are learning. *Lancer*'s been abandoned. Most of the crew survived. But I've got something else for you to worry about. Those Feddies on the ground are moving toward the downed pilot. They didn't start as early as you did, but they're still closer."

"We'll do what we can," David said, and he waved his men back to their feet.

The I&R platoon took one final rest before tackling the last mile. David sent Tory Kepner ahead with one fire team to make contact with the pilot.

"We'll be coming up behind you, not more than a minute or two off," David assured Tory. "Those Feddies are still two miles from him, but we don't have time to waste."

"As long as there's no ambush waiting between us and the plughead," Tory said. "We'll get him. He's not wounded, right?"

"Right. Said he didn't even get a scratch."

"Lucky buzzard," Tory mumbled as he led his men off.

41

Sheffield **came out** of Q-space ready to engage the Federation main battle line again, but it was gone. *Repulse* and *Sheffield* were alone, except for the crippled ships. The dreadnought that had lost its propulsion module had taken further hits since and was no longer a threat. The Federation transports were eight hundred miles away, accelerating, climbing away from Buchanan. The transports were still being harassed by a few Spacehawks, but most had broken off the contact. *Victoria* was in Q-space after retrieving *Lancer*'s survivors.

"Now it gets hairy," Truscott said, to no one in particular. "I'm surprised they needed this long to take the hint."

"They waited until the transports unloaded," Alonzo Rinaldi said. "Hadn't been for us, they'd have been able to keep their shuttles safe."

"No telling what they'll do now," Truscott said. "I'd guess their concern might be to protect those transports until they can shift to Q-space."

"Do we go after the transports or wait for the battle line to return?" Captain Hardesty asked over the complink.

"We wait, for now," Truscott replied. "We need to retrieve our Spacehawks. We'll use both *Repulse* and *Victoria* to cover the operation. *Victoria* hasn't that much in the way of armament, but we'll put everything we have into this. I want all of the ships ready to jump instantly though, just in case the Federation ships pop back right in our face.''

''We're ready as of right now,'' Hardesty said, stretching the sentence until the necessary ninety seconds had elapsed.

''Admiral, *Victoria* just emerged, out past Pebble,'' Gabby Bierce said from his console.

''Ask them when they'll be ready to jump again so we can pick up our birds,'' Truscott told him.

''Soon as their Nilssens recycle,'' Gabby reported.

''Tell them they'll help cover this maneuver. We'll get our birds in as quickly as we can.'' Truscott turned in his chair. ''Weapons. Any trace of the Federation ships yet?''

''No, sir. They must have withdrawn a considerable distance.'' The weapons officer looked at a clock. ''Certainly at least two light-minutes out. We may not know where they went until after they've left to come back.''

Another wrinkle, Truscott thought. *It still depends on where they come back, and when, not where they went for the interval.*

''What do we have from those Marines the prince is with?'' Truscott asked.

''Nothing recent, sir,'' Commander Estmann said. ''They had split up the last we heard. The I&R platoon went off to rescue that downed flyer. The rest were on the move as well, going off to rendezvous with the others after the pickup. There are Feddie troops in the area as well, this new lot.''

''Alonzo, after we get the fighters in, we'll all jump out past Boulder, rendezvous with *Thames,* and wait for the Federation battle line to show itself again. Get the coordinates set up, ready to transmit to the other ships.''

''Aye, sir.'' Rinaldi started working at his console. ''Won't take a minute to get the preliminaries.''

''Gabby, get me Hardesty and Murphy of *Repulse.*''

That connection took less then fifteen seconds.

''I want a full spread of missiles launched toward the

transports,'' Truscott told the two captains. "Make the spread wider than normal. Maybe we'll get lucky and catch part of the battle fleet when they jump back in. If we're still in position forty-five seconds after the first spread, launch a second. But leave a clear patch to pick up our fighters."

"Should I make a jump and send in the spread from another direction?" Murphy asked.

"Good idea, Captain," Truscott said. "Cut down on their maneuvering room. Just remember to leave room for our operations."

"Will do, Admiral."

"Okay, coordinate your releases but get it done as quickly as practical."

Truscott smiled after he broke the connection. The tactic might not do any good, but it would give the Federation skippers something new to worry about. And the transports might not be able to defend against that much fire all at once if the battle fleet didn't return in time to get caught.

"Weapons. Still nothing on the Federation ships?"

"No, sir."

When *Sheffield* made the jump to retrieve her remaining fighters, there were a lot of nervous people on all three Commonwealth ships, waiting for the Federation battle line to return. *Victoria* and *Repulse* were posted to shield *Sheffield*. Captain Hardesty threw away more pages of the rule book by bringing the Spacehawks in all at once instead of a squadron at a time. Still, it took twenty-five minutes to get all of the fighters in and the LRCs retracted.

One more Federation transport was out of commission, broken apart by one or more missiles that struck while the Commonwealth ships were in Q-space. Another appeared to have minor damage.

"Give the transports another spread just before we jump out," Truscott told Hardesty and Murphy.

As soon as the missiles were clear, the three Commonwealth ships made their Q-space transit, coming out behind the larger of Buchanan's two moons, the Boulder. There was still no sight of the Federation battle line.

Arias Rivero made sure that all of his injured got to hospital, and he talked to groups of the uninjured. Everyone seemed to be in shock. Responses were dull. Eyes stared blankly. People from *Victoria*'s crew moved among *Lancer*'s people, pushing tea carts and offering refreshment and words of encouragement. There were promises of a hot meal and beds.

"Keep on top of things here, Mel," Arias told his first officer. "I'm going to the bridge. I've got one more report to make to Admiral Truscott." *And I'm not looking forward to it.*

It was a long walk. Rivero was announced formally when he reached *Victoria*'s bridge. Captain Naughton got up from her seat to shake his hand.

"I wanted to thank you for picking up my people," Arias said.

"Glad to help. You and your people did a good job."

Arias shrugged. "Not all that good, or I'd still be on my own bridge."

"You did what you had to do," a new voice said. Arias turned and saw Admiral Greene, just coming onto the bridge.

"I lost my ship, sir, and too many good people," Arias said.

"I know it's not easy to face, but you'll get another ship," Greene said. "People can't be replaced, but your people didn't give their lives for nil. In large part due to your work, we've done for more Feddie ships than we had at the start of this donnybrook, and blunted their second attempt to take Buchanan. You and your people did your job, and came out of it luckier than you might have. You saved most of your crew. There are several Feddie ships out there that didn't manage that, even with superior assets.''

''Thank you, sir. Do I need to report to Admiral Truscott right away?''

''No. Unless you've come up with something that our ops people can use?''

''I can't think that far right now, Admiral,'' Rivero said. ''I've gone numb from the neck up.''

''The transports have gone to Q-space, two of them anyway,'' the flag duty officer reported. Truscott was working with his flatscreen, repeatedly adjusting the scale and orientation, looking for the Federation battle fleet. Nearly an hour had passed since the enemy dreadnoughts had jumped to Q-space.

''Ops, start moving us. Random jumps, location and timing. Keep all of the ships together, but we move. If anyone needs resupply urgently, set it up for when we're farthest out. I don't want us to stay in the same place longer than ten minutes, but don't get us too close to the ninety-second minimum for now. Let's not press our Nilssens any harder than we have to. As soon as you have the first jump plotted, get the fleet out.''

''Aye, sir.''

''Intelligence. We'll need a quick view of our surroundings each time. And updates to the Marines on the ground. With us moving in and out, they'll be guessing on the movement of the Federation troops.''

''Obviously, Admiral, you'd don't believe the Feddie fleet has simply gone home,'' Captain Rinaldi said.

''Not for a minute.'' Truscott watched his monitor as the gray of Q-space wrapped itself around *Sheffield*. ''They know they outnumber us. They've put more troops on the ground. They're here, somewhere. Once they decide on a way to counter our tactics, they'll come looking for us. Right now, we need to keep the Federation from interfering with our ground operations. As long as they can't fully support their troops, our Marines will hold the edge."

"Admiral, they may *not* know our strength," Rinaldi said. "If they assume that it takes more than ninety seconds to cycle for a jump, they may believe we have several times the number of ships we actually have. It depends on what they think is possible."

"We can't count on that," Truscott said. "The fact that none of our ships made it back from Camerein suggests that they use Q-space more efficiently than we used to. Until we know what *their* limits are, we have to assume that they can move in and out of Q-space at least as quickly as we can."

The Commonwealth ships passed through Q-space four more times before there was any change in the view around Buchanan. The Federation battle line was back.

"They're on a minimal deflection course for the settlements" was the report from weapons.

"Put *Repulse* and *Sheffield* on a head-on intercept," Truscott said without hesitation.

"Sir, by the time we can cycle back through, that'll mean coming out of Q-space little more than a hundred miles above the surface. That's awfully close, especially for *Sheffield*."

"So they'll never expect us there," Truscott said. "Do it."

When the two Commonwealth ships returned to normal-space, the Federation line was starting to separate. One dreadnought and two escort ships held an easterly course. The other two dreadnoughts and one escort were burning toward a polar orbit. Each formation stretched out into single file.

"Take the ships heading east," Truscott ordered.

"Looks like they plan to stick around, Admiral," Rinaldi said after he relayed the orders. "Give them a little time and they can stretch those formations to keep at least one ship on a line-of-sight to their troops on the surface constantly."

"That's one thing we want to avoid," Truscott told him.

There was little delay in the Federation's return of fire this time, but it was obvious that the Commonwealth ships *had* come from the heading that the enemy was least prepared for.

"Ninety seconds and out," Truscott said.

"Already laid in, sir," the navigator replied.

"We'll have to start crossing the tee," Truscott commented as *Sheffield* was rocked by a glancing blow. "Come across between ships again, limit their options."

Ninety seconds—the longest minute-and-a-half of the day, for *Sheffield* and *Repulse,* exposed to all the fire from three enemy ships, up close. *Repulse* lost the nozzle of one forward maneuvering rocket. *Sheffield* took another hit, one that sprung the gastight hull over a storage compartment.

"We can't go on like this indefinitely," Hardesty told Truscott after the ships jumped back to Q-space. "Even if they don't get lucky and do for us the way they did *Lancer,* the way they're degrading our abilities . . ." He didn't need to finish the thought.

"We have no choice," Truscott said. "We'll concentrate on that same formation. This time, we'll go in north to south, top acceleration, either end of the dreadnought. Time it so we make our jumps out when we're directly in the Federation line. Shade both ships close to the dreadnought. We've taken out two of them. Let's try for a third."

There was no way to know if it was coincidence or conscious timing on the part of the Federation ships. *Sheffield* passed ahead of the dreadnought. *Repulse* went behind. Neither Commonwealth ship scored or took any significant hits during their approach, but at almost precisely the same instant that they made their transit back to Q-space, the three Federation ships did the same thing.

As soon as *Sheffield* came out of Q-space, it was clear that something had finally gone wrong with a jump. There were twenty seconds of absolute confusion. Neither Commonwealth ship was where it was supposed to be, and they weren't as close together as they should have been.

"They jumped at the same time we did." The flag navigation officer said, guessing. "We're a million miles too far out. *Repulse* is even farther out of position."

"Any trace of the Federation ships?" Truscott asked.

"No . . . wait." The navigator squinted at his monitor and made several adjustments. "The dreadnought. It must have broken up into a million pieces. We can't track all of the debris."

"Just the dreadnought?" Truscott asked.

"Yes, sir. Everything we *can* trace comes from where it was."

"Get damage reports from *Sheffield* and *Repulse*," Truscott said. He adjusted his own monitor to show the debris from the Federation dreadnought, then ran it backwards to show the chunks moving back toward their origin. The computer complied, but it could only show where the pieces came from; it couldn't reassemble them.

"Any sign of where those escorts came out?" Truscott asked.

"No, sir. They must have gone out a considerable distance, like before. And if they're as off course as we are . . ."

"They'll recover. They were at the ends of the line. They

might not be as far out of position as we are," Truscott said. It was an intuitive conclusion. The dreadnought in the center had been destroyed, caught by Q-space bubbles on either end. Truscott frowned as he tried to reason out what had happened. Why had the Federation ship been destroyed while the Commonwealth ships had not? *They must have started their jump just an instant behind us,* he decided, *and got squashed in the middle.* The two nearest ships had been thrown off position, apparently in relation to their mass. The end ships: their deviation should be less than that of *Repulse* at least. It was something else that the theoreticians would have to look into, but Truscott could think of no other possible explanation.

"What about the other group of Federation ships?" Truscott asked.

"Still on course. No, hold that. They've just shifted to Q-space."

"We've bought ourselves a little more time," Truscott said softly. *Let's hope it's enough.*

42

"We can't count on our helmet displays or mapboards, not as far as current enemy positions are concerned," David said. Lieutenant Ewing and Sergeant Jawad from Delta Company, Lead Sergeant Hal Avriel of Alpha, Prince William, and Commander Shrikes were gathered around David in the center of the Marines' new defensive position. They had staked out an area four hundred yards long and seventy-five yards wide on and behind a low ridge.

"The fleet's jumping in and out so often that we're not getting constant position updates," David explained.

"That was the admiral's plan," Ian said. "But the Federation ships are jumping in and out now as well, so their information about us will also be suspect."

"Throw of the dice," Bandar Jawad said. "Depends who's got the most recent data and how much it's changed since."

"And how good the other side's detection gear is," the prince added. "We have to assume it's as good as ours, perhaps better."

"Sorry, sir, I disagree," Ewing said. "I think we can say with considerable confidence that our electronics are definitely better. Detection range. On those occasions when we both moved into a fight with helmets operating, early on, our people always picked up the Feddies first. I doubt they can pick up passive radiation at all, even with the ships. As long as we restrict ourselves to the most essential of communications, we should be safe until they're almost in our laps. Receivers open, no transmitting except in emergency conditions. Passive IR scan, no IR lights. That sort of thing.''

"I agree," Ian said. "They were too ready to forgo electronics altogether. They must not have much faith in their gear."

"We have another decision to make," Ewing said. "We've got an excellent defensive position here, but we were too free with our complinks after we arrived. The Feddies likely know where we are. Do we stay here because it's the best defensive position we're likely to find, or do we move on to make it harder for the Feddies to find us?" He directed the question at Ian, but David was the first to speak.

"I&R usually calls for movement over fixed defense, but I'd suggest staying put, at least for the night. It's getting dark. We have wounded who will make it impossible for us to move fast and silent. And there are still pockets of Feddies left from the original invasion. Tripping over an ambush in the dark is too likely now, and we'd really be on our own."

Jawad and Avriel were quick to agree. "I think it's the only way," Avriel said.

Ian nodded. "So do I. At least for tonight. See to your men. Have them sleep and stand watch in turns, half and half in each fire team. Passive sensors only. No radio transmissions unless we're under active attack. You men know the drill."

David's platoon slipped out of the defensive ring and planted snoops along approaches to the ridge. Then they came back in, to get a little rest before their next job.

Ewing's headquarters platoon set up a command post on the east slope of the ridge, digging a shallow bunker into the bottom of the hill and reinforcing it with logs and rocks.

"It's not a palace, but it might do for one night," Ewing said when he brought Prince William and Commander Shrikes in.

"I'm sure it'll be fine," Prince William said. "Your subtle way of suggesting that we keep out of the way?"

"Not at all, sir," Ewing said, much too quickly.

"Wrong answer," Ian said with a soft chuckle. Ewing looked confused, but Ian took him off the hook quickly. "Never mind, Lieutenant. We *are* the outsiders here."

"Yes, sir," Ewing said, almost stuttering. "Excuse me, I'd best take a look around the perimeter before it gets too dark."

"Don't shake the lad too much," William told Ian once they were alone. "We get in a fight, he'll need all the confidence he can muster."

Ian sighed. "I know. There are times when humor is out of place. But I'm not used to this kind of situation. I'm still learning. That's why I told Ewing that I wouldn't interfere with him running the show."

"If you hadn't, I might have clobbered you to keep you out of it."

Ian stared at him for a moment, then decided that the prince was serious. "That's gentler than what some of the Marines might have done. And they'd have had the right of it, no matter what *King's Regs* say."

"What do you think's going on up there?" William asked, gesturing upward with a thumb. "You've known Truscott longer than I have."

"We still have a fleet. After eight hours or more, that's quite a statement. Five dreadnoughts and six escorts against our lot."

"Truscott has certainly proved the value of his new tactics," William said. "I just hope he wins clear here to enjoy the fruits of his labors."

"Him and the rest of us," Ian said. "I hate to think that it all comes down to Long John's reaction to the admiral's dispatches."

"You don't think much of the First Lord of the Admiralty?"

"Let's just say that I don't know him as well as I know Admiral Truscott. I don't have any cause to doubt Raleigh's abilities, but he's never seemed particularly suited to innovation or spur-of-the-moment planning."

"You may be right, or we'd likely have had tests run on this Q-space routine years ago," the prince said. "We get back to Buckingham, the Admiralty will certainly come under close scrutiny." Ian noted that while the prince had avoided using the word "if," he had also shied away from "when."

Josef found himself shivering uncontrollably. He wasn't injured, having come out of this smash even better than the one back on Buckingham. The temperature was seventy degrees Fahrenheit, so it wasn't cold. He had his flight suit and helmet on, and that should have had him roasting. The flight suit was a major handicap moving through the jungle; it was heavy, bulky, and not particularly limber; but he needed its thermal shielding. He didn't want to stand out like a bonfire to enemy IR detectors.

The Marines had treated him right. One of their medical orderlies had given him a close once-over, even though they had *real* casualties to care for.

I'm proper useless here, he told himself as he got the shivering fit under control. *Fish out of water.* He was armed, but only with a slug-throwing pistol and his survival knife. The pistol had only the nine rounds in the magazine. He didn't carry spares. He hadn't even fired the gun in months, since his last annual appearance on the range to qualify with it.

I'm getting to be a bloody wastrel with fighters. They'll have me flying a desk if I'm not careful. At the moment, that wasn't the worst possible fate, but he knew he wouldn't be happy anywhere but in a fighter cockpit. He curled up on the ground in a fetal position, still shivering.

Kate, I hope you made it okay. He had tried to avoid thinking of her after his own fighter was blown. At least six other Spacehawks had been lost in the battle. He had heard that much over his complink while he waited for pickup, but he hadn't heard who the pilots were, or even which squadrons they were from.

By the time Josef got around to thinking that it was going to be a long, miserable night, he had slid into what was almost sleep, an uncomfortable, semiconscious state that made the minutes pass like hours.

Avoiding helmet complinks was no great hardship for veteran I&R Marines. Special operations often called for electronic silence. David cued Alfie, Jacky, Roger, and Sean to go out with him on patrol. They loaded themselves down with mines and snoopers, and slipped down the western face of the ridge. Before they left, David briefed his companions as completely as he could, spelling out precisely where they were going and what they were going to do. While the veterans scarcely needed the blueprint, Sean was too new for David to presume that he would know without initial coaching.

David led the way. He curved south, planning on a significant detour, hoping that the Federation troops would be concentrating too much on the direct route between them. The red blips had remained in one place for hours. The patrol was based on the assumption that the Feddies had made camp for the night.

Intelligence and Reconnaissance . . . and sometimes a bit of a commando raid. *Like now.* David smiled. This patrol had been his idea. Lieutenant Ewing had accepted the idea, almost gratefully. Commander Shrikes and Prince William had both seemed pleased at the prospect as well.

"It should cut down the odds against us, at least a little," David had told the others. "Make these new arrivals more cautious."

"Just don't get carried away," the prince had said. "You'll do us a lot more good back here safe and healthy when it's over than you would out there, dead or hurt. We don't know when we'll be able to get any medevac down."

"I'm aware of that, sir," David assured the prince. "That's why I'll only take four picked men, the best I've got for this sort of job."

The team had been out for an hour before David raised his hand, fist clenched, to signal for the team to stop.

Now, if my memory hasn't gone south, we're almost there. David motioned his men off to the right, spreading them out along the path. Each man knew his assignment. Once the others had time to reach their positions, David knelt down and started his own share of the work, planting one snoop and a half dozen small land mines that would be triggered when the snoop spotted human movement across the arc. The mines went into the underbrush, aimed out over the path to provide overlapping kill zones. David's batch would cover a stretch of thirty yards. The other Marines set up similar kill zones along the path. The computers running the system were programmed to permit intruders to get well along before the mines were detonated. Whichever end of the string the enemy came from, the snoops would wait to trigger the mines until the enemy's lead element reached the far end of the last kill zone, or until the rearguard came even with the first snoop.

One by one, the other Marines ran back down the path, crouched low. David counted, and he touched each man on the leg as he went past to let them know that he had seen him. Alfie was the last. Once Alfie went by, David got up and followed. The others waited for him fifty yards from the end of the booby-trapped stretch of path.

This was the predictably dangerous moment. For a few seconds, while David activated the snoops that would control the mines, he would be visible to anyone using electronic detection equipment.

The others gathered around David, all of them close enough to see what he was doing as he turned on the portable transmitter and keyed in the seven-character code that activated the system. Quick bleeps confirmed the activation. David shut down the transmitter as soon as the last confirmation sounded. He stood and waved the team on, back toward the ridge.

David slept easily, but lightly, after he brought his men back from patrol. He scarcely noticed the discomfort of simply spreading out on the ground to sleep. It was too familiar. His field skin kept him warm, his helmet all the pillow he needed. If he were wakened abruptly, the rifle at his side would be in his hands before his eyes were open. When he woke on his own, as he did frequently, it was different. There was a moment of awareness. He would open his eyes without moving, look around, listen. As soon as he could assure himself that nothing was amiss, he would slide back into sleep.

Half an hour before dawn, David got up and prowled behind the line of men on the ridge, then went down to the makeshift command bunker. Lieutenant Ewing was just waking, sitting across the entrance to the bunker. He stood and gestured David away from it.

"I didn't expect you up so soon," Ewing said.

David shrugged. "My body decided it was time."

"You got your packets planted?"

"Yes, sir. Unless the Feddies change their route, they

should run into our surprise no more a few minutes after they start out.''

Bandar Jawad came across the slope toward them. In the predawn darkness, his figure was no more than a light green ghost, the faceplate of his mask slightly reflective.

''A quiet night,'' Bandar said around a yawn. ''More than I expected.''

''Let's hope for a peaceful day,'' Ewing said. ''I'd just as soon save any fighting until after we deliver our guests to more senior officers.''

The two sergeants nodded. They understood completely: *Not on my watch.* They wouldn't want to be remembered in connection with the death or capture of the king's youngest brother.

''They get a break upstairs, I imagine the admiral will send a shuttle for the prince and our casualties,'' David said. ''Leastways, I hope he will.'' He glanced along the slope toward the bunker. Neither the prince nor Commander Shrikes had come out yet. ''We'd be in a lot better shape without them.''

''Be nice to get Gaffer Chou to the medics as well,'' Bandar said. ''Save him a lot of grief later.''

Both of Chou's legs had been shot up and broken. Chou had been treated with a variety of medpatches, both for pain and to fight infection. He had remained unconscious, or close to it, since. But if the Marines couldn't get him to a trauma tube soon . . . The nanoscrubbers could only do so much without the more complete molecular machinery of a trauma tube. Even if Gaffer didn't die, the legs might deteriorate so badly that they would have to be amputated. That would mean *weeks* in a trauma tube while the legs were regenerated, and more weeks of therapy before he would be able to function normally again.

Chou's men, the survivors of the squad he had brought down to protect Prince William, were arranged around the bunker as an inner line of defense. Prince William and Ian Shrikes were their primary responsibility.

"Let's spend the morning improving our positions here," Ewing said. "Unless we get new orders, we're still supposed to dig in and wait."

"We stay here instead of looking for a different spot?" David asked.

Ewing nodded. "Moving would kill Chou. Dig in and sit tight, and hope that friends get to us before the other lot."

"We'd best send a detail for water as well," Bandar said. "We may have to go a mile for that. We get locked into this position, we could run short in another day."

"Work it out with the other sergeants, Bandar," Ewing said. "Maybe two men from each platoon, a squad to run cover for them."

"Yes, sir."

"I wish we could afford the time and noise to give us clear kill zones around this place," Ewing said. The main ridge faced the known concentration of Federation forces. Two lower, gentler, hills blocked off the sides—somewhat. But there was little in the way of natural protection across the remaining side of the area. "Get some quick ramparts in across the east." Ewing gestured.

"If we're staying put, we have to do *something* about that side," Bandar said. "Bring down a few trees, something to give a little cover to the men there. Plant a few mines out far enough to slow an attack. The other sides will have to make do with what nature provided, but nature didn't provide a damn thing for us on the east."

"Do it quickly, and as quietly as possible," Ewing told him.

"Right, sir."

David glanced along the slope as two men came out of the bunker. "Looks like our VIPs are up," he said softly.

Ewing turned and nodded, then started toward them. Bandar and David followed.

"We made it through the night," Prince William said.

"Yes, sir," Ewing agreed. "I think it's time we had a look at a mapboard to see what sort of data we've got."

"Inside?" Ian suggested, jerking a thumb toward the bunker.

"Yes, sir. That will mute the electronics somewhat. A little bit of luck and they might not pick it up at all."

Five men crowded inside the narrow dugout. Ewing unfolded his mapboard and turned it on. Their own position was clear from the triangle showing the position of the mapboard. The group of red blips representing the Federation's soldiers west of them was a little closer than it had been the day before.

"Right where they'll have to stumble on our surprises if they come this way," David pointed out. That wasn't the problem. The problem was a second group of red blips, to the north, and only a little more distant.

"That other lot must have done a night march," Bandar said. "They were at least six miles farther off the last we looked." They had been so far away that the Marines had given them little thought.

"Coming toward us," the prince noted. "They must be acting in concert."

"They're coming for us," Bandar said.

"And it won't take them all that long, once they start moving again," Ewing said. "You'd best get those details working right now, Sergeant."

43

Admiral Truscott was feeling his age. He had lost count of the coffee and tea he had consumed in the last twenty hours. It was hard enough to keep track of the time. He had to stare at a clock and concentrate for the time to register. He had managed a couple of short naps, but it was hardly a down payment on the sleep he really needed. Tension, adrenaline, and willpower had been enough to carry him only so far. Beyond that point, the inevitable physical reaction had set in.

On the flag bridge of *Sheffield*, everyone seemed to be suffering the same waning alertness. Sending people off two or three at a time to rest hadn't done much good. They were all too acutely aware of their vulnerability to sleep even when they had the opportunity.

The early successes had been heady. The crews of *Sheffield* and *Repulse* had been ready to take on the galaxy, certain they could beat any odds. Then the Federation ships started to play by Truscott's new rules. There hadn't been any exchange of fire in fourteen hours. The sides played hide-and-seek, retreating to Q-space as soon as the enemy showed up, jumping to new positions, coming out over Buchanan just often enough to keep each other from fully supporting their ground forces.

Sunrise was approaching the settlements again.

Truscott rubbed his face with both hands. His ships were

far out in the Buchanan system, over the far side of the system's outer gas giant. The planet's electromagnetic signatures completely masked the ships'. They were nearly as invisible as they would be in Q-space. They were also almost as isolated as they would be there. The images they could see of Buchanan were too old to have any tactical value—ancient history for all practical purposes.

The hours of relative inaction had served some needs. The ships had been able to repair some battle damage. *Thames* had replenished the munitions stores of the other ships. There had been time to do extended checks on Nilssen generators and other essential equipment. But now . . .

"Alonzo, how do we draw them into combat on our terms?" Truscott asked, breaking several minutes of utter silence on the flag bridge.

"Put a couple of flights of Spacehawks out to go after their ground troops," Rinaldi said after a moment. "That means risking the fighters and maybe putting ourselves in a vulnerable position. If they come at us during launch or recovery, we're in a poor position to defend ourselves. Ties us down until we finish the operation and takes at least twenty percent of our weapons out of action."

"Any other ideas?"

"That's all I've been able to come up with so far."

"Put one flight of the alert squadron in their cockpits," Truscott said after two minutes of tapping his fingers on the arm of his chair. "We'll jump in and gang launch them. As soon as they're beyond the bubble radius, we return to Q-space and come out on the tail of Boulder, ready to jump back in when and if the Federation ships stand to against the fighters."

"Yes, sir," Rinaldi said. "How soon?"

"Twenty minutes. That'll make it light over all of the Federation troops on the ground. We want them to see our birds this time. If they're in radio contact with their ships, I want them to be able to call for help."

Josef groaned as he woke. Sleep had been a long time coming the night before, and it had been disturbed frequently. His flight suit hadn't been designed as camping gear.

"It'll get worse," one of the Marines had assured him the evening before. "Tomorrow afternoon, when it gets hotter than hell and you can't use your suit's air conditioning because of the electronics blackout."

The Marine had disturbed Josef's first attempt to sleep. He had a present for the pilot, the rifle that had belonged to one of the Marines who had been killed in the last ambush. The Marine took time to give Josef basic instructions. *You put the magazine in here; pull this bolt back to load the chamber and cock it; squeeze the trigger; remove the empty magazine; start all over.* He had ignored Josef's protests that he knew how to handle a rifle. The Marine's instructions had been to give the flyer a lesson, and that was what he was going to do.

Josef used the rifle to help him get to his feet when he woke in the predawn twilight. His joints were stiff, and his flight suit felt as if it had doubled its mass overnight. He stretched and groaned again, thinking how wonderful a cup of hot coffee would go down, how much he would like to have his berth back on *Sheffield* to crawl into for some real sleep . . . not to mention how much he would like a full, *hot* breakfast in place of barely edible field rations . . . and, most of all, Kate. But he couldn't think about her now. To think would be to worry.

Josef looked around. Marines were working on the open side of the bivouac, cutting down trees, trimming branches, building a barricade. Everyone else seemed to be digging holes, or enlarging holes they had started the evening before.

"Should I be digging too?" he asked himself. The night before, he had just found himself a place to sleep near the command bunker. He didn't have a shovel in any case, and no one had come around to give him one.

One of the Marine sergeants came up to Josef then and held out a breakfast pack. "I'm David Spencer."

Josef nodded and took the meal pack. No matter how the food tasted, it *was* food. "What the hell am I supposed to be doing?" Josef asked. "Should I be digging myself a hole, or what?"

"I'll have one of the men dig you a pit, sir. That'll be faster. There's quite a force of Feddies heading our way. Two different groups, coming from the west and from the north. The ones to our west were just a little slower reaching your location yesterday than we were."

"You mean they still want me?"

A smile found its way onto David's face. "I wouldn't take is so personal, sir. I'd say they want all of us, dead or captured, preferably dead. Prisoners are such a nuisance."

"They obviously know where we are," Ian told Ewing. "So there's not one bloody reason why we shouldn't use all the advantages we have."

"Maybe they *don't* know our exact position," Ewing countered. "We've kept everything on the hush all night. Maybe they'll assume we've moved."

"We need the mapboard to track them. And I want to contact *Sheffield* about air support, and to find out whether we still have ships up there. It makes a difference," Ian said.

"We can still minimize our exposure for now, sir," Ewing pressed. "There's no need to switch on everything. I'd best put the NCOs on full electronics to watch for incoming signals, but we can hold off on the rest until the Feddies are on top of us.''

Ian nodded. ''Yes, no reason to give them a head count. Get your sergeants notified. I'll wait till you get back before I switch on the mapboard and try to contact *Sheffield*.''

After Ewing left, Ian turned to the prince. ''I didn't hear you offering opinions.''

''Couldn't decide which I preferred. I can see both sides. Besides, it might have given the wrong impression if I'd come out in favor of contacting *Sheffield* for help. Might have looked as if I were simply trying to get myself out of a jam.''

Ian shook his head slowly. ''I haven't noticed you doing a lot of talking with Weintraub either.''

''He's on the line with the Marines,'' William countered. ''We did natter for a time last evening. Of course, most of the chat seemed to be of the 'If we get out of this alive' sort.''

''Yes, there is that.'' Ian picked up his needle rifle and checked the safety.

''Hardly the place for a senior naval officer to make his last stand, is it?'' the prince asked softly.

''Or a king's brother?'' Ian replied.

William shrugged. ''Who can tell? I might serve the Commonwealth more by dying in battle than I can do alive. Symbolism is important.''

''That lot north of us is moving.'' Bandar Jawad pointed at the mapboard. Josef had joined Prince William, Ian Shrikes, Asa Ewing, and Sergeants Spencer and Avriel around Bandar.

''If they're in communication, the other lot will be moving within the next few minutes,'' David said. ''That'll give them almost identical distances to cover to get to us.''

''We're going to get some help,'' Ian told the others.

"I've been on to *Sheffield*." He had needed three tries before he got an answer. The flagship had been off in Q-space. "They're launching a flight of Spacehawks to harass the enemy. Besides giving us a hand, they hope to draw in the rest of the Feddie fleet."

"One flight?" Josef asked, just joining the group. "Then the only real purpose is for them to be a lure for the enemy fleet. Any help they actually give us will be incidental."

"The fight up there is more important than anything we might face down here," Prince William said. "If we lose our ships, or if they can't do anything because of the Federation fleet, it doesn't matter how much havoc we wreak on the ground troops. They can wait us out or come in and hunt us down the way we were hunting them."

"We'll do what we can, sir," David said.

" 'England expects every man to do his duty,' " William quoted.

"What's that, sir?" David asked.

The prince shook his head. "Ancient history. What Admiral Nelson said to his men before the battle of Trafalgar."

It was David's turn to shake his head. "I didn't know that, sir, but, begging your pardon, we're all talking as if we were already dead. It wouldn't do for the lads to hear us talking this way." *It's not doing me any good either,* he thought.

The distant explosions were clearly audible to the Marines, but there were no cheers. Instead, the men got more alert, bringing weapons to the ready, looking off into the forest as if the enemy might appear that very second.

"Be an hour at least before they get here," David called out to the men on one stretch of the ridge. He headed back down to the command bunker. Lieutenant Ewing was shaking his head as David approached.

"Not near as much as we hoped for," Ewing said. "They left too much of a gap between their scouts and the main body. We only lost six red blips."

David shrugged. "Six less for us to face later. It should slow the rest a trifle. If those fighters take care of a few more, we'll be in fairly decent shape—least as far as these two groups are concerned."

"Yes, Spencer, I know. They don't outnumber us any more than three to two now and we've got the high ground and defensive positions. You *will* let me worry about the space fight, won't you?"

Six Spacehawks made runs against the Federation forces. The fighters came in two at a time and alternated between the two enemy columns. The newly landed Federation troops were more prepared for air defense than the ones who had been surprised on the ground by the arrival of the Commonwealth fleet. They had more than a few surface-to-air missiles. Two Spacehawks were destroyed in the first five minutes of the air raid. Another fighter was damaged. Its pilot pulled up and away, looking for altitude and a healthier neighborhood to eject in.

After that, the remaining three fighters were more cautious in their attacks, keeping more altitude and distance as they launched their missiles and made their strafing runs. The Federation troops blanked their electronics and moved under cover of the forest. Then the last three fighters went to full power and made a burn to orbit.

"The Feddie ships came out," Ian whispered to Prince William. "Down to all-or-nothing time."

David's platoon held the center of the main ridge. Alpha Company of the First Battalion was to their left, holding the south end of the ridge and stretching around to the flank and half of the rear. Delta of the Fourth completed the perimeter on the north—ridge, flank, and rear. The few remaining Marines from *Sheffield* were in a trench around the command bunker, with the VIPs, the wounded, and the flyer.

Doug Weintraub was on the ridge, his foxhole between those of David Spencer and Alfie Edwards.

The first attack came in the form of a few long-range rifle shots, unnervingly close for their length—over four hundred yards. Doug saw one bullet kick up dirt less than two feet from his foxhole. Slug-throwers were the only rifles with that sort of range.

A couple of minutes later, there were two explosions out in the forest, some distance and seconds apart. David nodded slightly. The explosions placed the enemy precisely for him. They had reached the first line of landmines I&R platoon had spread across the approaches to the firebase the night before, 250 yards out. There was one more line of mines, plus a few extras scattered at random to make the enemy think that the routes were more heavily mined than they actually were.

"Hold your fire," David told his men over the platoon circuit. "Squad leaders, make sure everyone's switched on." The first shots were meant to be the signal for that.

There was another explosion, off to the north, in front of the other group of advancing Federation troops, then a spate of firing as they opened up on Delta Company. Bandar Jawad's men held their fire. Lieutenant Ewing had given no command to return fire. The plan was to wait until the Federation troops were within one hundred yards. The Marines had no way to know how long their ammunition would have to last, and their reserves were finite, not to be wasted on futile sound effects at long range.

David had his mapboard open and on. The red blips that represented the enemy drew steadily nearer, nearing the second line of mines. David looked up as the first of those mines went off. Then there was a period of silence, followed by a number of rifle shots—that were, in turn, followed by a number of mine explosions as the Federation troops located and cleared the obstacles.

Too fast and too many, David thought, and he realized that it meant that the Federation must have superior mine detectors.

It doesn't matter. They don't outnumber us by more than three to two, and that's not enough to make up for position, David assured himself. But he was looking at his mapboard when the number of red blips almost doubled as more Federation helmets were turned on.

Alfie had his needle rifle at his side, but he held his grenade launcher. He would need that long before it was time to start spraying needles. He took long, slow breaths, focusing completely on the forest. Alfie had marked his kill zone, and knew its limits intimately. What lay to either side was of little concern. Other Marines would watch those zones, overlapping the edge of his. Once the fighting started, casualties would mean redefining zones of fire . . . but it was all part of the drill.

Don't kid yourself, Alfie boy. This is like nothing you've ever seen before. These aren't colonials who don't know right from left. These are professional soldiers, or conscripts trained by long-term pros. They'll know the drill as well as you do.

Alfie blinked three times quickly after staring for too long. *Too long.* The silence had lasted too long as well. He glanced over toward Sergeant Spencer, who was intent on the forest below. Alfie looked the other way. Everyone was watching, waiting. He moved his right hand away from his rifle long enough to wipe the sweat off on his trousers. *The waiting.*

• • • •

The first volley of grenades, the first sustained shooting, came from the south, where there were no red blips at all. The grenades looped in over the dug-in Marines, scattering shrapnel and white phosphorus over half the clearing. The phosphorus burned and set fire to whatever ground cover it touched.

David glanced to his left, but only for an instant. He knew he had to mind his own front, not worry about the flank. The largest concentrations of Federation troops had to be to the west and north. *That shouldn't be more than a single patrol,* he told himself, *sneaking around without their helmets on.* But he worried about how many more of the enemy might still be out there without electronics. *They're too damn willing to use that trick.*

Then it was time for the men on the ridge to duck. A dozen grenades exploded within a second or two. Most hit the west face of the ridge, but before the Marines could lift their heads after the last blast, Federation rifle fire raked their positions.

"Return fire when you have targets," Ewing ordered over the all-hands channel.

David smiled thinly as he brought his rifle up. There were no Feddies *visible* yet. But by linking his sights with his helmet's electronics, he could lock onto the enemy's helmets—as long as the marked positions weren't hopelessly obsolete by the time he fired. That depended on how recently the positions had been updated, how far away the ships of the Commonwealth fleet were. But David didn't demand perfection.

He fired short bursts, moving from blip to blip on the head-up display on his visor, scattering each burst over a narrow range to make up for random movements in the seconds, or minutes, since the projection's last update. Along the ridge, other Marines were firing as well. Closest to David, Doug held back. He didn't know how to link his rifle to his helmet, and it was too late to teach him.

"Just hold on, Doug," David told him over a private channel. "We're using our helmets for target acquisition. Wait until you see movement. Don't waste ammunition."

"Right," Doug answered, his voice tight.

David switched channels to talk to Bandar. "You showing any activity over there yet?"

"Just a few stray shots," Bandar said. "The bulk of this group seems to be trying to slide around to the east. The way they're going, you'd think they didn't know we can trace their helmets."

"Doesn't wash," David said. "They've spent too much effort hiding their electronics when it suited them."

"Yeah, that's what I thought," Bandar said. "The movement of helmets must be a feint. They want us to concentrate on them."

"Keep your arse down," David advised. "It's too inviting a target."

The first sustained assault came against the northeast corner of the firebase. With heavy supporting fire from grenades and rifles on the other sides, a company of Federation soldiers advanced against the shoulder of the low hill on the north side of the firebase, where the hill dropped to meet the makeshift barricades stretched across the east.

There was no mad charge of screaming warriors. The Federation soldiers were too professional. They knew the utter futility of such an antiquated tactic. A handful of needlers could wipe out battalions of running soldiers, even without the backup of beamers, slug throwers, and grenade launchers, and any modern army would have all four sorts of weapons, and soldiers trained to use them.

Instead, the assault was made by men crawling and firing, using every inch of available cover to cut down on the targets they offered, and using their weapons to minimize

incoming fire. The covering fire poured into the Commonwealth positions by other Federation troops was just as important.

David Spencer divided his attention between his own
front and keeping track of the fight on the far side of the
firebase. The men on the ridge had to be careful of fire
from both sides.

"Lieutenant, I think we can help if we turn one man
from every fire team on the ridge around to get a better
angle on the Feddies," David said over the command channel. "They can always turn back around if we get action
on this side."

"Do it," Ewing said.

Team by team, the best marksmen with slug throwers on
the ridge turned their fire against the Federation assault on
the far side. The range was impossible for needlers, and
extreme for the beamers. The attack faltered. The Federation soldiers improved their positions and tried to meet the
new fire as best they could. Behind them, their support
troops also redirected much of their fire.

A second assault was launched against the southern end
of the ridge, obviously to take pressure off the exposed
Federation troops on the northeast corner. This assault
started with another flurry of grenades. Soldiers moved in
behind the explosions. This attack was in greater strength
than the first.

"They've got to try to take the ridge," Ewing told Ian
and the prince. They were in the trench that had been dug
across the downhill side of the command bunker. "As long
as we hold the high ground, they're just sausage meat going
into the grinder."

"Is there anything we could do that we're not doing
now?" Ian asked.

"Not unless the Spacehawks come back," Ewing said.

"Not before nightfall, and that's an eternity and a half from now."

"Maybe we should have left Spencer's lot out in the forest," Prince William said. "I wish I'd thought of that when it might have done some good."

"You're not the only one," Ewing said. "And I'm the one who *should* have thought of it. Or Spencer himself. I can see me missing something like that. I'm surprised that he did. Or my own lead sergeant."

"No use wasting time on could-haves," Ian said.

The attacks on the opposite corners slowed. The Federation forces quit trying to advance. But there was no sign of any retreat; that might prove too costly. The soldiers stayed where they were, improving their positions in the small ways that meant so much for survival, sliding a little to one side or another to put trees between them and their enemy, grubbing at the dirt to get closer to the ground, changing their angle. Survival could often be measured in small fractions of an inch.

The respite was only relative, and another advance started within minutes, moving against the other end of the weak eastern side of the Commonwealth firebase.

"They've got far more soldiers than we thought," Ewing told Ian.

"Somehow, they've managed to gather a lot of the men who were stranded here," Prince William said. "I wonder if that means they have communications channels we can't detect."

"That's something to worry about later," Ewing said. "If we have a later. Commander Shrikes, you'd best get on to *Sheffield*. See if there's anything they can do for us."

"I've been trying," Ian replied. "They must be in Q-space again. I haven't been getting any response."

44

"They're coming in low and fast,'' Alonzo Rinaldi reported. ''They're learning. There's no room for us to get between them and atmosphere.''

Truscott nodded and opened a link to Captain Hardesty. ''Tell your fighters to scramble for cover. *Sheffield* and *Repulse* will jump in thirty seconds, coming out side by side. Our destination is five hundred yards in front of the lead dreadnought, slightly above and heading straight for it. We pass over the nose and zip out as soon as possible.''

''Yes, sir,'' Hardesty said.

Truscott relayed the order to *Repulse*. The alarm for Q-space insertion was already sounding on *Sheffield*.

''We really need to do something about those damn horns,'' Truscott said. ''We really don't need the blasted things any more.'' No one answered. The gray of Q-space closed off the view on the exterior monitors.

We can't keep at this much longer, Truscott thought. *Unless we get help from Buckingham . . .* But that was too depressing to continue with. It was time and past for *Khyber* to have returned, at the very least. *Long John should have sent* some *word,* the admiral told himself.

The crews of *Sheffield* and *Repulse* handled the drill as if they'd been doing it for years. The ships came out of Q-space and immediately opened fire on the Federation ships. Missile launchers, particle beamers, and lasers flooded the lead dreadnought with more incoming traffic than it could handle. The command module exploded, showering both Commonwealth ships with debris.

A siren sounded on *Sheffield.*

"A chuck of that Feddie pierced the hull, forward and low," Gabby Bierce reported. "The crew inside that compartment were able to get out."

Truscott nodded, closing his eyes briefly. *For small favors . . . ,* he started, then stopped.

"*Repulse* reports damage to her forward particle beam battery," Gabby reported. "No casualties, but the gun's scrap."

"How are we on time?" Truscott asked.

"Another forty-seven seconds," Rinaldi replied.

"Make to both ships, 'Sheer off,' " Truscott ordered. "Put our sterns to them. We've scored another dreadnought. Let's not get greedy just now."

"Aye, sir." Rinaldi relayed the orders and *Sheffield* immediately started firing attitude rockets.

"The Feddies jumped to Q-space," Rinaldi said. Truscott was staring at the monitor. He had seen the ships disappear. All but the one. The dreadnought that had been hit was drifting without power.

"Tell both captains to put everything they can into finishing that ship off. Delay the jump to Q-space. By a full minute if necessary."

It wasn't. Two more main modules of the dreadnought were breached, destroyed, and the ship's spine was broken.

"It's going atmospheric, sir," Rinaldi reported within seconds of the last hit. "They'll never be able to keep her up."

"Can you project an impact area?" Truscott asked.

"Navigation says far side of Buchanan, almost certainly in deep ocean."

Truscott nodded and started to turn his chair away.

"Admiral," Gabby said. "*Repulse*'s skipper." A holographic image of Captain Murphy appeared in front of Truscott.

"We're not going to be able to jump on schedule, sir," Murphy reported. "Our Nilssens have gone down, something in the control circuitry. Repair's going to take at least an hour."

"We'll cover you as long as possible," Truscott promised. "But if thing's get too hot, you'll be on your own while we jump out and back."

"I understand, sir." Murphy's image blinked out.

Truscott gave *Sheffield*'s captain new orders. This time, the admiral did manage to get his chair turned away from the main consoles.

"Now we're for it," he whispered.

The wooden barricades along the eastern side of the firebase were on fire. The Marines had been forced to retreat from the flames with heavy casualties. Once the men got out of their foxholes, most of them at least partially under the felled tree trunks, they made easy targets, even though the fires gave off thick smoke. Up on the ridge, half of the men were turned around to give them covering fire, but it wasn't enough. Two platoons of Marines, sixty men, had manned the eastern side. No more than twenty reached cover during the retreat. They stumbled into foxholes along the low hills to north and south. A few made it to the trench by the command bunker. Most fell in the open center of the firebase. Federation troops advanced all along the eastern front, while enough remained on the other sides to keep at least some of the Marines occupied.

Alfie reached for another clip of grenades, but there were none left. All he had left was his needle rifle. He had thousands of rounds for that.

"Save the needler for this side, Alfie," Spencer told him.

"They're too far away over there. Don't waste ammo."

Doug had finally found a comfortable position. He was facing east, leaning against the lower side of his foxhole. There were targets he could see . . . and every time he saw a target, he shot at it. He scored a fair percentage of hits, but it didn't seem to make any difference. The Federation soldiers kept coming.

When his magazine went empty, Doug slid back down into his hole, surprised at how far he had edged up. *Lucky some sod didn't slice me up,* he thought as he reloaded. *I guess I do need a minder.* But when he started shooting again, he edged out a little farther with each three-shot burst, his exposure becoming almost too dangerous before he caught himself and slid back.

Prince William Albert Windsor, Duke of Haven, Privy Councilor, picked his targets as carefully as if he were on a weekend's bird shoot back on Buckingham. There was no hint of panic to his marksmanship. He found his targets and diced them, his finger light on the needler's trigger, husbanding his ammunition professionally. Even as he worked methodically at his shooting, he had time to wonder at his complete lack of fear. He did not doubt that death might be near . . . but that simply made no difference at the moment. *Guess I've gone right round the bend,* he thought.

Ian was at the prince's right, and Asa Ewing was at his left, their needlers proving as effective as the prince's. They worked together well, like old hands in the same fire team. The trench at the command bunker was crowded with the addition of a few men from the east wall. The bunker itself housed only Gaffer Chou. He was delirious, probably unaware that there was fighting going on.

"We can't expect any help from *Sheffield* unless those fighters come back," Ian told Prince William and Ewing.

Speaking over a private channel, they talked without interrupting their fighting.

"Have you managed to contact the fighters directly?" William asked.

"Yes, but they were told to bug out when the Feddies came back above. It's going to take a bit for them to get back to us."

"They don't hurry, those Feddies will be in our laps," the prince said.

"I don't belong here." Jacky White repeated the phrase under his breath for perhaps the fiftieth time. "I'm a civilian. I don't belong here."

The litany didn't make any difference. Neither did the odd tear that welled up at the corner of an eye. There was no fairy godmother to whisk him back to Buckingham, or even just over the horizon, away from this battle. The only way home was through these Federation troops. He simply had to keep going, to stay alive until enough of the enemy were dead for them to call it quits.

Thick smoke from all the burning trees and underbrush drifted across the center of the Marine firebase. The flames made the infrared pickup of the helmets almost useless. Everything was blanked by the greater heat of the fires. Under those conditions, it would hardly have mattered when a shot caught Jacky's visor at an angle and starred it so thoroughly that he couldn't see through it at all—except that the next two shots in the burst caught him in the neck and in the upper left quadrant of his chest. The blood that bubbled out of his throat might have hidden his final curse.

Roger Zimmerman was down to the next to last battery pack for his beamer, so he was careful about picking targets. The last group of Federation troops finally started to climb the western slope of the ridge that was the strongpoint of the Marine defenses. The enemy came slowly and died quickly, but the Commonwealth fire was nowhere near as intense as it had been earlier.

Roger had his last power pack lying on the ground by his hand while he used its predecessor. He went methodically about his quiet brand of mayhem. The laser gun suited his style. He was always a quiet man.

He died as silently as he had lived. A burst of needle fire underscored his helmet, and took his head completely off.

"Here they come, Admiral," Alonzo Rinaldi said. *Repulse* was still at least thirty minutes from having its Nilssen generators repaired. She was maintaining jump speed, but that would do her no good. All of the remaining Federation vessels had just popped back into normal-space on an attack heading, with enough speed to catch *Repulse* and *Sheffield* in three minutes. They were already within range of Federation weapons.

Truscott linked to Captain Hardesty. "We'll engage the last dreadnought. Full speed. Put out all the firepower we have left. Start us on the Q-space countdown and hold at the one-second mark for manual insertion on my command. Keep this channel open for that."

"Aye, sir." There was no more emotion in Hardesty's voice than in his admiral's. Neither man had emotion left to give.

Truscott watched his monitor as the exchange of weaponry started to meet in the narrowing gap between *Sheffield* and the Federation ships. He had little doubt that this would be *Sheffield*'s last run. Even if she escaped to Q-space, *Repulse* would certainly be lost. And *Sheffield* would be a doubtful candidate for another return.

We'll have to rendezvous with Victoria *and head for home,* Truscott decided. *Bring back more ships if I have to personally hijack them.*

He thought about the Marines who would be stranded on Buchanan, and the pilots who would have to eject from their Spacehawks or trust their necks to risky landings on the world's only landing strip long enough to take them. There to be hunted down, killed or captured. As the moment of decision approached, Truscott wouldn't turn his thoughts away from even the most painful aspects of command. But neither would he hesitate to do what had to be done.

"Admiral!" The call—scream—came from Rinaldi. Truscott blinked rapidly and looked up. "Behind the Feddies, coming in high and fast." Rinaldi pointed at his monitor. Truscott looked at his own.

"Good God, sir!" Gabby Bierce said, his voice penetrating his boss's sudden excitement. "Looks like the whole bleedin' Navy come to help."

Truscott counted ships as Rinaldi read data off the complink. "It's *Dover, York, Calcutta,* and four more battlecruisers, at least a dozen frigates, and two troop carriers. Long John *himself* is commanding."

"Hardesty!" Truscott yelled at his complink. "Take us out and bring us right back in, behind our fleet, *now.* Launch all fighters as soon as we're back. We've got Marines to bail out."

The gray of Q-space was already closing in on *Sheffield* by the time he finished talking.

Only two Spacehawks of the original six made it back to support the Marines. They made runs down the east and west sides of the firebase, directed from the ground by Ian Shrikes. Then they went out, curled around, and made passes along the north and south sides. It-gave the Marines the least bit of time to breathe deeply and sort themselves out. But the Spacehawks didn't have enough munitions left to finish the job. One more pass was what the pilots told

Ian. They had missiles for one more pass, and perhaps ten seconds' of ammunition left for their cannons. And where did the Commander *want* those missiles and bullets?

"As close to the line of burning logs on our east as you can get. That's where most of the Feddies seem to be," Ian told them.

The two Spacehawks were just beginning their final run when Ian got the call from *Sheffield*. He listened intently, asked two questions, and then shouted in relief.

"What?" Prince William asked. Ian shook his head and switched his helmet to an all-hands frequency.

"Hang on," Ian said, too loudly. "Help's on its way. More ships than you ever hoped to see. The rest of *Sheffield*'s fighters will be launched in less than five minutes, coming straight to us. Fifteen minutes from now, we'll have a whole fighter wing to help out."

There were no cheers. There wasn't a man on the channel who was confident enough of holding on for another fifteen minutes.

As soon as the two Spacehawks pulled up from their last run, the Federation troops started advancing again. This assault was slower, almost run in a series of stop-frames. Men on both sides were exhausted, overloaded by the horror of the devastation around them. They continued to fight only because there was nothing else they could do. The shooting became more and more ragged.

On the crest of the ridge, David was down to his pistol. His rifle wasn't completely devoid of ammunition, but he was saving that. The targets that mattered were close enough for sidearms now. His left arm was throbbing. A grazing shot had ripped his fatigues, field skin, and his own skin, drawing blood until the field skin and his nanoscrubbers stopped the flow. The wrist and hand were still numb.

He could flex the hand, grasp with it, but the feel of everything was peculiar.

Fifteen minutes? David didn't have the slightest idea how long it had been since he heard that. It seemed hours, but couldn't have been. *We'd all have been long since dead.*

Then or now, David told himself. More than a third of his platoon was gone, dead or helmets out of commission. More were wounded, some badly. David avoided bringing up the schematic that would show him who and how many. If those extra fighters didn't show up in one hell of a hurry, there would be a blank slate.

The sonic boom startled everyone. *Enough to wake the dead,* Alfie thought, and he regretted it immediately. He didn't know how many of his mates had died, but he knew that no noise in the universe could wake them.

Alfie didn't let up from his work. He had two magazines left for his needler, and he was making his ammunition count. The Feddies were right out in the open, ripe for the picking. He switched his aim from point to point, squeezing off short bursts, satisfied with stopping Feddies, not intent on shredding them any longer.

He needed a moment to realize when he suddenly started seeing backs instead of fronts. The Feddies were breaking off the fight. Those who could run were, trying to get away from the fire of incoming Spacehawks. The fighters were making one hell of a racket shooting off rockets, braking, trying to get their airspeed low enough to use cannons. Supersonic, they would run into their own bullets.

The Spacehawks seemed to come in an endless string, raking the forest on all around the firebase, even strafing the western slope of the ridge. Trees erupted. Alfie saw one that seemed to lift off like a rocket, climbing twenty yards before it lost its momentum and tipped over as it started to fall back to earth.

For nearly five minutes the noise of the air assault was overpowering. The Marines on the ground could do nothing better than hunker down, and stay out of the line of fire and debris.

Then there was silence. At first, no one seemed to react to the change. Then, slowly, Marines started to straighten up. They looked out at the ruins of the forest around them. There wasn't a single tree standing within two hundred yards. Most were burning or smoking. There were no Federation soldiers moving anywhere in that devastation. Gradually, the Marines realized that the fight was over. A few stood. When no Federation fire came in, more Marines got to their feet.

"Let's get busy," David said over his platoon frequency. "Check the wounded. Let's do what we can." As soon as he had his people moving, he switched channels. Asa Ewing didn't answer, but Ian Shrikes did.

"We've got medevac shuttles on their way," Ian said. "There'll be shuttles for the rest of us as soon as we get the wounded moved."

David looked around from his position on the crest of the ridge. "We get the wounded loaded, we won't need many more shuttles."

Epilogue

Five days later, David Spencer led the survivors of First Battalion's I&R platoon back down to the surface of Buchanan. Only eighteen men survived of the thirty-two who had first landed on the world. Six of those eighteen men had spent time in trauma tubes, recovering from wounds received in the platoon's last battle.

This time, the platoon wasn't landing to fight. Along with representatives from the rest of the Second Regiment, and detachments from each ship and fighter wing, David and his men were landing to attend a ceremony.

The shuttle landed smoothly on the runway of Buchanan's spaceport and taxied to a stop near the ruins of what had once been the terminal building. David formed his men up as soon as they debarked—as two squads instead of four. For an instant he saw the faces of the dead standing in ranks with the survivors, and he bit his lip. The taste of blood brought David back to reality. He looked at the men who *were* there. They were wearing undress khakis, no field skins, helmets, or weapons.

David would have welcomed a helmet, or a pocket complink, so he could ask where he was supposed to take his men. Several other contingents of Marines had formed up in the grass at the side of the spaceport, and there were growing numbers of Buchananers a little farther off, beyond a small platform that had been built and draped in colorful banners over the past two days.

David called his men to attention and was ready to march them toward the other Marines when he saw a naval officer running toward them. It took David a moment to recognize Ian Shrikes in dress whites. David walked out to meet him, and saluted when they met.

"Good to see you again, Spencer," Ian said, smiling as he returned the salute. They walked back to the I&R platoon together. "Good to see all of you."

"Where do you want us for this ceremony, Commander?" David asked.

"Ah, I didn't know quite how to break this to you before, but you'll be right up front. You and your lads aren't here to witness the ceremony. I'm afraid you're part of it."

"Sir?" David asked.

"At the specific request of the Buchanan Planetary Commission, through its new chairman, Doug Weintraub," Ian explained.

"Do you know what's up for us?" David asked. He wanted to ask if there was any way to escape the formalities, but knew better.

"Not in any detail," Ian said. "Weintraub has been quite closemouthed about this. All he would say was that he wants to show some measure of the gratitude that he feels he and Buchanan owe you and your men."

"We're just part of the team, sir. Nothing special."

"I'm the wrong man to protest to, Sergeant. I'm as stuck as you are. All we can do is smile and hope that it doesn't take all day."

"Yes, sir."

"Let's give them a smart show marching in. At least your men won't have to stand through all the speechifying. As honored guests, you'll have chairs."

"That much is welcome," David said. Behind him, one

man cheered softly. David recognized Alfie's voice, but took no official notice. Not now.

There *were* speeches, more than enough for any Marine. Doug Weintraub and two other members of the Commission spoke. Prince William spoke. So did Admirals Truscott and Raleigh.

The major item on the agenda was a formal offer of membership in the Second Commonwealth, made by Prince William and accepted by Doug Weintraub—to the general cheers of the Buchananers who had come to watch this ceremony. More than 80 percent of the population had come out to be part of this moment.

After the offer and acceptance, Doug returned to the microphone on the platform.

"It is impossible for us to properly thank every man and woman who contributed to our liberation, but we would be terribly remiss if we didn't take special notice of at least a few of those brave souls. During the recent campaign, I lived and fought at the side of the Intelligence and Reconnaissance platoon of Headquarters and Service Company, First Battalion, Second Regiment of Royal Marines, led by Sergeant David Spencer."

From the row of seats behind David, Ian Shrikes whispered, "Get up, Spencer, you and your men. Time to take your bows."

David stood and gestured for his men to do the same. Looking around, David saw that his men were as flustered and uncomfortable as he was at being the center of attention for more than thirty thousand spectators.

"The platoon came to Buchanan with thirty-two men," Doug continued, looking directly at David. "Fourteen of those men have been buried here, sacrificed to help buy back our liberty. We will remember their names, and we will remember the names of these men here. Sergeant Spencer, would you come up here, please?''

David looked around as if he hoped for a last-minute reprieve, but no one came to his assistance. The people of Buchanan were applauding, stretching it out, waiting for him to get up on the platform. David moved slowly, and the last few steps were almost impossible to take.

''You've been a friend and mentor in addition to everything else,'' Doug said, shaking David's hand. ''We have this token of our appreciation.'' One of the other commission members handed him a large, framed document. ''Our commendation to you and your men, David. If you or any of your men should happen, someday, to leave the Royal Marines and want to settle on Buchanan, we will provide homesteads and all that is needed to start a new life here. That offer stands for all members of the Commonwealth forces who came to help us regain our freedom.''

Josef Langenkamp was limping when he moved away from the center of the ceremony after it ended. His right leg had been shredded badly during the last phase of what was already being called the Three Hills' Battle. Against the advice of the flight surgeon, Josef had come out of the trauma tube for this visit. He needed another day or more in the tube, and would be returning to it as soon as he returned to *Sheffield*. Kate Hicks was at his side now, holding on to him as if she were afraid he would disappear if she let go.

''I want a word with those Marines before we go back to the shuttle,'' Josef said. ''They're the lads who pulled me out of the forest. They deserve every medal the Commonwealth has to give, and a few new ones for good measure.''

''I'd give them a medal myself for getting you out of Spacehawks,'' Kate said. ''Ejecting twice in one month. I know you're not thrilled, but I'm glad they're going to put you on a desk back on Buckingham.''

"I still say it'll drive me crazy." He had argued against the new assignment, as well as he could from a trauma tube, but the flight surgeon had insisted. After another shock, his brain was rejecting its new neural implant. It had to be removed, and without an implant, no one could fly a Space-hawk. "If you weren't going back with me . . . ''

"But I am." Kate tightened her grip on his arm. "Train-ing command. Deputy operations officer for the Second Training Wing." Both of them were being advanced to lieutenant commander.

There were bundles of promotions being awarded in the wake of the Buchanan Campaign. Ian Shrikes made cap-tain, in line for a command of his own as soon as there was an opening. David Spencer had already been named Lead Sergeant for H&S Company of the First Battalion. Tory Kepner made sergeant to replace David as I&R platoon sergeant. Hugo Kassner hadn't survived the last battle. Six of the remaining privates in the platoon were being ad-vanced to corporal. They would provide the cadre for the platoon when it was remanned.

Even Admiral Truscott was receiving a promotion, but his was more a promotion of position rather than rank. Sir John Raleigh had named him the new chief of naval op-erations. "You came up with these cockeyed new tactics," Long John told Truscott when they met aboard *Sheffield* after the surrender of the last Federation ships. "Now you're going to put them into effect throughout the fleet. We've won one battle, but it's not the war, not by a long patch." It was only later that Stasys learned to his bemuse-ment that a knighthood went with the new job.

From national bestselling author
RICK SHELLEY

An explosive new series of future warfare...

__OFFICER-CADET   0-441-00526-8/$5.99

Lon Nolan, a young soldier expelled from Earth's presti-
gious North American Military Academy on trumped-up
charges, is seeking to prove his worthiness in the
Dirigent Mercenary Corps, where the bloody craft of battle has been refined into an art...

__LIEUTENANT   0-441-00568-3/$5.99

Lon Nolan returns as a lieutenant in a new adventure—
a tale of leadership and loyalty in the heart of combat.

Also by Rick Shelley:

__THE BUCHANAN CAMPAIGN

                                    0-441-00292-7/$5.99

__THE FIRES OF COVENTRY   0-441-00385-0/$5.99

__RETURN TO CAMEREIN   0-441-00496-2/$5.99

Prices slightly higher in Canada

Payable in U.S. funds only. No cash/COD accepted. Postage & handling: U.S./CAN. $2.75 for one
book, $1.00 for each additional, not to exceed $6.75; Int'l $5.00 for one book, $1.00 each additional. We accept Visa, Amex, MC ($10.00 min.), checks ($15.00 fee for returned checks) and money
orders. Call 800-788-6262 or 201-933-9292, fax 201-896-8569; refer to ad # 783 (12/99)

Penguin Putnam Inc.	Bill my: ☐ Visa ☐ MasterCard ☐ Amex _____(expires)
P.O. Box 12289, Dept. B	Card# _____
Newark, NJ 07101-5289	Signature _____
Please allow 4-6 weeks for delivery.	
Foreign and Canadian delivery 6-8 weeks.	

Bill to:

Name _____

Address _____ City _____

State/ZIP _____ Daytime Phone # _____

Ship to:

Name _____ Book Total $ _____

Address _____ Applicable Sales Tax $ _____

City _____ Postage & Handling $ _____

State/ZIP _____ Total Amount Due $ _____

This offer subject to change without notice.

"The best writer in America."
—Tom Clancy

John Varley

☐ **STEEL BEACH**   0-441-78565-4/$7.50

☐ **SUPERHEROES**   0-441-00307-9/$5.99
with Ricia Mainhardt

☐ **TITAN**   0-441-81304-6/$6.99

☐ **WIZARD**   0-441-90067-4/$6.99

☐ **DEMON**   0-441-14267-2/$6.99

Prices slightly higher in Canada

Payable in U.S. funds only. No cash/COD accepted. Postage & handling: U.S./CAN. $2.75 for one book, $1.00 for each additional, not to exceed $6.75; Int'l $5.00 for one book, $1.00 each additional. We accept Visa, Amex, MC ($10.00 min.), checks ($15.00 fee for returned checks) and money orders. Call 800-788-6262 or 201-933-9292, fax 201-896-8569; refer to ad # 810 (12/99)

Penguin Putnam Inc.
P.O. Box 12289, Dept. B
Newark, NJ 07101-5289
Please allow 4-6 weeks for delivery.
Foreign and Canadian delivery 6-8 weeks.

Bill my: ☐ Visa ☐ MasterCard ☐ Amex _____ (expires)
Card# _____
Signature _____

Bill to:
Name _____
Address _____ City _____
State/ZIP _____ Daytime Phone # _____

Ship to:
Name _____ Book Total $ _____
Address _____ Applicable Sales Tax $ _____
City _____ Postage & Handling $ _____
State/ZIP _____ Total Amount Due $ _____

This offer subject to change without notice.

PENGUIN PUTNAM INC.
Online

Your Internet gateway to a virtual environment with
hundreds of entertaining and enlightening books
from Penguin Putnam Inc.

*While you're there, get the latest buzz on
the best authors and books around—*

Tom Clancy, Patricia Cornwell, W.E.B. Griffin,
Nora Roberts, William Gibson, Robin Cook,
Brian Jacques, Catherine Coulter, Stephen King,
Jacquelyn Mitchard, and many more!

**Penguin Putnam Online is located at
http://www.penguinputnam.com**

PENGUIN PUTNAM NEWS

Every month you'll get an inside look at our upcoming books and new features on our site. This is an
ongoing effort to provide you with the most
up-to-date information about
our books and authors.

**Subscribe to Penguin Putnam News at
http://www.penguinputnam.com/ClubPPI**